"I PROMISE YOU A YEAR..."

Barth's voice was husky and urgent. He buried his face in the sensitive curve of Miel's neck, running warm breath and swift caresses along the ivory skin.

"Just you and me aboard the *Yancy*," he continued. "We could drink fig brandy and go around the Horn. I'll show you icebergs under moonlight, or the Grand Banks in fog. Whatever you want—just come with me."

Miel was paralyzed by the clamorous confusion of her mind. Suddenly he was closer, and she was in his arms. The kiss that began as a gentle inducement ended in a shattering blaze of unleashed passion. Only when Barth gazed into the depths of her eyes did he see what she herself was unable to admit.

She was afraid to go. Now. Maybe ever....

Books by Margaret Gayle

HARLEQUIN SUPERROMANCES
52—PRECIOUS INTERLUDE
118—TO CATCH THE WIND

These books may be available at your local bookseller.

For a list of all titles currently available,
send your name and address to:

Harlequin Reader Service
P.O. Box 52040, Phoenix, AZ 85072-2040
Canadian address: P.O. Box 2800, Postal Station A,
            5170 Yonge St., Willowdale, Ont. M2N 5T5

Margaret Gayle

TO CATCH THE WIND

Harlequin Books

TORONTO • NEW YORK • LONDON
AMSTERDAM • PARIS • SYDNEY • HAMBURG
STOCKHOLM • ATHENS • TOKYO • MILAN

Published June 1984

First printing April 1984

ISBN 0-373-70118-7

Printed in Canada

To Barb and company, the original fan club.

CHAPTER ONE

MIEL MCCRAE'S second departure from routine that splendid morning in spring was to open the sunroof of her Corvette, letting the wind at her disciplined auburn hair. Her first, in a life that allowed few departures, had been the stunning sea-blue outfit she was wearing. The fabric was raw silk of the sort that scooped up light and tossed it back to her frank hazel eyes and luminous peachbloom skin. The precious, fabulously expensive sample ought to have been reposing in its own individual garment bag as it had all the way over on the plane from France. But she had flitted into her apartment not an hour earlier and listened to a voice that so far had had very little to say these past four years at Crome's—a spirited, delightful voice counseling rebellion.

Go ahead, it had urged. *This trip you really earned it. Put the outfit on for James.*

Now she was speeding off to him, bearing her triumph like a gift. Her success would not become real to Miel until it was sealed with the warmth of James Crome's smile.

Cutting nimbly into Toronto's Bloor-Yonge shopping core, Miel drove into the hidden lot behind the graceful Italianate building. It was one of the few that had not been replaced by a glass tower like the ones bordering the charmed enclave of fashionable shops. For the past year Miel's assigned spot was right next to the understated gray and tan of James's Rolls-Royce. The letters of her name were neatly stenciled beneath the blue Crome's logo. For the whole first month she would catch herself checking her sign as she parked; in this world of accepted privilege her old and clinging habit was to feel she still had to earn every little perk.

Today, however, she bounced out onto the asphalt and rounded the building to stride regally through the tall glass-and-bronze front doors without even pausing to see what surprises Hildy had wrought in the display windows. An interior of mellow, sand-colored marble and fluted pilasters greeted her. What threatened to be a stuffy environment was now freshened and enlivened with hand-painted banners and spills of thriving greenery, thanks again to Hildy. Even the twin statues at the door, antique nymphs clutching pots of ferns, seemed to smile as Miel glided onto the thick dove-gray carpeting around the accessory counters, where bottles of perfume, like tiny, translucent sculptures, reposed in backlit niches. Silk scarves billowed from Mexican baskets at the foot of the escalator.

Most of the salespeople were busy. Only Marion Wallace, who managed lingerie, looked up and spotted the tall young figure wearing the shimmering blouson top, which fell with unmistakable authority of line over soft, front-gathered trousers. Fanciful stitching on the yoke managed to suggest waves and clouds. The combination of colors, in delicate, barely perceptible swirls of light and shade, could only have been conceived by an expert.

Marion's brows shot up. Miel waited one dramatic second, then raised two manicured fingers in an unabashed victory sign as the escalator bore her out of sight.

This performance was repeated on the second floor and the third and also on the fourth, where the designer fashions were sold. Miel left a hubbub in her wake as she walked through evening wear to the hidden staff elevator that would carry her to the administration offices.

When the doors swept open, delivering Miel into the hushed, mocha-toned reception area, Allison, the receptionist, looked up. Only the rigid Crome sense of propriety prevented her from actually leaping out of her chair.

"My God, you got the Gagnon designs. How many Frenchmen did you have to garrote?"

Miel halted, struck by the novelty of seeing Allison excited. Allison, like most of the Crome staff, was middle-aged and immaculately turned out in the calm earth tones considered de rigueur for those who worshipped at the altar of Good Taste. Miel forgot that she herself glowed like a brilliant aquamarine flame. In spite of his preference for traditional taste, James, consummate manager that he was, had instilled in everyone the importance of expanding the store's inventory to include avant-garde foreign design.

That decision was more important than any of them imagined, she reminded herself bleakly, having been privy to the grim financial statements of the past three years.

"I left a trail of bodies all the way to the Eiffel Tower. Where's James?"

"Pacing a hole in the carpet, I suppose. I give him about thirty seconds to realize you're here."

Unable, by any stretch of the imagination, to picture James pacing, Miel stepped into the inner regions of the executive offices. No sooner had she done so than the man himself appeared, urbane and dependably impeccable, no matter how much pacing he might be suspected of doing.

Miel paused breathlessly and was rewarded by his mild, but shrewd eyes widening in surprise as they swept up and down her impressive figure, taking in the boldly gorgeous color, the inimitable originality of cut that trumpeted the newest, most sought after of European designers, Hélène Gagnon. Tiny lines of strain suddenly smoothed his face. His wide mouth broke into a radiant grin of delight and relief.

"You did it! Congratulations, my dear! My heartiest!"

Miel had been standing motionless, her eyes shining, all that was crisply, efficiently business-like about her submerged in a moment of raw vulnerability. Now she swung toward him, her willowy limbs reflecting a new grace caused by her happiness. This was the moment she had been waiting for ever since Hélène Gagnon, in that startling Gallic manner of hers, had pointed a long finger and declared that permission to market the designs was hers. This was the one thing she had lived for since James had plucked her, four years before, from a hopeless wasteland and started her out as a humble inventory clerk.

James, in that fine, long-featured English way, was very handsome. Ashley, Miel had thought that first time she had seen him, Ashley in *Gone With the Wind*—although he was completely without Ashley's weakness of character, as any employee who shirked duty was swift to find out. If only he wouldn't cling to that charming but outmoded conservatism that was so painfully at odds with the changing times.

He didn't look conservative now. The sight of her had filled his eyes with gladness, and there was an uncharacteristic flush along his jaw. As if unable to contain himself, he grasped Miel's hand and pressed it in his own, eliciting by this gallantry a gasp of laughing astonishment.

"James!"

He straightened quickly, but the smile remained, as well as whatever was causing such eagerness in his expression. Yet something in the way he held himself caused Ashley to vanish and a ruff and rapier to leap into Miel's mind. They wouldn't be out of place, she thought. In one of the art history night courses she had taken to fill the gaps in her education, she had studied paintings of Elizabethan courtiers who displayed the same aplomb as the man before her.

A spill of warmth, a feeling very much like protectiveness, washed over her. Even those times when she had been tempted to tease him about his lovely, unconscious courtliness, she had to admit it made him more dear to her than ever. Long ago she had decided that James was that rarest of all finds: a true gentleman—not simply superficially, but bone deep, with a kindness, a gentleness at his core.

"Your due, Miel. You of all people should know what the Gagnon designs can do for us. What unbelievable luck that Hildy should discover a gap in their program. Did you have much trouble convincing them to take pity on one poor retailer out here in the bush?"

Miel shrugged, unable to resist a certain nonchalance, even though she knew perfectly well what a coup it was to persuade a top French designer to allow her work to be sold in one single store in Canada, when establishments from all over Europe had been at each other's throats for the privilege.

"There were certainly others vying for the rights," she replied casually. "*Madame* herself drew out the competition, mostly for the fun of seeing us scrap."

"And you, naturally, gave an excellent account of yourself."

"I did what I could," Miel returned modestly, smoothing one whispering sleeve.

As a matter of fact, she had spent a good deal of the time with very clammy palms, although she made very sure no one was aware of that. One whiff of weakness and the pack turned on you. That much she had learned the hard way before she was six years old. Before she had left for Paris, she had had her business proposal typed on the thickest, creamiest of paper. In France, she had followed her instincts, waiting for the right moment to cut into the stream of glib, eagerly animated representatives flowing in and out of *madame*'s office. Though unable to speak French and certainly at a loss when it came to continental suavity, Miel knew that when she tried she was a presence to be reckoned with. Commanding attention and respect was necessary in business, and heaven knew she had fought bitterly enough to learn how. Summoning her reserves of confidence, she had faced the Frenchwoman, whose black eyes were piercing and whose brusque manner was so much at odds with the flowing drama of her creations.

The proposal had seemed lost among a jumble of papers strewn across *madame*'s desk. *Madame* plucked it out with unerring precision.

"This is yours? *Oui?*"

A pause followed Miel's nod. *Madame* assessed her. Negotiations began. Madame Gagnon was tough, sometimes frighteningly so, and Miel almost had a sickening vision of everything slipping through her fingers until she became aware of another communication between them on a very different level. The negotiations continued—thrust and parry, contracts, obligations and percentages. After some time, as Miel consistently proved her business mettle, the eyes of the two women met and held. The recognition of a young but worthy equal gleamed under the Frenchwoman's lashes.

"Eh bien," she had said, suddenly relinquishing her expression of aggressive concentration. "You 'ave impressed me, *mademoiselle*. We will give this unknown store a try."

A little *acquéreur* from Toulon groaned in a corner and nibbled his mustache. Miel flew home with as many Gagnons as she could carry and her heart singing with success.

"I never had a moment's doubt since I saw you onto the plane." James was uncharacteristically emphatic, expressing in a few endearing words the faith he had put in her from the moment he had insisted she take on the mission, which was by all rights his own. Miel was glad, very glad, she did not have to bear the censure she would have heard in his voice had she failed—censure he knew all too well how to convey. Disapproval from James was as seemingly mild as the rest of him, yet it only took a word in that special tone to send any wrongdoer scuttling off to mend performance. Never had James spoken in that tone to Miel. But then, though it had often been a secret struggle on her part, she had taken care never to fall short of his expectations.

His hand found the small of her back as he guided her toward her office. The gesture startled Miel, for James was not given to touching, even with those most familiar to him. She responded quickly with a shy but grateful smile, lest he think she had disapproved.

"It's not all gravy," she hastened to say, for Madame Gagnon had driven a hard bargain as was only proper with a store as distant and untried as Crome's. The only reason they'd had a chance at all was because one of Madame Gagnon's regular outlets in Marseilles had had a fire, closing it down and making a portion of the limited Gagnon stock available for another distributor. "It's only on a trial basis and only for this season. It's May, you know. If we don't get the stuff selling right away we'll be stuck with some very pricey and very out-of-date inventory. All the way back I wondered if we were crazy trying to pull this stunt."

"Perhaps," replied James, his curious mood not allowing him to sober in the slightest, "but we have to do something. The store has been losing money since the last two years mother was in charge. Even the family fortune can't go on taking this sort of strain."

They both knew inheriting a family business was no longer protection against ravaging inflation and fickle fashion tastes. James was the third generation to operate Crome's from this location. For many years the store had been run by James's widowed mother, the late, formidable Lillian Crome, who had released her iron grip in death only a year and a half earlier. It had been Lillian, with her considerable personal fortune and vast social connections, who had turned the store into a bastion of dignity and quality. Maintaining her own particular standards, Lillian regarded the sprouting of high rises and costly boutiques in the area with the same jaundiced eye one might regard a particularly annoying cloud of gnats.

Unfortunately, the gnats had proved more than annoying. As competition intensified and the hub of fashion migrated a few blocks to the east, Crome's began to suffer, its faithful clientele thinning in number, aging and fading away. Why, just a month ago, Miel had seen a young woman in expensive boots and Mexican serape haul her companion away from the door.

"Are you kidding!" she had said. "That's Stodge Villa. My grandma buys her camel-hair coats there. Let's go look in Selks."

Selks! Always Avery Selks! It wasn't fair. Crome's stocked good solid classics, but so many of the replacement shoppers it so urgently needed were lured to the brash, glitzy establishment that had opened three years ago two blocks away— and two blocks closer to the Bloor-Yonge traffic flow. Exorbitant prices and too much flash, but the store had incredible luck nosing out even the front-runners of ever-changing fashion. In fact, it was a source of wonder to both James and Miel that Avery Selks hadn't snatched up the Gagnon opportunity before the news of it had even filtered through to Crome's. That single advantage in the capricious struggle for the tastes of the young and affluent might just have made Selks's stranglehold complete.

Countless times Miel had wondered if it was the store or the man himself that rankled her so. Avery Selks had come out of nowhere and set up on one of the best locations on the street—but then many a businessman had done that. No, it was something about his personality evident in the very loudness of the carpets and the ostentatious presentation of the store's display windows. Something that said, here is a man who isn't content to share trade, but must control it.

Miel had not guessed at the depth of her aversion to the fellow until she and James had met him at a convention a year ago. Avery Selks was a florid man with broken veins and large teeth and a swagger his Harris tweed couldn't hide. He had spotted the two of them half a room away. Knowing perfectly well who they were, he had still raised his glass and given Miel a rude, lascivious wink.

The moment had passed in a flash, yet the message remained, as if Selks were saying, Live it up while you can, for as soon as I'm able, I'll grind you into the sidewalk!

Now Miel flicked James a glance, remembering how he had stiffened furiously at her side.

"We shall just have to make the line sell," she suddenly declared with conviction. "A few more names like Gagnon, and the store will certainly be noticed. The first shipment is arriving air freight, and I've brought enough samples in my luggage for Hildy to start on right away."

"Of course."

Again, that strange preoccupation even in the

midst of this victory. Miel swung her head to find that James was flushed and his eyes were oddly, almost unnaturally, bright. For the first time a tiny thread of alarm shot through her excitement. In the four years they had worked together, in all the crises large and small through which James had guided her, she realized she had never seen his calmness shattered as it was shattered now. She stopped decisively.

"James, is something wrong?"

Two steps beyond her, he swung round. His eyes looked dazzled by the clean lines of the Gagnon creation that somehow on Miel seemed to cry out for a free wind and open sky to fully absorb the lustrous, rippling color.

"No, Miel," he said in a low, almost raspy voice. "I hope. . . very, very right."

And his outstretched hand invited her down the corridor again.

At least he isn't peeved I'm wearing a sample, Miel thought, for her behavior had been highly irregular even for one of her high status at the store. The moment she was alone in her office she meant to change. Her private closet always contained a dress that conformed to the same unspoken dictates that kept Allison in line.

Ironically, it was the same dress—actually the first really good piece of clothing Miel had ever owned—which Lillian had picked out for her that first month at the store. The fact that a modern belt or a new scarf could still transform the light ginger wool bore out the little lecture on the agelessness of classics Lillian, frowning, had delivered while scraping hangers along the rack.

"You have good strong bones, dear," she had said in tones that had made Miel question the propriety of a sturdy skeleton. "Plain, simple styles will last you forever. Don't even think about frills."

Today, under the infinitely more sensuous fabric of the Gagnon, her bones were as good and as strong as ever. She stood practically eye to eye with James. Her naturally athletic form was toned by fitness classes and the relentless tennis games she indulged in like a secret vice to burn off the excess energy her job could not absorb. She moved with quick, effortless grace and once, seeing her at a distance, a photographer had mistaken her for a model. Up close, he had changed his mind, for she had a wide, stubborn jaw and a stride much too purposeful for the runway. No fragile specimen of womanhood, she. And today, in the hall, it had never been more evident that she was blessed with something most high-fashion models generally lacked—the crackle of inner vitality that attracted covert glances everywhere she went.

Then James was opening the door of her private office, which, at that time of day, streamed with sunlight over the burnt sienna carpet and the Elena Roth abstract Miel had purchased with her very first salary increase. Yet it was not the yellow sunlight that halted Miel's entrance, but the vase that stood on her solid walnut desk, which was a sign of Miel's status here. The vase was pure crystal and scattered fragmented rainbows across the blotter and touched flecks of fire to the extravagant scarlet blaze of roses blooming above.

A weakness shot through the back of Miel's knees. She grasped for the back of a guest chair. Her lips formed a small, silent circle. Only then did she realize how much she had been wanting this—and how not once had she dared put that hope into words. Now the power of speech seemed to desert her.

"Oh. . . my," was all she could say.

James closed the door and stood waiting, gripped by inner tension. Miel half turned, all her poise forgotten as the implications of the gift began to sink in.

"I've been meaning to give you roses for a long time, Miel. I hope. . . you'll accept them."

Her throat closed. Now she knew the reason for that extraordinary fever in his eye. She wanted to look at him, but couldn't. They both knew this was no ordinary bouquet. James had a deep reserve about matters of the heart. It wasn't hard to interpret the question the roses represented—would Miel let him court her for her hand in marriage?

Momentarily dazed, Miel tried to cope with the sudden beating and rushing inside her. She had struggled so hard, pushing herself from success to success with a hunger James could not begin to guess. It had been a race, a scrambling uphill fight to be considered equal among these confident, self-assured, well-dressed people. Each time she had reached a resting place, another rugged vista had opened up. Now, just when she had finally learned to stop expecting it, James had turned around and handed her the prize.

Her hand flew to her throat in an unconscious gesture of womanly pleasure. There was never any doubt about her answer.

"They're very lovely, James. I'll be honored."

She could not help imitating the formality that, even in this intimate moment, he kept folded around him like a well-fitted evening cloak. For one wild moment, Miel wondered what she would do if he kissed her right there in the office. But he only ducked his head, allowing himself for the first time to give her a tender smile.

"Dinner, then. After work. To celebrate!"

Why . . . he's bashful, she thought incredulously. *James!*

Nonetheless, the dinner invitation was an instant signpost to their changed relationship. They had lunched together, and Miel had attended the cocktail gatherings—a custom inherited from Lillian—James was fond of giving for his more prestigious patrons in his rambling gray stone mansion. At no time had the two of them ever shared an intimate dinner. Miel grew flustered.

"Oh, I'll have to change, then. And I'm still on European time. It's well into the evening for me already."

"Then we'll go at once," James returned gal-

lantly, for it was the middle of the afternoon.
"And it would be an offense to change that outfit. We'll christen it with champagne!"

He took her hand in his again, this time as if
he had a right to. The wonder of what had just
taken place started to hit Miel like little waves
heralding a breaker. This James, who couldn't
abide plastic shrubbery, who could work all
night if he had to and appear fresh in the morning, who gave to Daffodil ladies and indigent
musicians and the Animal Rescue League, this
James wanted her, this James was going to be
hers.

Oh, no doubt she would spend time being
fondly realistic about him, counting off his foi-
bles on her fingers. Yet he had made her what
she was and that she would never forget. In her
eyes, on a completely different level, James
could do no wrong.

"In about an hour, say," she agreed. "As
soon as I get a little bit organized here. I'd love
to."

Really, she was begging for time to let the
breaker hit. James nodded, touching her with a
delicacy that expressed what he would not for a
long time say aloud, for James, above all, was
order and reason. In his mind the steps of his
courtship were already arranged with the subtlety and ritual of a minuet. The door closed noise-
lessly behind him, leaving Miel gazing at the
great buds whose first petals were just folding
back, a promise on their tips of the full glory of
the blossoms.

"James," she whispered. "My James!"

She was still motionless when the doorknob rattled and a petite dynamo composed entirely of color and motion burst in. Hildy!

"Miel," she yelped as soon as she caught sight of the Gagnon. "I just heard. Faaaantastic! Wish I had been the first to meet you at the door."

In complete disregard for Crome decorum, Hildy grabbed Miel in a vigorous hug. Miel extricated herself laughingly and straightened her outfit. Like everyone else at the store, she didn't quite know what to make of Hildy, though she had liked the disconcerting creature from the moment they had first shaken hands.

"You made it in record time anyway," Miel assured her. "Around here, you're the last person I'd expect to miss anything."

Which was true. Hildy had amazing perception, and everyone suspected her of being a genius, though of what sort they would be hard pressed to define.

Hildy had simply appeared one day not very long ago, walking into James's office and demanding to be hired. She had presented very good, recent credentials in advertising, merchandising and commercial art from a training institution of sterling reputation. Graduating penniless into a hostile economy, she had taken a couple of equally penniless boutiques and within a matter of weeks turned them into raging successes. Having proved her knack, she had offered her services to Crome's on the matter-of-fact assumption that a store in such obvious difficulties could not afford to do without them.

"Marched right past me," Allison exclaimed afterward, scandalized, "that mop of curls bouncing down her back, hardly bigger than a chipmunk, with her nose in the air as if she were being announced by her own brass band. My word, I expected James to warm her bottom and set her back out on the doorstep."

No one was sure what had gone on in his office, but it must have been the zippiest sales job this side of the St. Lawrence. James had hired her. Within an hour, while introducing her around, he had everyone gaping at the violent contrast between his own tall cool gentility and the irreverent flamboyance of the small person at his side.

Actually, James had looked a little bit as if he wasn't quite sure what hit him.

"Well, we need *somebody*," he had muttered to Miel's open-mouthed stare after Hildy marched off to commandeer art supplies. "Anyway," he had said, saving himself as he often did by his self-deprecating wit, "everyone is entitled to one piece of madness in a decade. Let's just say Hildy is mine."

Madness or not, the acquisition of Hildy was a sign of just how desperate the situation looked to him. And the staff was in shock for days as this alien sprite, like some possibly dangerous plague germ, was safely sequestered in an office at the very far end of the hall.

Hildy, however, intent upon gaining credibility, handled the mechanics of Crome's genteel, low-key advertising policy with sure-handed ease, never once deviating from the traditional, never even tempted to hint at the outrageous. Yet ever since she had passed on the tip about the Gagnon line, the air of placid obedience about her had quietly disappeared. The glint in her eyes said she had marked enough time. Free of restraint, she knew the Gagnon promotion was to be all hers.

She circled Miel again, great green eyes absorbing every detail of the exquisitely simple design, until one couldn't help feeling she understood the Gagnon intent quite as well as *madame* herself.

Miel watched Hildy in fascination, examining, as they all secretly did, what new persona the young woman had come up with today. Though Hildy was pretty, with cascades of tight chestnut curls surrounding her alabaster oval face, she attracted attention mainly by turning herself into a constantly moving, constantly changing piece of experimental art, different every day, blissfully oblivious to the revered Crome dress code.

Today, for instance, she had on enough gold eye shadow for a Persian princeling, a thin, turquoise bandana knotted through her hair and an antique top of eyelet lace tucked into baggy harem pants batiked with blossoms. Chunks of coral glowed against her bosom, and the whole ensemble was held together at her tiny waist by a sash that was probably once someone's hand-knitted winter scarf. The curious thing was that no matter how bizarre, how garish the separate pieces, nothing ever looked wrong on her. It was simply assimilated into the bundle of quick, dancing creativity that was Hildy.

"Beautiful," she chirped, fingering the stitching on the yoke. "First thing I've seen in this store that I'm dying to wear. I can't wait...."

Her eyes fell on the roses burning in their vase like a miniature bonfire. Though she had only been at Crome's a short time, Hildy grasped their meaning immediately. Her voice grew suddenly quite small.

"From James?"

Miel nodded, at once proud and shy and wanting intensely to share the joy of it with someone.

"Yes. We're going out for dinner shortly. James wants to celebrate. The designs and... everything."

For half a minute, Hildy went completely still, exactly as if a butterfly had achieved the impossible and hung frozen in midair. Her gaze was hidden behind a sweep of lashes. She seemed to have forgotten to breathe.

"Hildy?"

Right away a smile lit up the small features, restoring most of her animation. She hugged Miel again, but lightly this time, as if something of her energy had been diverted elsewhere.

"I'm... glad for you, Miel. It's just... goodness, I'm so surprised. Who would have thought that after all the time you two must have worked together...."

"Oh, James never jumps into anything, you

can be sure of that. But once he makes up his mind, he makes it up for good.''

Hildy greeted this observation with silence, as if the idea had never occurred to her. Hastily, she turned her back to the vase.

''Well, time will tell, I suppose. Now let's get another look at this Gagnon. You say you have samples in your luggage?''

And the next several minutes were passed in an intense business discussion before Hildy left the office to its normal state of dignified solitude. A thin, much-pruned maple, a refugee among acres of concrete, reached as far as the window and Miel gazed at it pensively, wondering why it hurt her that Hildy had not been more than politely pleased at her news. Silly, of course, for romances formed and dissolved so fast these days, one could hardly keep oneself informed, let alone be overjoyed. Miel felt awkward and schoolgirlish to know that she had, just for a moment, expected her whole little world to rejoice at her good fortune.

The maple had very little to say on the matter, so she passed some minutes moving papers around her desk and fingering the rose petals. She was twenty-four years old. Men had come and gone, but for the past seven years she had not allowed a thought of genuine romance to breach her tightly disciplined defenses. Naturally she was behind her contemporaries somewhat in savoir faire.

Absently, her fingers slid along a stem until a green thorn pricked her. Miel winced and just for a second was deeply afraid. A rugged face exploded from her memory, and the sear of a mouth that had burned away forever the shielding innocence of her young girl's heart.

Then she reminded herself that she had already paid her dues—amply—in shattered illusions and tear-stained pillowcases. This time she had earned the love of a good and decent man. This time, surely, there could be nothing in store for her but happiness.

CHAPTER TWO

LATER, JAMES AND MIEL stepped onto Bloor Street, which bisects the city north and south as nearby Yonge Street divides it east and west. The forces of change had elbowed hard here. Glass structures all but overwhelmed the two- and three-story converted houses that nervously protected themselves with lots of display windows and clever little names stenciled in gold above the doors.

Light and warmth flooded all the open spaces, so that even the well-to-do shoppers and business people shed jackets and sweaters in some atavistic urge to bare their skins. A little to the southwest, on campus, students would be lying on the new grass of Queen's Park, trying to concentrate while the sun of a new season beat down on their backs. Wherever there was a bench, there was someone on it blinking in the sunshine, marveling at the recurrent Canadian wonder, spring—a hot sudden spring—which had burned through to touch them once again.

Miel, no less than the others, was subject to the urgings of the season. Not a few passersby spared a glance for the handsome couple—the attentive man with the neat pin-striped suit and the lissome young woman in blue who looked, if she had not been so carefully measuring her steps to those of her companion, as if she just might be able to fly.

James offered his arm and Miel took it, thinking for the first time of the muscles under the good fabric of his sleeve.

I shall have to get used to touching him, she thought with a start as they reached the university's first outlying building, with its cream stone and perfect Greek temple facade, once thought to inspire students of domestic science. *Someday our whole bodies. . . .*

Her spasm of trepidation was unnoticed amid the blare and activity at the intersection of Bloor Street and Avenue Road. They turned north, leaving behind the long gray galleries of the Royal Ontario Museum and the little church that, freshly sandblasted, held its own on an exceedingly valuable corner, as churches were apt to do in the city formerly known as Toronto the Good.

Two blocks north was Yorkville, once a genuine village in a time when stump fences lay between it and the thriving settlement of York— Muddy York, this time of year. The community itself had long ago been engulfed by the burgeoning city, but not quite swallowed. Several rows of narrow gabled brick houses were charmingly preserved despite the expensive boutiques, galleries and restaurants honeycombed throughout.

The very green of the new leaves danced, and through an archway Miel glimpsed white wrought-iron outdoor tables in a little courtyard.

"Oh, do let's sit outside, James. There's such a lovely breeze."

But James glanced at her oddly, and she reminded herself she was wearing the precious Gagnon sample.

"We came for champagne," he said with the gentlest reproach. "Remember?"

Guiding her away from the laughing, cappuccino-sipping crowd behind railings all along the street, he led her through a polished cherrywood door, with lilies etched in its window. Inside, wicker chairs and small tables were scattered artfully among lacquered Chinese screens and cascades of lush tropical plants. Ornate sconces spread light onto the deep rose walls.

In contrast to the buzz of people outside, this place was almost empty. The maître d', like most in the city Miel guessed, welcomed James as if he were a personal friend and seated them discreetly against a gathered burgundy curtain whose deep ruddiness was the only hit of the intense sunshine it shut out.

"It's awfully early for you to eat, James. Are you sure it's really all right?"

James touched a napkin. A lock of fine brown hair loosened at his brow, accenting that very elegant sex appeal that was, had he but guessed, why many of the female customers returned to Crome's as often as they did. His smile singled her out, one very special person in his private universe.

"Food is incidental. This is a victory celebration. I mean us to be awash in bubbly, and I'm giving you the day off tomorrow to recuperate."

He signaled their waiter and ordered, that cachet of privilege and private schools commanding instant, unobtrusive compliance. Miel watched, pleased and comforted. She herself had long ceased to be intimidated by such places, but there had once been a time. . . .

Lord, would she ever forget the evening she had first encountered a real fish fork!

Very shortly, James and the waiter made a small and charming ceremony of opening the bottle of champagne. When the cork was popped and the excellent vintage was poured, they lifted their glasses.

"To the future."

James said it so significantly that, just for an instant, Miel struggled with a panicky catch in her throat before she could bring herself to swallow. Those brown eyes of his looked at her so. . . expectantly. Yet she knew he would never call her darling in public or drape his arm around her as if to indicate some entertaining new acquisition. Her respect for him increased. She lifted her glass again without hesitation.

"Yes, the future."

The champagne slid down her throat, cool, prickly, just slightly sweet. She examined James with fresh interest, noting with surprise he had a small scar hidden in the arch of his eyebrow.

"And do I look delectable?" he teased, for

they were at once diffident and very familiar with each other.

"Delectable enough, right down to the cleft in your chin. Did you know that half the store wonders why you never kicked up your heels as a ladies' man?"

For a moment James appeared amused. He could have offered a snappy comeback, but he favored the more honest approach.

"Games, Miel. I was never good at them. Seems to me you either commit yourself or you don't. Is that old-fashioned?"

"Delightfully."

"Time passes, of course." He looked into the golden liquid releasing bubbles in his glass. "Then one day...a man looks around for an equal. When he finds one, he ought to pay attention, don't you think?"

In his quiet way, he was paying Miel his highest compliment. In the back of her mind she wondered if the trip to France had been a final test and was infinitely grateful she had passed.

Later, when they were eating and the wine had mellowed them, James brushed her hand lightly.

"I've been thinking, Miel. All the time we've been together, I hardly know a thing about you. Your life, I mean. How, for instance, did you ever get that lovely name?"

Miel, they both knew, was the French word for sweetness or honey.

Miel felt her grip tighten instinctively on the fragile stem of her wineglass. This new intimacy between them meant that James would be naturally curious about her childhood. One by one she loosened her fingers and shrugged casually, careful not to look into his warm gaze.

"There's hardly anything to tell. My mother lived just long enough after I was born to give me the name. My dad died in a van accident. I was brought up in a pint-size village on Lake Ontario."

This was the skeleton biography given out to those who pressed her. So far as it went, it was true. No need to explain that her mother, not even eighteen and half mad from boredom, had run off with a French Canadian singer who had played the village hall for a night. Pregnancy was immediate, marriage was not, though they stayed together through all the one-night gigs up and down the length of the St. Lawrence. When the baby started to come, they had been snowed in at an isolated motel. They decided, with the blind optimism of youth, to deliver it themselves.

Complications had developed. Before the horrified, helpless eyes of her young lover, Miel's mother had quickly died. In the ensuing official brouhaha, the young man fled and was later assumed to be a passenger, burned beyond recognition when, miles to the west, a van piled into a tree. Baby Miel had been claimed by a raging grandfather who had just been pulled from a freighter hauling wheat from the Lakehead. Her cherished name was the only proof a lonely child could cling to that her mother and father had wanted her, despite everything.

"You never told me about your grandfather. Wasn't it tough for him to raise a little girl alone?"

If she hadn't known better, Miel might have suspected James of probing, ever so delicately, the suitability of her background. All the years at Crome's when she had been cultivating the right approach, both personal and professional, she had pretended she had no past. Now she found she was extremely sensitive. She winced from a painful memory.

"He was a sailor. Lakers mostly. He'd been taking shorter and shorter hitches. When I came along he opened a...a marine-supply business and retired completely to shore."

Truly exquisite chicken Kiev appeared, served by a waiter smiling at the sophisticated young couple who had been so impetuous as to order good champagne at four o'clock in the afternoon. James took a thoughtful bite. Miel, with a small breath of relief, saw he was diverted.

Not, of course, that she was afraid he would look down on her. It was just that, a long time ago, she had determined that no one should look down on her ever again, and she could not break the iron habit of reticence. Besides, James came from a background of drinks before dinner and black-tie social functions; he could not be counted upon to understand. Why bother him with the fact that the marine-supply business had been an unpainted, ramshackle repair shack leaning toward the lake. The downstairs had been crammed with engines in various states of oily disrepair, while Miel and her grandfather occupied the cramped, mildewed rooms overhead.

Nor did James need to know that the first scent she had been aware of in the world, the one that meant security, was the reek of raw chewing tobacco in the old man's beard. And as for the impressive array of cutlery before them—could James possibly see eye to eye with an old tar who thought his granddaughter magnificently equipped for society if she didn't spit on the sidewalk and knew how to use a knife!

She fingered the thick table linen and tried to banish her disturbing thoughts. With any luck, James would drop the subject. The last thing she expected was his subsequent flight of nostalgia for smalltown Ontario.

"How wonderful to grow up in one of those really close-knit places where everybody knows everybody and helps out. The kind of community we city folks can only imagine. Was it really like that?"

"Um—" Miel stopped with a forkful of tiny Brussels sprouts halfway to her mouth "—sort of," she said, recognizing the romantic notions urbanites cherished for the life that never was. "Depended on who you were."

And if you lived with a grease-spotted old curmudgeon at the bottom of the street and it was known that your mother never married and other kids called you "Mailbag," or "Mealy Mealy," then the village was not half so idyllic as affluent Torontonians supposed.

They finished their chicken and were silent briefly as the waiter cleared the plates away.

"He's not still alive, is he?" James asked as if it had suddenly occurred to him there might be a new family responsibility he should presently consider.

"Who?"

"Your grandfather."

"Oh no. He died when I was still in my teens. I left the village then." In a lower voice she added, "I've never been back."

Now James was sure to press for all the gory details of a time she was determined to forget. She braced herself to fend him off, forgetting for a moment that James was made of more considerate stuff. His hand closed briefly over hers.

"You must have loved him very much."

This was so unforeseen that Miel actually started, jarring the table. Out of the past where it was meant to stay leaped the image of her grandfather's contorted face calling her tramp, trash, fool and all those other terrible words only someone of his generation could fling out. She saw again the horrible paleness seeping over him just seconds before that final crippling stroke. . . .

Her fist clenched on James's surprised palm.

"Yes," she muttered fiercely. "Yes, I did! He was everything I had in the world!"

Swiftly, James laid down his fork.

"Oh Miel, I'm sorry. How thoughtless of me. I know how it was when mother died. Why are we talking this way when we came here to enjoy ourselves?''

Behind a slightly crooked smile, Miel made her typical and admirable recovery. The past was packed away. Once again she became the cosmopolitan woman at home with baba au rhum and matched silver. No one would ever guess she had once been a grubby, jam-faced urchin playing with scrap in the corner of a broken-down repair shop and staying up half the night to keep the old man company. She leaned forward and lifted her glass, the Gagnon silk lit like sea fire against the dusky folds of the shadowed drape.

"More champagne?''

She was determined to restore the festivity, and in a moment they were toasting each other playfully over the small centerpiece of cut carnations.

"Glad you hired me now?'' she asked mischievously.

"I drink to the day. I can still see you standing there in the middle of my office, that chin of yours stuck out, insisting you'd do any job I asked.''

"Is that what decided you?''

Miel had long harbored a secret embarrassment over her outburst that day. It hadn't been brazenness that had motivated her but sheer desperation. She knew there were other applicants more suitable than herself, waiting in the hall.

"Quite frankly, yes. Pure spunk. You showed you had possibilities. I thought you could be brought along.''

"And if I had been bluffing?"

"Then you would have shortly been unemployed again," James returned cheerfully, swirling his wine in his glass. Miel's glimpse of his underlying steel made her shiver, and she was thankful she had been up to snuff. Would they ever be old enough or comfortable enough together for her to tell him she had spent her last nickel on a haircut for the interview and that only a few weeks previous to her hiring, she had been scraping carrots at a pitted sink in a third-rate hotel with nothing ahead of her but masses more vegetable peelings and despair?

The restaurant was almost full now, and the background noises grew more noticeable—little laughs lifting, cutlery clinking discreetly. It grew time for the candles on the tables to be lit. When their candle was lit, Miel could not help but feel that the soft glow had created an island upon which she and James would drift together from now on. Bonds of loyalty, affection, deep regard would hold her steadfast through all weathers. If James wanted her, nothing, she vowed, would blow out their little flame.

"Hey there, two pennies for your thoughts. Why are those eyes so dreamy?"

Caught out, she stumbled badly.

"I . . . well, actually, I was thinking of the Gagnon campaign. And Hildy. Do you suppose she's really up to it?"

Oh, how could she have evaded him so instantly and so readily? The past was one thing but she had been thinking about the present, and her natural candor warned her there should be no barriers now. Dismay touched her. She should share herself more easily. But then. . . this was all so new.

James, missing her evasion, turned all too eagerly back to business. His brows took that odd slant they always took whenever Hildy was mentioned—slightly quizzical, as if reminding himself all over again that he was the one who had hired her.

"The whole thing's a gamble because we've got to get the right kind of coverage fast. I'll bet—" he chuckled in the direction of an exceedingly healthy asparagus fern "—I'll bet she chooses something very watery. The theme of the whole collection this year is the sea. I hope," he said soberly, "we don't drown."

It was true. Hélène Gagnon, who did her best work holed up in a crumbling villa clutching an unfashionable cliff on the Atlantic coast, had named the collection Seascape, turning it out in colors like shrimp, pebble, aqua and so on. Some of it was deckwear meant for pleasure boats.

Silenced by a new reticence, Miel bit into her crème caramel. Things nautical. She hated them. Now what was James going to think when he found *that* out about her?

At length the champagne bottle in its bath of melting ice was whisked away and coffee came, strong and fragrant in dainty china cups. Miel poured cream and stirred it round and round, the action of the silver spoon vaguely hypnotic until she set it clumsily back in the saucer and spilled dark drops onto the snowy cloth.

"Oh!"

James peered at her anxiously.

"I'm sorry, Miel. I forgot. It must be God knows what hour of the morning for you."

"I... well, yes, I guess. Jet lag and all that champagne...."

The candle and the glimmering wall scones had in fact begun to fuzz slightly under her drooping lids. James took charge, flicking his hand with authority for the check, gathering her up from her chair, shepherding her toward the door. It was so comfortable the way he did it, yet she felt she had to grasp his elbow to slow his determined speed.

"It's been wonderful, James. Really."

He smiled and tucked his arm around her waist. Outside, she was surprised to find it still light, though now the sun was low, slanting light along Yorkville, gilding the café railings, and turning the pavement into a city version of the yellow brick road. She shook her hair in the reviving evening breeze and cast a wistful glance toward the still-crowded outdoor tables. Then James was taking her home, insisting on driving her in her own car. Before they left, Miel asked to stop to get the roses from her office. Now she sat in the passenger seat, cradling the delicate, fragrant buds.

The Corvette had a gearshift sweet to the palm and a gas pedal light as a leaf. At the first intersection the car almost leaped out of James's hands into the tail of a plumber's pickup just ahead.

"Phew! Talk about having a mind of its own. Why did you buy a beast like this?"

Why indeed? Something about the thrust of the seat into the small of her back as it roared off the freeway ramp, the long growl of the motor up through the frame and into her bones. It appealed to an embarrassing wildness still left in her, the same that on certain bright windy days would make her take her tennis racket and slam and slam and slam....

"Oh, it's quick and handy," she heard herself say, laughing. "And there's so little cargo space, it keeps my shopping in line."

I'm doing it again. Will it always be like this with James?

He saw her to the fifteenth floor of the building he himself had recommended almost two years before—a good address on St. Clair. He had wanted her to have a better view of the lake, but Miel was content not to look at it. From her living-room window that distant band of blue beyond the monoliths of King and Bay was quite enough to cope with.

"Coffee?" she asked, determined to be gracious even though the jet lag was making it difficult to decide which of her keys fitted the lock.

The corners of James's mouth dipped gently. He shook his head. Once again, Miel detected that slight awkwardness in the midst of all his urbanity. Hesitating, he bent, brushing her lips just enough to make a promise, sweet and firm for another day.

"For luck," he murmured. He took her by the shoulders, meaning, perhaps, to say a calm good-night. The warm firmness of her under the silk arrested him, and his hands suddenly gripped her as if he had just then realized that flesh and blood and desire were what the whole thing was supposed to be about.

"Has anyone ever told you how beautiful you are, Miel? Hélène Gagnon was right about the name, Seascape. In that outfit you ought to be standing on the prow of a boat with a smart breeze and the sunset behind you...."

A gasp tore from Miel's throat.

"Don't, James! Please don't say things like...."

She stopped herself too late. James had let go of her, his eagerness abruptly, brutally extinguished.

"I'm very sorry. You're tired, Miel, and I... didn't mean to upset you. Goodbye."

Then he was gone, leaving her clutching a mass of roses and staring after his retreating back. She was horrified to think he had revealed a tender spot and she nad trodden on it.

I didn't mean it that way, she wanted to call after him. *I didn't.*

But she made no sound. She sagged back against the doorjamb, knowing what James could not—that after all these years her heart could still hurt when she thought of herself against sails taut with wind.

She listened until she could no longer hear the hum of the elevator carrying him away. Then she stepped inside, kicking off her shoes on the thick carpet. Shutting her eyes, she inhaled the fragrance from the crimson flowers in her arms until the champagne-tinged euphoria came back and she could think of sleep.

CHAPTER THREE

MIEL WAS SOUND ASLEEP at ten the next morning when the phone made her stir drowsily in the depths of her lavender-scented sheets.

"Mmmmnnnn," she groaned.

The ringing persisted. She opened one eye and searched for the receiver.

"Hi," laughed James. "Had your beauty sleep?"

The pleasure and surprise of yesterday came flooding back. Miel tipped her head and smiled, a languid, dewy drowsiness upon her lids.

"Champagne buzz, I think, is the term. I haven't twitched a muscle since I hit the mattress. It's sweet of you to call."

"Sweet indeed," he returned with that dry wit that so often saved his sobriety. "Just an excuse to zing you with the first problem of the day."

"Don't tell me! The samples didn't arrive!"

Miel righted herself against the pillows, apricot lace falling away to reveal the whiteness, like fine cream, along her collarbone.

"Oh, they're here all right. It's Hildy. She's been going like a miniature fury ever since you arrived. Taken up the sea theme and run with it.

She insists we rent a yacht at the very least to shoot the ads on.''

"So?''

She was sitting up straight now, her hand tighter on the phone.

"Crome's doesn't usually go in for his kind of grandstanding, so I'm afraid I gave her some flak about our image. She promptly inspected the entire harbor and decided there was only one thing afloat ritzy enough for the Gagnon line. Of course the fellow who owns it has totally refused to lease.''

"Can't Hildy offer him more money? What's so special about it anyway?''

"She's says it's old-fashioned and romantic looking. Fancy carved wood instead of plain old fiberglass. And yes, she did offer more money—an outrageous sum as a matter of fact—and he still isn't biting. I could have told her anyone rich enough to own that sort of transportation isn't about to be tempted by mere cash.''

Miel became uncomfortably aware of what he was leading up to. She swung her legs over the edge of the bed and frowned at her bare knees.

"I was planning to go over the new lingerie order today.''

"One try, Miel. How about it?''

In the early days his voice had held a calm authority she had responded to at once. Lately, as her competence and status grew and he shared more and more of the management with her, he always made her feel that whatever she did was the result of consultation between two rational individuals. Now it struck her that he was almost cajoling her. This was so untypical of James her stomach contracted.

It's the mention of boats, she thought. *After last night.*

The memory of her own clumsiness surfaced to haunt her. She would do what she could to make amends. Already she was reaching with her toes for her slippers.

"Okay, sure. Where do I find the guilty party?"

"Down in that slip next to Harbourfront. He lives aboard, I think. Check with Hildy about his name."

Miel hung up, pausing to rub the remaining sleep from her eyes. If she had refused, James would have stepped in himself, offering no reproaches but noting her reluctance. Well, she did not intend to stain her record at this point. This fellow would rent his yacht if she had to bring him back to the office in a sack.

A small job really, even if it did display a rather unusual indulgence on James's part toward Hildy. She ignored the tick of tension building inside her but dressed with particular care, choosing a wheat-colored linen dress, nylons and her fawn kid heels—in short, everything unsuitable for climbing around on a boat. The last thing she did was phone Hildy in an effort to confirm the owners name. She reached Jan, the assistant.

"Hildy's out for a sandwich. One of those things full of alfalfa sprouts. I can't find any name, but you can't miss the boat. Big yummy-looking thing tied up in the last spot next to the wall.''

Miel bucked traffic all the way down Spadina, a broad, raucous avenue piercing the garment district. At the foot she rumbled over a blackened iron bridge spanning the bunched ganglia of railway tracks where diesels gulped fuel from underground tanks and trans-Canada passenger trains slid into the gray caverns of Union Station just beyond.

Turning east onto Queen's Quay, which ran parallel to the harbor, she parked next to Harbourfront, a former warehouse converted into a cultural resource, gay with flags and landscaping, craft shops, art gallery, theater and even an airy outdoor café. The boat slip was next to it. The harbor itself was sheltered by the green and cradling arm of Toronto Island, actually a curving spit composed of interconnected islands and lagoons, which were serviced by ponderous black-and-white ferries chugging through the sunny waves.

The boat basin was spanned by an arching footbridge. Inside, connected by floating catwalks, were tethered dozens of pleasure boats of every size and description, all of them swarming with sunburned owners making ready for the coming summer afloat.

The moment Miel shut her car door, the excruciatingly familiar scent of the lake assailed her. Involuntarily, she took a hungry gulp, then regretted it. Into her mind sprang a similar shore perhaps a hundred miles to the east. The massive old dock with its pilons being eaten away. The Queen Anne's lace that used to look so white and intricate against the weathered boards of the shop. The foam turning over and over again the gray pebbles at the water's edge.

Dismissing the images, she found the steps that gave access down to the bobbing craft. Because of the bridge and the swaying tangle of masts she could see nothing clearly, and she had to concentrate on keeping her heels out of the cracks between the boards. Two children giggling on the stern of a jaunty red cutter distracted her. A woman lugging two bags of groceries stared pointedly down at the troublemaking shoes.

Finally Miel reached the very end of the slip, where she steadied herself by placing her fingers on the rough wall beside her and looked up. A startled, agonized cry ripped from her throat. There before her, a specter with solid planking and furled sails! The *Yancy*.

No wonder she had missed it at a distance. Instead of the flaking hulk on which she had once so humbly scrubbed and scraped her fingers raw, the *Yancy* now gleamed, flawlessly restored, masts soaring against the clouds, brightwork shining, solid teak appointments mellow in the morning light. Here, at the end of the slip, the yacht was unmistakable, its aristocratic, faintly antiquated lines standing out vividly among all the fiberglass and plastic—hand-fashioned royalty amid a crowd of factory-stamped pretenders.

For the first few seconds of shock, Miel could not get enough oxygen into her lungs. The muscles of her diaphragm heaved. She felt herself shrinking smaller and smaller until she became a tiny dot in the center of an all-engulfing faintness. Only the greatest effort of will kept the scene from reeling drunkenly before her eyes. Blindly, she began to back away until one of her foolish heels jammed in the catwalk, pitching her toward the dark green water at the side.

Powerful hands grasped her before she even had a chance to cry out. Her foot came out of the caught shoe. She found herself righted and turned.

"Careful, lady, these walkways are no place for high heels. You might have...."

That voice, that oh-so-well-remembered voice stopped dead, and Miel found herself staring into eyes suddenly gray as storm scud. Seven years had bleached his hair and darkened his tan to a permanent ruddy stain. The sailor's creases had deepened at the corners of his eyes, and his shirt, instead of the tattered, paint-stained garments he used to favor, was a respectable polo knit, with not a spatter on it.

But his mouth was exactly the same. Easy, sensuous—and for Miel, the cruelest mouth in the world.

The gray gaze narrowed, scanning her swiftly, fiercely. It only took a moment before his eyes widened in recognition. She was vaguely aware of the electricity in the air, but the sight of him had hit her like an explosion. An explosion named Barth Tramande.

"Miel! My God! Is it really you?"

His voice sank to a scraping whisper. He seemed almost to blanch.

For many, many months after he had abandoned her, Miel used to long for just this moment, this very opportunity to spit out her hatred, strike at his heart as he deserved. In the empty dark of the night she had lain hatching scathing, withering rejoinders. In the long hours slaving at the greasy hamburger joint in an effort to support herself and her newly invalid grandfather, she invented bitter curses to impale him like a crawling insect should he ever be so unfortunate as to cross her path again.

That was seven years ago. Now, after the shock of seeing him, she felt her mind was a deep and yawning blank filled only by the inane observation that his forelock was as tangled and his lashes as golden as that first day he had tossed her a mooring line on the Bay Point dock.

In slow motion, the horrible moment passed. Blood returned to her heart. Her awareness of his fingers gripping her arms became an overwhelming burning sensation scorching her to her marrow. In a single violent movement she wrenched herself free. Her remaining shoe tumbled to join its mate.

The man was still bereft of speech. He kept looking at her as if a water sprite had material-

ized between his callused palms. When finally
he did speak, the words tumbled over each other
as if there were seven years of things to say and
only a moment to say them in.

"Miel! If I'd had the slightest idea you were
in this city. . . . What are you doing down here at
the harbor? Of course you must have your own
boat now and. . . ."

"No, I don't have a boat. I was sent. . .to
rent yours!"

"Mine?" he asked incredulously. "Don't tell
me you're with those cream-puff fashion people!"

"I. . . ."

After one attempt at speech her mouth began
to go dry. A rushing swirled in her ears. Her
dress had to be quivering from the hammering
in her breast. He was leaning so close to her she
picked up the scent of that soap he must still use
and the smell of clean sun-dried cotton. The
combination evoked that time, so long ago,
when he had crushed her to him. Her brain
rapped out one frantic signal. *Get away,* it said.
Just get away!

She tried to slip past him on the narrow catwalk, but he jumped quickly to block her way.

"Hey, wait! You just can't go barreling off.
At least come aboard the *Yancy.* We'll. . .we'll
talk."

She knew he was groping for something to
hold her and for some reason this brought on a
savage burst of energy. She felt quite up to
throttling him with her bare hands. Her child-

hood and her present fell away, leaving only the explosion that had strewn its wreckage through the best of her young years.

"Go to hell!" she snapped. "You and your boat both!"

Unconscious of her bare feet, she dodged him and bolted, her expensive nylons shredding as she sped up the embankment to her car. The powerful engine earned its reputation as Miel gained the street and drove and drove until the car was deposited in her underground garage and she herself fled into the refuge of her apartment.

Numb and panicked, she wanted nothing more than to be able to call James and crawl straight into his arms, but she knew that she could not. She could just imagine the startled look on his handsome face should she ever burst into his office in such a state. Even now the blaze of scarlet roses on her little parson's table glowed a gentle accusation at her, as if she had done something already to betray his trust.

The first thing she did was pull the drapes, for the lake had suddenly become an insupportable blue presence just beyond the downtown skyline. And the CN Tower, dominating everything, might even then be pouring its enormous shadow over the *Yancy*. She wanted to keep the roses separate, to sit enclosed with their light reassuring scent. But again and again, she returned to ponder why meeting this man, whom she had many times assured herself was utterly forgotten, should affect her like a lightning bolt on a clear and peaceful day.

When she had taken off her ruined nylons, washed her face and poured a small brandy, she found she felt much better. Once she was comfortable in the embrace of her many-cushioned sofa, her muscles finally relaxed, though her mind began to surge and swell like a dark sea feeling for the first time in a century the winds of turmoil and change. Laying her head against the yielding surface, she closed her eyes.

INSTANTLY, SHE WAS TRANSPORTED back to a beautiful day in Bay Point, a day much like this one, with gulls turning lazy loops and Lake Ontario the color of dark sapphire, flung with foam in the stiff breeze tumbling the waves toward the shore.

Miel was almost seventeen then, a skinny, mop-topped creature compounded of elbows and knees and a flapping old shirt torn under the arm. Sprawled on the sagging dock, she scraped patterns in the wood with the stub of a nail. The sharpness of the gouges had a great deal to do with the fact that all the other kids her age were at Melanie Spencer's barbecue, and she hadn't exactly been invited.

Her exclusion was an old story, and much of the time she brought it upon herself. She supposed she had been blissfully happy as a tot perched on grandpa's blackened workbench. With a marmalade sandwich in one hand and a perfectly grubby stuffed duck in the other, she watched the old man work. The two of them kept to themselves. She had no idea then that they were considered the village scandal owing in part to the fact that they never bought a decent stick of furniture and the atrocious way the old man swore in front of the child.

The first day of school changed all that. Her blouse had an egg stain from breakfast, her hair was ragged, she toted her lunch in an ugly battered bucket left over from grandpa's stint at a shipyard. Miel had remained pretty good-natured despite all the teasing until they started pulling her hair. Then she kicked and bit until Mrs. Brower yanked her by the waistband and made her sit in the corner as an example of a naughty, naughty girl. Miel had sat. Never once did she cry.

The kids weren't so eager to pick on her after that, and Miel soon learned to protect herself with an attitude of splendidly careless defiance. It got her through grade school fine and dandy but cost her the help of those who might have proved refining influences on her life. She continued to wear her mismatched clothes and her wild hair. And when the pangs of adolescence struck her, she hid them just as proudly—all the little hurts and spurts of joy and the terrible longings that had no name.

She squelched them so well that day, that finally she dozed in the sun and so missed the approach of a large, scruffy vessel, which slid around the point and up to the long, dilapidated pier that had once served lake-fishing boats.

The yacht bumped against the leaning uprights. It was a pleasure yacht, though its finery had fallen into unbelievable disrepair. Miel had practically leaped straight into the air, before she recovered her senses and scrambled to her feet. The yacht was missing its masts, ancient paint peeled off in blisters, the wooden deck was gray and unvarnished and one of the portholes was staved in. Nevertheless, speed, courage and beauty stood out in every unkempt line. A man leaned over the side. With unerring aim, he tossed out a line.

"Here, young lady, give this a couple of turns."

Miel froze as the heavy rope slapped down at her feet and began to slide toward the water.

"Hey, it's getting away!"

Instinctively, she moved. With the same competence as the man, she grasped the line and looped it fast while the fellow leaped to the dock to secure the yacht aft.

Miel remembered how she had stared at him. How he was like nothing she had ever seen before. Tall, rippling with muscles, bristling with energy and moving with the agile, leonine grace of a born sailor. To anyone else, a young man so obviously at ease with the water, combined with a yacht in such deplorable condition, might simply have spelled boat bum. To Miel, however, he looked like a spangled sea god springing miraculously onto the Bay Point shore.

The fellow surveyed the village, then tossed his teenage spectator a grin.

"Kind of pretty here. Might stay a while and work on my boat. Where can I get some grub?"

His voice had seemed impossibly rich, so that it mattered not the least that his torn green T-shirt was shrunk over his ribs or that his dungarees, cut off at the knees, trailed a tattered fringe when he moved. Though clearly only in his early twenties, his face was tanned enough for a dozen years at sea, and his eyes had that piercing quality that comes from constant scanning of far horizons.

"Your ladyship, I'm looking for a grocery store."

Miel jerked back, suddenly, mortifyingly aware of how she had been gaping.

"Up there," she blurted. "Palmer's. You can see it when you get onto the road."

The man rubbed a hand through fair hair bleached to the color and texture of new straw.

"Great. I've been wrestling that wheel all night, and I could eat a shark. Thanks, peanut."

He strode off up the tipsy planks leaving Miel with a dull red sting seeping up along her cheekbones.

"Boy, has he got a nerve!"

After a time the fellow reappeared laden with two huge grocery bags. Miel realized she was still standing in the same spot. He would think she had been gawking at his boat all that time. Well, she didn't have to gawk at any old boat. She had her own.

She zoomed off to the bank by the shop where a scarred sailing dinghy was tied up, ostensibly in case anyone wanted to buy it. Really, it was

Miel's boat, the one her grandfather had taught her to sail in. Sailing was her one certain escape from the growing pains Bay Point had thrust upon her.

She paused, noting the curl of the whitecaps and the silvery poplar leaves. Grandpa would yell if he saw her going out, but he was changing the bearings in a chain saw, so she knew he was occupied for the day.

Pointedly ignoring the visitor, Miel loosened the painter and cast off. Out in the open she ran up the sail, grasped the tiller and headed the bow of the fragile craft out into the lake. Instantly the wind took the canvas, sending the dinghy leaping joyously into the long green waves.

In a few moments the sound of water hissing under the hull sent the familiar exhilaration singing through her, and the way she changed was quite extraordinary. On land she was a collection of uncoordinated growing bones, hunching her shoulders and bumping into things. In the boat she turned into a mariner, at one with her craft, alive to every lift and shudder under the spread sail, balancing like a seabird every time the dinghy struck a wave and heeled. Add to that her natural teenage recklessness and Miel made a truly heart-stopping sight, scudding madly through the foam.

The moment she was past the sheltering point, the wind took her in earnest, propelling the dinghy so forcefully that spray broke over the bow, and water splashed in at the port gun-

wale that was even with the waves. A more sedate sort would have reefed the sail and worked
back toward the protection of land. Not Miel.
Unperturbed, she ran as far out in the lake as
she dared, shifted the boom and tacked about,
all the while bucking crests that threatened to
swamp the little boat. With the wind behind her,
she raced to the east. Then, for the hell of it,
turned and sailed, close-hauled as much into the
wind as she could go, zipping past the harbor
mouth and back again.

She stayed out, running dares with the gusts
until a sudden blast all but knocked the sail into
the water. Only by the speediest action did Miel
save herself. Cold spray caught her in the chest.
Even she realized it was time to go in.

Shaking herself, laughing at the water dripping from her elbows, she worked back and
skimmed with a swanlike flourish up to the
shop. As she leaped ashore she saw out of the
edge of her eye a tall figure perched on the
yacht's cabin roof devouring an enormous sandwich. That same figure had sat there all the time
Miel had been out. She hadn't looked at it. Nor
for all the world would she admit she had been
showing off, though that's exactly what she had
been doing.

Taking her own sweet time, she tested the fabric of her plaid shirt, which had been whipped
dry in minutes by the boisterous breeze. Then,
lifting her chin toward the rooftops, she strolled
past the end of the larger dock, the joy of having sailed keeping her youthful awkwardness at

bay and giving a glimpse of the grace that would be hers when her body finally stopped growing.

"Hey, kid, come here. You could have drowned yourself taking that cockleshell out on a day like this."

Miel fumed at being thus addressed.

"I sail whenever I like," she answered loftily. "And if you don't mind, I'm not a kid!"

That was the first time she'd heard his laugh—a low husky sound that vibrated like caressing, playful fingers up and down her vertabrae. His eyes, smoky and direct, ran over her, head to toe.

"I see. Well then, Miss All-Grown-Up, come and let me talk to you."

Miel felt her old, earthbound gaucherie return, and she hesitated, suspicious of his lightly teasing manner.

"It's okay. I won't bite. I need to find out a few things about this place."

Already the spell of this man was working on her. Unable to help herself, she strolled toward the big yacht. The man finished his sandwich in two lusty bites and came to the side. A shock of wind-ruffled hair fell across his forehead. He waited until Miel was opposite.

"I was going to say you're quite a sailor, miss, and I'd ship you on as crew anytime. Think it would be all right if I tied up here for a few weeks? I need a quiet place to scrape down this boat."

Miel shrugged as if to say he could scrape down the whole dock if he wanted to. Her eyes strayed over the dilapidated vessel, and the man laughed again.

"Sure needs work, doesn't it? Just bought it this week from a Thousand Islands estate. Millionaire named Sperry had it built specially, but the next two generations left it in the boathouse to molder." He ran his hands along the curved wood with a gesture as close to love as Miel had ever seen. "Solid mahogany on grown-oak frames. And look at the lines of the hull. Can't wait to see it cut the side out of a good Grand Banks nor'easter."

Miel referred to the missing masts.

"How'd you get here? Motor?"

"All the way. Took three days just to get the antique started. Got new diesels ordered in the city along with masts and sails, but nothing'll be delivered inside a month. I might as well stick around here and start on the woodwork."

Blisters, bare patches, large stains ran from bow to stern. Over sixty feet of painful scrubbing, sanding, varnishing and painting looked Miel in the eye. Her heart speeded up. Some wild impulse took possession of her tongue.

"You don't need any help, do you? I mean... I could use an afterschool job."

The man's brow lifted slowly in speculation, while his forthright scrutiny made Miel flush.

"Sure—if it won't interfere with your studies."

Studies! She studied when she felt like it, and that was that. The rest of the time she wandered the shore or sat in the shop listening to the salty talk of the local men.

"It won't bother me. I want to make some money."

"Okay, then. Barth Tramande's the name. What's your's?"

"Miel McCrae."

"Miel. That's a new one. Means something in French."

Miel had been braced for this, as always, when someone new had occasion to learn what she was called. She cherished her name and was always afraid that once people discovered the translation they'd use it in some cheap, casual way. If anyone tried, she was quite prepared to flatten them.

"It means...something sweet," she muttered, defying him with her whole thin body.

She waited for the wisecrack to come, but it didn't. Barth seemed to be amused, but in a kindly manner.

"I know, I know. And I won't call you Honey. Now let's see what we can do about some scrapers."

He understood. Her heart soared up and up. And that was the moment she fell helplessly, fatally and unreservedly in love!

THE TELEPHONE SHRILL interrupted her reverie. Miel leaped up from the sofa and was momentarily disoriented. The sun was still shining and she had never actually left her luxurious apartment. Gratefully, she grasped the receiver. Thank heaven! The warm, steady voice of James. A voice touched with elation.

"Miel! Hildy is dancing in the aisles. I don't know what kind of persuasion you used, but that Tramande fellow phoned and said we're welcome to the yacht as long as we need it."

"He did?"

"Yes. He's really taken with you, apparently. Made it a condition of the contract that you be present personally to oversee everything we do even though I assured him that our advertising staff is perfectly competent...."

"James, you didn't agree!"

Her dismay caused James to pause in bafflement.

"Certainly I did. I knew it might be a bit of an annoyance for you, but Hildy was so overjoyed that I had the papers made up right away. She's down now getting them signed." He hesitated. Then, "You really don't mind, do you? Probably be just a couple of times or so."

"I...."

Words half formed in her mind suddenly dissolved. To say she objected would mean explaining her former acquaintance to James. James would get talking with Barth and then... oh, how would she bear it if the whole idiotic, hurtful, embarrassing episode was dragged out into the open....

"I...I guess it's all right," she managed. "I just hate to take time from the office now that there's so much to do."

"Don't worry. Maybe we can spare somebody else to go down. I don't see why he'd be that particular."

"Maybe."

But as she hung up, Miel knew that Barth would be very particular. He would accept no substitute, would demand her presence every moment Crome's was near his boat. Her hands began to shake, and she balled them into fists to keep them still. Barth Tramande had rented his yacht to Crome's for one reason only—to gain access to her.

Why, she wondered irritably, why did he want near her now? Why, after what he had done, after the horrid way he had cast her away did he suddenly insist on thrusting himself upon her once again?

Did he still, so many years afterward, want to look at his handiwork? Did he think she could like him again? Did he have the unutterable arrogance to imagine he could rekindle her infatuation enough to provide him with casual amusement while he lingered in this port?

She began to pace rapidly, mindless of the glass coffee table she jolted in her fury and alarm. For the first time since she had moved in, the lovely apartment seemed too small, too cramped, too much like a trap shutting her off from open air and escape. Finally, she flung herself down on the sofa and stared miserably at the ceiling.

Curse that man for reappearing in her life right now. Just when she was about to win the calm, protective safety of James's arms!

CHAPTER FOUR

AT DUSK MIEL WAS STANDING in front of her mirror, brushing her hair with firm, calm strokes. A confrontation. Yes, a confrontation might be best after all. Her future had changed irrevocably with James's roses. She ought to rake it clean of ghosts like Barth.

The convolutions of logic that had brought her to this conclusion did not bear looking at, and Miel had no desire to. Her reaction earlier in the day had now assumed a disturbing dimension of melodrama. Surely everyone in the world had some disaster in his or her life. What an embarrassment to find herself still so sensitive underneath.

When she was finished with her hair, she touched a little blusher to the unusual pallor of her cheeks, then adjusted the jabot of her peach silk blouse, for she had long ago embraced Lillian Crome's dictum that good clothes were a comfort to the soul. She would make herself tea in her Staffordshire pot. Later, of course, James would call.

The tea was just steeping and the cup set out when a rap at the door disturbed her painfully won peace. Dabbing on a last drop of perfume,

Miel flew across the carpet, not even pausing to think how unlike James it was to arrive without announcing himself through the intercom. She pulled the door open—then froze with her hand halfway to the chain.

"You!" she gasped.

She had not realized how much she had been counting on James until she met those keen gray eyes.

"I brought your shoes back, Miel."

Burly and brawny, with his shirt opening to reveal a mat of bleached hair, he was as out of place in that hushed, gold-papered hall as a gust of March wind. Miel stood staring at him, wanting to slam the door, catching herself in time to be ashamed of the fierce childishness of the desire. Slowly, very slowly, she lifted her hand the rest of the way, and the chain fell from the slot.

He stepped in without being asked, then stopped in the center of her lush carpet to look at her. Miel, at a loss for words, was only able to think that he was the first person who had ever made the scale of her apartment look so tiny. The shoes were neatly packaged as if he had had them cleaned and repaired. Miel took them dumbly.

"I'll just put them away," she managed, playing for time.

She opened a closet, painfully aware, in the silence, of the rasp of silk along her upper arms and the burning up her back that told her Barth hadn't lifted his gaze from her since he had entered the room.

"Tea?" she asked, turning to the now hope-lessly dainty teapot.

"I'd rather have a drink, if I could."

Automatically, she went to the small side-board and poured out a whiskey, only aware, at the last moment, why she chose this. There use to be an old blue cup perched on the *Yancy*'s cabin roof, and surely as not, it was filled with whiskey. Every evening at six Barth allowed himself this one drink. Miel had had no idea that the whiskey was the finest. She'd only known that Barth was there, lounging against the cockpit rim, radiating that clean, strong masculinity that had become the very fabric of her dreams.

Her fingers shook slightly as she handed him the glass. He sat down on her wine-colored sofa. Miel, after some hesitation, took the wing chair opposite, still grappling with the implausibility of entertaining this man in her home.

"I suppose you found out where I live from James."

"James Crome? Yes. He was very obliging, as a matter of fact. I told him I had something to return."

Poor James. Was there no limit to that unfail-ing courtesy? What would he have said had he known how the shoes were lost?

They both sipped their drinks. Barth's eyes swept boldly around the apartment, over the airy chintzes and little framed English water-colors and then back.

"So then, Miel, how are you?"

"Just fine."

Though she had meant to sound neutral, she knew she sounded defensive, which made Barth lift his head just slightly. He had matured since Bay Point. If anything, broadened and grown more hard and sinewy. Miel had forgotten how a hardy strength could accompany even the tiniest of his movements.

"I see you're working for a store now."

"Yes."

Still gripped by the surprise of each other's presence, they could manage no more than these brief, clipped words. Miel stared at the center of the coffee table, but out of the corner of her eye she could see the fingers of his free hand slide over the material of the sofa. They were as hard and callused as ever and grated slightly on the delicate slubbed silk. He must still do front-line work, she thought, in spite of being the owner of a large marine-salvage company.

If he still owned it, that is. The brief idyll relaxing in Bay Point, restoring the *Yancy* for his personal use, had been but a long holiday, a sort of ritual farewell to youth before he made his way out to sea to take the brunt of the business from his father's shoulders. And what about Frank, his younger brother who had been just about Miel's age and "immured," as Barth referred to it, in one of those international boarding schools while she was growing up at Bay Point.

Miel fought a brief, unexpected skirmish with curiosity before she opted to remain silent. It was bad enough to know that Barth was examining her.

"Actually, I thought you would have been a marine biologist by now."

A stab of pain caught her under the ribs and she winced. If he meant to be cruel, he had certainly made an efficient start. More likely he was just being thoughtless in the manner of those habitually negligent with other people's lives. She was surprised he even remembered those languid summer evenings spent filling her head with this dream.

"Things don't always turn out the way we expect," she said, relieved by the calmness still in her voice. She was, after all, determined to be terribly adult about all this.

"In your case, might I ask why?"

Why! A fuse inside her flared and was put quickly out. She had her pride. After so many years, it occurred to her for the first time that the truth might make him feel sorry for her, and she'd be damned if she'd tell him anything.

"I changed my mind," she tossed out from behind a wintry smile. "When I got to the city I was lucky enough to find a job at Crome's. James has been very good to me. I worked my way up."

If only he would stop looking at her like that—so intently, taking in every pore of her skin, every tendril of her hair. The corner of his mouth flicked slightly at the mention of James.

"What about your grandfather, then?"

"He died. A stroke."

Deliberately, she made it sound quick and simple, with no hint of the attendant agonies. She didn't want Barth to connect the trauma of her grandfather's illness to the turmoil left behind in the *Yancy*'s wake.

"I'm sorry, Miel. I liked the old man. Was it soon after. . . I left?"

His eyes darkened. They were widely set and tilted slightly so that, at times, they could give the impression of immense kindness and concern. It had been this look, perhaps more than anything else about him, that Miel, a young, gawky thing famished for just that kind of understanding, had fallen for. Even now the old response fluttered in her like the senseless reflex kick left in the legs of a creature otherwise quite dead. Well, she knew about his look. She turned her face toward the dimming window.

"About a year."

A year to the day, almost. And ten months after that first stroke had dropped him across the kitchen table—the day she brought home her final report card, the day he had learned that because of Barth she had failed every one of her final exams.

Silence again. Barth peered into his drink and Miel made a conscious effort not to fiddle with the cuffs of her blouse. He was so big, she thought again, as the dimensions of her sofa were dwarfed by his six feet plus. Hard physical labor gave him a barrel chest and broad shoulders. No suit jacket for this man.

Once she had thought him a veritable Viking

incarnate. Now she was much too sophisticated to fall for the type. If anything, he made her admire all the more the lean, civilized elegance she had come to appreciate in James—and she closed her mind against this living reminder of how much her world had changed since those easy carefree days the two of them had spent in Bay Point.

She caught the tiny line between his brows and knew he must be ruminating. In a moment he would be asking what became of her university career. She roused herself to divert him.

"So, Barth, what brings you here? Surely it isn't the fishing."

"No, not the fishing." For the first time a hint of a smile tugged at his mouth, for one of his pet peeves in Bay Point had been the pollution of the Great Lakes and the decline in numbers of even reasonably edible fish. "Mostly I wanted a holiday, to get away and think. I'm having trouble in the company now with Frank."

So Frank had grown up too, putting away soccer for adult things.

"Frank's a big boy now," Barth continued as if sensing her thoughts. "Couldn't get out of school and into business fast enough. A mover and a shaker, if you know what I mean. He likes to win in the salvage business as much as he did on the old school team. We've already had a number of clashes."

"Clashes?"

Barth had showed her a picture once of a

stocky, jut-jawed kid in sweaty team colors.
Tough, she had thought then, and probably
tougher now. Clashes between Tramandes
would be on an elephantine scale, and it only
now occurred to her what a formidable oppo-
nent Barth might be.

"Doesn't your dad keep things in line?" she
asked in spite of herself.

"Dad's been dead for three years now."

"Oh."

That caught her off guard, having to concede
that death had touched him too. She toyed uneasily with the handle of her cup.

"Frank's damned good, but he can't think of
anything but profit. Give him one ship, he
wants five. Give him one sector, he wants three.
He can't help it. Just something in his bones.
Soon the company won't be big enough for the
two of us."

So the intervening years have been filled with
trouble and change for him too.

"So what are you going to do?" Miel inquired casually, unable to deny her interest.

He cocked his head exactly the way he used to
when the two of them discussed what kind of
varnish to use on the forepeak—discussions
made intensely sensual for Miel by the brush of
his body as he bent close and the sunlight that
tangled in the little golden hairs on the backs of
his hands as he turned over unopened cans.

"I don't know yet, but we're headed for a
blowout because Frank is one of those people
who just can't share command. In an outright

scrap, of course, I'd win hands down. I've got the authority and the experience, and the crews are loyal. But my own brother!" He grimaced. "I'd never be able to look myself in the face again."

Carefully, Miel put down her cool tea.

"Why not simply split the company?"

Barth snorted.

"That would be worse. Two outfits fighting like dogs for what business there is. Frank would have nothing to restrain him then, and times are just as hard out there as they are here. Salvage ships don't grow on trees."

Despite the concern in his voice, something of his old easiness was coming back. His constantly wandering life had made him quick to adapt to new situations—and no doubt take them over. He was obviously relaxed, spreading out all over the cushions, his tone becoming richly husky and much too personal.

Miel recoiled to find she had been following the swing of his voice, the lilt of that accent that had seemed so exotic against the plain, flat vowels of Bay Point. Though Canadian, Barth had spent his childhood in boarding schools scattered around the world where his father happened to be working. She could hear accents from Britain and Australia spiced with the Côte d'Azur and a hint of Martinique.

She knew there was a big house somewhere too, on the wild coast of Nova Scotia, but except for a caretaker it remained painfully empty. Barth's mother had died shortly after the birth of Frank. The boys had spent all their free time dashing about the sea on a ship with their dad.

Odd how her perceptions remained locked in the past. There could well be a wife in the big house now and a platoon of children shrieking through the halls. Without thinking, her gaze dropped to his left hand. Barth laughed and extended the bareness for her to see.

"There aren't that many women on the high seas, Miel. I'm still disgustingly available."

He started to grin, then had the decency to stop. Miel felt the flush climb up her neck.

I used to imagine I'd be your wife, cried out a voice inside her with more anguish than Miel thought possible. In an instant, she was back in Bay Point—callow, moonstruck, going faint from love each time he knelt on the deck beside her. She had been buoyed by the easy camaraderie as they worked together, her dazzled youthful vision unable to extend beyond the wish to ride beside him, in his glorious, vital presence, all the days of her life.

And then he had torn it all away. . . .

She pursed her lips, angry with all this turmoil over simply another teenage crush, surely as benign and ordinary as thousands just like it. She had fallen harder than most because of her loneliness and a headful of romantic notions, thanks to her grandfather's endless yarns of the sea. Barth had a scar from a stonefish sting on his left ankle and could talk of giant waterspouts and coral reefs and tiny Galapagos finches that would drink fresh water from the palm of his hand. He was the one who had told her about marine biology, and she had seized the idea hungrily as one way she could satisfy her wanderlust. Oh yes, he had encouraged her to dream but hadn't inquired into what she was doing about her final exams, which were scant days away.

"I used to call you Wild Thing. Remember?"

Now he was eyeing her dainty sleeves and polished nails ironically, saying more clearly than any words that he did not think much of her tailored look or bandbox apartment. She shrugged irritably.

"You used to call me lots of things," she said negligently. "You can hardly expect me to remember now."

But she did remember. To her dismay, the memory came back vividly—the way he used to tousle her hair when he called her Wild Thing, and the way she used to secretly shut her eyes and hug the precious moment to her. She had thought the name so dashingly romantic. Now she guessed it was probably his private joke about the unkempt ragamuffin she had once been. She ran her fingers down the crease of her expensive trousers, silently thanking Lillian Crome for teaching her about good taste.

"I don't know what I expected," he returned in a voice curiously flat, "but I...really thought you'd remember that."

Her head came up, her face both hot and pale. What did he want from her, this man who had casually announced between bites of a sandwich that the new masts and engine had come in. After they were installed in the city, he was off up the St. Lawrence to the sea.

Distinctly she remembered the sensation of blood draining from her face. She must have gone white that time, for he had stopped eating and tucked a finger under her chin.

"Hey, no need to look like that. Let's see a smile."

She had curved her mouth into something that satisfied him and turned away. In her inarticulate, adolescent mind, she could not have said what she was longing for, but in her heart she needed her desperate love to be recognized. If only Barth would speak to her, make promises, arrangements, admit outright he cared.

How she'd worked that last afternoon, her heart sinking as each hammer and screwdriver was packed away. When the very last moment had come, he handed her an envelope, fat with pay, and slipped his arm around her waist. At the foot of the dock, his playfulness had been replaced by a mood Miel had not experienced before—remote, contemplative, silent. Surely, her stuttering heart had cried, surely this was the moment!

Barth took her face in his hands, his thumbs tracing the outline of her jaw, his touch sending her into agonies of longing and expectation.

"Goodbye, Wild Thing. There's a good life waiting out there for you. You're so damned young. Someday, maybe, we just might meet again.''

With a brief brush of his lips on her forehead he dismissed her and vanished into the *Yancy*. Miel stumbled home, unable to believe that, with a few shallow words, he had sent her off the boat and out of his life. ''Goodbye, Miel. You're so damned young!''

His farewell throbbed like an angry welt on her psyche until midnight, when she had sat bolt upright in bed. In one flash of insight she was possessed of the answer. Barth thought she was too young. No matter how much he liked her he'd never make a move. He was too much of a gentleman.

He could really love me, she had thought in a stupendous leap of consciousness. *He could, he could! If only he understood how I feel. If only... before he sails away!*

She agonized for another half hour as she worked up to the grimmest, most desperately courageous act of her young life. Barth could not leave without knowing. She must go down to the *Yancy* and explain.

She would never forget that night, the soft slap of the dock planks underfoot, the wild rushing of her blood at the base of her throat, the cold fear in the pit of her stomach. The *Yancy*, portholes still burning bright, quivered slightly as she boarded. Almost instantly, Barth appeared.

''Miel! What the devil....''

He was naked to the waist, clad only in denim cutoffs, and Miel, with a speed born of sheer panic, bolted past him into the glowing interior. Once inside she spun round, urgent and vital, her eyes like dark pools in the gentle light.

"I came because you're leaving and...I had to tell you something."

Barth stepped back in, his face wary and serious. Miel had pulled on her best ruffled blouse, which managed to expose most of her thin shoulders. The cabin rapidly filled with the scent of gardenias from a bottle she'd bought at the five-and-dime. She stood awkwardly, feet wide apart, clutching her hands nervously.

"You can't leave without me, Barth. I...love you!"

She had thought he was never going to speak. His jaw dropped, and the muscles of his face flexed as if he was grinding his teeth. Miel trembled, all the passionate yearning of her heart exposed. Throbbing with anticipation, she watched him anxiously as he groped for something to say.

"You're hardly more than a child, Miel. You don't know what you're saying. You shouldn't be...."

"But I am!" The dismay in his face made her even more anguished. "And don't call me a child. I'm old enough to...to want you!"

Her own mother had been scarcely this age when she had run away!

Miel's eyes blurred with hot, gathering tears and Barth's face faded in and out of focus. A series of strange expressions crossed his face and then his eyes grew hard. Miel realized what he was going to say and couldn't bear to hear it. Impelled by a violent surge of emotion, she swayed forward, gripping his arms.

"Barth! Barth. . . darling. . . ."

The unfamiliar endearment came out clumsily, and then she pressed her lips to his with all the innocent force of her untutored fervor.

She would never forget that precise moment. What a shock it had been, the tough but tender feel of a man—the unexpected heat of his skin as her arms reached up to clasp his neck. He remained still as stone, as if waiting for her to weary and drop away. She refused, pressing her young womanly curves against him. She clung until at last the flame that scorched Miel had leaped out to lick him too. With a low moan, he leaned forward, his lips answering hers with excrutiating sweetness.

After a split second of surprise, Miel melted like wax in a furnace. Utterly inexperienced, she was instantly overwhelmed. Veils caught fire and burned away one after another so that her young soul was suddenly faced with staggering vistas of totally unsuspected passion—glorious, terrifying knowledge only a mature woman was equipped to handle. In her wildest dreams she had not thought such ecstasy was possible. Determined to experience everything, she flung herself even closer.

"Oh, take me," she sobbed out, "take me, Barth. Oh. . . please. . . I'm yours!"

The next second she felt herself jerked back by the scruff of her neck like an alley cat. Barth's face was a violent, dreadful red. His teeth were bared in a snarl.

"You damned silly kid. Your grandpa ought to spank the britches off you. Five more minutes and you'd have had bad, bad trouble. Now get your butt out of here and don't come back. I don't fool around with babies!"

Miel had merely stood there, staring in stunned silence, her senses still swooning with desire. Barth emitted an exasperated hiss and moved her himself. Two blinks later she found herself chucked headlong into the dark of night and the hatch slammed behind her.

"Get home this minute," spat a furious voice. "And don't show up here again. Ever!"

The harsh words tore cruelly at Miel. She stumbled against the cockpit, skinned her knees and finally fell as she groped over the gap between the boat and the dock. On her hands and knees she crouched there, shaking and sobbing. Her tears turned the night into a black, star-smeared blur. If she'd thought of it, she would have just plunged herself into the lake, but right then her only instinct was like that of a wounded creature heading for its lair. Scrambling to her feet, she began to run toward the shop, uncaring that she stumbled against two strolling shapes near the bottom of the planks. By the time she crashed her way up the narrow stairs to her room, her breath was like fire in her throat and the noise of her entry woke her grandfather.

"Miel? What the hell? Is that you?"

By then the girl was hunched against her pillows. She didn't answer when the old man called out one more time, then, mumbling darkly, fell back to sleep.

He slept, but Miel lay face down across her bed, all her illusions brought to an abrupt and brutal end, her fledgling heart torn by a wound too bitter, surely, to ever, ever heal. She cried all night. And in the stark clear light of dawn, the *Yancy* was gone!

CHAPTER FIVE

WHAT AN EERIE, UNCOMFORTABLE FEELING it was
for Miel to be sitting in her own airy living room
entertaining such memories. She found herself
staring at her knuckles and praying Barth
hadn't noticed the emotional turmoil beneath
her calm exterior.

Too bad the episode hadn't ended the night
the *Yancy* sailed. Miel might very well have survived it. Many another teenage infatuation had
been ended just as abruptly and forgotten in a
week. However, in Miel's case, being abandoned on the dock wasn't even half of it. Yet
now the past was long gone, and she had sworn
not to let it interfere.

She smoothed the soft creases along her
thigh, uncomfortably aware that Barth's gaze
followed the motion of her hand. *Down, girl,*
she admonished herself. *We are going to keep
our cool, remember!*

After a moment he began fingering the pillow
at his elbow.

"You know," he said suddenly, "I can't get
over this place of yours. It's kind of, I don't
know—" his palms came up in a slightly baffled
gesture "—like a doll's house. You used to be

such an outdoor type, especially when it came to the water. Somehow I never expected to find you in a high-rise and selling clothes.''

"Oh, really?"

Her tone of voice was detached, even faintly amused, but the effort cost her a great deal. The challenge in her eyes made Barth backpedal.

"Oh, I don't mean it's not an okay job—if you like that sort of thing. But you were so bright. Back on the *Yancy* I used to look at you and think, there's a girl who's really going places. Full of capabilities you didn't even suspect you had."

Ignorance might be his excuse, but Miel wouldn't bear this sort of talk for long.

"Oh, so you don't think I need capabilities to pretty well run a store. You should try it sometime—sitting up late over invoices, wondering whether to sink your last cent of capital into stock nobody might buy, worrying with James...."

She stopped, suddenly aware she had been talking about the store as if it were her own—or as if she and James were truly partners instead of employee—employer. Barth's eyes narrowed imperceptibly at the mention of James, but soon he was grinning easily and spreading his palms in a gesture of surrender.

"Hey, I run a business too, remember? I know all about it."

Dusk had come and gone and the city wore a glittering evening coat beyond the undrawn drapes. Miel switched on a small table lamp and immediately a pool of warm yellow light enveloped them, turning Barth's arms to a beautiful gilded umber. Dragging her eyes away from this wide, strong wrists, she resumed her cool exterior as Barth continued.

"Actually, that Crome fellow told me you were his good right hand. Only natural, of course—you're top-notch stuff." He paused, then looked probingly at her. "What did you study at university, then? Business administration?"

A little drumroll of alarm sounded in Miel's breast. *Here it comes,* she thought. *Might as well get it over with.*

"I never went," she returned shortly.

For a moment, he was astonished, then he set down his empty glass sharply and frowned.

"You didn't? Why not?"

"I changed my mind," she lied. "Anyway, after you left I had other things to do."

"Like what?" he demanded, ignoring the edge of anger she had been unable to keep from her voice.

"Just things!"

He was getting too near the truth and Miel was panicked. *Why can't you just go away and leave me alone,* she wanted to shout, but instead she dropped her gaze, astounded by the emotions this man brought out in her.

"I can't imagine what *things* could be more important than a university education," Barth said with infuriating evenness, fastening onto this line of inquiry. Under his scrutiny Miel tried stubborn silence, then could no longer contain herself.

"Grandfather was an invalid for nearly a year. He couldn't talk and barely shuffled around the kitchen. The shop had to be closed up, of course."

"Oh." He was taken aback to have the idea of a swift, painless death dispelled. "So you wouldn't leave him."

"Somebody had to look after him. I took a job in the village."

Even now the sickening scent of hamburger grease came back to her, and all the graveyard shifts she had worked in order to see that the old man was fed and washed and properly put to bed.

A look of what—sympathy, dismay, astonishment—crossed Barth's face and took her by surprise. For some reason, she found it odd that he should have to question her. She suddenly realized she had, for all these years, assumed he had been following the events of her life, knowing each failure as if he had planned it, feeling each triumph as if she had beaten him. How much, she wondered, had this imaginary rivalry motivated her over the years?

"Then he didn't die from the first stroke?"

"No. He lived until the following spring. The second stroke was quick. I left for the city right after the funeral."

"You could have applied for university then."

Oh sure, with a report card full of failures because the finals had been written scarcely a week after Barth left, and she hadn't been able to see straight for grief.

"Look, what is this, some kind of inquisition? I didn't want to go to college. Can't you swallow that?"

That wasn't true either, of course. It was just that the university dream had been so beaten out of her by the time she reached Toronto she hadn't even considered it. Beaten out by her grandfather's tirades and the villagers' sneers during that long, soul-destroying year working at the grill. The trouble had begun the moment she stumbled from the boat, for her humiliation had been witnessed, almost in full, by Myra Baker and Cookie Weston, out for a late-night stroll. By morning the news was all over the village that Miel McCrae, that stuck-up hoyden, had finally made a fool of herself over a man— and a strange sailor at that. By noon grandpa had heard the gossip and blundered furiously into her room. Miel was instantly damned by the yellow blouse flung over a chair and by the reek of gardenia perfume that hung in the close little space. Fixed with ideas two generations removed, baffled a second time by a young female who had grown suddenly and intractably into a woman without his noticing, the old man raged so frightfully Miel shrank beneath her tear-stained sheets. She huddled there most of the week until forced to go to write her exams. When she brought home the damning report card her grandfather had suffered the final blow and had plunged forward, stricken by stroke, crashing over the kitchen furniture to her feet. When he came home from the hospital he had not only lost his speech and physical control, he had lost his authority. No power on earth could have forced Miel back to school.

"And you looked after him until he died," Barth said softly.

"Yes. And then I came straight to the city."

The funeral costs had horrified her. And by then there had been all those unmanageable little debts. A local speculator had offered cash for the shop. Miel sold out without knowing she was handing over valuable waterfront property for a song. She only needed enough to get to the city where she wanted a job—any job—to put Bay Point as far behind her as she could.

The formal finality of her words finally derailed Barth. He made a small apologetic gesture with the hand that lay against the sofa—brown, brawny and jarringly out of place.

"Look, I'm sorry. I guess I don't have the right to pry, but honestly, Miel, I'm interested. I want to know."

"Really! How very *kind* of you!"

Her temper, made savage by the resurrected past, was now barely leashed. Barth's gray eyes were seeking hers, but she allied herself with her present surroundings—and with all that was tasteful, controlled and very, very civilized. She was glad of her fine clothing and her expensive haircut. She belonged to a different world now, and she wanted nothing else but to let him know he was absolutely not a part of it.

Quietly, with a sigh, Barth rose, his frame unfolding with slow, supple ease.

"It's been a long time, Miel. I came thinking perhaps we could talk but you're...different now. I'd better be going."

Incredibly, she felt a pang of something that surely, surely could not be regret. Then, as he moved away, regret changed to relief. As every good hostess does, she, too, rose to show him out.

At the door, Barth paused with his hand on the knob. Miel held her breath, waiting for him to leave. Once again she was impressed by his size and the evidence of muscle showing plainly under his snug shirt. He was really a natural man, totally foreign to the lean, urbane men Miel mixed with nowadays, men fit from squash instead of tough physical labor, men grown indoors like healthy hothouse plants. Once again he was gazing down at her with that disconcerting concentration so different from the cavalier manner she chose to remember.

Why won't he say goodbye, she agonized silently as a nameless tension mounted. *Why won't he simply* go?

Instead, he lifted one of those great hands and touched her cheek—a light, wistful, oddly inquisitive gesture as if he wanted to assure himself that the flesh and blood before him were quite real.

She was so utterly unprepared for his touch

that she jerked away as if scorched, the old rending pain flooding into her eyes for him to see. Immediately, Miel hated herself for her transparency. Without saying a word, Barth smiled—and it was astonishing how sad a smile could be. He lifted his hand again, this time to ruffle, so lightly she barely felt it, her shining hair.

"I knew it," he murmured, a husky softness coming from deep in his throat. "You're not entirely gloss and polish yet, Miel. There's still something in you I recognize. The Wild Thing is still a little bit alive."

She clenched her jaw, and her mouth tightened into a thin line. Barth leaned forward, frowning.

"Are you still angry with me, Miel?"

Angry? Angry!

Her control burst, and red fury swam before her eyes. All the rage of all the years, all the rage she didn't even know she had, came boiling up out of nowhere.

"What do you think, Barth! Just guess! Don't you suppose I know you only leased the *Yancy* to get near me—although for what reason I can't imagine. As you've probably just noticed, we have very little to say to each other. I'll see the ads are shot as quickly as possible. After that, let's forget the social stuff for good!"

Miel stood breathing quickly, her face either very white or very red—she couldn't tell which. Now that all pretense was gone, she felt released. She hated this man who had hurt her so cruelly when she was the most vulnerable—and she no longer cared how juvenile it might be to rant and rave so long after the fact. It felt good. It felt very, very good. And the devil take him anyway!

Bracing herself, she waited for Barth to thunder back. Instead, the eerie silence lengthened. He seemed to be simply waiting for the reverberations of her explosion to die away. There was a certain wistfulness in his expression and when at last he spoke, his voice reached out, low and quiet, caressing her like velvet.

"You were always a very special person, Miel, even half grown in Bay Point. Regardless of what you may think, I never forgot you. After I left, I thought about you a lot, and four years ago I sailed back up the Seaway to the village, meaning to get a line on a pretty fantastic grown-up woman. When I found you had disappeared without a trace, I guess it was one of the biggest disappointments in my life."

Miel's anger was shattered. Whatever she had expected from him, it was not this—not this gentleness, this note of regret. There seemed nothing at all she could reply. She stood in a daze, hazel eyes hopelessly misty, lips parted. Barth had his own way of dealing with the moment. He leaned forward. His mouth brushed hers, poignantly, as if by this slow, questing kiss he might find out the truth.

Miel could not even draw a stifled gasp. His mouth was cool but the warmth of his breath spilled along her cheek, causing her heart to leap madly. Yet by the time she had gathered her wits to push him away, he had already slipped out into the corridor and was gone.

She was left alone in the silence of her empty apartment. Slowly, she lifted one hand and pressed the back of it against the heated pink of her face. Her heart lurched again at the thought that Barth had crossed half the watery world to look for her, and she hadn't even known.

And if he had found her...?

What would have happened? What?

A shudder was wrenched from her very soul, and she clenched her eyes shut. She of all people should know the futility of wondering, What if. The past was gone. Her loyalty and, yes, her love, now lay with James. Barth could not be allowed to mess up her life, ever again!

CHAPTER SIX

THE RESTAURANT WAS ONE OF THOSE little cozy marvels that Toronto seemed to sprout so easily in the corners of lovingly restored Victorian homes. Good northern white pine wainscotting and plants, of course, hanging from newly installed skylights. Faded postcards, antique farm tools scattered on the walls. Their wineglasses were empty and plates, which had contained *quiche à la mer*, were cleared. Only the dark aromatic coffee remained.

"Dessert?" James asked.

"Oh, goodness no. I'm stuffed. Anyway, we spent so much time sipping that glorious Riesling we haven't time. We should be getting back."

James, usually so punctual, made an expansive gesture with his hands and leaned back, clearly suffused with the pleasure of being out to lunch with Miel. Another small, private tradition was being born in this biweekly outing. Really, Miel thought, James, if he was not watched, could become such a creature of habit. If lifeblood were to be kept flowing in the store, her task in the future would be to do what she could to counter that tendency.

"It won't be a catastrophe if we stop for apple strudel."

His grin became just slightly self-conscious as she lifted her hand to the jaunty nosegay pinned at her lapel. Another tradition, she suspected, for she had discovered it on her desk that morning, a fragile blossom surrounded by bits of fabric and colored straw, the forerunner of a lifetime of those charming, thoughtful gifts so much a part of James's style.

"I'll pass, nevertheless," she returned lightly, dropping her fingers at his look of chagrin. "Let's just finish our coffee in peace."

Despite her own automatic concern for the store, Miel, too, wanted to linger in this little hideaway. She was feeling particularly tender toward James today, aware just how much she needed him—his calmness, his discipline, the gentle way he accepted her for what she was and didn't probe and probe and probe the way Barth had done. He would always be a refuge for her, she decided, for despite all her successes the hunger for safety still remained. And she knew from past experience that true refuges are precious few and very far between.

James gazed at her pensively from across the width of checkered tablecloth.

"Take all the time you want, Miel. If I do say so, you're looking a little tired."

Miel's coffee splashed, and she quickly put the cup back in its saucer. She had hoped her sleeplessness didn't show. That single, inquisitive kiss had lingered upon her lips long after the lights were out. Now a faint feeling of guilt caused her to chatter brightly about the Gagnon samples. James was looking very serious.

"Do you really think this boat idea is the right way to go?" he asked as they emerged, finally, into a leafy sunlight.

Miel hesitated, sensing that a word from her could cancel the entire project, for she knew he was unsure and had come to trust her judgment immensely. Part of her leaped eagerly toward this avenue of escape but her own basic integrity stopped her firmly. The Gagnons needed some kind of brilliant campaign and needed it now, and she had no alternative to offer. As cheerfully as she could, she took the plunge.

"Of course it is. The colors will look fabulous photographed against the lake. And that... yacht really is the final word in class."

James still frowned as they swung along the sidewalk.

"Oh, James, you're worrying." Miel laughed, taking his arm. She knew she had to tease him out of this mood instantly. Things were bad enough without James's fretting. He looked at her, a little startled.

"Yes, I am," he said slowly, and Miel knew that a week ago, before she had returned from France, he would not have admitted as much. He was determined to be open with her no matter what it cost him. *Is it so hard for you,* she thought with a sudden tug at her heart. *Is it really so hard?*

She broke into a stream of spontaneous wit as they strolled back along a route which tacitly avoided the vicinity of Avery Selks's store, although it would probably have been to their advantage to look in his windows. Perhaps they would have discovered some clue to the devastating talent he had for drawing in exactly the sort of shoppers needed by Crome's. Both stores had no choice but to resist the suicidal temptation to cater less to the already overcrowded middle markets and go instead for the wealthy. But people with more money to spare were a flighty lot, flocking here and there, subject to trends and fads and even location. When the fashion district had shifted, Crome's had lost some important customers. Miel had once heard the process of gaining clientele referred to as the same as herding cattle. Just corral the leader and the rest of them are yours.

Miel closed her lips firmly. No, she would not be tricked into thinking of her work like that. Nor would she be haunted by Barth's keen gray eyes glancing around her apartment as he passed judgment.

They paused outside James's office.

"Coffee later?" he asked, as he opened the door.

Miel shook her head. "Afraid not. Hildy and I have to go over that . . . yacht we hired."

Hildy was not immediately in evidence, so Miel returned to her own office to straighten papers and try to put the upcoming ordeal out of her mind. Then, peering at her watch, she stepped back into the corridor and found she could see through James's open door. She spotted him leaning back in his huge leather chair, with his eyes half closed and a small dreamy smile on his face. He was drifting in a fog in a way Miel, very poignantly, recognized. Years ago, that first day she had worked aboard the *Yancy*, she had been hopelessly adrift in that same dreamy fog.

Why...he really is falling in love, she thought with a kind of sharp wonder. And instantly she forgave him for his awkwardness back on the street. Instinct told her something infinitely precious was forming—and it was up to her to take care of it.

She moved away lest James see her, and she was surprised to come upon Hildy, also standing in the hall staring into James's office. Once again that mobile little body was completely stilled and something quite unreadable filled the bird-bright eyes. As Miel appeared she hastily turned, clutching a sheaf of layouts, which much have been approved by James but moments before.

"Well, mate, ready to hit the high seas?"

They both laughed, and the sound was oddly brittle—the start of a strange, uncomfortable mood that accompanied them all the way down to the harbor. Miel chatted feverishly while Hildy, dwarfed by the rainbow-colored tote bag in which she seemed to keep all her worldly possessions, answered absently. It wasn't until Barth's brawny form loomed out of the cabin of the *Yancy* that they both became completely silent.

He was wearing a T-shirt this time, well-faded navy cotton that clung to him like a second skin. His current shorts were actually neat along the bottom. His bare feet slapped softly along the deck as he moved to greet them.

"Ah, ladies, come aboard."

Miel looked him straight in the eye and willed herself not to blush. Barth acknowledged her with the lift of one brow, and she was relieved when those gray eyes did not provoke her with the memory of his kiss. All charm, he shepherded the two women solicitously onto the deck. When they had taken their moment to peer up at the clean, taut rigging and over the side, as visitors will, he leaned against the cockpit rim.

"I'm all ready to give the grand tour. Where would you like to start?"

"Oh, we want to see everything," put in Hildy who, despite her frivolous, tie-dyed coveralls, was now wielding a very officious-looking clipboard. "I've never been through a really beautiful yacht. Miel either, probably. I need to take it all in before deciding which outfits to send."

Miel ignored the ironic glance Barth shot her over that small head. He shrugged and padded along the deck with that surefooted ease she remembered so well. He began by taking Hildy forward, explaining about the two masts that made the *Yancy* a schooner, the long, unswept bowsprit, the furled mainsail under its carefully lashed cover. Miel followed at a distance, holding herself painfully tight, as if anything she touched might burn her. Barth's words faded in and out of her consciousness as she turned her face to the cool lake breeze, shielding her eyes against the sunlight bouncing from the wavelets, just as it had that first day Barth sailed into Bay Point. Oh, how vividly it was all evoked by the gentle shift of the *Yancy* under her feet and the familiar lap and gurgle of lake water under the bow. She might have been reporting for duty that morning. It was almost as if she had never been away.

Hildy scrambled among the masts and stays with the agility of a curly goat, squinting along the gunwales and scribbling quick, illegible notes. Miel drifted down into the cockpit, where she found herself running her hands over the beautiful honey-red wood of the wheel and gazing into the cast-iron features of Neptune, which ornamented the hub. She had not realized just how much she had dreaded boarding the *Yancy* until she actually stood on the sundrenched decks, how much she had braced herself for the inevitable shock she had suffered at the sight of that majestic metal face. With what devotion had she labored over it years ago, her mute adoration transformed into tireless energy for scraping years of dirt and corrosion from the sea god's curls and polishing his cheeks into round miniature suns.

"I keep him shipshape," said a deep voice close to her ear. "And the binnacle too. After the way you made the brightwork shine, I could never bear to let it turn green.''

He brushed a finger around the blustering deity and rested it next to Miel's, where it looked very dark and rough next to her pale, smooth skin. Once, when she had worked aboard the *Yancy*, her fingers had been as brown as his, the nails carelessly ragged to the quick. Now she couldn't remember when she had broken one of her manicured nails doing anything.

''You've finished the *Yancy* very well,'' she murmured in a noncommittal voice, glancing toward the forepeak where Hildy, planning for the models, was making unconscious, slightly comic poses.

''You haven't told any of them about knowing me, have you?''

Instant scarlet stung Miel's cheekbones.

''No, I haven't,'' she shot back. ''I have a different life now, and I didn't ask you back into it. My past is really not their business or concern.''

''Not even for James Crome?''

''James and I. . . .'' She shut her mouth emphatically and averted her eyes, lest he guess what a shrewd strike he had made, how close to home. In that brief pause, they seemed very close in the well of the cockpit. Miel really had nowhere to look except at Barth's legs, which were dusted with short, sunbleached hairs. His sinewy muscles made a mockery of the old saying that a sailor's legs were the weakest part of him. His bare toes gripped the cockpit sole naturally, and Miel knew he would move as lightly as a cat among the small forest of rigging necessary to any sailing vessel.

"I'm ready to go downstairs now—or below—or whatever you call it."

Miel jumped. How had Hildy managed to approach them without making a sound? Barth lifted his hand from the wheel and leaned rather lazily back.

"Right this way, ladies. There's coffee and there's drinks—whatever you prefer."

Hildy tucked her clipboard under one arm and prepared to follow, but her quick eyes darted from Barth to Miel and back again, catching the telltale pinkness in Miel's cheeks. Miel was too preoccupied with calming herself to notice the faint speculation in Hildy's gaze or the increased spring in her step.

Actually, it was all Miel could do to force herself through that same richly varnished door through which she had been so ignominiously ejected long ago. She expected the interior of the main salon to be changed, and of course it was. But in another way, it wasn't, for there was the scrollwork on the roof that was inextricably mixed with the image of Barth's head bending over her that ill-fated night. And there were the portholes whose light had been so treacherously inviting. There, also, was the chart table that had bruised her thigh so cruelly as Barth shoved her away. A throb started on the side of her leg, as if she still carried the pain. Just as she had expected, this return visit caused her eyes to glisten suspiciously, making her thankful for the turned backs of Hildy and Barth.

She recovered somewhat in the galley, partly from the surprise of seeing, of all things in that familiar space, a microwave oven. The stove was new too, with a practically invisible exhaust hood. The freezer was full of the ice that had been so amusingly scarce in Bay Point. Everything was new, Miel realized, running her hands over the costly modern conveniences, all of them custom designed so that the lovely teak cabinetry was in no way disturbed.

"But what do you do about bottles and things?" Hildy asked, eternally, engagingly curious, "when the cupboards start heaving up and down in a storm?"

"Lockers, not cupboards. Look."

A door revealed the racks that kept everything secure even in the roughest weather. Hildy was delighted with the locker and obviously equally delighted with Barth. Her small face was alive, her huge eyes bright. Apparently his overwhelming masculinity was having its effect on her too. Miel bit her lip, suddenly realizing how very protective she felt toward the young promotional manager and how fond of her she was.

"Let's get on with the tour," she said, moving between them, doing what she could to break up the dangerous moment.

They went through the rest of the interior, which, besides the luxurious salon, consisted of a large stateroom to the stern and an even larger one, the master cabin, in the bow. Smaller berths were fitted ingeniously into the sides along with the heads, or washrooms. The richly varnished wood and rather sybaritic carvings and scrollwork of the millionaire builder contrasted with the masculine clutter that indicated the boat was inhabited. Miel wasn't fooled. Perfect order, a necessary habit ingrained by a life at sea, was but a few minutes' tidying away.

"I'll have that coffee now," Hildy announced, perching herself expectantly on the deeply padded settee behind the salon table. She had examined everything down below but had made few notes because most of the advertising shots would no doubt be taken in the open air and natural light of the deck. Both women watched as Barth made coffee with that same easy economy of movement Miel remembered so well. And, tall as he was, he really didn't have to duck his head under the generously curved ceiling.

"This boat is really built for you, isn't it?" Hildy commented as he produced cream and sugar.

He laughed, a low rippling sound that filled the salon.

"I like to think so." And he told again the tale of wanting a personal yacht and stumbling upon the *Yancy*.

"Love at first sight. It really does happen, even though the object of affection was very seedy at the time. We had a fair bit to work out but now we're mated for life, I hope. I've been through many a nasty sea and rocked gently to sleep on the loneliest of nights.''

Mischief glinted in his eyes and when Miel felt them resting on her, she clenched her hand around her mug and stared heatedly back. Was he doing it to provoke her, she wondered, speaking in passionate terms of a collection of rigging and plank.

Of course, the boat really did seem to fit him—a legacy of the original owner's weakness for luxury and space. And everything around Miel had been lovingly and carefully restored, the wood just now beginning to acquire that little patina of care and use that gives good cabinetry its style.

When Miel remembered to turn away from Barth, she was dismayed to find Hildy more animated than she had been all day, looking at Barth and then Miel and then Barth again, her eyes shining with a brightness Miel prayed was merely creative speculation. Like others at Crome's, Miel was nervous of the razor-sharp perceptions lurking under that deceptively childlike face. With one foot tucked beneath her, Hildy picked up her clipboard and began to make notes with sudden, furious energy. Then Miel's embarrassment of the moment before turned to concern as she saw her young companion fix her gaze intently upon Barth's superb tanned forearms and the unique planes of his face. Just a little afraid, that Hildy was becoming fascinated with Barth, Miel reminded herself that despite her air of competence and breezy vivacity, Hildy was very young.

How many other women, she suddenly wondered, had been susceptible to Barth's charms.

Oh, Hildy, she silently cautioned, as if trying to save some more youthful vestige of herself, *please, please don't fall into this trap!*

"More coffee?" Barth asked, refilling their mugs. Relaxed as he was, he presented such a seductive picture of virility that Miel struggled with moments of unnerving dizziness. Though his presence filled the cabin with a subtle sensuality, she refused to acknowledge it. It was simply, she told herself, seeing him in his natural element that was causing her mind to play tricks.

Hildy fiddled with her pen and shifted position.

"You know what this campaign really needs," she began, looking from Miel to Barth with faintly mischievous green eyes. "Some kind of male focus. A handsome, burly, seagoing type would add so much authority, especially in the boat shots. By sheer contrast, the Seascape line would look breezy and feminine. Conclusion— the customers who buy them would have no trouble at all attracting a man. How about it, Barth? Are you up for the job?"

This kind of lightning-flash inspiration was already part of Hildy's legend, but neither Barth nor Miel was at all prepared. Barth let out a great guffaw.

"You mean get my picture taken next to a bunch of frilly clothes? Pose?"

Hildy nodded with that perfect innocence

Miel was coming to recognize as her most wily device.

"Oh, lady, you've got to be kidding!" And Barth boomed again with incredulous merriment, the sound of his laughter sending Miel's mind skidding back to the sunny fragments of their former days. Across the table Hildy pouted prettily.

"Why not?" she demanded with just enough indignation to make Barth look to his manners. "I was already planning a male model but none would hold a candle to your kind of authenticity."

"Forget it." Barth still chuckled with amusement and he looked at Hildy as if she were more than a little mad. "I'm a salvager, remember. If the fellows back on the ships caught wind of this, I'd never live it down."

Miel braced for the next exchange, knowing as she did that Hildy never gave up. To her astonishment, Hildy merely shrugged and dropped the subject with exceedingly little argument, her attention seeming to wander. She swallowed the remainder of her coffee then stepped up the companionway to look topside again. Miel followed hastily, lest she be left alone with Barth. Hildy poked around in a desultory manner for a few moments. Then, waiting until Miel was right where she wanted her, she dropped her clipboard swiftly into her monster tote.

"I want that man in my ads, Miel," she declared in a low, confidential voice. "God, with those biceps, he could make women faint. Getting him in front of the camera should be a piece of cake, especially since I think he really likes you. I've got all the info I need just now. I'll hop back to the office and leave you to it.''

With that, she sprang lightly to the catwalk and vanished in a flurry of color among the forest of masts. Before Miel could even respond, Hildy had disappeared into a taxi on Queen's Quay West.

At that moment, Barth emerged and remarked on Hildy's absence. Finding herself thus abandoned, Miel whirled and prepared to make her dash for dry land. Deftly, Barth intervened.

"Hey, what's the rush? Your working day must be over now."

Actually it was, but Miel was certainly not going to admit it.

"Not necessarily. Hildy had to scoot. I should go too."

Barth smiled down at her, the corners of his mouth creating attractive creases in his weathered cheeks.

"No, you shouldn't. Hildy clearly bolted. I think she left you behind to sweet-talk me into that male-model job."

He had caught her there and did not fail to press his advantage.

"Well, stay and try. I'll take you to dinner at the Harbourfront café.''

CHAPTER SEVEN

THEY SAT TOGETHER at one of the white outdoor tables on a deck that faced the lake and projected cleverly over a reflecting pool, bringing the ripple of water to their very feet. Below them, gulls and mallards competed raucously for crumbs. The warm evening breeze plucked mischievously and persistently at Miel's carefully controlled hair. She gazed uncomfortably down at the remains of the scrumptious cabbage roll resting on her plate and the carafe of red wine Barth had insisted on ordering. The fact that she was there at all made her feel as if she had been the victim of a conjuring trick. Barth, apparently, retained a fragment of his old magical power.

"Took my time up the Seaway," he was saying, as he lounged back against the chair. "The locks are full of freighters this time of year and, farther down, there's a mean river current you have to look out for. Then a squall hit me just this side of Kingston. Small one, thankfully, or I wouldn't have been able to get the mainsail down in time. Sometimes there's nothing in the world like these lakes for treacherous weather."

He chatted easily and pleasantly, eating with

the gusto of a healthy animal and at the same time filling in all the pauses himself so that the conversation appeared a seamless whole rather than what it actually was—a masculine monologue punctuated only by one-word comments from Miel.

He was more respectful now, more mature, but he hadn't lost his gift of gab. Miel was strongly reminded of the cheerful banter that had kept her entranced for hours long ago as they chipped away at the aging varnish on the *Yancy*'s decks. Her answers were short because she wished to remain angry with him, but it was becoming increasingly easy to be drawn in. Something had broken her resolve, and she knew very well it was the unexpected image of his searching Bay Point for her four years earlier, and standing baffled and disappointed on the shore.

She was dismayed to discover how much she had cherished her anger all this time, and now, when he was at last before her, she didn't want to feel cheated of it. Childish, childish, her mature and usually sensible self accused her, but still she could not contain her feeling of perverse loss.

"I stay away from marinas whenever I can," he said, tipping his magnificent blond head to indicate the harbor. "What I like is to anchor in those little Ontario bays where you can hear the loons at night and where the cedars hang right down over the shore."

Miel knew he was trying to placate her, lull

her with that lilting, yarn-spinning tongue that had worked so devastatingly well when she was young. And to a certain extent it was working, for it made her entertain ideas of entering into the conversation. Besides, on another less conscious level she was becoming aware that this meeting was really a test—the strange, bristling dance of sleek animals inspecting each other at the dark edge of a forest, where their territories unexpectedly met and overlapped.

Miel watched Barth warily as he drank from his wineglass with uncomplicated relish. She knew what he wanted, of course. He wanted her to join in the lightness and camaraderie of the moment, to finally smile and laugh with him—by so doing to tacitly admit that the past was the past and everything now was all right.

But she was firm. She would be polite to him. But deep down, a stubborn little voice insisted that it would never be all right. Never!

"So you're calmer now," he commented when she rather decisively poured herself more wine.

"Yes, I suppose so."

"Good. For a few minutes back at your apartment there, I thought I was going to lose a limb."

He was teasing her, those warm gray eyes inviting her to drop her somber mood and enter into the fun. But to do so would be to drop claim on her grievances, and Miel had no intention of being so easily disarmed. Even for the duration of the ad campaign she would not be bought off by that breezy charm. The problem must be faced—and head-on too.

"I've never forgotten it," she said, a sort of deadly softness in her voice, "the way you threw me off the *Yancy* in Bay Point as if I were some mangy cat. It's a little much to expect me to greet you now with a smile and open arms."

She had built him into such an irresponsible womanizer that she fully expected to see those eyes go perfectly blank with not a trace of memory remaining. Instead, the sudden, tautness of his face told her exactly the contrary, doing serious damage to the picture she had been carrying with her all the embittered, intervening years. He raked one hand through his sunbleached hair so abruptly that the wineglasses rocked on the table.

"What did you expect me to do, Miel? You were only a kid. What—fifteen? Sixteen?"

"Seventeen a month after you left."

That had been one birthday quite uncelebrated—except for the angry crashing of her grandfather in the shop below.

What remained of the cabbage rolls began to congeal on their plates. A gull lit boldly on the rail near their elbows, fixing them with greedy, inquisitive yellow eyes.

What had she expected? Oddly enough, she had never made herself consider the episode from his point of view. She had been concerned only for her thwarted desire and the subsequent longing that he should return to whisk her away from Bay Point and hold her to him tenderly forever. Having matured, she had learned shelter was not to be stumbled upon that easily. Now that she had insisted on dragging the incident out into the light of day, she had no choice but to look at it.

"You might have been. . . kinder about it, at least," she said weakly, tearing her paper napkin into uneven little shreds.

The silence was filled with the laughter of other diners and the whir of a motor launch as the harbor police headed home to their mooring. Barth seemed withdrawn now. He spoke roughly, but with the unmistakable defensiveness that accompanies vulnerability.

"You took me by surprise in the middle of the night. I hadn't a clue what you were up to until I smelled all that perfume. If I got you out of there fast, it was only for your own good. I ought to have warmed your bottom to boot!"

For the first time that day she felt a flicker of fury sparked by old embers that refused to die. It only pained her more to couple this with adult understanding, to think to oneself—really think—what else a grown man could do with a moonstruck, skinny teenager who had flung herself around his neck.

But you kissed me back, she cried out in silent outrage. *First you kissed me back!*

And that had made all the difference!

Her gaze slid to the pebbles lying with such brown clarity on the bottom of the pool. Then ripples caused by a scrounging mallard made them shimmer and become indistinct, just like her grip on all these rapidly shifting realities.

"Would it help if I said I'm sorry?" Barth asked rather grimly. "I'm not really, you know. What I did back there was certainly for the best."

A certain husky note in his voice touched her, and Miel brought up her head, searching his face. For a long moment he allowed her to scrutinize him as he stroked the fragile wineglass with his large, work-hardened fingers.

"It's true," he continued so quietly she barely heard him. "Though you probably hadn't the slightest idea, you managed to make yourself very beautiful that night—all huge eyes and trembling, long-legged grace. I had to get you out of there fast."

She experienced a moment of breathless hopefulness as she suddenly read the message in his expression. He *had* been affected by the madness of desire that had suffused her young limbs. He had felt the same fire that had reduced her to such trembling mindlessness. That, and not sheer cruelty, was the reason he had thrust her so hastily and so roughly away from him.

Tearing her gaze away, she stared down at the ruins of the napkin in her lap. Suddenly, after all the passing years, she found her heart was pounding in her breast and her blood making a great rushing sound in her ears. This singular attack of emotion paralyzed her, and she might have remained so, unable to move or speak, had not the gull that had been examining them turned its attention to the couple next to them and made a calculated lunge for the remains of the woman's roll. The woman yelped, tipping over her drink, which poured over the edge of the table and splashed onto Miel's trousers.

"Oh, I'm so sorry! Oh dear! That nasty thief!"

The woman tried to apologize as the gull ferried its booty to a post well beyond reach of human fury. Smugly, it tore the crusty tidbit while Miel stood up quickly, trying to reassure her neighbor no real damage had been done.

"It's quite all right," rumbled Barth, scraping back his chair and rising to his full height. "Come on, Miel, we can have coffee in peace back on the boat."

Without the bubbling presence of Hildy, the *Yancy* seemed weirdly silent as Barth and Miel stepped aboard. Most of the other boaters in the slip had either gone home or settled down to a meal in the cabins of their crafts.

"It's too nice to sit below. Just give me a minute and I'll be back with a couple of mugs."

Barth disappeared into the galley, leaving Miel to wonder topside. It was the first time she had really been alone with the *Yancy*. Turning her face toward the coral and lavender of the sunset beyond the Western Gap, she drifted forward, her hands lingering on the stays and running along the boom where the great white mainsail lay furled. This moment of solitude allowed her to realize all over again just how beautiful the *Yancy* was, how pure and frankly sensuous the curving sweep running from the taffrail to the nobly rising bowsprit. Under her feet, like all boats at anchor, the *Yancy* stirred, responding to the wash and ripple of the lake. Placing her hand against the stout mainmast, Miel tipped her head back to look up at the softly swaying tip. In Bay Point, she used to take her breaks sprawled on her back on the hot deck. She used to imagine that it was not the clouds but the *Yancy* rushing swiftly away, carrying her to unheard-of adventures over water so smooth not even a ripple could be felt beneath the bow.

"I'm back."

Barth stood in the cockpit, two mugs in his hand, the sunset gilding one side of him with a glowing sheen of golden light. Miel started, wondering how long he had been standing there and why there was such an oddly measuring look in his eye.

Instinctively, the two of them shunned the cockpit seats to hoist themselves onto the cabin roof as they always had. Barth handed her her coffee.

"Queen Victoria is still under the mainmast. First thing I saw to when I stepped it in."

He was still watching her carefully and, in spite of her resolve to remain objective, a few scalding drops spilled over onto her fingers. He seemed to be deliberately laying verbal land mines among the casual chat.

"My, my, this is an evening for sentiment," she tossed back lightly, determined to sidestep his intentions.

Queen Victoria had been her childhood treasure, a great old English penny from the 1800s that her grandfather had fished up from his sea chest for her sixth birthday. As soon as Barth had told her that the lore of the sea demanded a coin be slipped, for luck, at the base of a mast as it was raised, Miel sped home and eagerly sacrificed the worn, much-beloved old coin. There was, in those days, no end to her generosity.

Barth smiled at her, sailor's creases fanning warmly at the corners of his eyes, his expression faintly melancholy.

"Perhaps it is. More than we both suppose."

And the old companionable silence enveloped them as they watched small planes drift down like moths to the island airport and the distant trees turn sepia in the fading light.

Oh, the seduction of it all. Miel tried to resist but the combination of dusk on the water, the scent of the lake and the all too poignantly remembered peace were too much for her.

Was it really so much his fault, she asked herself suddenly—all the rest of it, the things that had happened afterward? How could he have even guessed about her failed exams and her grandfather's stroke or the hotel kitchen where she had worked until the kindly cook threw her out to do something better with her life—the things that had turned what should have been only one more awkward incident of adolescence into catastrophe?

Was she at last forgiving him, then? After so many inflexible years?

Novel and unbelievable as the idea appeared, it seemed to be so—in her mind, at least. For now she would not think about that small, stubborn corner of her heart that remained rigidly cold.

A gull, perhaps the same one that had disrupted them at the restaurant, lit on the boom and examined them for handouts. Miel grinned and spread her palms, for there was not a scrap to be had.

"Cheeky lady, isn't she?"

Miel laughed. "I like gulls. Beautiful in the air and brash on the ground. No one does them out of a meal."

"Well, the picking's no good here. Perhaps by the time I leave, she'll know not to hang around the *Yancy*."

Leave! Miel's mouth went suddenly dry, and she wet her lips with her tongue. Of course. Eventually, as in Bay Point, he must go.

"Have you got any plans? I mean, about going back to the company?"

He leaned back pensively, and she could see the compact line of his lower ribs.

"I don't know. I've had this idea rattling around in my head for a few years now. Might be time to get it rolling."

Miel waited expectantly as the breeze pressed her sleeve against the firm flesh of her arm.

"I've seen a lot of messes in my day. Oil spills, chemical dumping, slaughtered whales, the most pristine tropical paradises stripped for lumber and left to erode into the sea. Salvagers tend to be on the front line, you know, and it gets more sickening every year. Sometimes, in spite of all the so-called conferences and regulations, it's hard to believe that anyone really gives a damn about what's happening.''

The sea! How long had it been since anyone had spoken to her of the sea. No one since Barth had left. Miel was surprised how easily her old obsession was rekindled.

''I've been. . . out of touch for a long time. Is it really that bad?''

''That bad!'' Barth grunted, wrapping his arm around one sinewy knee. ''Did you know you can hardly travel two days together in any part of the ocean without running into those big tarry globes of oil. I was called to a tanker wreck up the coast of Carolina once. Gulls and sandpipers and cormorants staggering and dying under all that sticky stuff. Most pathetic calamity you ever saw.''

Their attendant gull croaked impatiently, its wings, lucky creature, still a clean and snowy white.

''I know the pollution is dreadful. I thought they were really tightening up on tankers.''

''Tankers just get the publicity. Actually, they think most of the oil comes from automobiles. Every time a garage changes the crankcase oil, the old stuff goes down the drain. Eventually, most of it's bound to end up in the ocean.''

He was warming to his topic now, not even looking at Miel but staring off at the dim horizon, the muscles of his mouth unconsciously knotting at all the disasters he had seen. His attitude, one that she had never known about, gave Miel a queer sensation in the hollow of her stomach. Quietly she waited to see if he would go on. He flicked a lock of hair from his forehead and rested his weight on one sturdy arm.

"Oh, it's not just oil. Miles of it are covered by soapsuds, all the oxygen cut off. There's leaking nerve gas, mercury poisoning and the U.S. army is even talking about dumping obsolete nuclear submarines. People seem to suppose the ocean is some kind of infinite disposal sink and if they just don't think about it, the ocean will take care of it."

"Not so, I guess," Miel commented a little nervously, fascinated by the silhouette of his jaw against the clutter of masts behind him.

"No way, even though the ocean is capable of an incredible number of things. If we finally dump enough chemical in the ocean to destroy the oxygen-producing plankton the composition of the atmosphere might change and we'd all keel over and die!"

Miel was quite visibly rattled, both by his fervor and by the sudden, powerful focusing of his personality on her. She couldn't suppress her sudden anger, for if she'd studied to be a marine biologist, she would have been involved with all this.

"It's an awfully big problem," she returned, masking her emotion. "What are you planning to do about it?"

He rubbed his chin pensively, his broad shoulders lifting into something of a half shrug.

"I'm not sure, but I just can't let it go. I have to try. Nothing to do, I suppose, but to start yet another organization devoted to ecology. Something completely free of politics and governments. Maybe a kind of network among the sailors so that an engineer or a deckhand from, say, Jakarta or Ankara or Sydney or Buenos Aires could just come in and tell us what he saw. Even Frank. Be a way to work with my brother instead of always clashing."

"Why, of course it would," cried Miel enthusiastically, picking up the idea with that effortlessness that was so much a result of her intensive training at Crome's and her own hard-won self-confidence. "You could call it Operation Seawatch."

"Hey, a name already. You are fast, aren't you?"

Miel felt absurdly pleased and began to fiddle with one of the stays.

"Where would you headquarter it?"

"Somewhere near the sea lanes, naturally. Start with some regional offices and a skeleton office staff. After that, I'd have to find some scientific consultants I could trust."

"And lawyers."

"Yes, I'll certainly need some smart cookies in the legal department."

"And, of course, if there's to be genuine change—" Miel broke off, realizing how easily she had fallen into this rhythm with him, eagerly snatching up his concept and tossing it back and forth until he had become, as now, intensely alert. But there was something else in his eyes that made her feel faint. He was afire with something, and Miel prayed it was only the excitement of his burgeoning project and the last glints of sunset caught in those deep gray eyes. Uncomfortably, she shifted away.

"Anyway, it all sounds good," she mumbled with no trace of her former, betraying energy. "I suppose you'll want to get to work on it right away."

"Maybe. I don't know."

"Why not? Surely the sooner the better."

It was hard to discard the old careless selfish image she had carried of him and now imagine him willing to tilt at such gigantic windmills. The whole alteration knocked her a little cockeyed.

"Getting together a thing like that would be a lonely job," he answered, after a seemingly endless interval. "Sometimes I wonder if I haven't had enough of lonely jobs in my life."

A prickling of alarm went off in the back of Miel's mind. Suddenly she could picture Barth on the bridge of a salvage ship, a tough, scarred iron tramp whose business was to speed through icy seas or blistering tropics to places of shipwreck and disaster. A ship crewed by hardbitten, taciturn but competent men and clanking with tools and cables and diving gear. This, perhaps, was the reality he had spared her when spinning out those fanciful seagoing tales in Bay Point.

Yes, there were lines there, deeply etched in cheek and brow, confirming the existence of worry and responsibility. Were they new or had they already been there in Bay Point? Typical of her years, she had been unable to look beyond his expansive, good-natured charm. He had been so shining to her then and so black afterward. Why now did it hurt with an almost physical pain to admit that he was a complex human being like everyone else?

Beside her, she sensed that Barth was waiting for some kind of response from her. Not an ordinary response—but something more than she was prepared to give. She slapped the first mosquito of the evening away from her wrist and rose abruptly.

"I'd better be going. I had no idea it was so late."

She descended into the dimming interior of the yacht to retrieve her notebook and briefcase. Barth followed but didn't switch on the light, so he appeared only in shadow. Miel, hearing him, turned rather too quickly and found him leaning against the chart table, looming between herself and the open sky behind him. Too strongly, it reminded her of another time in the confines of this cabin. Her nerves began to hum. She lifted her head in silent defiance, but her obvious discomfort had no effect on his easy demeanor.

"You are good at your job, aren't you,

Miel?'' he murmured as he surveyed the proud set of her head and her long, graceful neck. "Have you ever thought of changing your field of endeavor?''

"No!''

The word was a sharp eruption made all the more emphatic by a wild surmise of what he was getting at. The sooner she was out of there the better. Grasping her briefcase, she made to push past him.

"Don't rush off, Miel. I was merely thinking out loud.''

Although he was plainly sincere, Miel refused to back down.

"I really am quite happy in my career, Barth. Please don't block the door.''

He made no move whatsoever, his vital presence extending into all the darkened recesses of the salon. Miel had forgotten what a truly physical person he was, how incredibly masculine. The very nearness of him seemed to charge the air around her, paralyzing her immediate desire to leave. Nervously, she wetted her lips with her tongue—then saw, too late, that he was watching this too.

"Quite happy?'' he challenged softly. "I wonder if you've made much of an effort to really find out. Gilded cages can be very comfortable—but I sensed a decided lack of oxygen in that apartment of yours. Perhaps its time for a little fresh air in your life.''

She should have been outraged by his unsolicited interpretation of her life, but the gentle, caressing way he spoke and the mellow tones of his voice combined to make music to her ears.

Then he was closer. How did he do that—glide forward until she could feel his heat mere inches away along her lake-cooled skin. His arms moved to encircle her—big, immensely strong, but holding her so lightly she was only aware of them by the faintest of pressure on her shoulders.

"Barth. . .no. . . ."

But his lips claimed hers with a delicacy one would have imagined impossible in such a large, rough-hewn man.

At his first touch, Miel went rigid, refusing to respond. Instinctively she shut her eyes against the increasing rain of kisses on her lashes and cheekbones and the silk-smooth skin across her temples. But in mere moments she stood trembling like a creature caught in a storm with nowhere to hide.

She felt his arms tighten until she lay against the light cotton of his shirt, feeling his heart pounding beneath her palm. Distantly she heard a small thud as her briefcase slipped from her fingers and fell to the floor. The *Yancy*, bobbing gently, tipped her yet closer into his embrace.

Barth held her as if he had a perfect right to, rocking her slightly, burying his face in the sensitive curve of her neck, running warm breath and swift caresses along ivory skin no other man had been allowed to so ardently enjoy. Miel was paralyzed by a clamorous confusion of the senses, her bearings lost in the familiarity and the newness of being in his arms. Feeling fearfully dizzy, she reached for him simply to steady herself. It only took the feel of him beneath her palms, his smoky murmur against her ear, to ignite a wild flame that leaped along her limbs and turned her own soft grip into a convulsive clinging.

A flame raged exactly like the passion she had experienced those last moments in Barth's arms aboard the *Yancy* years ago.

It was this parallel that shocked her—shocked her as much as if she had casually opened a broom closet and a dragon had leaped out, all tongued with fire and roaring. And it terrified her exactly as much, for she realized the madness was not dead. All these years it had been merely lying in wait, treacherously dozing, awaiting just this opportunity to lash out and destroy once again the fragile, carefully balanced stability that was her present life.

Violently she tore herself away from Barth and backed against the paneling, her words coming in short, furious bursts.

"How dare you! How dare you touch me! Haven't you done enough to my life? Haven't you made a big enough mess without waltzing in now to try again. You're...contemptible!"

In the red-tinged twilight of the cabin she could have sworn he flinched, yet he didn't take his eyes from her. But there was something in those gray eyes now that frightened her.

"Contemptible? There's nothing contemptible about wanting to kiss a beautiful woman. And you are a woman now, Miel. I've just had indisputable proof. Someday you're going to have to grow up and accept that fact."

"Whatever I am, it doesn't concern you," she spat, flinging away recklessly and without regret the tenuous rapport they had built up over dinner and coffee. "I won't be subjected to this. If you must know, I'll soon be engaged to James Crome!"

The astonishment in his eyes was quite gratifying. She bent and snatched up her briefcase again from where it lay tilted against Barth's strong brown ankle. Seconds later she was flying out of the cockpit and onto the floating catwalk. Calling her name, Barth emerged into the light-spangled dusk. Miel spun, her cheeks scarlet, her mouth pale and very fierce.

"I don't want this, Barth. Any of it! I'll thank you to keep your advances to yourself through the rest of the ad campaign!"

The boards shuddered under her retreating steps and sent out angry ripples from their edges. She escaped full of resolute indignation strongly tinged with fear. The familiar, the secure, so painfully fought for, so arduously won, was shaking around her, precarious and threatened. She fled from the source of this upheaval. She had had enough upheavals in her life. Now she wanted James. Only James—and safety.

CHAPTER EIGHT

THE VOICES REACHED HER FIRST as she stepped
into the office corridor the following morning—
Hildy's bright and merry, as it had not been all
week, and James's cultured chuckle drawn up
and down the scale by the sheer infectiousness
of the young sales-promotion manager. As Miel
reached the open door of James's office she saw
their heads bent, almost touching, over an as-
sortment of paper only Hildy could fan out with
such energy. When Miel startled them, they almost looked guilty before their faces took on
the smug, pleased expressions of successful co-
conspirators.

"You sure have the magic touch," Hildy de-
creed. "Barth Tramande has offered to model
after all—on condition that you do the primary
female stuff."

"Pardon?"

Hildy, leaning so comfortably close to James
as to brush his sleeve, started to repeat herself,
but Miel shook her head, the small, suspended
pearls at her lobes quivering with emphasis.

"The idea is ridiculous. I can't model!"

"Of course you can," James piped up loyal-
ly, his eyes clearly indicating that contact with

Hildy had energized him for the morning. "I don't honestly know why we never thought of it before. You have that special kind of...glow about you, you know. Could be dynamite in front of a camera."

Damn Barth! How had he managed to put so many suggestions into their heads in such a short time? It was one more trap, and she was having none of it.

"No way, James. I'm much too busy here. I have absolutely no intention of modeling."

Hildy and James exchanged a knowing glance. Clearly they had planned this conversation. And it wasn't the end. Hildy touched James lightly on the wrist as if to prompt him. He gathered the scattered papers into order and began in the calm, reasonable, slightly deferential voice Miel had little defense against.

"Actually, I'd really appreciate it if you'd give it a shot. You see, as part of the deal, Tramande has come up with a joint advertising package from a manufacturer of sailing dinghies. The company will ante up a large chunk of money toward our own costs just to get some really good shots for themselves.

"Yes," Hildy broke in excitedly. "They claim it's a devil of a job finding models who can sail convincingly and still look appealing to a camera. Mr. Tramande seems to have discovered you're a fair hand with a boat."

Miel must have gaped openly, for suddenly two pairs of eyes were riveted to her face. A little wildly, she wondered what else the man had confided.

"Well, you are, aren't you?" James pressed, seeming just a little piqued that this man, this acquaintance of a few days, this *stranger*, should know something so interesting about her that James himself did not.

Forcibly, Miel calmed herself, though her fingers silently curled into fists at her side.

"I used to sail a little bit when I was young," she offered weakly, waiting for more details of her own intimate and appalling past to come tumbling from their lips. Only when James looked up at her in complete innocence did she realize it was her own uneasy conscience that had made her misinterpret him. His brown eyes regarded her with a concern that made her wince. There are so many things I don't know about you, his gaze was saying. What a pleasure it will be to find them out, every one.

"If you do it even a little, then you'll do it well," he added, with total confidence in any ability she might show. "I'm satisfied. What do you say? Shall I give the company a call?"

Miel saw there was no escape. James was already absorbed in his cost sheets and Hildy ablaze with this new campaign. She bent her head in reluctant concession, thinking that it was the least she could do for James and for Crome's. The memory of Barth's embrace had haunted her throughout the night.

"A LITTLE TO THE LEFT, MIEL. That's right. Up against the sailor. Make it look as if you're really enjoying yourself."

Chuck, the free-lance photographer Hildy had hired, backed up along the deck of the *Yancy*, avoiding stays and cleats with preternatural dexterity. Miel, arrayed in a long-sleeved fuschia sashed top and natty white deck pants, was getting the feel of modeling while Barth leaned against the mainmast. His only concession to the Seascape collection was a blue T-shirt that graphically hugged all the tantalizing muscles of his chest. The yacht was still tied up in the slip because Chuck wanted to experiment with the background—the drama of bare poles against the busy and crowded basin.

Obediently, Miel backed up, close enough now to Barth to sense his energy, yet keeping enough distance to avoid being engulfed by it. Hildy, standing directly behind the photographer, frowned intently.

"Closer," she instructed over Chuck's shoulder. "Barth, put your arm around her. We've got to suggest that element of romance."

Barth obliged. Miel found herself leaning against his solid length, the muscles of his upper chest against her shoulder blade. The sensation of their body heat mingling was immediate and acute, shooting through her so that she stiffened in order to prevent a gasp.

"Heads to the right. That's it. Both of you at the same time. Let the breeze just ruffle the hair at your foreheads."

Chuck picked up one of the three cameras dangling around his neck and began snapping rapidly, adroitly avoiding the drop of the cock-

pit and sort of flowing over the salon roof. His
catlike sureness was fascinating for one built
like a linebacker running to flab.

"Hey, *great!*" He picked up a second camera
and squinted through it, changing the angle.
"Wonderful color, Miel. Just the sort of excitement that comes across in an ad."

Wonderful color! How could it be otherwise
when her cheeks were burning and her heart was
slamming against its cage of ribs. Nerves, she
told herself. Just nerves—and panic. For whenever he came near she recalled that lingering kiss
that roused all the memories in the sensual dusk
of the *Yancy*'s salon.

Barth had made no more advances since that
evening. He had had little opportunity, with
Chuck and Hildy swarming over the boat and
Jenny from the store toting the precious garments in their bags. Now he stood firm as a
rock, his arm around Miel's waist, pressing her
to him, his hand resting underneath the firm rise
of her bosom, his fingers lightly but significantly planted on her flesh.

The closeness seemed interminable as Chuck
crouched and tilted and snapped. Through each
agonizing moment, Miel was thinking that if
this was a sample of what was to come, she had
a mind to quit right now. As soon as a break
was called, she headed for Hildy, meaning to get
in a word or two about being forced into that intimate pose. Hildy began to bubble immediately.

"Miel, you're terrific. Both of you. So out-

doorsy and vigorous. So...I don't know...
healthy. I never even guessed how glorious
you'd look once we got you away from the office.''

Those large, fringed, shining eyes made Miel
feel her objections were piddling and unsporting. After all, models did this sort of thing every
day, and how was Hildy to know Miel found
this particular man so objectionable. Hildy's
creative schemes were only enthusiasm for her
job. Besides, a picture of James smiling with
Hildy flashed into Miel's mind. She could not
let James down.

They did shots in three more outfits while
Barth, most obligingly, played the rugged
sailor. Hadn't he been concerned that his bud-
dies might laugh him out of the ranks? Yet there
he was, letting the activity swirl around him
while he stood like the calm at the eye of a
storm. And if there was more than a trace of
irony in those gray eyes, no one was going to
comment and thus endanger Barth's generous
mood. Eventually, cloud moved in, making
Chuck purse his lips and fiddle with his equipment. Finally, he shook his head.

"Light's going, folks. Have to call it a day.
Everybody can get changed.''

Miel slipped down to the stern cabin to don
the plaid shirt and fashionable jeans she had arrived in. She stayed in there, smoothing the garment bags until everyone else had clattered back
on deck. Then she stepped into the salon, now
temporarily deserted in the hurry to get ashore.

About to leave also, she hesitated, noticing that the door of the large forward cabin, Barth's cabin, was just slightly ajar. Unable to help herself, she tiptoed forward and pressed her fingers to the wood. Just one look, that was all, and then she would be gone.

She peered in, noticing not the rigorous order or the millionaire's carving, but the great main berth. It came back to her all at once, how long ago she had flung herself full length into that softness, her face pressed into the pillow. She had inhaled with a secret, guilty joy the male scent of him, imagining him lying there in the darkness of night, his soft breathing mingling with the gentle creaks and murmurs of the *Yancy* at anchor. Half-formed yet unbearably exciting visions of herself snuggled against him under the blankets had thrilled her, making her young heart hammer and filling her with a heated restlessness when she tried to sleep that night. Now the embarrassment of the memory scorched Miel's cheeks. She slammed the door and fled to the deck.

"Over there," Barth was saying as she skidded into the cockpit. "I've made arrangements for them to be tied up at the sailing school."

A man and a woman in blue coveralls stood there, while a truck in matching colors idled on the shoulder of Queen's Quay. Barth noticed Miel had turned.

"It's the dinghies being delivered. Let's go and see what they've brought."

"Yes, go on, Miel," put in Hildy, stuffing her

clipboard back into her satchel. "The day's shot anyway, so it would be great if you two could get those dinghies into the water as soon as you can. I'll just hop back to James with today's report."

Without waiting for an answer, she set off, leaving Miel vastly discomfited but unable to think of an objection. Avoiding Barth's offered hand, she sprang down and followed him to the other small slip where the boats were being lifted from the truck and having the final fittings installed. There were two of them, dazzling white with a long red racing stripe down the side of each. They were as far from the old wooden dinghy Miel had learned to sail in as a Ferrari is from a Model T.

"There," said the woman, attaching the brilliant red-and-white-striped sail. "All ready to go. If there's anything, anything at all you need or want to know, just give the factory a call. Ms Fowler phoned personally to make sure the ads come off well—and believe me, that's the first time the boss ever heard personally from her. You folks the models, by the way?"

Miel nodded and the woman, sturdy from her job, straightened. Her gaze slid over Barth with visible appreciation.

"Well, you sure do look the part, I must say. Actually, there's a nice little breeze blowing right now. Why don't you go out for a little spin?"

"Well, how about it, Miel?" Barth said, after the truck had lumbered off into the first of rush-hour traffic.

Miel bit her lip, struggling with the rush of panic invading her. It had been so long since she had sailed, and she had put it all so finally and firmly behind her.

"Oh, not now. Really, it's been a tiring day."

She tried to sound weary, cavalier, but he wasn't taken in.

"And since when wasn't sailing exactly the thing to put you back together again? I know you, Miel, perhaps a whole lot better than that crowd you chum around with."

Oh, do you now! she wanted to snap, but caught herself. She would not be baited by the conceit of such a statement. She shoved her hands in her pockets and looked resolutely at her toes.

"I haven't been sailing since. . . that summer you left. I might not even remember how."

"Haven't. . . ." Barth's head came up and he stared at her, disbelieving. "You're kidding me!"

He looked truly dumbfounded. So much so that Miel gazed uncomfortably back toward Queen's Quay where Hildy had disappeared. Hildy was all too ready, she thought, to dump her into Barth's lap whenever she could. How foolish Miel had been that first day to imagine Hildy interested in Barth for herself. Young as she was, Hildy was much too clever for that.

Barth took the painter of one of the cocky little vessels and balanced easily on the edge of the retaining wall where the green harbor water lapped in. He had changed back into his old denim shorts and a T-shirt from which the sleeves had been removed. He saw that Miel was not kidding.

"All the more reason to give it a whirl, then. I'll go with you. I believe these things are designed to take two people when necessary."

"Oh no, really...."

Miel stiffened at the idea of those long arms reaching for the boom across her breasts, those hard thighs crashing into hers each time the boat heeled over in the wind. The memory awakened in his cabin still loomed in her mind, and she drew back even as he tossed her a life jacket. She hesitated, then forced herself to buckle it on. The sooner she got this over with the better.

The dinghy tipped, then steadied as Barth got in and turned to Miel expectantly. She stood on the low concrete embankment and swallowed hard. She had no idea why climbing into a toy-like sailboat should be so much like stepping off a precipice, but it was. Fear snaked through her veins—fear of her past and the half-forgotten joy that was sailing, waiting to claim her heart once again.

"Come on." Barth stood with one hand on the newly erected mast and the other stretched out to her. When she didn't move, his eyes narrowed as he searched her face. Miel lifted a hand to her mouth in a futile attempt to hide her vulnerability. "Hey, you can do it," Barth persisted softly, as if she had turned into a wobbly creature starved for encouragement. "You can do it. Just slide down. Nothing to it."

Oddly enough, though she could not make herself admit it, his words were soothing, as was the invitation of his outstretched hand. It would be so easy to like him, to trust him, to fall into that trap again.

Momentarily she drew back. Then, seeing she had no choice, she mastered the terrible tightening in her chest and, taking his hand, stepped down. As the dinghy rocked, she was forced to grasp Barth's other wrist for support and even after she had quickly let go, she was conscious, much too conscious, of the tingle the contact had left along her palms. Barth raised the jib and the mainsail and pushed off with such a lusty shove that the bow slid away from the retaining walls and pointed out toward the harbor. The next second Miel felt her own hand placed firmly on the tiller. Barth grinned.

"All yours now. I'm just a passenger."

How could he know that exactly what she needed at that moment was command, even though everything in her shrank from it. And of course, what could she fear in a sheltered harbor scantly traveled at that hour and rippled by the friendliest of breezes?

Even with the combined weight of the two of them the boat seemed lighter in the water than anything Miel had been accustomed to. She worked the tiller gingerly to maintain momentum, then, free of the slip, she swung hard. At that moment, the limply flapping sails snapped to and took the air immediately, heeling the dinghy to the side and spinning it dangerously toward a rusting construction barge moored to the side. Barth merely clung to his perch waiting until Miel instinctively scrambled down to shift the jib and swing the boom clear to the other side. At once, the bow veered away, and the breeze pushed the little boat silkily into the open harbor waters.

Miel's fingers and movements had been stiff and nervous, but only for those first few moments. The hiss of the water under the hull, the sudden, clean crack of a sail never before touched by wind burst upon her. Her body leaned out, balancing naturally as the little craft seemed to actually lift itself and skim along beneath her as if it were a gull. She knew at a touch that she had under her hand the very latest of nautical design, for all its brightly frivolous appearance. Her old Bay Point dinghy wallowed like a washtub compared to this. A kind of awe clutched her as it responded to her lightest touch and strained with almost living eagerness to be out in the heart of the water.

"Why...it's beautiful," she gasped softly. "Beautiful!" And in that instant her old love of sailing came flooding back like the singing and surging of a long-forgotten tide. How had she ever lived so long without it? How had she ever imagined that tennis and fitness classes could substitute for this?

Forgetting all else but the pure joy of it, she threw back her head, grasped the tiller and pointed the bow directly for the far side of the harbor. It was all back now—the deep, instant rapport with the boat, the instinctive knowledge of all the wind's vagaries, the aching desire to sail and sail and sail. Her hazel eyes shone, her hair whipped back from her pale forehead as, with unbelievable speed, she sped toward the Eastern Ship Channel where the great black freighters lumbered in and out. She ran a race with the ferry, darting fearlessly across the course of its blunt heavy snout. And when it came time to tack around, the stern of the dinghy swung wide and beautiful in a white, bubbling curve.

"Pretty glorious, isn't it?" Barth said over the slap of the waves and the crackle of the sail.

Miel jumped, realizing that she had been so swept up in the exhilaration of it all that she had almost forgotten him.

"Yes, wonderful."

She smiled, a wide, enchanting smile because she was too happy to care what he thought anymore. Barth, ruddy in the flecks of sunlight that slipped through the race of cloud above, gazed at her, drinking in the sight as if it was something he had long been thirsting for. Then the breeze gusted so that the two of them, laughing, tucked their feet under the hiking strap and leaned far out over the water, balancing gracefully in unison as if they had been born sailing together.

Miel's creamy ankles peeped from beneath her cuff beside Barth's browned bare legs. With a pang she remembered herself in Bay Point, her skinny, coltish legs tanned like leather, tight as springs with nervous, youthful vigor. As the dinghy strained back toward the boat slip she glanced at Barth and drew her breath in sharply, for a glimmer of lowering light had turned him momentarily into an Inca sculpture sheeted in beaten gold. His infectious laughter drew her in even as she made the spume fly from under the bow and the sail strain eagerly at its lines. They were free—free as young animals let out to play.

They finished back at the ramp of the slip, wind-tousled and charged with energy. For the first time since Bay Point, Miel was brimming with the old recklessness, the same that had made her run dares with a dangerous wind that day when Barth had sailed to the village dock. How easy and agile they both were now as they hauled down the sail and lifted the centerboard, their arms brushing, their fingers meeting as they worked with boom and halyard, readying the boat to glide that last calm yard across the glassy water.

Only when the hull ground to a final halt on the concrete did Miel sober. She looked at Barth and was suddenly, excruciatingly aware of herself, all rosy and carefree and full of banter. Could this be she—the woman who had detested Barth and was almost promised to James Crome?

This just wouldn't do. Quickly, she leaped ashore and was silent through all the mundane packing away of sails and mast and centerboard and the tying up of the boat in the place arranged for it. Barth followed her up to level ground and laid his fingers on her bare forearm so unexpectedly that she barely controlled a yelp of nerves.

"There's no law against enjoying yourself, Miel," he said with a quiet and disconcerting seriousness.

Miel was still feeling the afterglow, her cheeks flushed with excitement and pleasure, her blood pumping madly through her veins. She turned away from him deliberately, flicking back her auburn hair.

"I didn't know you were an authority," she threw out breezily but with enough of an edge to make Barth's brows draw together.

"Don't, Miel. It does me good to see you happy."

"Oh, does it!" She suppressed a brief, bitter flash of him pushing her out into the night, breaking her heart, not caring the least about her happiness. "You'd better look more closely then, since I seem to be enjoying life pretty well these days."

"But not like now, like today. Out in the harbor you were really living. That's what I want for you, Miel. For both of us."

Miel's eyes widened and for a moment, only a brief instant, she actually believed it was so. The deeply etched lines at the sides of his mouth and on his forehead seemed to have disappeared, making him almost boyish again, the way she had remembered him. But the boyishness vanished as their gazes locked, and she discovered herself the object of a slow, hungry, smoldering look.

He took her hand and drew her to him, his thumbs sliding sensuously into the hollow of her palms, his face drawing closer and closer until he was almost touching her lips. Miel was terribly frightened, yet at the same time she felt drawn by the magnetic spell he was casting on her. She could only lower her lids and stand immobile as his lips found her nape and the delicate, sensitive skin below her ears. The flight of his butterfly kisses sent achingly delicious tremors along the nerves of her shoulders and throat, straight down to her solar plexus. Her stomach tightened involuntarily at the unaccustomed sensations invading her very soul. As his mouth found hers and tipped back her head the reality of the situation suddenly made her limbs tense and her conscious mind wake again to alarm. Her eyes flew open and she pulled away from him, dismayed by the look of unmistakable need in his eyes.

If his hands had tightened the slightest bit, if he had pulled her toward him one more centimeter, she would have fought. But he didn't try. Something in him, deep and carefully attuned, let him sense her changed mood. With a sigh, he released her.

"There's no law against this either," he murmured. "In case you didn't know, it's called desire."

"Barth, I'm sorry. I . . . ."

"Sssh. Until tomorrow, then. If the sun shines, we'll take the *Yancy* out onto the lake."

She couldn't be angry with him this time, couldn't even think to ask herself why. And since he didn't insist on her lips again, she thought her hand was a small price to pay as he held it all the way back to her car.

CHAPTER NINE

"HEY, MIEL. They really did a job on you in makeup."

James rose from behind his desk and Miel, who had just hurried down the corridor for a very early business meeting before the day's modeling, looked startled.

"I haven't been to makeup yet, James."

He came round, taking her hand as the door swung half shut behind her. His brown eyes glowed a warm greeting and a little bit of wonder.

"Then something out there certainly agrees with you. I've never seen you look so...well, blooming. Or," he added in a softer voice, "more beautiful."

Glancing swiftly at the deserted hall, James brushed her cheek with his lips, for both of them were still self-conscious about this business of stealing kisses on the premises. Perhaps when they got more used to each other they might become a little more adventurous. Miel offered her extraordinarily soft cheek and closed her eyes. Unconsciously, she braced herself for a leaping, electric rush. When she felt only a kind of tenderness, she realized what she had been doing—expecting poor James to over-match Barth.

Her heart contracted. How could she? How could she let the loose ends of her old life come back to entangle even this innocent moment with foolish discontent?

Benevolently, in restitution, she paused, then kissed James back, trying to tuck all her respect and caring for him into the deliberate caress. She ended by sliding the back of her hand along his jaw, feeling how fresh and cool and smooth it was from his morning shave and the expensive lotion he used.

"You really are...precious," she half blurted, suddenly making of the word one of those deeply meant endearments that are often so hard to say.

James flushed, then covered his obvious plea-sure by saying rather heartily, "I'll have to come with you sometime before the shooting is over just to see what's going on aboard that boat. More power to it for making you this way."

Oh God! Her heart thudded guiltily and she was suddenly possessed of an urgent need to straighten the leg of her vanilla pantsuit. The simple trust and joy between herself and James was changing, confused already by her unmen-tioned interludes with a sunburned sailor. As she smoothed the fine material, Miel was filled with a horrible resentment against Barth, that he should once again intrude in her life, muddy-ing up with his damnably tempting lips all that she had waited for between herself and James.

"Of course you must," she tossed over her shoulder, praying he wouldn't. "A day in the sun would be good for you. The open sea and all that—or the open lake, at least."

And then, because her attempted witticism sounded so weak, and her accompanying laugh so brittle, she straightened and kissed James again, this time lingering on his mouth. James was both surprised and delighted. She was lifting her fingers to his hair when both of them were frozen in action by the sound of the door as it opened.

"Oh!"

The voice behind them was very small and very shocked. Miel and James broke sheepishly apart to find Hildy standing there, a bundle of Gagnon promotions under her arm. Her green eyes were painfully wide and the color was draining away from the delicious little mouth, leaving only a pink slash in the midst of a pale white oval. Miel forgot her own embarrassment in astonishment at the young woman's face. Good grief! Hildy could not still be so naive as to blanch at two people smooching on the sly at the office.

"Hildy?" she questioned, taking a half step forward, torn between amusement and concern.

Hildy scrambled to recover herself, clutching the promos tightly and tossing that mop of curls the way she did when she was agitated. She must have read Miel's thoughts for the paleness was swiftly replaced by two spots of high color, like flags, upon her cheeks.

"I...well, I just thought I'd tell you we'd better be going. Chuck and the other models will be ready on the boat by ten thirty, and we have to get you made up before we go."

By ten, Miel stepped from the salon of a professional makeup artist looking not a great deal different than when she had gone in. Partly because of her fine-pored creamy skin, and partly because in the direct light of day she had to appear as natural and wholesome as possible, she had only been lightly touched up. Her short hair, with its body and magnificent natural sheen, had been styled simply with a blow dryer and left to the wind. The Gagnon outfits had already been ferried down to the yacht in Chuck's van, along with the two extra models Hildy had hired. Miel, in her Corvette, picked Hildy up at the door.

"Beautiful day for pictures," Miel commented as they swung along Queen Street past the long arches and dancing fountains of City Hall square. She felt an unusual need to make conversation because Hildy was so silent, making no comment even as Miel indicated the gorgeous chestnut trees leaning over the iron railing of Osgoode Hall. "Good sun and just the right bit of wind. We ought to hit the papers right on schedule with the finished ads."

"Guess so," came the laconic reply.

They took a corner and pulled up at a light. Miel saw that Hildy was staring far off at the black monolith of the Toronto Dominion Centre, looking decidedly disturbed by some inner thought. It occurred to Miel that, for all the instant rapport, for all the shared laughter and growing professional respect, she really didn't know Hildy very well at all. Ordinarily, Miel was rarely curious about people's private lives, but now, perhaps, she ought to show an interest.

"You know, you've never exactly told me if you were always a city girl or not," Miel tossed out just a little awkwardly in response to her young friend's retreat into silence.

"Mostly the city, yes."

The light changed. The white car sped smoothly off the mark.

"Your family must live here, then. Do you get to see them very often?"

The small features suddenly became drawn, as if the subject had all the appeal of a harsh cruel wind. "I really have no family," she said in a light, cheery voice bizarrely at odds with her appearance. Her fingers worked in her lap, and she stared fixedly ahead into the sunlit streets and the traffic streaming toward them.

Miel said, "Oh!" in a faint voice and turned, ready to extend sympathy, then stopped. There was a look about Hildy, even in her yellow, flouncing finery, a look she knew all too well. It had been on her own face many times—the scarcely veiled hostility that warns a speaker, through simple messages from the nerve ends, not to probe any more into the past.

So she is not as carefree and sunny as she would have us believe, Miel thought, and sank back pensively into her bucket seat.

Hildy remained extraordinarily quiet until they reached the harbor, where she launched into an exaggerated flurry of activity, getting the models aboard and seeing that the clothes were stowed away for their use. This campaign would make or break her career, and the season was already racing past them. It was vital they hit the papers in time, and she had even dreamed up a headline about Barth: "Passionate Fashion Draws the Seascape Man." Miel had gaped a little when Hildy had shown her her headline, accompanied by naughty copy, the day before. She suppressed her own slightly scandalized amusement to wonder aloud how they were to get such florid prose past their rugged sea captain. Hildy merely shrugged in that flamboyant way of hers.

"Simple. We won't tell him. He signed the model releases the same as you. We can pretty well do what we like with the photographs."

Now the copy lay safe and sound in the bottom of Miel's desk drawer while they all swarmed over the *Yancy*. They had had to wait out two days of intermittent showers before Chuck, liking the look of the sky, had sent out the call. Miel, who had only just got out of bed, replaced the receiver with a small burst of anticipation, not wanting to admit to herself that every moment of delay had been secretly chafing her.

Barth stepped out into the sunlight, breathtakingly handsome in the white canvas trousers and navy nylon shell jacket the photos would require. He greeted Miel with a wink and a flashy smile that made her mute and breathless as she stepped past him into the cockpit. Everyone stood back as Barth cast off the lines and headed the *Yancy*, propelled by a powerful but barely audible diesel engine, toward the Western Gap.

Miel found herself in an odd state, her excitement over being out for the first time on the *Yancy* mixed with considerable shyness. She was careful to hide her reactions from Barth's sharp gaze. She stuck close to Chuck, who perched against the mainmast, fiddling with his camera bag. The other two models, quite blasé about yacht trips, had retired below to protect their hair and to dress. Miel, having changed after her makeup job, already wore the wide-sleeved raw silk overblouse and button-cuff trousers in turquoise required for the day. She reveled in the swift, almost silent glide of the *Yancy* over the harbor.

When they passed the island airport and skipped out into the lake itself, the breeze picked up, sending wavelets in small slaps against the steadily knifing bow of the yacht. The warmth of the day was already felt in the decks, and Barth nodded to Chuck.

"I've fixed something tall and cool down in the galley. You'll need it before the day is out."

Chuck rose appreciatively, necklace of cameras dangling against his incipient paunch.

"Sure thing. Thanks."

And then there were only Miel and Barth left on the deck of the *Yancy*.

"Come and hold the boat steady, Miel. We better get some sail up if this advertising deal is to look at all authentic."

The breeze was now very respectable. Miel stepped back into the cockpit with the silk of her blouse dimpling against her, unaware that the curves of her body flowed as effortlessly as music. Barth, who never took his eyes off her, brought the *Yancy* up into the wind, then slid from behind the wheel to give Miel room. The smile he gave her faintly reminded her of a pirate's. As Miel brushed his thigh, she distinctly felt his muscles respond before he stepped away.

She took the great mahogany spokes in her hands and felt the satiny wood warmth both from the sun and Barth's fingers. When Barth shut down the diesel there was a long moment as the *Yancy* skimmed forward under its own momentum. Miel watched in fascination as Barth padded forward with totally unconscious agility to unfurl and raise first the working jib and then the great white mainsail, which swept up the mast in a magnificent cloud of fabric. Miel held the bow straight ahead so that neither of the large sails would be caught before they were ready. Barth secured the halyards and then set the main and jib sheets, handling with the authority of experience what others only arrived at through trial and error. When everything was rigged to his satisfaction, he dropped back into the cockpit with a lithe, soundless leap.

"Now, Miel," he rumbled, his eyes shining

brightly and intimately, "swing the *Yancy* over."

Realizing he meant her to stay in command, she gripped the wheel and spun it so that the bow raked sharply away from the direction of the breeze. The *Yancy* trembled slightly and, in an instant, forgot all about the slow and stately motion imposed by the diesel. The sails bellied out with a spine-tingling ripple and snap. Immediately, the yacht heeled to the wind and sprang forward with a thrilling burst of power. Miel gave a yelp of delight as the wheel kicked alive in her hand, telling her this lively, responsive yacht needed a vigilant person at the helm.

Barth, watching her, let out a gusty laugh at Miel's reaction, then their gazes locked. For several seconds, while spray flew from the bow, something leaped between them—a pure joy, a perfect, vital understanding of that wonderful instant when spread sails snap hard with the wind and a true sailboat finds its soul.

Miel was enthralled with the swift, racing glide, the rush of glittering water to the sides, the long white wake, like a veil, frothing behind them. From where she stood there was only the graceful bowsprit pointing into the endless, hazy blue horizon of the immense lake. When she glanced at Barth again all the pretense was washed from her wonderstruck hazel eyes.

"I...didn't know it could be like this!" she whispered, barely heard above the hiss of foam. "It's...just incredible!"

And then she realized he had arranged this,

gotten everyone else off the deck so that her first real experience sailing the *Yancy* could be shared only by the two of them.

"Yes, incredible! The old saying is very true. A sailboat is the closest people have ever come to creating a living creature."

His voice husked just enough to remind Miel of that day she had first met him in Bay Point, when he had run his fingers along the wood of the *Yancy* with just such emotion. Now, by the mere inflection in his voice, Miel finally understood the passion this man had for sailing and the sea—a passion so strong he might even abandon his livelihood in an attempt to corral the forces destroying the oceans he loved. The attempt might be insignificant and ultimately futile, but the only honor was to try.

And his passion showed now, in every angle of his face, in the set of his shoulders, in the deep, intense light of his eyes. Miel shuddered, feeling as if his passion had suddenly reached out and touched her body. Unbelievably, Miel felt as if she was about to cry, tears pricking at the corners of her lashes, emotion tugging madly at the softness of her mouth. A flame somewhere deep in her soul quivered and leaped, responding with the same headlong delight as the *Yancy*.

Standing together in the open cockpit, bound by the awareness racing between them, neither seemed able to move. The tug of the wheel and the long cry of a gull barely penetrated Miel's fascination. Barth's eyes, almost hooded with impetuous desire, lingered upon her mouth so that her lips parted instinctively to welcome his touch. Endlessly, endlessly, she waited for him to step forward from where he balanced like an athlete on the slanting cockpit sole. Then, just when he seemed about to move, a lightning series of soft clicks behind them, followed by a clatter, broke the mood.

It was Chuck, camera tilted, emerging from the salon.

"Hey, dynamite," he enthused, circling them, still clicking furiously. "Dy-na-mite! That's the kind of stuff I like to get on film!"

Miel burned scarlet to the roots of her hair and Barth was about to make a sharp, angry gesture that would have stopped Chuck cold had not Hildy's voice floated up behind him.

"Hey, Miel. There's a jacket that's supposed to go with that outfit too. Come and get it."

Miel handed the wheel back to Barth and bolted below where she found Hildy leaning against the chart locker, sparkle and color restored to her small face, as she held out a natty pea jacket. Just as Miel was reaching for it, carefully avoiding those acute eyes, Hildy paused, stroking the sleeve with a kind of deliberate dreaminess. "That Barth," she sighed. "He really is one fantastic hunk. If the shots come out well, we'll have them pouring into the store on the strength of his sex appeal alone!"

Miel winced at the baldness of the statement

but could not deny it was true, even to herself. Not after the electricity that had passed between them but moments before.

The shooting went well, though Miel remembered very little except for the discovery that serious modeling was also very hard work. She had to admire the two beauties Hildy had hired, Cheryl and Louise, for their sporty, unflagging professionalism. Barth set the yacht on automatic steering so that he would be free when required. Without supervision, the *Yancy* glided, through the aquamarine waves, the gentle tilt of the deck providing just the right amount of marine authenticity to the glorious cottons and silks of the Seascape collection. Cheryl, a limber brunette, and Louise, a honey blonde, turned in a smart job, but it was still Miel and Barth that Chuck zeroed in on every moment, for with every glance, every motion of their vibrant bodies, they made unconscious love to the lake and boat and the sky.

Hildy, today a windswept bundle of yellow with huge drop earrings, attended them, hopping this way and that, tilting her head, checking, rechecking, scribbling on her clipboard. Then, suddenly, the sunlight was snatched away, and Hildy was thrown rather unceremoniously against a stay. They looked up to find storm clouds billowing overhead and foam whitening the tops of the waves below. The *Yancy* heeled more sharply, spilling the models awkwardly across the deck so that they had to grab Chuck for support. Imperturbably, Chuck began packing up.

"Can't work without full sun," he announced. "We'll have to call it quits for today."

Released, Cheryl and Louise escaped below, hoping to protect their borrowed finery. Hildy followed, claiming the chart table to organize her latest mass of notes. Barth released the steering device and grinned at Miel.

"Take the wheel. We're going to come about."

Unable to stop the surge of excitement she felt, Miel scrambled into place, enjoying the added bite of the wind as she swung the bow directly into it so that the sails lost their hardness and began to flutter noisily. Barth worked forward, the nylon shell unzipping and whipping casually behind him. He loosened the jib sheet then glanced back at Miel.

"Steady now. I'm going to swing the boom."

Miel tensed. He was trusting her with the whole yacht as she swung the bow, careful not to veer too quickly, or else the huge mainsail and the loosened boom might swing out of control, perhaps tearing the rigging or slamming into anyone too slow to duck. She threw her weight into it, holding steady as the tack was completed and the boom and jib secured in their new positions. From this direction the wind was even stiffer, pushing the *Yancy* forward in long dipping leaps.

"Hey, double dynamite!"

Chuck had his half-packed camera out again, snapping the careless beauty of Miel's total absorption and the rippling lines of the Gagnon creation against the incomparable curves of her body. Barth was back beside her, his eyes running over her every bit as admiringly as Chuck's.

"You take us in. You're doing just dandy."

Miel forgot Chuck altogether as she relished the thrust of the wheel against the palms of her hands and the sight of the slim bow bounding like a greyhound toward the city skyline. The breeze, once so congenial, had turned into a wind that whipped spray up from the lake and flung it across the deck. Chuck, still taking pictures, lasted until a handful of flying spume struck him sharply on the back of the neck. Then, afraid for his precious equipment, he tucked everything away inside the protective cases.

"Don't you think you better take down a little more sail?" he shouted apprehensively. "It's too rough for the big one you've got up."

Barth, looking every bit the amiable Nordic mariner, leaned into the wind toward him.

"We can't capsize. Look who's at the helm."

Chuck might have stuck it out had not the water threatened his camera bags. Very shortly he retreated to the shelter of the salon with Hildy and the models.

Miel, oblivious to his departure, was caught up in the increasingly bucketing race across waves toward the harbor. But she wasn't oblivious to the presence of Barth standing beside her, emanating that pervasive sensuality no woman could ignore. Nor did she miss the pleasure on his face as he watched her, so graceful in her elegant Gagnon, nevertheless keeping the bow straight as a sure and speeding arrow.

The Western Gap, heralded by the silvery geodesic dome of Ontario Place, approached with swiftness. Barth eased forward to furl the mainsail and take down the jib. As soon as the billowing fabric had been lashed down, the *Yancy* lost its fine exuberance, coasting to a staid halt near the mouth of the channel. Barth started the engine and took over the wheel, aware of the disappointment clouding Miel's face.

"I know. I always hate this moment too. When I take the sails down I feel as if, somehow, I've stolen the life from the *Yancy*."

No wonder seamen and engineers and pilots endowed their big, beautiful machines with names and personalities. Barth loved this yacht with the mysterious bond that bound all sailors to their boats. Miel was profoundly moved that he had shown this love to her, for she had begun to suspect that, despite his apparently easygoing nature, there were parts of himself that he did not easily reveal. She had been there at Bay Point when the first tentative restorations to the yacht had been made. Perhaps, in her own tenuous way, she, too, was bound to the *Yancy*.

They lost the chance for further conversation as the stillness of the yacht and the proximity of the harbor brought their passengers out on deck again to watch the docking. At Harbourfront, they poured over the side, Hildy gamely helping Jenny, who had arrived from the store, to tote garment bags.

"Wait for me," Miel called, heading below to gather up her scattered things and shed the Gagnon she was wearing. "I won't be a minute."

"I haven't got a minute," Hildy called over her shoulder. "I have to get these back and meet a bunch of people for dinner. See you in the morning."

So Hildy had succeeded in dumping her once again. Miel shook her head and went down to change. Chuck was commandeering the models to carry cases to the van so there was really nothing for Miel to do but change into her street clothes. When she stepped from the stern cabin into the salon she was not surprised to find the *Yancy* deserted and Barth pouring a couple of drinks from the surprisingly well-stocked bar. This time she didn't even protest. A deep inner glow that matched the ravishing honey of her newborn tan made her want to extend the afternoon as far as it would go.

"Well, Coconut Princess, did you have a good time?"

She smiled softly at one of the many nicknames he had used for her. *Yancy* at its mooring lulled her into perfect contentment. The teasing now in Barth's voice—familiar and suddenly dear—warmed her. She was in no hurry to leave.

"You always used to call me that. I was too shy to ask why."

Astonishingly, it no longer hurt to make casual mention of the past.

"Perhaps I was too shy to tell you," he bantered back, and was rewarded with the lightness of her laughter.

"I can't imagine you being shy about anything."

"Can't you?" He slipped a glass tinkling with ice cubes into her hand. "Then you haven't thought much about what it was like for a cocky, roughneck sea tramp like myself to meet this perplexing collection of growing bones and prickly defiance. You really were wild then. Entrancingly so, I might say—even though you really weren't aware of it. I couldn't think what to do about you except make jokes while we worked. Besides—" he took a large gulp from his glass "—you were just . . . well, a kid."

Her breath caught. There it was again—that hint, that suggestion that he had cared, at least a little, the way she had wanted him to. Her lashes made shadows on her cheek.

"So Coconut Princess—that was a joke too?"

"Hardly. It's a legend from Fiji, where once upon a time the king fell hopelessly in love with a beautiful native girl. Actually, it tells how the coconut tree came to be."

He ran his hand down a section of paneling and stood, half turned away from Miel, gazing out the porthole at Centre Island as if it were suddenly landscaped with white sands and clumps of palms. The slanting light cast thin bright streamers along his cheekbones and tangled in the thickness of hair touching his nape.

"I fail to see what the coconut palm has to do with a king in love," Miel ventured, intensely curious about his pensiveness.

"Quite a lot. You see the native girl was reluctant and fled. The king searched for her, following her from island to island in the shape of a gigantic, many-colored eel. Sina—that was the girl—got so upset he finally relented. Quite humbly, he told her that if she buried him at her feet in the sand he would provide her with food and drink and shade forever. She planted him and up sprang the coconut palm. The king of Fiji had kept his word."

"Very noble." Miel arched her lovely brows. "Sina got a useful food item but the poor king of Fiji seems to have done himself out of the romance market forever."

"Oh no." Barth swung back to her, his voice too low, his smile too sultry for ordinary purposes. "Every time Sina drank coconut milk she knew she was kissing her royal lover's lips."

How could the comfortable companionship slip away in a few seconds and the atmosphere thicken with sensual urgency? The smile faded from Barth's lips, and Miel found her gaze helplessly held by his. She watched as he moved closer and closer, his gray eyes clearly indicating that he wanted her. For endless electric moments he searched her eyes for signs that she was after all bright water rife with shoals.

She missed the faint clink of his glass being set down on the table. The sound was lost in a small, muffled groan as his large hands took her shoulders and pressed her close to him. His mouth found hers with a passionate fury and when the first starving urge was satisfied, he gently bent his head to rain light butterfly kisses along her cheeks and forehead and the tender, trembling corners of her eyelids.

Deep in some hidden corner of her heart Miel must have been expecting this, though she was once again paralyzed by the sweet shock. She mustn't think, couldn't think, could only close her eyes and drink in the strength of the fingers gripping her firm flesh and enjoy the surprise of the slow, delicious warmth stealing over her. She swayed against him gently, like an underwater plant in the tide. She lifted her arms and one of her hands touched his face, touched it wonderingly, as if exploring what she had so often seen in dreams, so desperately loved but never never in the flesh possessed.

The pads of her fingers became so sensitive they could distinguish the tiny creases at the corners of his eyes. Barth withstood the seduction of her touch until cords stood out along his throat from the enormous control he exerted.

"I...don't want to spoil it," he murmured. "I don't want to spoil it the way I did before...but oh, Miel...."

A low groan escaped him, and the next instant Miel was crushed against the rampart of his chest. His tongue invaded her mouth and urgently sought the moist honeyed secrets she had never before fully yielded to any man. Her senses roared like a conflagration out of control. She was dizzy, reeling—and she jerked herself away, her breath coming in short, frightened sobs. Barth made a brief, blind movement toward her, then caught himself. Every muscle in his body was straining against his self-imposed withdrawal. Wide-eyed at the sight of such obvious desire, Miel ran the back of her hand across her mouth and would have bolted had not Barth reached swiftly, grasping her wrist.

"Don't go, Miel. Don't run away!"

His touch stopped her. Slowly, very slowly, he turned her and drew her hand to him. Though his face was fiery and his breathing erratic, he was looking at her closely and in surprise.

"It isn't fear, is it, Miel? Surely, now, you're an experienced woman. You must know all about the effect men and women have on each other."

Her mouth flew half open as if to speak, and her face drained of color. She didn't know what to tell him. She was experienced and she wasn't. There had been men, kisses, but they had all left her cold. She hadn't felt anything like this since Bay Point aboard the *Yancy*. She had assumed she never would. . .until now. It was no wonder she wanted to flee as fast as she could!

"Hey, hey, it's perfectly natural," Barth soothed. "Look."

Taking the palm of her hand, he pressed it to his lips and to his face, then let it go free. Once again she felt a thrill clear down to her toes. Fascinated, Miel felt her fingers drawn irresistibly to his flesh again. She explored the bridge of his nose and the hollows at the sides of his temples. He remained still as she tangled her hands in the wonderful wiry sun-bleached hair, shoving it back and discovering, with a small intake of breath, a new scar, white and years old now, that hadn't been there at Bay Point.

He tilted his head back, encouraging Miel to stroke the bronzed column of his throat. Half closed, his eyes were flooded with desire, but desire he held rigidly in check as Miel progressed to the wings of his collarbones and the rippling layers of muscle that made up the breadth of his shoulders. She rested one hand lightly on his jugular vein, and to her amazement she felt the flow of his blood speed and pound as her other hand slid into the opening of his shirt to lose itself in the mat of curling hair.

"See what you do to me, Miel," he whispered raspily. "See the power you have. No other woman has been able to drive me half mad with only a touch. . . ."

Now he was visibly restraining himself as he bent his head close to hers. In the diffused yellow light of the cabin Miel stared openly at him, amazed at the control he was commanding over the forces surging through him—forces her mere presence, her nearness had aroused.

Without warning, an answering surge struck her, and again the dark flame of passion danced through her nerve ends. Only this time, instead of being afraid, she was overwhelmed by an intoxicating sense of power. In just a few minutes, Barth had taught her more about desire than all those young men who had tried to embrace her, than dear discreet James ever dreamed of with his polite, diffident caresses.

James! Her hazel eyes flickered momentarily, but not even that reproachful image could make her turn away from this awesome new discovery she had fought against for so long. She was stunned by the vistas before her. How could she possibly have reached the age of twenty-four without confronting this elemental part of human knowledge?

Barth was closer now, pulling her hips against his own. His hands slid up under her blouse and found the sweet indentation of her spine. "We could take the *Yancy* out again," he whispered, so near that the warmth from his mouth poured over her cheeks like molten joy. "We could run to the horizon if you like and throw down a sea anchor. It'll be calm tonight with buckets of stars, and the city will look like a heap of Christmas lights. Oh, sweetheart, you haven't seen anything until you've looked up at the sky from the arms of someone you've just made love to. . . ."

The snap of her bra giving way penetrated her swirling senses, then was lost in the incredibly delicious sensation of Barth's hand cupping her breast and finding her nipple, which eagerly responded beneath his touch. She quivered clear to her bones as Barth loosened the buttons at the front of her shirt so that it dropped open. As she moved, feebly, to draw it shut again, Barth brushed away her fingers.

"Don't, darling. I want to look at you. Your skin...it shimmers in the light. I want...oh, I want to touch it forever...."

Mesmerized, she stood there, her nakedness the color of pale amber as his gaze seemed to consume her. Then, swiftly, Barth bent his head to the fragrant valley between her naked breasts. Miel stiffened and tried to lift her forehead away from his neck. He was mad, surely, to tempt her away with such sweet honey. Yet she had had her part in driving him to it. Her female instincts and this new knowledge of her own desirability, knowledge that ran like hot wine in her veins, urged her on, lured her toward the yawning chasm opening at her feet.

Extraordinary means were required to resist. Her imagination responded by providing a very clear picture of herself as she walked into the office in the morning, her eyes glazed, her lips swollen from Barth's ardor, while James rose to greet her, asking with gentle, unsuspecting concern how she had slept that night.

"Stop. Oh, Barth...no!"

She wanted him to stop and she wanted him to stop her, for his seductive blandishments still possessed every cell of her body. She longed for the wildness of the lake air and the million stars, obscured for years by the city glare, shining huge and white against the ghostly rigging. The stars and Barth's warm arms. . . .

"Miel, it's not a crime!"

But it was—against herself and James and everything she had struggled to build for herself. Miel thrust Barth away and tried valiantly to ignore his groan of protest as she did so. Fully aware now that her shirt gaped, she turned away and struggled with the buttons, feeling suddenly, unbearably exposed. The shining dream fled before a hounding guilt. So this was what people meant when they said they had been swept away by passion, a blind calling of flesh to flesh trampling every other consideration in the world. Thank heaven she had caught herself before she had managed to betray James totally and hurt without repair the dearest, kindest man she would ever have the luck to meet. Frantic to leave before it was entirely too late, she fumbled for her briefcase and the brown garment bag that hid the splendor of the Gagnon she had been wearing.

"Miel, wait. . . ."

"I can't, Barth. Don't you see? I have to go."

She could not look into those gray eyes again for fear of what she might find, so she fled up the companionway with a light, swift movement that carried her over the catwalks and along the aging concrete to her car.

Yet when she arrived at her apartment, the powerful experience of being with Barth refused

to leave her, soaking through her like some ex-
alted drunkenness, making it impossible for her
to see to the practical matter of heating a quiche
for dinner or washing her morning coffee cup.
Instead, she wandered, disoriented, floating,
toward the window where the low sun breathed
reddish fire up the sides of the office towers and
sent fanciful shadows curling around her living
room. The familiar surroundings of her home
became strange, divorced from reality just as
Miel herself was.

It seems she had lost both her reason and her
memory. On the yacht she had swallowed a
heady intoxicant and now could only follow its
delicious progress through her limbs. On impulse she flung wide the tall glass doors to her
balcony to let the breeze in, regardless of how it
buffeted her prized French sheers. The smell of
the city drifted up—exhaust fumes and asphalt
she hadn't noticed in ages. Now, with her senses
so vividly alive, it quickly became intolerable.

Instead, there flashed into her mind a vision
of a warm lagoon with swaying palms and the
Yancy lying like a seabird at rest in water so
clear it seemed as if the yacht were lying cradled
in the air. Gripping the balcony rail, Miel was
suffused with an almost insupportable longing
to soak her body in the vital tropic sun, then
dive, lithe and tanned, from the forepeak down,
down into the transparent coolness until she
floated above coral red as blood, blue as uncut
sapphires. Just to be free there, oh, just to be
free. And later, under a moon as big as a

Chinese gong, sleep on deck wearing nothing but a wisp of a sarong with Barth's hungry arms to hold her.

The sun sank behind the western apartment towers with a lavender blink, and Miel shook herself, recognizing her old wanderlust, a fever she had not allowed to touch her since those young and smitten days in Bay Point. Summoning her will, she shut her heart against the temptation. The world, as much of the world as she wanted, was about to be all hers. Why torment herself with troubling fantasies that rightly belonged only in her foolish adolescence?

But that other thing she had learned tonight, that undeniable knowledge of passion, had become emblazoned in her very core, and Miel could not leave it alone. The memory of Barth's embrace drew her back again and again, each time sending a pulse of liquid fire through her veins. And the last thing she could think of when she went to bed that night was that she had stepped into another country, another sunlight, and she wondered if there was any way she could find her way back to the ordinary light of day again.

CHAPTER TEN

SHOWERS AND A CEILING of uncooperative clouds had interfered for three days since the last time the crew had been out on the *Yancy*. But finally they welcomed a sunny, albeit somewhat misty, day. Everyone sprang into action, for Hildy was prodding to get this first, urgent stage of photography over with. She had planned an ambitious direct-mail campaign to introduce the Gagnon line to names carefully chosen from the social register. This would coincide with a newspaper blitz and fashion show Hildy and James had dreamed up to bring in important customers. Each of these warm, heady days reminded everyone how imperative it was to get the summer stock of Gagnons moving so that later seasonal lines, with new loyal patrons, could be promoted at leisure.

Listening to his own suggestion, James had abandoned his office to see for himself what all the ferment aboard the *Yancy* was about. Then, too, he probably wanted to reassure himself that the radical new concepts Hildy had convinced the store to gamble on were getting the best possible exposure. At least that's what Miel prayed it was and not the blush of Barth's caresses that must lie as clear as a banner across her honey-tinted skin.

She had not spoken to Barth since that moment when she had lifted her arms from his neck and fled from the *Yancy*'s deck.

Reckless, racing dreams had troubled her sleep that night. The next morning she had awakened like someone with a hangover, wondering why her coffee cup tilted and slipped so clumsily in her hands. At work, when she should have been busiest, she spent time staring into space, only to blush furiously whenever Hildy or Allison or James came into view. Especially James, for she was a loyal, honest person and it would be foolish to say that guilt, darkening and deepening with the passing hours, did not leave its bitter and recurrent sting upon her.

Yet something else had happened to her too. She had become intensely, too intensely perhaps, aware of the world around her—of clouds glimpsed between soaring skyscrapers, of the dull roar that is the pulse of any city, but mostly of the small things close around her. Miel would find herself forgetting everything else to stare at the intricate wood-grain patterns on the top of her desk, or the way the sunlight turned the leaves of her very ordinary office plant into blades of gold. It was during these moments that the memory of the *Yancy* was apt to creep back to her—her weakness for the sun-drenched decks, the passion for the open sea would seep into her bones so easily.

Last night James had taken her to Giorgio's, an oregano-scented Italian hideaway in the midst of Toronto's huge Italian community. It had thick cotton tablecloths, real candles in the heavy iron sconces and a good earthy bite to its house wine.

"Salute!" she had cried, brightly trying the Italian she had overheard at nearby tables. And then she had curled her hand like a lost thing into James's palm.

She tried as hard as she could to be her old self—more than her old self—but James grew silent. He peered at her so strangely Miel realized her laugh had been altogether too brittle and her words suspiciously light. A small icy tremor ran swiftly, like a mouse, through the corridors of her heart.

"My dear, I believe you're just a little drunk," he said in the car, smiling in that gallant, faintly puzzled manner that always made her feel so sad. Vehemently, and for the umpteenth time, she tried to suppress the upheaval Barth was causing in her life.

"Oh, James," she whispered, a bare edge of tears in her voice. And she had slid her arms seekingly, hungrily, around his neck.

He had taken her into his embrace, carefully, waiting until she turned her face up before he kissed her, holding her in the prescribed way, as if he had been reading about it in a book. Miel had closed her eyes as their lips met, giving herself up to him, yet braced for an ambush of fire.

But there was only the gentleness of James, the respect he had for her, the longing much too gentlemanly ever to break down into crushing caresses and hot moans against the fine upholstery of his car. In the end, Miel had brushed a brown lock from his temple and smiled into his eyes. Yet when she dashed up the steps of her building, her fists had been squeezed tight. She knew now that the encounter on the yacht had changed her irrevocably in ways she had never thought she could be changed.

"Why me?" she had asked the silence of her apartment. "Why now?"

And the worst of it was that when she thought of Barth, these hot and cold needles of desire shot through her without a moment's notice, and some deep part of her, some smoldering sensuality, was glad, glad, glad!

That was why today, when James had mentioned he might come along, Miel had acquiesced with eagerness. Surely, with James at her side, she would have a safe, sure shield against the further dangerous appeal of Barth Tramande.

Clad in T-shirt and simple white shorts, which showed off more than usual how beautifully she was put together, Miel stood ready with the stern line as the last of the passengers trooped aboard, making the *Yancy* shiver in the water.

James stepped over the toerail very carefully as if he had had little to do with boats before. Of course Miel had expected to see him perfectly turned out, but it was hard to get used to James without his business suit. He wore white trousers, white deck shoes and a white cotton shirt open at the neck under a blue blazer, which anywhere else would have looked exceedingly casual. Here, next to Barth, who was barefoot, as usual, and sporting a battered Greek sailor's cap, it managed to look excruciatingly formal, more suitable for a drink in the Commodore's Lounge than a stint at the mast out on the lake.

A gusty erratic breeze and low chop told of some passing weather disturbance far out on the water. The sun, however, was strong and bright and that was what Chuck was mainly concerned about, even though there was a very high, white scatter of thin cloud. They glided out again through the Western Gap, past the gaily roofed beer kiosks of Ontario Place and the futuristic dome of Cinesphere, with its six-story curving movie screen where Miel had once actually yelped aloud at the realism of a forest fire.

She saw that James was firmly settled into a cockpit seat before the sails went up. Her heart lurched at the sight of Barth so alive in the sun, putting the last turn in the mainsheet. Quickly, she scrambled down to the salon. The other two models were in the stern cabin unzipping garment bags. Their voices—and Barth's name—stopped Miel just as she was about to grasp the doorhandle.

"That sailor's some specimen," Louise commented from behind the lovely carved door hanging just slightly ajar. "What does he do for a living? Just drift around on this yummy yacht?"

"Uh-uh. I hear he's a very big cheese in marine salvage. This yacht is just a little holiday toy."

"No kidding! Then he's rich."

"Yup. Bet he's got a girl in every port too. You know what they say about sailors. Remember Adam Ryker who used to run that trimaran out of Ashbridge's Bay?" Cheryl's voice was momentarily muffled by a garment sliding over her head. "I went out with him a few times. Then he came round one day just reeking with perfume, so I broke it up. Boy, did he get mad. Said he had women, *willing women*, stashed all up and down the St. Lawrence, so who did I think I was. Positively smirked about it. And the awful thing was, I knew just from the look on his face that it was perfectly true!"

"The louse!" Louise sputtered darkly.

"Yeah, that's what I say. I stay away from sailors now except for just a fling. Something about floating around the world does it to them. They can't take people seriously. And why should they, when all they have to do is hoist the sail and take off somewhere else. Neat way to avoid any little messes they might have left behind."

"But I saw you looking this one over," Louise ventured mischievously.

A moment of sheepish silence died in a wash of laughter.

"Who could help it? And don't tell me you wouldn't like to have him bronzed and put on your mantelpiece too. Quite a morsel—but he's already got his eye on someone to fill up his idle hours in Toronto.''

"Do tell. Who?"

"Why Ms McCrae, of course. Our toothsome employer from Crome's. Spotted it first time I stepped aboard.''

"Oh, poor girl. Do you think she's. . . .''

"Ssssh. She's up on deck, you know.''

The voices dropped immediately but remained painfully audible.

"Are you going to drop her a word of warning, then?''

"Oh sure! Last time I tried to be a good samaritan my best friend froze me out for six months. She's a big girl. She'll have to take her chances.''

Miel heard the click of Louise's makeup case but was unable to move.

"Yeah, I guess. But I can't help feeling kind of sorry for her. She seems kind of innocent. Just something about her, even though she's far too pretty not to know about guys. Anyway. . . . Hey, look at the time. We'd better scoot!''

Ears afire, Miel retreated ignominiously and just managed to be coming back down as the two models emerged and favored her with a bright and—surely not—pitying smile. Alone in the stern cabin amid a muddle of discarded street clothes, scattered lipsticks and the overpowering smell of hair spray, Miel slumped down on the bunk and hugged her knees, the words of the models looming luridly in her mind.

"Oh, the poor girl...I can't help feeling kind of sorry for her...she's kind of innocent...."

Oh God, was it like that? Really? She was twenty-four years old and the casual remarks of these two stunning, sophisticated women hit her savagely. And they didn't make her feel like an innocent. They made her feel like a fool!

Yet what did she actually know of Barth? Only what he chose to tell her, weaving a gripping tale of the dangers, the storms, the lonely missions across the trackless seas. But he had been decidedly silent on the other side of it, the days and weeks the great salvage tugs lay idle, sitting in port in, say, the Azores or Rio de Janeiro waiting for the distress call to come from a broken-down or grounded ship to spur them into action. What then would a handsome sailor do to while away the idle sunny days and the long, hibiscus-scented nights?

With a shudder that was part memory, part present pain, she remembered too vividly that last encounter. Barth pretending to be vulnerable, all the time urging her fingers over his flesh, awakening her consciously and deliberately. And when at last she realized her feminine powers, she would weaken and give into his seductive promise to take the *Yancy* out for the night.

In the darkness behind her eyelids other images were recalled. Barth in the café, his face positively glowing as he passionately outlined his concern for the sea. The ghost of his deep laughter, which could tingle all the way down her spine. That special look as he handed over, for the first time, the wheel of the *Yancy*. Miel didn't want these images. She rejected them frantically and grasped at the ones the models had left. As her own insecurities surfaced she recounted every unhappy thing they had said about Barth. Without her even knowing why, some part of her seemed determined to erect a spiky fence. She wanted to stand behind it with James, who was totally incapable of such deceit....

"Hey, Miel. Everybody's ready up here."

Miel whipped into a bell-sleeved Gagnon jump suit of pale heliotrope silk and was out on deck, the humidity laying a dewy shine on the delicate honey tones of her skin.

"That's it," cried Chuck, as Miel hauled on a line for the camera. "Put some energy into it. Look as if you mean it!"

She did, with a vigor whose boiling source not a single one of them guessed. She kept her face turned away from Barth and into the breeze. She took a perverse satisfaction in interposing the other two models between herself and that rugged body of his.

"Damn!" sputtered Chuck, and they all knew what it was. Cloud again, low, heavy and gray this time, thickening as they slid toward the city. In a race for the last of the sunlight, Chuck set up one final shot, a dramatic arrangement of belted cotton tunics against the splendid proportions of Barth's body, which, this time, was left in his ragged denims and sleeveless T-shirt for contrast. Miel, holding herself taut, took great care not to touch him in any way.

"Okay. *Finito*, ladies. We'll have to head back."

Miel sped down to change into her green trousers and short-sleeved safari shirt. With Cheryl and Louise she was scrupulously polite and acutely conscious of their eyes fastened on her. *They're wondering,* she thought, *just how far I've gone with Barth!*

A wave knocked her into the doorframe as Chuck and Hildy clattered with their gear into the shelter of the salon. It gave Miel a queer, queasy feeling to be leaning against all that remembered wood, but the queasiness was soon replaced with fear when she realized that now only James and Barth were left together topside.

James. . . oh, James!

She rushed out to look for him and found him clutching the foremast, where he had apparently gone to leave the cockpit free for Barth and the activity buzzing around the companionway. One look at him, one good close look, caused Miel to catch her breath in dismay. It was the first time in her life she had seen James painfully at a disadvantage.

Instead of becoming lustily windblown the way Barth did, he was simply disheveled. His jacket kept blowing open and his normally elegant body was stiff and awkward in his efforts to keep his grip as the *Yancy* bucked in the increasingly short, steep chop. His hair, always so impeccably combed, was being blown forward in points. The muscles of his face were bravely set but intensely grim, and for the first time it occurred to Miel that he might be subject to seasickness. A sharp pang of failed responsibility shot through her. How could she have neglected him so, even with her modeling duties?

"Hey, Miel, want to take the *Yancy* in?"

Behind her, Barth was offering her the wheel again, expecting her to leap for joy. Yet now his vigor, his ease, even the rough and ready way he looked, seemed somehow affronts to her loyalties, indictments against James. How could she even think of taking the helm when James, to whom she owed everything, absolutely everything, was here in distress and needing her?

Yes, needing her. A vast surge of protectiveness began to flow through Miel, and she flung up her head to Barth.

"Not today," she tossed back pointedly. "I'm going to stay with James."

Not even waiting to see the effect her answer had on Barth, she hurried forward to where James hung on to the mast with one hand and with the other kept trying to smooth his hair back in place. Her heart twisted when she saw that what he was trying to protect was a tiny bald spot that until that moment no one would ever have suspected was there. She took his arm. He looked down at her, his face flooded with relief.

"How are you doing?"

"Fine, just fine," he replied, though his

pinched mouth contradicted every word. It was, once again, a source of wonder to Miel that there were people in the world who didn't take to the pleasures of sailing like fish to water.

"Come below. I'll make you a cup of coffee."

Patiently she led him back, negotiating the wall of sail and forest of stays. Barth watched steadily as they stepped down into the cockpit, his obvious robust health making a mockery of James. As they made their way down the companionway under that gray gaze, the high color on Miel's cheek had nothing whatever to do with the freshness of the wind. James eased himself gratefully into one of the luxurious settees and immediately looked much better. Besides, from the marked gentling of the *Yancy*'s dip, Miel knew that Barth had reefed in the main so that all his squeamish passengers could have an easy ride. Miel pursed her lips, wondering if this small action was Barth's way of commenting on the people he had aboard.

Oh, stop it, she told herself, and got up to make coffee, working quickly and efficiently, completely unaware that she was imitating the actions of Barth at the same homey chore. Fortunately, James was much too delighted with the interior comfort to notice that she was displaying an overfamiliarity with the kitchen area. When the brew was ready, Louise and Chuck gulped theirs down and made their way back up on deck, followed by Cheryl who didn't drink coffee. Only Hildy hovered around, sipping from her mug nervously and pacing a little in front of the table Miel and James shared.

"Why don't you go up top for a while, Miel," she urged. "It's lovely. And I don't know how you could refuse when Barth actually offered you the wheel."

Miel shook her head, though a small part of her longed briefly for the wheel's familiarity in her hands.

"I'm staying with James. You go up if you like. Maybe Barth'll let you steer today."

She refilled James's mug and handed it to him. Smiling, he lingered over the warmth of her fingers, a gesture that Hildy watched rather closely. Next, Hildy tossed back the rest of her own coffee with an utter disregard for the burnable membranes of her throat and hurried without another word into the whipping breeze. Miel gazed after her quizzically before she was distracted by James, who was attempting to smooth his hair into some kind of order.

"I'm afraid I'm not much of a sailor," he said apologetically, feeling considerably recovered. "The sport always struck me as something either too wet and too cold or too hot and too windy. Living quarters like a linen closet and all that murky water going up and down beneath one's feet. For the life of me, I've never been able to understand why people do it."

These few half-joking words reminded Miel once again just how alien all this wind and casualness was to James's ordered world. He could sweat on a squash court or do her proud in doubles at tennis, but he would be dressed in crisp whites and the game would be played within the precincts of a prestigious club. A city-bred thing, this refinement of his, admirable the way an intricate sculpture was admirable, but certainly not built to stand up to nature in the raw.

Bracing against the heel of the *Yancy*, Miel was far from chagrined by these revelations. She felt enormously tender toward James as she played with the edge of his cuff. It was as if she had stumbled on something fragile and beautiful and knew it must be protected from the elements. James was so out of his environment here that she only wanted to get him home.

The coffee had restored him and he leaned back, peering out the port when the closeness of the buildings and the telltale slowing of the boat indicated that the sails were being lowered and the engine would soon start. The tap of feet above them and the chatter from the cockpit gave the almost deserted salon a sense of intimacy. James reached over and took Miel's hand.

"You make one helluva model, Miel. Smashing. Why do I have this feeling that I've only glimpsed a hidden reservoir of talents?

Miel laughed rather shortly. A number of those talents, learned or rediscovered, might be not at all the sort to bring comfort to their lives.

"I try, James. I just try to do what's asked."

He traced a line in her palm, the one commonly known as the lifeline.

"I wonder, Miel," he ruminated almost to himself, "I wonder if you'll do what I want to ask of you—when the time comes."

Miel looked up sharply. James remained stubbornly silent, merely smiling that well-bred smile of his. Yet there was something eager and trusting in his eyes, something that ought to have filled Miel with joy but somehow only managed to dismay her.

Bringing her other palm up, she covered the back of his hand. James responded and the two of them remained that way, motionless, as if joined in the most solemn of pledges, until the *Yancy* bumped against the fenders at the slip and the companionway door was thrown open by a large and ruddy presence.

"We're tied up now. I thought . . . ."

For the first time ever, Miel heard Barth's voice stumble as his gaze fell upon the knot of hands. James and Miel broke up hastily as the others bustled down to collect their things. The models and Chuck vanished immediately while Hildy, normally so swift to take off, now hung around fussing with papers. Barth was suddenly mightily busy with lashing on the sail cover as he waited for the jumble of people and things to clear. A gray ceiling of cloud was lowering over them, and the air smelled distinctly of rain.

When only the four of them were left, he hopped down into the cockpit, his face now very bland. "You know," he explained with what Miel could later only put down to mischievous intent, "I haven't really had a chance to take in any of the city sights yet. I sleep here under that huge CN Tower every night, for instance, and I've never been up to it, though I've sure heard a lot about the view. Maybe if some of you aren't busy right now you could show me how to get to the top.''

He glanced at his complicated watch as if to say that the afternoon was yet young and there was plenty of time for such an expedition. James, with his unfailing courtesy, nodded agreeably and Hildy, oddly enough, leaped onto the bandwagon.

"Oh, it's marvelous up there, Barth. I'm surprised you've waited this long. Normally it's the very first thing a visitor goes to see."

"I suppose we could all go up," pondered James, "but it's getting a little cloudy."

Hildy waved away his objection with a flick of her clipboard.

"Nonsense, James. It won't close in for ages yet. But I've been carrying these layouts around all day waiting to see you. We still have to make a decision about which Gagnons to run in the flyer. And if I don't firm up the newspaper space very soon, somebody else...."

In seconds James was drawn deeply and adroitly back into the concerns of the business and only paused to wave his hand at Miel.

"Do take Mr. Tramande up the tower, Miel. You can still catch the view if you hurry. Hildy and I had better go back to the office and take care of this."

"But shouldn't I...."

Miel was used to being included in the planning, and suddenly neither of them was paying attention to her. She was dismayed to find her lower lip trembled a little. "I can't take anyone up the tower," she insisted. "I'll go back to the office, too."

James stopped in the midst of reaching for Hildy's papers and looked at Miel, making her realize all at once how very rude she was sounding. Her cheeks burned with two bright spots of color as she reminded herself not to protest too much or James might guess that something odd was going on between herself and Barth. She cringed as she imagined how hurt he would be. He didn't deserve that.

So, to save James from possible pain, she agreed to conduct Barth on a tour. Barth was looking clearly pleased, so it was with a perverse sense of satisfaction she noticed that the topmost spike of the tower was suspended in a fog that would probably veil the observation deck by the time they got there.

"You engineered that," she said accusingly as they slid into the bucket seats of her car.

Barth was now clad in a cinnamon oxford-cloth shirt and deep chocolate trousers that actually looked pressed. And of course he was perfectly shameless.

"Naturally. I saw you and James holding hands like that. I thought I had better do something."

She was enraged. How dared he! *How dared he!* She whirled on him, hazel eyes shooting off sparks of green-and-gold fire, but he met her with a straight unwavering gaze that more than belied the banter in his words. In the end, it was the dismal voice of her own conscience that stopped the retorts hovering on her lips. Wrenching the steering wheel, she roared under the Bay Street railway bridge and somehow found her way into the parking lot that served the CN Tower. When she had backed into a slot and taken her handbag into her lap, she felt more capable of speech.

"James and I have something very special. I don't want...I won't allow anything to interfere with it."

Small words, full of bravado, somehow like throwing pebbles at a tiger, though she meant them nevertheless. She waited for Barth to recall their slight indiscretion aboard the *Yancy*, but he was either a gentleman or much wilier than she thought.

"The only thing that can interfere," he returned very quietly, "is yourself. Now shall we go?"

Miel reached for the door handle, but a glance up the dizzying curve of the three immense supports told her that billows of cloud had already obscured the podlike observation deck, and a fine mist of raindrops dampened the windshield of her car.

"Look, we're not going to be able to see a thing up there. Why don't we just call this off?"

She was unreasonably irritable and acutely

aware that James was going back to the office without her.

"Certainly not. I'm glad of the clouds. It never hurts to look at the world from a different perspective."

They got out and Miel acquired a crown of droplets in her already windblown hair, while Barth, apparently impervious to rain, looked down at her, more rakishly appealing than ought to have been legal in such surroundings. They marched over the arched causeway supported on its orange girders just above the railway tracks. The blue-carpeted area at the base of the tower, normally packed, was virtually deserted today because of the weather. Only a few stragglers hung around the souvenir displays. The ticket seller, accustomed to virtual shutdown when cloud rolled in, was surprised that Barth and Miel wanted to go up. The elevator operator was even more so, though she went gamely into her spiel about the tower's being more than 1,800 feet high and heavier than 20,000 elephants.

"Elephants?" chuckled Barth. And the attendant, who looked like a student, blushed easily and instantly.

Miel gripped her handbag and clenched her teeth as the glass panels all around her showed the harbor dropping away with frightening speed, while her ears began to pop as if she were aboard an airplane.

"Actually," she said somewhat nervously, "I

haven't been up this thing before, either. Then, in answer to the sharp lift of Barth's brows, "Well, you know—local attraction and all that."

She fought a disconcerting urge to press herself closer to the back of the elevator where Barth was.

"Look," said Barth. "Down there. There's the *Yancy*."

And Miel, too, felt a small surge as the distinctive white boat grew small and smaller as they climbed up to the sky.

The elevator disgorged them onto more blue carpet, leading to the great outer circle walled with glass. As predicted, not a soul was in the area. Also as predicted, nothing could be seen except banks of gray white cloud swirling around as if Miel and Barth had suddenly found themselves lost in space.

"Oh. . . it's beautiful," cried Miel, rushing up to the glass. "I never would have thought!"

With one of those spontaneous bursts of enthusiasm so much a part of Miel's nature and so often repressed, she pushed herself against the glass like a child and stared at the milky white coils of cloud. Barth gripped her hand.

"Come outside. Let's see what it's really like."

There were stairs to a lower level and a revolving door to let them out onto a platform that was completely open to the elements except for a waist-high rail. This area was also unpeopled. The clouds rolled in so close as to obscure the very rods of the discreet silver grille installed to discourage suicides. There was a breeze too, warm and humid, heavy with rain. The way it moved the clouds was ethereal, magical. If she didn't know better, she might have simply stepped out to lie down in a pillow of cotton cloud.

A thicker cloud rolled in, like a night mist, reaching tendrils around them so that Barth's face, partially obscured, looked like a face in a dream. Arm in arm, they walked all the way around the platform. When they reached the west side again a fissure in the cloud coverage opened—and below them lay the city, all shining with rain.

"Why, we're actually above the weather," Miel exclaimed in sudden wonder, grasping at last the true height at which they stood.

"I told you a different perspective would be a surprise. It doesn't always pay to plod a comfortable rut."

At once some of the magic retreated.

"Some of us search very hard for that comfortable rut, Barth. It might just be the only place we can keep alive."

"Then you get a medal, Miel. I know it can't have been easy."

He could make his voice so very calm and kind, but she sensed only a limited sympathy mixed with a stubborn challenge.

"It wasn't," she returned, irked. "I was all alone when I came up from Bay Point, without a single idea about how to get along. The job at Crome's was a very lucky chance for me."

"The old Pygmalion story."

"What?"

The reference refused to emerge from the layers of miscellany deposited by her night courses. Barth could not hide his amusement.

"Aha, I see it comes as a shock to you that a ruffian such as I could have a smattering of culture too. One tends to read a lot those long evenings out to sea. Pygmalion was a Greek sculptor who couldn't find anywhere what he wanted in a wife, so he got himself a piece of ivory and carved a woman. Some obliging goddess brought her to life, and she kept the studio tidy ever after. James must have worked very hard on you."

"We worked together. And I'm not sure I like the kind of implications you're making with that little story."

"Why not? I thought it was a charming tale."

He was very big and easy on the edge of that balcony so very, very far above the solid earth. A drift of mist floated between them like a phantom streamer. He was looking at her intently, but with that kind of enigmatic gaze that she realized was probably a mask for deeper emotions.

"I don't care who knows that James made me what I am," she said very quietly and very steadily, as a damp gust lifted the hair from her forehead. "I owe James everything."

"And now, loyal soul that you are, you're about to give him everything. Is that really very wise, Miel?"

"Oh, so now you think you have the right to judge me?"

She turned away, trying to control the edge of anger again in her voice. She felt inexplicably shaky, as if being forced to walk over hot coals and feeling them burning through the soles of her shoes. Her ancient rancor frayed the edge of her emotions, and she did not see the effort working in Barth's face.

"I have all the right of someone who. . . cares about you, Miel. James is a fine man—but I don't think he's man enough for you."

It was as if she could feel the ramparts breaking down all around her. Fear rushed through Miel, making her fingernails scar the fine Moroccan leather of her handbag. The fear transmuted itself into irrational fury, draining the color from her cheeks.

"How dare you make such casual judgments. I love James!"

There, it was out. The first time she had ever said it to anybody, including herself. She was jarred by the unfamiliar shrillness of her own voice.

But her words had their effect on Barth. His whole body tensed, and his expression became hard in the mist.

"Can you say that to me again, Miel? Can you say it and look me in the eye?"

Oh, why did her skin feel suddenly chilled and the air laden with a terrible emotional urgency?

"Of course I can. I love. . . ."

Before she could finish, his mouth claimed

hers and she was crushed close in those powerful seaman's arms. He might be able to kiss away the words but not her anger. She would not be taken this way. She would not! Their embrace turned into a deadly struggle, with Barth ravaging her face and neck with swift hot kisses while Miel squeezed her fists against his chest and thrust with all her might. In a moment, her own considerable strength communicated itself to him and he let her go.

"Oh, Miel," he groaned, stepping away and splaying both his hands on the top of the mist-darkened concrete wall, "you don't belong in that store anymore. Not to be turned into some kind of small-time executive. You're better than that. Stronger than that. I want you to be with me, Miel. The other half of Operation Seawatch."

She could only stare at him, her breath laboring in her lungs, red heat marks rising along her jaw from his kisses. She was truly shaken that such an apparently easygoing man could react this way, with such explosive passion. Slowly she became aware of just what he had said.

The other half of Operation Seawatch! Be with him. . . .

A sudden warmth infused her body. His lingering touch mingled with an all-too-vivid image of the *Yancy* reaching smartly in a dawn wind, spray dancing from the bow, while Barth, cradling Miel against his side. . . . She shut her eyes. Oh, God, how was it she hadn't realized how deeply the sea fever had inflamed her again?

Drawing in a shaky breath, Miel walked abruptly away from Barth and stood staring down. Another hole in the clouds opened up, letting her see the cars speeding, like tiny metal corpuscles, along the dark artery of the Gardiner Expressway. Directly below, a white, segmented GO train with its green locomotive head, slipped under the Spadina bridge. Everywhere the buildings had taken on that extraordinary fragility and precision objects acquire when viewed from a great height. When the tension had ebbed enough, she ventured a look in Barth's direction. He raked his fingers roughly through his hair.

"Sorry. That wasn't very cool, was it?"

"No."

"But look, Miel...."

"Don't, Barth. I don't want to talk about this anymore."

He opened his mouth again but something in the set of Miel's face made him understand the futility. His shoulders dropped into a painful half shrug.

"All right, then. Let's go."

The clouds closed in again, only all the magic was gone. They were merely blank and thick and stifling. Miel was glad to get on the elevator, even though the young attendant stared openly at them, lingering meaningfully on the uneven redness down Miel's neck. Not a bad place for a lovers' tryst, she was probably thinking, though these two certainly didn't stay long. Unrecognizable as a half-drawn map, the lakeshore rose to meet them, then the poplars, and finally, the pool, with its abandoned paddle boats, around the base of the tower. The attendant let them out, thinking she would have at least one story to tell her pals at break.

It was raining rather heavily as Miel and Barth made their way toward the parking lot, but neither seemed to notice. Miel's hair was quickly plastered to her forehead, and the downpour spread wet patches across the shoulders of her blouse and down the front, touching the firm curve of her bosom. Briskly, she began unlocking her car.

"Never mind," said Barth. "I think I'll walk back."

"Walk?"

His face was bleak and cold, and his fists were clenched at his sides.

"But the rain. . . ."

"It's only a little way. I'd rather."

Oblivious to her protests, he strode off into the watery grayness, his hulking form looking curiously defeated. Miel stood staring after him, a large, unexplained knot of pain gathering in her throat. A madness in her wanted to go after him, heedless of blurred stoplights and the hounding traffic of Front Street. But of course she didn't. She got into her car and sat with her wet head streaming against the headrest.

Passion, she thought. *Sex. That's what this is all about. A mighty engine once set in motion. . . .*

She sat for a very long time in that parking

lot, the rain beating against the windshield, the streetlights, activated by the rainstorm, making dim white smudges through the scurrying drops. She could not forget the taste of Barth's mouth upon her own, or that intoxication that was somehow like the rushing of a train when she was in his arms. Miel closed her eyes and leaned her forehead against the coolness of the leather-covered steering wheel. In spite of everything Cheryl and Louise had said, in spite of her own loyalties and all the warning signals of her heart, she had no choice but to admit that Barth Tramande had gotten into her blood once again.

CHAPTER ELEVEN

"HEY, MIEL, LOOK AT THIS. Even better than the proofs."

Hildy sashayed in, waving a newspaper as if it were a triumphal banner. Miel tried to remain deliberately businesslike as she looked up from her desk. Looked up and felt the office floor drop away from under her feet.

There, splashed across the entire back page, was the first of the ads for the Seascape line. She and Barth in full living color. It was not one of the posed shots they had all worked so hard to produce but rather one of the candid ones Chuck had shot. This one showed the exact moment when Barth had handed over the wheel and Miel felt for the very first time the quiver of the *Yancy* under sail.

Smoothing out the paper, Hildy held it up dramatically so that Miel could absorb the entire effect. She watched as Miel stared at it in a kind of horrified fascination. The photo was indeed beautiful, showing Miel against a staggering sweep of sky and lake, the Gagnon practically leaping to life, while Barth, impossibly masculine and self-assured, hovered just far enough away to let the Gagnon have center focus.

All this was nothing to Miel compared to what Chuck had caught between the two of them during those few charged seconds when their eyes had met. Every virile inch of Barth was focused on Miel. And as for Miel, she had been caught with her head thrown back, a fantasy beauty, with a magnificence she couldn't possibly conceive of possessing in real life.

But worst of all, her eyes were riveted on Barth and her lips parted in unmistakable invitation. Her body swayed toward his. The expression on her face was both innocent and hungry—and melting with naked infatuation.

The shock made Miel lift her fingers to her mouth and her eyes widen. It was as if something unbearably private and intimate had been published for all the world to see—and she was alarmed by the palpable sexual tension that crackled throughout the entire ad.

"Oh, Hildy...."

"It's a beaut, isn't it? With Barth looking as sexy as that, we'll have them stampeding into the store!"

Sex! Sex to sell clothes. For the first time Miel felt her gorge rise against a reality of the garment trade everyone took for granted. Fearfully, she lifted her gaze to Hildy's face, wondering if there could be more there than simple delight with an ad well done.

"Has...James seen this yet?"

"Just a few minutes ago. Thought it was jim-dandy."

Miel let out a long shaky breath. Perhaps she

was just imagining it after all—the effect of too many late-night hauntings by that face, those sun-bronzed arms.

Hildy showed no inclination to go. She pirouetted around the office, the ad held high, tiny elephant earrings dancing from her lobes.

"Boy, getting Barth to pose was an inspiration, don't you think? Lucky woman who gets her hands on him."

Conscious or not, Hildy was pushing this thing a little too far. Miel picked up her pen quickly.

"Yes, lucky, living all cramped in a boat like that and being dragged forever around the water!"

Hildy laughed merrily, folding the paper and tucking it neatly under her arm.

"Ooooh yes, all cramped in that yummy yacht. Nothing but misery all the way around the Caribbean, slaving over a hot suntan. Nothing but headaches from gazing into those hypnotic eyes!"

Miel was on her feet so fast her chair tipped and crashed against the side of the desk. Hildy froze, her rosy mouth dropping open.

"Gosh, Miel, I was only teasing."

When Miel realized what she had just done, she sat down and rubbed her temples. Talk about feeling like an idiot!

"I'm sorry. I seem to be getting jumpy these days. All that outdoor work."

It might have been her imagination that Hildy shot her a look at once wise and sympathetic.

She left wordlessly, leaving Miel to a silence that thundered in her ears.

Silence that gave her only the briefest respite before the door opened again and James came in, that selfsame newspaper in his hands. He was smiling as he shook the ad out for their mutual admiration.

"Star quality, Miel. That's what I call it. Don't know why I didn't spot it the first day I hired you. Bet you ten to a dollar we end up sold out of everything."

There was actually pride in his voice and warmth in those brown eyes.

Can he really be that innocent, Miel asked herself, wincing. How could he look at that ad and not know?

No, not innocent. Honorable. It would not occur to him that anyone he was courting could look that way at another man.

"All in a day's work," she said hastily and with false lightness, coming around to kiss him on the cheek and take the ad from his hand. He regarded the doubled-over paper with a proprietary pride.

"If this campaign has the effect I think it's going to have, we'll have to use you a lot more in the future. Your talents just never seem to end."

She turned away, embarrassed.

"I think I can pass on the modeling, James. I've quite enough to do keeping up at the office."

"I suppose you do, but you're good at that

too. I don't tell you often enough, Miel. In fact, you're a natural administrator. It would be nothing for you to run a whole store by yourself.''

Halfway back to her chair, Miel paused. It was not like James to make idle speculations. He tugged a bit at the knot of his tie and raised one brow at her.

''Silly to say so when we're so deeply in the red, but I've always wanted to open a second store. Maybe two or three. Who else, of course, to take command but you?''

So James, too, had dreams. Miel was so used to thinking of him as content to confine his aspirations within the present walls of Crome's that she had not suspected this other dimension existed. She walked back to him and laid her fingers on his sleeve. He should not be cheated of his heart's desire.

''A whole chain, perhaps, if this campaign comes off!''

He squeezed her fingers in acknowledgment, and once again she felt she was sharing something special.

''Is everything ready for tomorrow?''

''Yes. The caterer and the club. Much to her surprise, Hildy got a yes from most of the people on the guest list.''

This, once again Hildy's brainchild, was to be the gala event of the Gagnon promotion—a cocktail party at one of the most select of the island yacht clubs. The *Yancy* would tie up there temporarily. A fashion show featuring the dressiest and most glamourous of the Seascape line would flow glitteringly across the decks.

"Amazing what Hildy thinks up," James murmured, his face assuming that usual quizzical expression when he spoke of their young sales-promotion manager. After their curious start together, James's admiration seemed to be growing every day.

And well he ought to admire this latest idea. In a way, it was brilliant, designed by Hildy specifically as a set piece for James. As host, in that rarefied setting, he would be at his very best, winning over by the sheer charm of his personality those of the privileged few who had not met him yet.

Miel would appear at his side, of course, both as hostess and as the centerpiece of the ads. Barth would be in charge of the *Yancy*, glorious scenery for the man-watchers.

THE NEXT DAY couldn't have dawned better. Yellow sun soaking its brightness into the green island grass. High, brilliantly azure sky scoured by a breeze that carried the tang of a hundred miles of lake. Dense families of trees chuckling and rustling around the expensive, dignified clubhouse, where a fine buffet was being set up on the lawn.

Miel was dressed in green for the occasion, silk shantung in a big tunic belted grandly over a tiered skirt with an irregular hemline. Stylish shoulder pads and her natural grace gave her the air of a royal huntress out for a dashing afternoon. She conversed briefly with James as they both watched, from a careful distance, the last of the tasseled ropes being attached to the two walkways, which would lead the models on then off the *Yancy*. Barth was double-checking the mooring lines and showing remarkable forebearance with the caterer's lad who was installing trays of edible dainties in the main salon lest any of the guests, bound to wander, weaken for lack of suitable provender.

Miel tried to avoid looking directly at him but found it next to impossible. For the occasion, Barth had dressed entirely in sailing whites, making himself more effectively the center of the scene than even the magnificent *Yancy*. While James pointed out the first of the approaching launches bearing invited socialites, Miel felt her gaze slip helplessly over Barth's glowing tan, admiring the splendid proportions of that body moving with such ease over the deck of his seagoing home. His image had not left her mind since the episode atop the CN Tower. The warmth of his caresses had whispered even when she had looked at that offending ad.

Only when James turned did she pull her eyes away, only to find his gaze sliding right past her to the clubhouse. With a sparkle and a suddenly expectant half smile, he fixed upon a small figure emerging from the rather intimidating doors and rushing toward them. Miel looked too and, for the moment, forgot her own discomposure.

Hildy, in a completely unprecedented effort to be haute monde, had abandoned her usual creative mode of dressing in favor of a Gagnon. And what a Gagnon! A delicate foam of pink-and-lemon challis supported by two spaghetti straps floated around Hildy's body, leaving her fine-boned shoulders delectably bare. The mass of hair had been tamed into respectability by two curving gold combs. Simple coral studs adorned her lobes, and her makeup was a wonder of subtlety, evincing not the slightest hint of her usual theatrical flamboyance. Indeed, without the aura of eccentricity that normally enclosed her like a protective cocoon, Hildy, Miel was startled to see, was really gently beautiful. Never had she looked more ethereal and more appealing, and James's eyes widened with surprise as she approached.

"Why, she's lovely," James cried. "Isn't she lovely, Miel! Here, let's have a look."

He actually took Hildy's hand and led her around in a small circle before he realized what he was doing and hastily let go. Hildy twirled again, daintily, and finished next to James, peeping sideways to see if the smile was still on his face.

"Hildy, you're blushing!" Miel laughed. "Even your ears are turning pink. Don't you know that dressed the way you are you're a positive peril to the men?"

Hildy turned from pink to scarlet and very suddenly grabbed James's arm with one hand and pointed to the docking launch with the other.

"We'd better get down there. People are starting to come in."

Miel, wanting to avoid the pier area, let them march off without her. James was halfway across the intervening space of grass before he came to a halt, remembering her. She smiled weakly and waved them on, though she was just a little surprised when James, apparently still bedazzled by Hildy's company, continued without so much as a token protest.

Miel drifted toward the clubhouse as Hildy and James were swallowed up by the little mob pouring from that first launch. In the second launch, two matrons, bosom friends of Lillian's, laid claim to James, and Hildy was elbowed out. For a moment the tiny figure tried gamely to make her way through the crowd before giving up and trotting back to join Miel. The blush had turned into an excited glow? The soft challis floated about her like fairy smoke as she moved.

"Did you know James has real dimples when he smiles?" she exclaimed incredulously, craning her neck at the milling people now moving toward the lawn buffet and sustenance.

Miel paused and bit her lower lip. No, she didn't know. In four years James had never smiled like that for her.

"Hey, hey look! She really did come. Cora Fowler!" Hildy began to hop up and down, completely demolishing the image of sedate grace she had striven so hard to maintain. "I phoned her personally. She said she'd only

what I hear. I got the lowdown from this junior PR person at the Fowler head office. Do you know that she once stowed away on an eighteen-wheeler just for the hell of it. The driver was a limp but happy dishrag by the time they pulled into Thunder Bay.''

"Oh now, Hildy!"

"I'm serious. She has this...way with men and more money than she'll ever know what to do with. Not that she's a nymphomaniac or anything. Just a connoisseur in the true sense of the word. A dish is a dish wherever she happens to find him. And once she sees one, she doesn't easily let go."

The two women, both so beautiful in their own way, stood watching the milling turmoil where Cora had to be.

"You know," Hildy continued thoughtfully, "the odd thing is that women really like her too. They admire her chutzpah, I guess, and the way she seems to be incapable of jealousy."

Curiously, Miel could understand that. Cora would reach out and grasp her pleasures with the simple directness of a child in a licorice factory, so firmly certain of her own allure that it would not occur to her that other women might not have as easy and immediate access to the goodies. Hence she would share easily or pass on when her current amour grew boring.

"There! See."

Hildy pointed to where Cora, emerging with her drink, at once developed a feminine entourage. Friends of hers, mostly, Miel guessed, who now streamed around her like pieces in a kaleidoscope, all of them wearing brilliant, staggeringly expensive outfits, as if a fashion show were in some way a challenge to their wardrobes. Cora herself swept around in a togalike confection of mango and cerise. Exactly the sort of thing, Miel thought with a tick of irritation, one might pluck from the overpriced inner regions of Avery Selks.

Whales are dying, admonished a voice from some deep recess in her head, *and you're trying to sell people like these more clothes?*

Miel blinked and the thought went away although she felt oddly disturbed. She mustn't start thinking of her job this way, she mustn't. No cracks were allowed in the perfect facade that was her present life.

Cora remained chatting breezily, yet constantly scanning the scene, much as a lioness might in its search for game. Miel knew the exact instant Cora spotted Barth, for the woman's mobile face and form became completely still— and that stillness conveyed so much intended action that Miel half expected the woman to scatter her cohorts in a beeline to the yacht and drag the object of her attention off by the leg.

But Cora did, after all, have some regard for the convention. Barth vanished below deck, and a buzz of new arrivals claimed her attention. Miel sighed. In her life she had seen one or two women such as Cora, who would never have to worry about age or looks. Though one day, perhaps, she might be encased in wrinkles, shaped like a flowerpot and confined to a wing chair from an excess of good living, still there would be that swirl of activity around her, the cheerful flow of friends, the line of men waiting to bestow gifts and compliments upon her. No matter how aged she was, men would always seek her out, for she had once been, and would always be, a legend of breathtaking sensuality.

The last launch arrived and when everyone had had sufficient to eat and drink, James lifted the microphone of the cleverly hidden PA system. After an amusing little speech of welcome, he drew Miel close to him.

"Ladies and gentlemen, for your delight today, the fabulous Seascape collection. Your commentator, my good right hand at Crome's, Miel McCrae!"

Stepping up onto the small raised dais, Miel licked her lips nervously. Because of her own high profile in the Gagnon promotion it was natural she do the commentary. However, as a sea of exceedingly influential eyes fixed themselves upon her and she realized just how much was riding on her words, she suddenly faltered. She turned to James, who immediately gave her a big smile and one of those heartrending "you can do it" looks. Courage and pride surged back into her breast. She picked up her copious program notes.

"What a privilege to introduce, for the first time in North America, the inspired creations of Hélène Gagnon...."

The show had been meticulously organized.

Models even then readying in the back rooms of the yacht club were to glide up the carpeted walkway onto the *Yancy*. After a whirl around the deck, each one would go below where a new outfit would be waiting. She would change while the following model was monopolizing attention, then reappear for a sweep back to the clubhouse base. Dresses, evening wear and the dramatic pieces of loungewear were to dominate this show. To one side, orders would be taken discreetly and appointments for fittings made. Later the entire event was to be topped off by a gentle cruise around the harbor aboard the *Yancy* for those who had been truly swept away by the Seascape theme.

"And now, ladies, here's Cheryl in a wonderful little afternoon dress. Paper-sheer silk sprinkled all over with miniature crescent moons, it moves with a certain silvery swish about the knees...."

Miel was surprised how clear and pleasant the microphone made her voice sound. Another dress passed by, summery pink with a huge necklace of white shells swinging at the neckline. Then a lounge outfit with baggy pockets and daring top, distinctly reminiscent of fisherman's netting.

Anxiously, Miel kept skimming the crowd, trying to glean some clue as to the show's reception. The women, drinks in hand, sat or stood around watching the ongoing spectacle with close attention disguised by blasé expressions. Cheryl and Louise strode on, doing yeoman's duty in silk suiting, belted linen and romantic organdy.

Yet as the presentation moved inexorably toward its climax of evening wear, Miel felt the pace pick up and interest increase. More and more often a murmur would run through the audience, like a gust through leaves, at the particular boldness and wit of this pair of tulip sleeves or that little wrap in crepe georgette. Her pulse began to quicken. Success might just be theirs—if only that curiously blank look could be erased from those faces.

The look persisted stubbornly despite Miel's most lilting tones over the PA. Her spurt of exhilaration began to give way to a gnawing worry, for she had seen that look before and knew exactly what it was: herd instinct. The Seascape collection had lived up to its promise and met with secret approval in practically every bosom. Now they were all waiting for something to happen, some kind of signal that the rest of the crowd also approved and it was all right to show one liked the fashions.

However, if the moment passed without the signal, if that influential gathering dispersed without placing a decent order, then the Gagnons would probably be ignored for the duration of the season—or even worse, declared unchic.

As this veiled wariness continued right up to the last numbers, Miel began to actively despair. James was trying gamely not to frown and the models, two extra besides Cheryl and Louise, sensed the tension. It showed in the animation of their gestures and the sparkle of their smiles as they exerted themselves to push the mood of the audience over that vital edge. Finally there was but one design left, and this had been assigned to Rifa, whose hour that day cost more than the fee of the other three models put together.

Rifa, of some exotic, undefined Asian extraction, had been hired for her awesome and sultry beauty. She had hair darker than burnt ebony and the grace of a captive leopard—and when she merged from the *Yancy*'s salon dressed in yards of scarlet taffeta, a gasp, quickly muffled, rose from the onlookers. Caught at one shoulder with a huge gold pin, the dress fell away in oblique tiers that rustled and gleamed against the honeyed duskiness of Rifa's skin.

Rifa turned this way and that, posing on the deck, doing her best to elicit the buzz and chatter and spates of applause that would mean the Gagnons had made it. When only a tentative politeness was forthcoming, Miel crumbled a little inside, thinking Rifa would have to finally make her exit. But Rifa was a professional, and it was actually the brains inside that queenly head that warranted her exorbitant fee.

Instead of leaving the yacht, she turned to where Barth was leaning, well out of the way, against the foremast. Before Barth could realize what was happening, she flowed up to him and fitted her body next to his in a long, simmering curve. The result was a stunningly dramatic

tableau of white and crimson against the un-
clouded azure of the sky. She then ran long fingers along Barth's face and lifted her lips in a
pantomine of a kiss so evocative that Miel was
shaken. The next moment, Rifa was shimmering
down the walkway and Cora was waving one be-
jeweled wrist high in the air.

"I must have that one," she declared enthusiastically. "That red one. Where do I place
my order?"

That was all that was necessary. A roar of applause went up, accompanied by much nodding
and chattering and comparisons of choice. Miel
thanked everyone and stepped down, feeling at
once the warmth of James's hand in the small of
her back as he shared the triumph. She should
have been overjoyed—and on one level she was.

On another level she shriveled inside, for she
knew that Cora's delight in the dress was simply
her way of announcing to the hills that she
wanted Barth Tramande.

The crowd broke, swirled, and in moments
claimed James from Miel's side. The empty spot
was filled by Hildy, dancing from one toe to the
other, eyes sparkling, fingers clutching Miel's
arm excitedly.

"We really knocked 'em dead, didn't we!"
she exclaimed, chortling. "James is going to be
so proud!"

Miel looked down at her small companion
and agreed with a smile so enormous and so me-
chanical she could feel the creaking in her
cheeks. All her attention was focused in her

hearing, which, with hypersensitivity, picked out from the hubbub Cora's racy cocktail chatter and responses in that mellow baritone Miel knew so well. At this gathering Barth had been expected to do nothing except be visible and circulate, if he wished. Well, he was circulating all right. And Cora Fowler had had no trouble at all drawing him into the fascinating brightness of her orbit.

Miel held out until Barth, only the broad back of his shoulders visible, laughed boomingly. Then she recognized the pain. Jealousy. Jealousy mixed with something she had not felt for years. Yet now she suffered as keenly as if she had just whipped back the curtain of a window and had seen the faces of all her old classmates staring at her there. The hurt of being left out, left aside. No date for the tenth-grade prom. Those times when the little clique of popular girls had fallen silent as she passed in the hall.

Tossing back her head, Miel stared far out over the funnel of a departing freighter, a kind of despair rising within her. So much for imagining herself mature, impervious and secure. Of all the things she could find out about herself, the last she wanted to know was that she was still as vulnerable as ever. Would she never be free of Barth or her inconvenient past?

"Hey, Miel, they're getting ready for the cruise. You're wanted on the *Yancy*."

The voice was Hildy's as she flitted off to join James, who was solicitously seeing those of Lillian's generation into lawn chairs in the shade.

By unspoken agreement, James was to cover the yacht-club base, while Miel would act as official hostess aboard the *Yancy* for the harbor cruise. People were gathering on the dock, and the more adventurous had already stepped aboard. Barth was seating Cora in the place of honor by the wheel. He was smiling and nodding and being so relentlessly charming that Miel suddenly wondered if she recognized him anymore. He had become a stranger, dispensing the wonderful, beguiling force of his personality to all and sundry because it happened to suit his purpose that day.

"Something about floating around the world does it to them. They can't take people seriously."

Cheryl's remembered words echoed like a dull brass bell at the back of Miel's head. She had another vision of Barth aboard the restless iron ships of his trade, a sense of the rootlessness that kind of life must engender, the lack of real attachment to anyone or anything. A form of self-protection, really. A pleasant, amoral selfishness that let him fit in easily and gave him the illusion of caring, which could he put away instantly the moment a call to action came. Why get involved when one could leave with no muss, no fuss, at the end of the month? As silent proof, there was that great family mansion forsaken on its promontory because neither of the brothers could bother to fill it once again with life.

"Yoo hoo, Miel. All aboard," Hildy prompted from somewhere just behind James. "Don't let Cora make off with Barth from right under our noses!"

"As if there's anything *I* could do about it," Miel muttered, and with a resigned sigh forced herself to join the small but very lively crowd testing the decks of the *Yancy*. She met Barth's eyes with an icy politeness, not even having time to nod before Cora scrambled to be near him, displaying a surprising, telltale awkwardness in the cockpit.

"You'd be amazed how little attention I've paid to boats in my life," she said, laughing with a provocatively self-deprecating gesture. "Time I learned, perhaps—if I could get the right someone to teach me."

Again, Miel felt a sickening twist in the pit of her stomach and turned to see that all of the handropes had been replaced, lest any of their pampered cargo be lost overboard. Barth inched the *Yancy* slowly into open water and began skirting the wake of the ferry at a pace so sedate not even one drink stood in danger of being spilled. Miel made pained small talk for several minutes, then fled to the shelter of the main salon, where she could preside in relative obscurity over the passing out of lobster canapés and tiny glazed shrimp on whole-wheat thins.

At first there was a steady stream of people, curious about the rich interior, through the spacious salon. When nearly everyone had had a look, however, they returned topside where

Cora, center of attention as always, was practically a one-woman show. Miel, finding herself alone, sank down on one of the wide settees and pressed her head back against the paneling. Through the ports she glimpsed the pure white of a lovely little sloop as it slipped past. Nowhere on the vessel was there respite from Cora's laughter sailing up to the sky.

Eventually, she felt the turn at Hanlan's Point and knew they would soon be back at the club. Wanting to be busy, she got up and went to the large master stateroom, which Barth had generously opened up to the models. Fashion wear, hastily abandoned by the models in their efforts to get on with the show, lay scattered around, and Miel sat down among them, closing her eyes for a moment as she tried to let the accumulated tension seep out of her. It was a trick she had learned early in her career at Crome's, a trick that now failed somehow to work its customary magic. She shouldn't be feeling this way at all, she told herself. The day was an unmitigated success, and never had she been on closer terms with James, who needed such a success so badly.

Cora and Barth, of course. Their faces, their laughter, their image was the only blemish on this glowing afternoon—that and having to admit their mere casual closeness bore a whiplash sting.

Miel closed her eyes tightly, suddenly very tired of the party, the voices, the constant smiling facades behind which, however genteelly hidden, always lurked the need to sell somebody something. That seemed to be a great capitalist tradition, of course, but she could not help but wonder if, deep down, Barth did not harbor a seed of contempt for all the busy goings-on. She saw herself through Barth's eyes, bustling about in her green designer creation, seeing that the overfed had yet one more bite of caviar to eat. She saw James holding his breath, awaiting the whims of the trendsetters while so many bright wisps of fabric were paraded before their eyes.

The mere thought of Barth's passing judgment on James was enough to make Miel grit her teeth and sink her fingers into the softness she rested upon. About herself she didn't much care, but if Barth had looked at James with the least bit of contempt, she couldn't bear it! Not this dear man, who in his own way was trying so very hard. Trying and succeeding, she added to herself, getting up abruptly and looking around the cabin, which had been absolutely bare of any personal traces for the duration of the show. She had been sitting on Barth's bed and once again, unbidden, came the memory of that girlhood time when she had flung herself upon it, inhaling the scent of musk and after-shave that still clung there. For an instant, she actually felt dizzy. Then Cora's laughter drifted down, piercing the cloud of memory and challenging that steadfast courage that had carried Miel through so often these past years. This madness for Barth, this longing, this...this way he affected her was getting out of hand. She would overcome this, take control. She must!

Methodically, with a perfectly expressionless face, she began to gather up the scattered Gagnons, smoothing them and inspecting them for any damage inflicted by the speedy changes during the show. So intent was she on imposing order upon the brilliant chaos around her that she quite missed the gentle bump of the *Yancy* against the clubhouse dock and the fading away of people sounds as the passengers slipped off toward the bar.

What did rouse her was the renewed cough of the motor and the barely perceptible subsequent motion. A glance through the portholes revealed the smooth lawn receding once again across an expanse of pale turquoise water. Why, she wondered, was Barth heading back to the Harbourfront slip so soon?

Collecting garment bags, she finished her task slowly, waiting for the foot of the city to glide up. She was exasperated because she had looked forward to going ashore to be with James, and now she would have to take the island ferry back. It was her own fault, of course, for not getting off when she should have, but she'd be darned if she'd ask Barth to turn around.

Only when the busy pavilions of Ontario Place passed through her view did she realize that they were threading through the Western Gap into the lake itself. Alarmed and angry she marched through the main salon. One foot was actually on the companionway before a gust of earthy feminine laughter froze her instantly. Through the opening she saw Barth at the wheel and Cora draped breezily over the taffrail looking as if she was having the time of her life. Damn! The two of them thought they were slipping off to be alone together!

Before she could retreat, two heads turned and spotted her. The intimate little nothing Cora was leaning over to say died on her lips. Barth, considering the surprise this must have been to him, regarded Miel with admirable aplomb before making a beckoning gesture with his free hand.

"We thought everyone had gone ashore," Cora declared with the kind of inflection that brought spots to Miel's cheeks. It was all too obvious what Cora's intentions had been on this little expedition. Stepping out, Miel stood miserably in the opposite corner of the cockpit.

"I was just...putting away some of the clothes the models left when they changed."

"And quiet as a mouse too." Barth swung the wheel to avoid a rather wobbly young man on a sail board. Miel felt a coldness invade her when she realized he hadn't suspected she was aboard, either.

"Are you going out into the lake?" she asked rather idiotically.

"Yes. Cora wanted a real run in the *Yancy*. I thought I would oblige."

I'll just bet, Miel thought, when he didn't even have the decency to look abashed. Cora, whose very presence seemed to vibrate in the stern of the *Yancy*, gazed from one to the other with those perpetually interested eyes of hers, waiting for the next turn of events. But finally her eyes came to rest on Barth, giving Miel the distinct impression that it would be unsporting of her to stick around.

"I still have to put the outfits in their bags," Miel muttered quickly. "I'll go do it now."

"Miel. . . ."

But she was already back inside the main stateroom with the door shut behind her. *Let them keep the deck for themselves if they want to,* she told herself stiffly. After all, Cora Fowler was much too important a customer to alienate at this late date. If she thought Barth was part of the deal, let her help herself!

Then, because her sentiments did not echo pleasantly in her ears, she did busy herself with the garment bags, rustling them vigorously to cut out the intermittent rumble of Barth's chuckle and Cora's husky response. Miel was very angry, mostly at herself, for caring, for being upset. She was just informing herself that she was much too old for this when her name floated through the salon.

"Miel, could you come out here, please? We need you."

Only when the cabin door opened and Cora put her head in did Miel move.

"Barth is in an uproar about getting you on deck, dear. Something about changing a sail."

Looking windblown and quite flushed, Cora

radiated an aura of pleasure that extended to include her. Miel winced at her benevolence and went on deck, where Barth shifted from behind the wheel.

"Hold it steady, will you? Cora wants a bit of a ride under sail."

Miel took the helm mutinously, for in the easy breeze that day there was not the least need for her assistance. In a few minutes the jib was set and the mainsail up and the *Yancy* heeling through the short chop with the ease of a pleased porpoise. When Miel yielded the wheel and tried to go below again, Barth stopped her with a broad hand on her wrist.

"Stay up top. The view is so much better."

"It certainly is," put in Cora, running her eye appreciatively over the crisp, pressed whiteness of Barth's clothing. She glanced at Miel and back again, smiling, as if extending an invitation to a friend to admire a particularly gripping example of visual appeal. "The most beautiful boat, the most beautiful sailor. How lucky can a couple of gals get in a single day!"

She really isn't competitive, Miel thought incredulously. She just thinks Barth is the cat's meow and doesn't mind sharing the knowledge with anybody within shouting distance.

Leaning back against the hand-rubbed teak, Cora lifted her face to the sun and let the breeze ruffle the extravagant folds of her dress back against her body, revealing earth-mother breasts and wide hips and a length of rather powerful thigh. Never once did she remove her heavy-lidded gaze from the man at the helm.

"He really is quite splendid, isn't he?" Cora said in that lush, slightly raspy voice that was her trademark. "Look at how he stands. How I like a man who can stand that way, as if he didn't give a damn whether the devil himself popped out of the lake. Of course his hands are mighty fine too. I think you can really tell a man by his hands. You know—" Cora shifted herself and gave way to a spontaneous laugh "—I guess everybody in the country has heard that story about me and the truck driver. Well, it was his hands that did it. Just like Barth's here. Strong but sort of kind and maaarvelously sensitive. Just ran into him at one of those service-center places and, darlings, I was gone right over the moon. His truck was a long-distance outfit with plenty of room, so naturally. . . ."

She related the tale with unabashed glee, all the while emitting a flow of genial, completely uninhibited sexuality that purred and curled, like an invisible embrace, all around Barth. By this time Miel was beyond all thought of escape. In total fascination she watched the interplay unfolding, saw Cora making love to Barth with her eyes, her voice, the very drape of that opulent body against the cockpit rim. She couldn't even find it in her heart to be put out with Cora, for Miel felt as if she were watching a force of nature at work.

And Barth stood calmly behind the wheel, a

small smile on his face as this woman paid open tribute to the corded breadth of his shoulders and the very touchable thickness of hair curling down his nape. It was this smile and not Cora's extravagance that finally nettled Miel—a smile that widened fraction by fraction as Cora dropped broad hints about her car, parked not far from where the launches had set out.

"I intend to toss you over my shoulder, laddie, as soon as this boat ties up. A good dinner, maybe at The Wharf. It's very important to feed them up well first." She turned suddenly to Miel, grinning wickedly. "A man with low blood sugar makes for a dull, dull evening. Take it from me!"

I'll bet you know for sure, Miel commented silently as Cora flung out her arm toward the tip of the long eastern spit of land that curved like a crooked arm around the entrance to the ship channel.

"What's over there?"

"Sea gulls," Barth answered laconically. "Thousands of them. That's where they all nest. If they keep multiplying, the city might as well hand over the rest of the waterfront."

"I know. You can hardly eat a sandwich out of doors anymore. Greedy things!" Cora licked her lips and ran a sparkling look down Barth's thighs. "Can we go look?"

"Why, sure."

"But it's...."

Miel's involuntary protest died as Barth, in easy compliance, brought the yacht around in a lazy loop, even though it was clear that Cora had no idea what she was asking. If they took that route, it would be ages before they got back—giving Cora that much more time to work her seduction.

Miel resigned herself. Leaning back over the taffrail, which was warm against her elbows, she watched a big jet from the airport leave a thin, disintegrating trail of white across the sky. Fortunate people, flying off into the wild blue and leaving all their troubles behind them.

Yet as the jet vanished, Miel became quietly aware that something was wrong. Her senses, rather acutely tuned to the *Yancy*, informed her that the vessel was not sailing as true and as smooth as it ought to. The lake had roughened a little and the bow, moving in the direction necessary to get back round the island, was hitting the marching waves at an awkward angle so that a series of small stuttering thuds vibrated through the hull.

Without thinking, Miel did a half turn exactly as if she wanted to straighten the wheel. She caught Barth looking her full in the face. Before she could twist away, he delivered a broad wink.

Her cheeks flamed and she remained staring rigidly past him at the low, gravelly spit until she noticed something else—a most peculiar silence on board. Cora's endless, outrageous chatter had thinned out to nothing, and the woman now seemed to be avoiding the scenery. In fact, her whole interest had shrunk to her own two hands folded in her lap.

Miel's eyes flew open as she suddenly understood. Barth was grinning and Miel suffered a huge and grateful surge of relief very quickly followed by suppressed mirth. Barth was doing his best not to let the *Yancy* wallow but the wind was against him. As a result, Cora was growing slowly, inexorably seasick.

To her credit, Cora lasted most of the way back to the ship channel before plucking rather whitely at Barth's arm.

"If you don't mind, I think we should go in now. And...maybe we could skip that dinner for today. The thought of eating fish...." The skin under her eyes began to match her green mascara. "Something out here isn't agreeing with me as much as I thought."

Barth and Miel both registered massive disappointment.

"What a shame," murmured Barth. "I really was looking forward to a nice long spin down the wind."

"Yes, well...another day, of course," returned Cora gamely even while crumpling deeper into the corner of the cockpit.

Miel fetched a glass of water from the galley and smiled her best-customer smile.

"We won't even stop at the island, then. Just slip on back to the city so you can go straight to your car."

Cora kept taking little swallows from the glass until the *Yancy* coasted up to its usual mooring. Then, looking infinitely relieved, she thanked Barth for his concern and headed off, quickly but unsteadily, toward the parking lot. The last thing she did before she was out of sight was cast a look of regret over her shoulder at Barth's biceps.

CHAPTER TWELVE

"WE DON'T HAVE TO GO BACK there, do we?"

Barth nodded toward the yacht club barely visible across the harbor through the phalanx of trees. Miel could make out the launches beginning to bring the guests back to the city and spotted a colorful contingent heading for the ferry dock, apparently having lingered too long. James would be very busy seeing to the final details with Hildy, of course, at his side. The *Yancy* had served its purpose. Neither James nor Hildy would expect it to return. The yacht seemed very peaceful without Cora and to go back to tired caterers and racks of garment bags was thoroughly unappealing.

"No."

All her former emotions of the day made her now feel slightly like a hypocrite and she was vaguely uneasy, as if she had done something tacky. She was also acutely aware of Barth who, with raised brows, was looking at her very much as if he was about to make some rather pointed comment. Instead, he stepped back behind the wheel of the *Yancy*, which, without mooring, had been gently drifting away from the slip. The idling motor coughed to life, and they nosed out into the green harbor again.

"Hey, what are you doing?"

"Kidnapping you. Do you realize that in all this silly campaign, you and I have not had the fun of just sailing this boat all by ourselves?"

Dark panic poured through Miel's bones. To go out alone with him was madness. She must stay ashore. She must! The day had gone so well because they had kept their distance and played their roles. Now he was sabotaging everything.

Miel grasped the handropes and watched as the sleek side of the *Yancy* moved away from the cement. To her wildly beating heart, the gap seemed to be widening in slow motion, so that for a very long time it seemed she could leap easily across the narrow patch of water to certain safety. Then, as the bow angled away, she knew the yacht had so little momentum it could be stopped with a flick of Barth's wrist. *Speak up,* cried an urgent voice at the back of her mind. *Tell him! Tell him to moor the boat this minute!*

Somehow, this clamor of reason and instinct was unable to reach her vocal cords. Miel felt her hands growing clammy as she became acutely aware of every tiny movement of the man at the wheel. The yacht turned in a smooth half circle and began to glide east toward the freighters and cranes of the cargo depots and the bobbing buoys tipped jauntily with ribbed blue lights. A small plane took off from the island airport and arched away into the sky above them. A power boat bumped along at the head of its streamer of foam, and a small red cutter with a yellow jib preceded them toward the ship channel.

"Sit down and take it easy," Barth said calmly, though Miel knew his eyes had not missed the paleness of her knuckles.

Even as he spoke, the hidden diesel softly revved, making a small plume of water whisper away from the bow. His words were a challenge to her, a test to see if she would resist.

The yacht club slid past, shrouded in willows, seeming very distant. Here and there a tiny figure scurried, clearing away the chairs and the outdoor buffet. James would be one of the last to leave, smoothing over final details with club officials, seeing that not a single guest or garment was left behind. And even if he did know Miel was aboard the *Yancy*, he would no doubt think that she deserved a little recreational spin on the water. She had earned it.

When she could see the club no longer, Miel turned and sat silently on the cockpit rim. At once the tautness inside her gave way and her breath released in a small rush.

I want this! she thought with a kind of dismayed wonder. *I want to stay with the* Yancy. Oh, James!

The moment they were clear of the ship channel, Barth ran up the sails. The *Yancy*, like a fleet white sea creature, danced around the spit that guarded the outer harbor and bounded through open water until the city sank back and the shore became a rugged panorama of deeply eroded buff cliffs. Barth swung the yacht around and dropped the sails so that the vessel ceased moving and lay quietly rocked by the slow waves curling in from the horizon.

"I've always wanted to have a look at this spot. What's it called, so near the city?"

Could she speak to him as if this was a perfectly ordinary conversation, as if she had no idea how dangerous it was for her to be here?

"Scarborough Bluffs. The weather eats them back constantly, and people are always having to move out of their houses. Funny, I never imagined how wild and abandoned they would look from this particular angle."

Nor did she imagine what an arresting sight she herself made against such a backdrop, for she had shed the oversize belt that bound her outfit and the green silk fell in rustling folds all along the length of her torso.

"A lot of things are different when you see them from the water. You'd be surprised."

Miel frowned, reminded of the scene at the CN Tower. He didn't pursue it, however, and proceeded to lower a small anchor over the side. The breeze, as it was apt to this time of day, had dropped, so that it was now only a cool breath on Miel's forehead. The silence, broken only by the lapping of the water and Barth's soft movements, began to soothe her, unwinding the painful tension that had carried her through the day. Unconsciously, she tipped back her head and pulled off her earrings, which had been pinching her lobes. One of them dropped from her fingers, rolling along the cockpit sole until it wedged in a slot in the wood.

"Oh dear!"

She was half bent down before she remem-

bered that the costly garment she wore would
not take kindly to crawling around on deck.
Barth was past her in a moment, but his fingers
were too large to rescue the small glittering thing
from its hiding place.

"Just a minute. I'll have to lift the engine
cowl. If I'm lucky, it won't fall in."

Deftly, he unlatched the fitted section that
gave access to the engine and lifted it just
enough to slip in his palm and catch the piece of
jewelry as it teetered into the darkness. Miel
took it quickly, unable to avoid his fingers, and
stood there as he sealed the cowl and straightened.

"Hungry?" he asked.

Miel merely inclined her head, for she had
been transfixed by the sharp scent of diesel that
had drifted up when Barth uncovered the
engine. Barth gestured toward the main salon,
which was still laden with the provisions of the
caterers' feast.

"There's certainly plenty to choose from.
Look at all the goodies left over from the party."

Rousing herself, Miel became all too aware of
a pang gnawing at her stomach. She hadn't
eaten since that pumpernickel toast she'd gulped
for breakfast. Yet when she followed Barth into
the interior, she flung herself down as far away
as she could from the lavish spread.

"I've had enough fancy stuff. It's not really
what I have a yen for."

Barth lounged against the bare maple drainboard of the galley, the planes of his face softened by the shade.

"And what do you have a yen for?"

His voice was quiet now, friendly. Had there been the least trace of abrasiveness, the faintest hint of mockery, she would have kept her thoughts to herself. But he stood there, arms folded across his chest rising and falling a little with the rhythm of his breathing. Miel could feel him waiting patiently while she searched for what was tugging so persistently at the edge of her mind.

"Wieners and beans!" she exclaimed with a sudden recognition. Suddenly, poignantly, she was overwhelmed with a memory, yet it was something she hadn't thought about since she had fled Bay Point. "Grandpa and I used to make them a lot when I was small."

She paused to rub her forehead, a little shaken by the vividness of the image that had chosen this moment to leap from the vaults of the past.

"I guess it's the smell of that diesel fuel that triggered it. Like in grandpa's shop. When he was really busy, on a motor or something, and it got to be suppertime, we'd both be really hungry. He'd give me some money—I still remember how the dollar bills used to crinkle up in my hand—and send me up the street to the store. I'd get a package of wieners and a big can of those brown Boston beans with all that spicy tomato stuff in them. When I got back, grandpa'd give me his pen knife and let me chop up all the wieners into little pieces on the anvil. We kept this old black pot hanging on the wall. He'd put in the beans and I'd put in the wieners, and then he'd make this big show for me, heating up the pot with the welding torch. Boy, that was really something!''

Miel's hazel eyes softened with faraway pleasure as she recalled the big knobbly old fingers holding the pot handle and the acrid hiss of that hot blue flame—a flame she had seen cutting through iron as if it were butter, now heating her dinner without even scorching the bottom of the battered saucepan. "Then he'd get a spoon and I'd get a spoon, and we'd set the pot between us on this monster of a hardwood block he kept for hammering on. The whole time we were eating, he'd be telling me these perfectly hair-raising tales about shoals and storms on the Great Lakes and getting caught in the pack ice in the North Atlantic during the war.''

Through all this, Barth hadn't moved a muscle. His arms remained folded, his eyes unfathomable. Miel stopped short in her narrative, both from the power of his gaze and the realization of just what she had been telling. Before the moment could become awkward, a slow grin creased Barth's face. He leaned across the trays of caterers' dainties and opened a storage-locker door. From the interior he extracted a large can of baked beans. With his other hand he delved into the top-loading freezer and produced plump wieners encased in plastic.

"I'm not to be outdone, lady. Your wish is my command!''

Wonder turning to laughter bubbled up in Miel. She clapped a hand over her mouth.

"You're not going to!"

"I am. Watch me."

Sweeping aside the trays of canapés, he took out a wicked-looking knife and chopped the wieners, frozen as they were, into a pot, then poured the canned beans in on top.

"And now for the crowning flourish. Not for me the mundane stove. At least I can try to match your grandfather."

Another locker yielded a small but very efficient-looking brass blowtorch. He pumped it quickly, then, motioning her out with him into the open cockpit, he lit it with a match. There was a violent hiss and a blast of orange flame which Barth quickly tamed into a steady blue tongue.

In the sunlight, with great skill, he swept the torch back and forth under the pan, allowing Miel a glimpse of the cool competence of his hands when there was a job to be done. Soon the beans began to bubble and gurgle, and when Barth judged them done, he extinguished the flame with a flick of his thumb and set the pot down on the gunwale next to Miel. It was darkened with flame patterns up the sides and smelled delicious. Barth got two spoons and handed one to his guest.

"There, eat your fill. See if it's as good as you got at home."

Miel had been laughing until she was weak, delighted by his craziness. He dug in with gusto and she did too—but as soon as the familiar

smoky taste struck her mouth she found she
could not swallow a bite. To her horror and
dismay, she felt her eyes filling up with tears.
Barth's figure began to waver through a thick
film of moisture and she heard a sob bursting
unchecked from her throat.

Immediately Barth set down his spoon and
gathered her into his arms. She tried feebly to
struggle, but one of his large hands pressed
against her hair to rest her head against the
warm and comforting hollow of his shoulder. It
seemed such a safe haven, such a marvelously
close and secure haven, that she gave in after a
few seconds and burrowed her cheek into the
fresh whiteness of his short-sleeved shirt. The
fabric was heated by his flesh, and through it
she could hear the deep and solemn beating of
his heart.

Almost at once, she found herself in the grip
of an emotion so powerful it racked her entire
body and yet she could not put a name to it. She
only knew her chest hurt horribly, tightening
and tightening until the pressure broke and
great ragged sobs were tearing themselves out
into the air. Against this incredible emotional
eruption, there was no question of resistance.
Miel could only give herself up to it until the
thing that clutched her breast weakened little by
little and she was finally spent.

"I'm so sorry. I can't imagine. . . ."

Her words died in a final sob. Barth, who had
been holding her tenderly all this time, placed
one hand soothingly on the middle of her back.

She could feel his breath whispering next to her ear.

"You've never really allowed yourself to grieve for him, have you?"

"Wh...what?"

"Your grandfather. You've been hoarding it all inside. It just took this one bit of nostalgia to push you over the edge."

To her astonishment, Miel realized this was true. That one mouthful from the heated pot had flooded her with memories of the old shop, all the smells of oil and metal, the clink of wrenches, the rusting chains heaped in corners, the never-ending wash of lake water where her sailboat was tied. But the force of this explosion from her subconscious left her bewildered and stunned, though since Barth had appeared these things had been striking her from nowhere. She had recovered enough to be deeply embarrassed.

"Oh, what an awful fool I've just made of myself. I...."

"Ssssh, don't talk. You don't have to explain anything. It's all right."

There was so much softness in his voice that it reached out and enveloped her like a protective cocoon. Eventually, Miel surrendered herself, for she felt very weak inside, drained—and deeply grateful for the burly arms that held her.

For a long while she just lay there, listening to the calm steadiness of his breathing while a distant sail pricked the blue smudge of the horizon and the white reflection of the *Yancy* quivered in the water at their side. Finally, Barth's hand moved up to stroke her hair lightly, pensively.

"You know," he said at last, "I've never told you what finally drove me to take off on my own and think about founding Operation Seawatch. It was a whaling ship. I hate whalers. There isn't a single product the whale provides that can't be manufactured cheaply and synthetically, yet certain nations simply won't give up. And I don't find it funny that everyone imagines the days of Moby Dick to be the great killing times, when in fact modern efficiency destroys more whales today than those old sailing ships could ever dream of."

He paused, and Miel could feel him tip his head back, as if to stare far, far out at the few wandering clouds.

"Anyway," he continued, "this whaler ran aground on a godforsaken shoal off the coast of Brazil. Not in real danger, mind. Just sitting out of production until it could be hauled off and a dandy hole in the bow cobbled up. The crew, except for a watchman, had been taken off to the mainland and were living it up in town while the call for a salvager went out. My ship was in the area but it wasn't the only one. I said to let another company grab that one, but Frank had a fit. Business was business, he said, and we weren't going to hand money to the competition. In short, we had a royal row. To appease him, I agreed to patch up the whaler after all."

He stroked Miel's back, hypnotizing her by the movement. Her wet lashes were closed as she bathed in the glow of his nearness.

"What happened?" she asked, wanting only the sound of his voice.

"Nothing at first. There was a fair bit of diving involved, inspecting the hull and welding on a temporary plate. I did most of it myself, wanting to get out of there as fast as I could. Then, wouldn't you know, this pod of Right whales decided to linger in the area. A young one, about half grown, a really curious youngster, started hanging around watching what we were doing. I wasn't too keen at first because when something weighing several tons gets playful, you look out. But the whale turned out to have unbelievable control over all that bulk and such intelligent eyes. It poked and hovered and let me scratch its nose. Its tail fluke alone was ten feet across and could have flattened me with a flick, yet I never felt afraid. By the time the job was done I felt I had made a friend for life."

His words were somber and slow, washing over Miel and conjuring images of him drifting almost naked below the sea-green waters while breakers all the way from the coast of Africa rolled above his head and the shadowy gentle shape of the whale hovered in the depths. When his voice trailed off, Miel noticed his heartbeat speeding up and was startled by a sharp deep breath as if he were in pain.

"Barth?"

"Sorry. I guess I got really sentimental over that young whale. It disappeared a couple of days before the repairs were finished. I hated to see it go but I was glad. Sticking around a whaler was not at all healthy for it. Then the crew flew back, and we hauled the ship back out into open water good as new. The captain was just giving me the high sign from the deck when along came my friend, dipping along and blowing off great lungfuls of air. Our own boat was backing away and there wasn't a thing I could do. Inside of a minute the harpoon was through it and there was blood everywhere.''

A shudder passed through Barth, and Miel pressed her forehead to his chest, clenching her jaw against this unexpected horror.

"Oh God, how...awful!"

"Awful is the word. I had to stand there and watch the poor desperate thing writhing and plunging as the great power winches drew it in. It was dead before I could even get down from the bridge.''

"And that was your very last job?"

"It was. I handed things over to Frank and got straight aboard the *Yancy* for a good long think. Strangely enough—" he halted, then went on in a different voice "—the struggles of that young creature reminded me somehow of you. You were so much like that in Bay Point. Eager to grow up, so full of brightness and curiosity. And then...."

"You left."

"Yes."

The jagged regret in his voice stunned Miel, making her go very still, almost rigid, in his arms. Comprehension almost knocked her over like a violent gust of wind. He understood! He really and truly understood how much he had hurt her that night he pushed her out onto the Bay Point dock.

"Oh, Barth...."

She was the one who now gathered him into her embrace, pressing him as close to her heart as her strength would allow. A fever was beating in her now, testing her defences, tormenting her with a terrible urge to tell him everything, get it out, be free of it at last.

His lips trailed along her temple.

"It must have been...hard for you, Miel. I'm not entirely dense about small towns, you know."

"It was. Somebody saw me running off the pier. They were snickering everywhere by morning. I could hardly...bring myself to write my exams."

The feathery caresses stopped. She could almost feel Barth frowning.

"Is that the real reason you never went to university? Those exams?"

For a long moment, she remained silent, knowing it was no use trying to hide anything from him now. Slowly, she released a sigh and nodded.

"I failed them. When the report card came, grandpa got so angry he...he...."

She couldn't actually say it. With a tiny, half-stifled cry, she turned her face in to the comfort of his chest again. Barth hugged her to him fiercely, remorsefully.

"Oh, no! I had no idea. No wonder you hated me."

"I did blame it on you for a long time, but it wasn't your fault. Or mine either, I guess. I was just a lovesick kid acting the only way a lovesick kid could act. I should never have gone near the boat so late. What choice did you have but to throw me out?"

"I know, but damn! I should have written or called or done some fool thing to see how you were getting on."

"I would have burned a letter. And as for the phone—" she cringed "—do you think you could have talked to me over a party line? It was all just... circumstances. And with my grandpa getting sick like that, wild horses wouldn't have dragged me back to school."

His cheek rested on the top of her head, nestled in the softness of her hair. The *Yancy* creaked gently, while behind them the lowering sun dropped a path of golden sequins into the lake.

"I feel very sorry about your grandfather. I liked the old man, liked getting things for the *Yancy* done in his shop. It's tough to find out he thought I was, well... betraying him."

Images of her grandfather loomed again in Miel's mind, images of engine grease ground indelibly into the creases of his hands, of his grizzled cheeks and that funny half scowl beaten in by decades of rough weather on the lakes. Grief caught in her throat again and she fought it, pushing back damp hair from her eyes.

"I... I don't know what's wrong with me, Barth. I... all this just came over me after a p... perfectly fine party. You must think I'm crazy, breaking all to pieces like this."

Barth looked down at her. *Oh, such a good face,* she thought in a rush, and knew he would laugh if she told him. A good-natured face, which only in certain lights revealed the lines that spoke otherwise of lonely, grievous responsibility.

"Perhaps there's a reason, Miel. Things are...changing for you. You're growing, getting rid of the burdens of an old life so you can go on with a new. Maybe what's breaking away is simply your shell."

Miel uncurled a fraction and looked at the pot of beans that had triggered all this. A shell was at least a wall, a resistance. If it were cracked, gone—what then? She began to stretch her mind a little, testing around her, and indeed felt a curious imbalance as if some prop she took for granted was no longer there.

A flight of Canada geese arrowed toward the island and, dominating as always, the CN Tower now appeared to rise dynamically out of a cloud of trees. Miel could not help but remember the taste of Barth's lips up there among the drifts of mist, and she began to understand that it was Barth's very presence that had allowed her to weep for her grandfather. For the first time since she had left Bay Point she was with someone who had known her as she was before and had known the old man too. With him, she had no reason to pretend.

"He...loved me the best he could," she said sincerely. "And if he got very harsh in the end, it's because he came from a generation that just...couldn't understand. I never realized before what he must have suffered when my mother ran away. What happened on the boat was such a silly little incident, yet it must have seemed just like that other time all over again to him.''

Barth produced a large white handkerchief and handed it over with an oddly gruff gesture. Miel wiped her eyes with it and felt comforted, for something in his very manner reminded her, though she was too embarrassed to show it, that her grandfather had cared about her too. Now her mind wandered back to those childhood days when she had sat on the workbench and watched dismantled motors miraculously cough back to life. Yes, they had this in common, she realized—she the shop, he those working ships. They had both been raised almost entirely around men.

And now she knew why she no longer felt the constrictions around her. With the tears had melted the last of the grief and anger she had harbored all these years. If, before, she had cleared herself intellectually, now at last her emotions were free.

Free! Miel could feel herself trembling under the folds of silk, for it was such a strange condition. This last relinquishing of old and ingrown prejudices had uncovered a void. Nothing had been left to fill its place.

The breeze lifted tendrils of hair and played with them gently around the edges of a face that was growing pale from a new vulnerability. She could not bear to look at Barth and so stared past him at white and pink houses clinging high along the shore. She felt exposed and soft inside. If anything touched her now, she just might take the imprint forever.

She didn't know when she had separated herself from Barth or when his hands had slowly slid to her shoulders and turned her to face him. His gray eyes had picked up flecks of color from the first of the sunset. He was no longer easy and casual. A terrible tautness around his mouth and cheeks made her heart stumble and skip.

"I love you, Miel," he said simply.

She stared at him, her heart beginning to hammer. His voice had been devastatingly clear in the blue silence of the lake, and the words struck her like shocks, one after the other. Her brain began to swim. Briefly, she began to wonder if she'd lost her powers of understanding.

"I've never said that to any woman before, believe me!"

His face testified to the truth. Dimly, Miel knew she ought to make some response but found herself quite incapable of speech. All known reality seemed to be splintering around her. The most she could do was lift long fingers to touch the vein pulsing at his jaw. The movement proved encouragement enough. Barth gathered her to him again, his arms rough this time, as he was driven by emotion barely under control. When he met no resistance, he buried his face as deeply as he could in her hair.

"Oh my beautiful Miel, I want to lay you

down under the open sky and make love to you. My darling, sweet as honey. . . ."

He kissed her eyes and her throat and somehow found the delicate hook that held the silk together. Parting around her shoulders, it fell into an emerald froth tangled with his arms and only when the cool breeze whispered over her did Miel realize her entire back was bare.

She didn't care, for they had glided down into the shelter of the cockpit, long-grained teak gleaming round them like a wall. The woman in her reacted to his nearness and her hands stole around his neck. His head bent, paying homage to the ivory swell of her breasts, and when his fingers explored the two tiny dimples at the base of her spine, she was treated to the most astonishing sensation of exquisite joy.

"Barth, Barth. . . oh. . . ."

Desire fell upon her then, dropping like an incendiary bomb from the heavens, exploding, filling her private universe with burning stars and streaming pinwheels. It surrounded her like thunder, pulled at her with the determination of an undertow until she felt herself rushing away. And that was what, finally, frightened her—the utter loss of control, which she could not bear. She became a struggling mass of disheveled silk and Barth held her now as one might hold someone thrashing in delirium. Miel went very still, aware of her own pulse pounding in her breast and the tension that surrounded them, dense and dangerous.

"You're not ready for this, are you?" Barth said thickly.

Miel's mouth drew into a thin, tremulous line. She shook her head and leaned her temple against his breastbone. *Idiot!* she berated herself as the rigging creaked softly and Barth's hands remained motionless upon her body.

"It's all right," he moaned at last. "Never mind."

Reaching behind him, he grabbed a sailbag for them to rest against. His arms loosened, and he turned his face away for a while so that Miel could not see him. But she could hear him. The raggedness of his sigh and the tremor he was fighting to subdue told her just what his calmness cost him. Her stomach tightened with regret, for she knew then that he had chosen just this moment to try to reach her, and now the effort was in tatters because of this involuntary panic of hers.

One by one, a string of tiny pink clouds trooped by the masthead, and then Miel felt his breath on her forehead again, the brush of lips no longer demanding as she was nestled against him.

"I meant what I said on top of the CN Tower," he murmured, "about Operation Seawatch. But first, my sweet, before the real work starts, I promise you a year. Just you and me aboard the *Yancy*. We could drink fig brandy and go around the Horn, if you wanted. It's a devil of a passage, but the *Yancy*'s up to it. We'll stop at Tonga and dive for conch and listen to the old women able to call up the grandmother of turtles. I want you to smell the island flowers, Miel. For miles out in the ocean—hibiscus and honeysuckle. I'll show you icebergs under moonlight, or the Grand Banks in fog. Whatever you have a yen for—if only to get you out of that clothing store and show you that you belong to the sea.''

His voice rolled on, painting the world for her as she lay against him, warm and secure, carried away by the dream. She lost consciousness of all else save the seduction of his words and the warmth of his arms around her. *He loves me,* she thought in nascent wonder. *Barth Tramande loves me!* A great happiness blossomed in her, making her blood sing like the water of a stream dancing over bright stones. It was like being gathered into a sunny place, and she felt she could lie there forever, simply savoring it. This couldn't be, however, for a power boat roared rudely past, jolting the *Yancy* with its wake.

The two of them struggled upright, astonished at the deep pearl dusk stealing across the water. Miel shrugged the whispering Gagnon back up over her shoulders and did up the tiny catch. Barth knelt beside her, the wheel behind him making a spoked arc against the sky.

''Miel, say you will.''

She knew what he was asking. Again, there was that swell of joy inside her and a deep, deep sense of connectedness with him. She searched for words, remembering, with a twinge of pain, another man.

''There's James to consider,'' she murmured barely audibly. ''I have to speak to him. I couldn't just...leave.''

She saw the smile dawning in Barth's eyes. He nodded and understood, they both understood, that James had been part of the reason they couldn't consummate their love. Not yet.

Barth kissed her eyelids.

"We'll go back, then. Do what you have to do. I'll be here for you always. I promise."

And when their eyes met, a pact, a bond, was made between them. Rising to her feet, Miel knew it was only a matter of time before Barth would expect it to be fulfilled.

CHAPTER THIRTEEN

THE MORNING DAWNED gray and blustery, waking Miel to a patter of rain on her balcony and a cool wind whipping in through the window she had dreamily opened wide the previous night. Hopping out of bed, she pulled it shut with a solid bang. Spring had been like summer. Now the leading edge of real summer had capriciously decided to act like another season.

She twirled once and stopped in the center of her little Azerbaijan rug, the previous day flooding back to her in a kind of ghostly glow. As she looked round her apartment at her own small treasures—the china shepherdess she was so fond of, the clock under glass, her antique brass library lamp—she was quite incapable of grasping their reality.

Why, I've actually been asked to run away to sea, she thought and, most uncharacteristically, giggled, for the romance of it at least had not been lost on her. She supposed she was suffering some kind of emotional hangover. She felt breathless and disoriented, just as one might after a whirlwind party. So much had happened yesterday that she could only float giddily into the shower. Almost immediately the sensuous play of the water woke her body to the voluptuous memory of Barth's lips and hands and stunningly potent virility.

As she left for work and stepped outside, she turned her face up to the sky, though the stinging drops flew persistently at her as if attempting to remind her of ordinary reality. The effort was useless. The bubbling continued in her heart and her simple seersucker dress felt diaphanous around her. A gust blew her scarf to a rainbow at her throat and she waved to a flower seller outside the subway entrance.

In this condition she scurried in the front entrance of the store and was immediately enclosed in a dry, sheltering warmth. Marion nodded to her from lingerie as the first customers of the day were already folding damp, expensive umbrellas. When the elevator doors opened to the top floor she was brushing raindrops from her briefcase and was consequently not in the least prepared for the rage of voices that greeted her. She glanced at Allison, who was staring with helpless dismay down the corridor to James's office from where all the commotion was issuing.

"What on earth?"

Allison jumped to her feet, rattling all the pencils on her desk.

"Oh, Miel, thank heaven! You've got to go in there and do something about that awful man."

"Who? What awful man?"

"That Avery Selks from down the street. He just roared right past me in to see James and started yelling fit to bring down the walls. All about something Hildy's done. I didn't have a hope of stopping him.''

Miel sped down the corridor to where James's door hung half open, revealing the broad back of Avery Selks himself as one of his arms gesticulated furiously in the air. James stood facing him, his mouth white with control. Between them, her back almost against the wall, her face ashen, hovered Hildy, her small body rigid from some enormous determination.

"I tell you, she stole that Gagnon line from me outright!" Selks was bellowing. "I've got contacts in Europe too, you know. That juicy tidbit about the Marseilles fire was sent to me! Registered mail as a matter of fact, and marked Confidential—but this scheming little weasel managed to have the letter intercepted. How else could she tell you that part of the Gagnon stock was up for grabs because the Marseilles distributor was out of commission!"

"I hate you!" Hildy exploded back. "I hate your guts! You bet I intercepted your mail. Anything I take from you, you owe me. Your whole vulgar store down there was started with money you stole from my mother!"

The natural floridity of Selks's face deepened instantly to a weltlike scarlet.

"Listen to you, Miss High and Mighty. With a kid on her hands and a business to run, your mother was damned lucky to latch onto me. Yet the minute she was buried you took off like a stuck-up little rabbit!"

Hildy's eyes grew frighteningly big, and her breath labored in little hoarse pants as if she were preparing to fly at the man's fleshy throat. And for all his size and outrage, at that moment Hildy looked as if she might be the fiercer of the two.

"Do you think I would have stayed anywhere near you after what you did to my mother? You married her for her store and then you killed her with all your sleazy running around. My dearest hope is that you go bankrupt before the year is out!"

"Why, you miserable...."

"Mr. Selks! You've made your point. Now I'll thank you to remove yourself from the premises." James's voice was low and calm but chillingly cold. As always, when he used this tone, he got immediate attention. Selks and Hildy stopped glaring at each other and looked at him.

"I want her dealt with," sputtered Selks. "Right now I ought to call the police. As it is, I'm going to put that sneaking confederate of yours out on her pretty ear!"

"Oh, not Janet...."

Hildy clapped a hand over her mouth but it was too late. A distinctly reptilian smile slid along Selks's lips.

"So! It really is Janet who's your inside stooge. I knew I could make you let the cat out of the bag!"

Hildy began to shake with impotent rage.

"Oh... oh, you're despicable!"

"Mr. Selks, please leave or I'll be the one who calls the police!"

James was gripping the edge of his desk now, the knuckles of his fine hands showing white from strain. Avery Selks whirled on him.

"Damn it, Crome, don't threaten me. You and your lame-duck store. You're going under so fast you can't even see the bubbles—and you're quite desperate enough to put this sly minion of yours up to anything!"

A horrified stillness penetrated the office but James only lifted the telephone. "Out!" he snapped in a voice so taut even Avery Selks was daunted. The man glowered, a violent retort hanging on his lips. Then, thinking better of the whole thing, he thumped out into the hall, almost flattening Miel in the process. James, Hildy and Miel remained grimly motionless until the distant closing of the elevator doors informed them that Selks had indeed gone. All the heads along the corridor, attracted by the ruckus, vanished like turtles'. James met Miel's eyes and motioned her impatiently to come in.

"And shut the door. We have a serious matter here to straighten out."

His face was drawn, and his hands seemed actually to be shaking slightly. The room felt charged and close as if some painful but invisible electricity were leaping about. Hildy stayed against the wall, pathetically cornered, yet still furious and resolute, her head thrown back and that mass of tiny curls cascading wildly down her back. Never once did she take her eyes from James.

Miel waited while James struggled visibly to get hold of himself. Not even at Lillian's death had Miel seen him in such a state. *He really can't stand upsets,* she thought, aching to go to him. *Somehow, he hasn't the emotional armor.* Nevertheless, he drew a deep breath and began.

"You'd better hear this from the beginning, Miel. I want you in on everything."

Hildy turned her face away so wretchedly that Miel suddenly would rather have been on the moon than become privy to whatever could so embarrass her friend. However, there was no escaping. Another instinct told her she must share this thing with James. If she herself was wincing, his own sensibilities must be making him suffer double measure. Right now he needed her at his side.

He began, painfully, to fill in the parts Miel had missed. It was common knowledge that in a business as shifting and cutthroat as the garment trade, there existed a network of spies and gossip sometimes more efficient than satellite transmissions. One of Selks's contacts had evidently sent him a tip indicating that Gagnon stock was available if one could swiftly impress the hard-nosed Hélène Gagnon. Then Janet, a close friend of Hildy's working at Selks's, had spotted the letter. Hildy convinced Janet to hand over the information and brought it to James instead. Only now had Avery Selks discovered the deception and galloped over in a rage. Miel cast a deeply chagrined look at the little sales-promotion director.

"Why, Hildy? Why would you do such a thing?"

"Didn't you hear me? Because I hate him. Anything's fair as far as I'm concerned if I can just get back at him. He's my stepfather. He married my mother and took everything she had!"

The very admission seemed wrenched from Hildy's soul, and James frowned heavily.

"I gather there's some kind of family quarrel behind all this?"

"You bet there is. My mother had a store, you see, in Montreal. When I was thirteen, Avery Selks married her and elbowed his way into control. As soon as he was sure he had everything in his own name, he started running around with other women. Just broke my mother's heart, he did! It killed her. The minute she was dead he sold out for a big profit and came to Toronto. I left the day of the funeral and waitressed my own way through school."

"But to steal the information about the Gagnons...."

"Oh, so what!" Hildy turned like a goaded animal, her formerly waxen cheeks now battle flags of color. "It wasn't the formula for a nuclear bomb. As far as I'm concerned it was a great big stroke of luck—for all of us. And that's all I've got—talent and luck—but I mean to beat him at his own game!"

Defiance glittered around the small figure, but Miel noticed she was afraid to look at James.

"So that's why you were so determined to get a job in my store?" To Miel's amazement,

James sounded as if the very idea devastated him. Hildy edged closer to her boss as if drawn by a magnet.

"If you must know, yes. Crome's was the most logical competitor. At first, all I wanted was to make the store so strong and up to date no one would dream of going back to that gaudy barn of Avery Selks's. Then later, after I'd been here a while. . . ."

Her words trailed off as if she'd almost made some terrible slip. James stared at her with a concentration that unnerved Miel.

"Later what?"

"Nothing!"

"I don't take 'nothing' for an answer."

James's face was drawn tight, yet he recoiled from the force with which Hildy suddenly lashed out at him.

"What does it matter?" she cried. "I got you the Gagnon designs, didn't I? And the campaign I designed is so damned good Crome's is going to shoot straight back up out of the hole. Who cares what Avery Selks rants about? Let him scream. We both know there isn't a thing he can do."

"But there are one or two things I'll have to do."

James dropped these last words into a sudden well of silence. The stiffness in his tone, the look of haggard desperation that crossed his face, sent a frisson of alarm skittering up the back of Miel's neck. *Oh, don't go too far,* she pleaded silently. *Don't do something everybody is going to regret!*

For several unearthly seconds they could hear the infinitesimal hum of James's digital clock and a metallic creak in the air vents. Hildy's gaze was locked into that of James. His eyes seemed to burn into hers. When at last he brought himself to speak, Miel had never heard those cultivated tones so raveled.

"I appreciate your great talent, Hildy, but I had no idea you found out about the Gagnons through what amounts to an act of retail espionage. I feel that the store has been disgraced and my own personal honor sullied by all this deviousness. No member of my staff is to use Crome's as a tool in a personal vendetta, no matter how justified it seems. As of today, we'll discontinue the Gagnon line. And—" he wavered, as if he could barely get it out "—I have no other choice, Hildy, but to fire you at once!"

Hildy's wounded gasp sliced through the air, and Miel felt her own jaw drop as she gaped at James. They had both expected something in the nature of a severe reprimand—but this!

"You're mad, James, stark raving mad!" Miel whispered so quietly that James couldn't hear it. Until this moment, Miel had not actually understood how deeply James's code of honor really penetrated. Reluctantly, her admiration soared in proportion to her dismay at the implications of what he was doing. In one stroke he was wiping out completely the only hopes Crome's had for recovery—Hildy's whimsical genius and the expensively promoted

Gagnon line. Without the vital new business they were just on the verge of winning, the store might not survive another year.

Then she glanced at Hildy's anguished face and her heart contracted.

"Oh, James, you can't!" ventured Miel.

"I can," he answered in frozen determination, "and I will. You'll have ample severance pay, Hildy, but I'd appreciate it if you'd remove yourself from the office by this afternoon."

If a bomb had gone off two feet away, Hildy couldn't have looked more shattered. She continued to stare at James with huge and stricken eyes as if hoping some miracle would drop from the sky and change things to what they used to be. James remained perfectly rigid until Hildy, uttering a wounded cry, turned and bolted from the office, her gaily embroidered peasant skirt and beaded sandals flying behind her. Miel was left reeling from the scene.

"Oh, James," she breathed, shaken by the pallor of his cheeks. She took a step forward, wanting only to touch him, give him comfort from the overflowing compassion welling up in her breast. Unexpectedly, almost brutally, he stepped out of reach.

"I don't want to hear it," he warned woodenly. "Now if you'll excuse me, I'd like to have my office to myself so I can get on with my work."

Such rudeness was so unthinkable in James that Miel halted as if from a blow. Only the look of total misery on his face made her understand.

Whatever he was feeling was too personal, too vulnerable to be exposed even to her. If she had any sensitivity at all, she would retreat at once, letting him have what he seemed to need most badly right then—his privacy.

"All right. But I'll be around the corner—if you need me."

Reaching for the telephone, James gave only a half-perceptible nod. "Jenny," Miel heard him say as she closed the door behind her, "I want the Gagnons removed from display immediately. Yes, that's right, every last one. . . ."

Miel took refuge in her own office for a moment, resting her forehead against her palms and listening to the rustling of the maple above the traffic sounds. She couldn't stay in solitude long, of course. Not if she were to run interference for James. There would be questions to answer and the store grapevine, which must already be ablaze with extravagant rumor, had to be dealt with. And Hildy! Poor Hildy!

Leaping from her chair, Miel walked quickly down the hall toward the promotion department, bent on comforting the young woman. There, Hildy was nowhere to be found, and her assistant, Jan, was sitting motionless at a much-littered drawing board, obviously in distress.

"She just grabbed her bag and ran off—in such a state that she could hardly talk. Is it really true that she was fired?"

"I'm afraid so."

"Poor kid. She looked as if the whole world had dropped right out from underneath her feet. I had no idea she cared so much about this job."

You don't know the half of it, Miel added silently, knowing soon enough that the in-store gossip would provide Jan, so isolated down here, with all the juicy details. Dejectedly, she walked back to her desk and tried dialing Hildy's apartment. There was no answer, and no wonder. It would probably be hours and hours before the little artist calmed down enough to finally straggle home.

For the remainder of the day Miel kept to the administrative floor, partly because she could not bear to go down and see the Gagnon display being dismantled and partly because she wanted to be nearby when James, as he inevitably would, called for her. It was hard enough, as the hours passed, to meet the curious, half-frightened looks of the staff, but harder still when no call came from behind the tightly closed door. What was wrong with James? Surely this wasn't the first time he had ever fired anyone.

But of course she knew what the matter was— the prospects of Crome's without the Gagnon line now that all the money had been sunk into its promotion was a loss.

That had to be the matter!

At James's door Miel poised one hand to knock, then, changing her mind, sought the privacy of her own office to dial the interoffice phone.

"Hello, James," she said softly when he answered. "Feel like some company yet?"

She could hear him quite audibly drawing in a breath.

"No, Miel. Not now. And if you don't mind, I don't want to talk about it all either. Okay?"

He hung up quietly, leaving Miel staring at the receiver in disbelief. James had shut her out! No doubt for perfectly good reasons of his own, but nevertheless he *had* shut her out. And never had she calculated just how much this unexpected coldness could hurt!

She had just taken her hand from the instrument and was plucking distractedly at a button on her cuff when the phone rang again, almost causing her to knock over the vase with the single scarlet rose, which was a poignant, daily-renewed reminder of James's affections. Knowing instinctively that he had relented and was calling her back, Miel leaped to answer.

"Dear James," she cried, bright with relief, "I knew you'd come round. Shall we pack it all in and go have dinner?"

The silence at the end of the line was disconcerting, and then forbidding.

"I'm sorry to have intruded on anything, Miel," a voice touched with ice said at last. "I was under the impression that this was a business phone."

"Barth!" Miel felt a little cold touch down her spine. "I wasn't expecting.... There have been such upsets here today...."

"You don't have to explain anything."

"But you don't understand...."

"On the contrary. I think I do. I called to see how you were getting on, but I see you have everything under control. I'll try again when you've had a chance to get properly squared away with 'dear James.' "

"Wait...."

Only the distant click of the receiver answered her. Miel hung up to find that the speeding of her heart made dull thunder against the turmoil of her thoughts. Barth! The memory of yesterday aboard the *Yancy*, the sweetness of his lips, the tenderness that was so much at odds with this abruptness today, came flooding back in honeyed waves. She savored the memory, firmly rejected it. In this building, with James so near, it still seemed a betrayal, improper and hopelessly out of place.

The maple spoke outside her window, reminding her how far, how very far, she was now from the dreamlike state in which she had drifted to work that morning. The dreadful scene with Hildy had quite shattered it so that now she was very much awake. And as she sobered, she realized fully, at last, the meaning of Barth's words aboard the yacht. They meant she must make a decision between these two men. Choose!

She frowned, for her heart and spirit flew toward Barth, but her loyalty, her compassion remained with James. The problem became a pressure, and soon a weight looming over her. She looked down the hall where she was sure James needed her, but she only sat impotently in her office chair.

NIGHT HAS A WAY of creeping darkly up on those who are lonely or distressed. Miel, at that moment, fitted both categories and she paced in her living room, taking periodic glances into the blue twilight interrupted regularly by the staggered night illumination of office buildings. To the east, not very far away, James's mansion was not to be seen for the density of leaves on the trees. Farther out was the broad blackness of the lake where the *Yancy* lay quietly waiting.

Waiting for her, Miel thought before pushing the idea away. Concern for both men filled her mind, driving her to this flurry of restless, aimless activity. Most of all she worried about James. He had gone straight home from the office at some moment when she hadn't been near the corridor to see him depart. Immediately, she had gone home herself and waited by the phone, which, for hours now, had stubbornly refused to ring. Yet she also regarded the phone with some alarm, lest Barth call again. He was a man of action and would want answers. She was faintly resentful that he should wish this of her in the midst of so much unexpected turmoil.

Turning on her heel, she stepped out onto the balcony and made another idle attempt to pick out James's roof, even though she knew perfectly well it was impossible to see in summer. Many times she had been to the house to attend Lillian's gatherings. She had a distinctly uneasy feeling now to think of him as he rattled around alone in those gracious, polished spaces. She herself remembered the place only when it was filled with people or the mellow afterglow of hospitality. Without Lillian or the presence of the couple who cared for it—they had their own apartment elsewhere—Miel could imagine all too painfully the hollow chiming of the ornate timepieces and the shadows spilling unchallenged across the silent halls, while James hunched in the corner of Lillian's huge divan and contemplated the ruin of his business.

Never would he sink to losing himself in the blare of a television or the depths of a case of beer. No, he would probably drink too much Napoleon brandy and stand just inside the French doors staring morosely out over the Rosedale Ravine, perhaps with only one tiny lamp switched on behind him to break the gloom.

He really did need someone to look after him, Miel thought, for the first time seriously wondering about his domestic arrangements. It wasn't good for him at all to be alone in that echoing house. How could he help but become slowly turned in upon himself and hidebound. He needed someone to bring light and air into his life and shake him up once in a while to cure that creeping pin-stripe conservatism. Someone to bring children.

Children! Miel's hand flew to her cheek in a helpless little gesture, for she had a startling vision of James standing astonished and full of pride before a row of well-behaved little copies of himself. Scenes of fireside comfort and security beckoned. She would never have to worry that James would run off to foreign parts in a white and wayward yacht!

Hurriedly, she turned back to the city, now blanketed in soft blackness, strewn with acres of twinkling lights. *Call, please call, James,* she pleaded, knowing she was helpless to go to him, for he had erected barriers she dared not cross until invited. Nor could she deny how bitterly painful it was to be cut off from him, even now when she hovered on the verge of running to another man. It made her frantic inside to realize James would not reach for her when he needed her most, even though she knew very well that no one, after all, likes his or her nearest and dearest to witness defeat.

Nor was it like James to get so emotional. It all had something to do with Hildy, perhaps—to have to do this to her. Who could appreciate better than James the real value of her enormous talent, or could imagine the humiliation of being released so ignominiously from her first important job.

Well, Miel hoped, perhaps things would be better on the morrow. And she spent the remainder of the evening gazing helplessly from her own darkened window.

THE FRAGRANCE, THE BLAZE OF ROSES took her breath away the moment Miel opened her office door. There were at least two dozen this time, lighting up the entire room with ruby red extravagance. The tall woman felt something go bump inside her as she touched a wondering finger to the gently folded softness of the petals.

"It's my way of apologizing to you, Miel,"

said James, for he had been waiting beside them. "I was beastly yesterday."

As she turned, he took her hands. His palms were smooth and very dry, though what shocked Miel was how truly haggard his face looked. Hollows seemed to have appeared in his cheeks overnight, and there was just enough disorder about his hair and suit to wring Miel's heart.

"Oh, James, you don't have to be perfect all the time. I only wish...."

"What?" he prompted when her voice faltered uncertainly.

"That you had let me...be with you. I know how upsetting everything must have been."

She meant this as an expression of solidarity, but his expression closed as if she'd offered a reproach. His effort to maintain his old, cheerful gallantry fell flat.

"I said I came to apologize. As you mentioned, I can't be perfect all the time."

Again, a hint of irritability so totally alien to James that Miel wanted to cry out for what he must be going through. Yet neither could speak of the main issue, and Miel could only offer hollow consolation.

"I know everything will work out, James. Really."

His grip tightened suddenly, as if he was wanting something, seeking something from her. The brown eyes searched her face beseechingly, yet all Miel could do was gaze back helplessly. After a second, he released her, and she suffered a terrible sense of failure. Why was there always this inability to ever quite fully connect?

"James. . . ."

"Not now, Miel. I know there's a lot to talk about. More than you imagine. It'll all be dealt with later."

Now, beyond the weariness, there was a curious, almost feverish brightness about his eyes that betokened some hidden excitement. Licking her lips, Miel grasped at hope and decided to broach the topic that truly rankled her.

"James, we at least have to discuss Hildy. Really, firing her like that. . . ."

In an instant, his expression hardened again, and a spasm of pain was revealed in his eyes. Miel could have kicked herself. Now she had really overstepped propriety, and James would be distant for the rest of the day.

"I'm sorry," she amended quickly. "You're right. This isn't the time to go into things. Would you like to meet for lunch?"

He looked as if he might have wanted it very much but he shook his head.

"No. I've got a lot of phoning to do and people to meet. I'll just have a sandwich in the office."

He brushed her hand again and bent toward her, but it was only a ghost of his old self. Despite this reconciliation effort he was deeply and unhappily preoccupied. How could it be otherwise? Coming up the escalator that morning, she had had to turn her eyes away from the large empty display space where the Gagnons had been. It looked like a gaping hole torn out of the heart of the store.

At the door, he stopped.

"You haven't forgotten about Friday night, have you?"

"Friday? Oh!"

She had—completely. Ages ago, James had planned another cocktail gathering à la Lillian at his home. However, the new people, Cora Fowler and followers in particular, had been invited, and the event was to have been another sophisticated and low-key promotion of the Gagnon designs. Without the Gagnons what were they going to do?

"Strictly social now," he said with a sad suggestion of a smile.

Smiling bravely back, Miel kissed him and murmured her thanks for the roses. Then he left her to contemplate the scarlet spill that once again illuminated her desk.

By today, of course, the entire staff knew what had happened, and a subdued hush hovered in the store. People moved more slowly at their tasks and looked away when James or Miel came by. These changes, imperceptible to a stranger perhaps, were the ones that worried Miel the most, for they signaled a subtle but definite loss of morale. Indeed, many of the clerks resembled the glum-faced crew of a sinking ship. If this mood was not promptly changed, then the beginning of the end was upon them for sure.

With a sigh, Miel tried Hildy's home number again, as she had already done twice that morning. As before, she got no answer. Worry creased her face and she dialed Jan.

"It's all right, Miel," Jan told her over a distant rustle of papers. "She called earlier. She's holed up somewhere but she won't say where. Only wanted her things put in a box so she can pick them up when she feels up to it."

"How did she sound?"

There was a long hesitation. The sound of rustling papers stopped.

"Well...perfectly awful, to tell you the truth. I thought she was going to cry right there on the phone, but of course she didn't. You know Hildy. I just wish she'd get back to her apartment so somebody could go see her."

Miel did not miss the implied reproach in Jan's voice, as if this disastrous dismissal had somehow been Miel's fault or at least Miel's to prevent. She suppressed a despairing ache.

"All right, then. There's nothing else we can do except keep trying to reach her."

CHAPTER FOURTEEN

FRIDAY, THERE WAS STILL NO SIGN of Hildy. Nor had Barth made any attempt to contact Miel. So it was not surprising that she felt at loose ends when she pulled into the semicircular drive in front of James's gray stone mansion. The house exuded the kind of comfortable unpretentiousness that bespoke old money and placid self-confidence. Cars already crammed every available parking space and through the lit windows she could see the movement of people, their hands animated in conversation, their heads thrown back in periodic laughter. How many of those affluent guests, she asked herself, knew this event held all the gaiety of a wake? Cora was coming for sure. She wondered if Barth would be.

Barth! She tucked her small clutch bag to her side and heard her heels echo hollowly on the long stone walk. Of course he had been invited, but now, perhaps, that the whole Gagnon affair had been called off, he might well avoid such a formal evening. For just one moment she closed her eyes, remembering his sudden smiles and the liquid tenderness that had melted her from his kiss. This man had said he loved her. Yes, he had. She hugged the wonder of it to her and longed for his touch as for a kind of nourishment. So much to think about, to decide. But not now. Not in the midst of all this trouble with James. Drawing a great breath to clear her head, she lifted a finger to the bell.

James was the first to greet her, a swift delight illuminating his face.

"Ah, Miel, how charming you look."

In an effort to keep up appearances and support James, Miel had spent the entire previous afternoon choosing a cocktail dress of moiré taffeta in a stunning off-the-shoulder design. The deep russet fairly lit her pale honey skin, and the constant rustle drew attention to her every tiny move. To Miel, this unusually daring foray into haute couture had begun merely as her answer to the Gagnons she could no longer wear. However, some new sensitivity, some delicious awareness of herself as a woman had caused her to listen to its whisper, savor its movement across the bareness of her back.

And it certainly had its desired effect on James. He reached out and took her hands as if she were something very welcome and very precious. With him, she stepped into the warmth and light and laughter that now made the huge old house so warm and inviting. Without further ado they plunged into the crowd, which contained, besides many of the old regulars, a strong spattering of new faces, there, no doubt, because of Cora's influence. Miel wondered what would happen when Cora discovered the Gagnons were no longer available. A lot less, probably, than when she found out it was Barth who was the least available.

"You ought to say hello to Cora presently," James told her, slipping his hand under her elbow. "She's over there, in the living room somewhere."

That unmistakable laugh attracted her attention. The people parted a little and there stood Cora, visible as a beacon in outrageous daffodil yellow. She was dispensing charm in dollops in the midst of her usual adoring circle of men. And one of the men was Barth!

Instantly, Miel forgot everything but the sheer impact of his physical presence. Also, this was the first time she had seen him in other than the casual, sometimes definitely tatty gear he usually wore. Tonight he gleamed in impeccable evening dress, a simple, severe but snowy shirt against a dark jacket with satin lapels and a black bow tie. Miel's practiced eyes told her that the suit was no rental but a top-quality tailoring job custom-fitted for those huge shoulders and breadth of arm. It surprised her to think that all this time the suit had been stowed somewhere in the depths of the *Yancy*'s lockers waiting for just such an occasion. A small voice suggested that perhaps his life had not been quite so rough and ready as she supposed.

She had barely a moment to study him before some sixth sense informed him that she had arrived. His head came up. His gray eyes met hers, obliterating all else with the magnetism that

flowed between them. The masculine aura
about him seemed to spread and grow more intense. Breaking away from Cora's group, he
came straight over.

"Hello, Miel," he said quietly, his mere presence greeting enough. "I've been waiting for
you."

There was such warmth and sincerity in his
voice that Miel's heart leaped in response. Then,
tuning into the confident undercurrent of his
smile, she realized he thought himself still sure
of her—as sure as when he had held her to his
breast aboard the *Yancy*. She had been sure then
too—or almost. Back at the office, the sureness
had slipped beneath the tumble of events. Now,
so close to him, she could feel the world of
Crome's receding and became intimately aware
of the vortex around Barth that continually exerted power to draw her in. But she felt the
movement of James's fingers on her elbow and
made a valiant effort to check any outward
show of her emotions.

"Let me get you a drink," Barth began, extending a hand toward her.

"Oh, that's all right," put in James who had
been scanning the room and, fortunately,
missed the whole charged interchange. "I'll get
her one in a minute. Miel, there are some people
you ought to meet."

Nodding to Barth he started off, and Miel
automatically followed, although not before she
saw the sharp frown Barth presented her. He
had expected her to break away and stay with

him. Her final look was apologetic. She guessed that her employer would need all the protecting she could manage. Much as she might want to, there was no way she was going to abandon James this evening. As they went, she felt Barth's eyes fixed on her all the way past the turn of the L-shaped living room until they were out of sight.

Automatically assuming her role as hostess, she circulated close to James, smiling and chatting under the high ceilings with their stylized plaster borders. Table lamps with fluted shades cast pools of light on marble-topped tables beginning to be dotted with empty glasses and used ashtrays. Expensively shod feet dimpled the carpeting. Some of the newcomers examined the paintings, for Lillian had had, of all things, a startling taste for nineteenth-century battle scenes.

As promised, James had provided Miel with a spritzer. Clutching it in the swirl of people, she found herself next to Ruth Conning and Willa Spencer, both longtime friends of Lillian's. Both of them had caught sight of Cora Fowler and were craning their necks in bemused shock. Tensing for friction, Miel moved in, pleasantries ready to smooth whatever feathers might be ruffled. Mrs. Conning merely looked at her through bifocals and smiled in that dainty lavender manner she cultivated.

"My dear, this isn't your usual crowd, is it? I'm glad *somebody* got James to liven things up at last. Does my heart good to see a girl showing a little life—like that one over there.'' She wagged her silver-gray head toward Cora. ''Just look at her reel in that big good-looking pack of muscles with the tan.''

Willa, beside her, broke into a surprisingly feisty laugh, so that the brown, flowered jersey covering her began to quiver.

''Well, Ruth, we didn't do so badly ourselves when we were young. Remember that time at the tennis tournaments. . . .''

''Oh hush! At least we got one each. . . .''

Miel was no longer listening. She too was aching to see what Cora was up to and soon enough caught sight of Barth, once again lounging comfortably, well inside Cora's orbit. Cora was making a determined play for his attention and seemed to be succeeding. Laughing at some quip, he fixed his eyes with pleasure on her broad, wonderfully alive face. However, with some uncanny sense, he seemed to be aware that Miel was watching him. He stepped back a pace from the ring of suits and bare little dresses, inclining his head toward her in clear invitation. Feeling James at her side, Miel shook her head ever so slightly and saw the corners of Barth's mouth flex. Seconds later, Cora was touching his cuff in such an earthy, inviting gesture it would have been beyond any man to refuse.

Miel turned away, ridiculously wounded by the sight. Yet she could not help but be relieved that the milling of guests precluded any private words between herself and this towering man who had shaken her life so, for what could she possibly say if he again asked her to fly off with him aboard the *Yancy*?

"Look, Miel, there's Jane Swynford. We'd better go and have a word or two with her."

James, free of his office glumness, was now being so extraordinarily brisk in his duties as host that one would have thought the store had just turned over a million-dollar profit. *This is true valor in the face of adversity,* Miel decided in admiration, feeling herself once again swept along at his side. The other times she had been here, she had simply drifted freely among the guests. This time, James's fingers were either at her elbow or resting lightly on her waist, as if he was afraid that if he let her go she might disappear. "Clinging" was not a word one dared apply to James, but there could be no mistaking his need to keep her exceedingly close.

The house was one of roomy arches and vistas, with hardwood floors that creaked even under carpeting and a central staircase of dark oak. It was by this staircase that Jane stopped and, after the ritual chitchat with James, lifted her stylishly cropped head.

"Where's Cora? I'm sure I can hear her laughing."

Jane Swynford was a very handsome woman in her early thirties who was one of the more levelheaded members of Cora's coterie. Graciously, James opened a path for her to the hub of action and Cora, grabbing her friend away from James, greeted her with a series of delighted little cries.

"Jane! Good to see you. Come over and stand beside me. I need all the help I can get in properly admiring this magnificent sea dog here. Lord, couldn't you just picture him a pirate!"

Jane, seeming to draw energy directly from Cora's heartiness, turned immediately to Barth and looked him up and down with almond-shaped eyes.

"Pshaw, Cora, pirates aren't blond. They have thick black shaggy locks and handlebar mustaches. . . ."

They continued this utterly frivolous banter, which Cora's rich voice made so fascinating, so plausible. All their attention was focused on Barth, who stood without so much as a blush, soaking it all in and looking amused. Ruth had more or less been snatched away from James, so that he stood at the rim of the group, appearing just a little at a loss. This was the first time that evening Miel had seen James and Barth in close proximity, and the contrast gave her a sudden pain deep in her breast.

James, as usual, was immaculate, his jacket sleek, his hair a careful wave above those fine Saxon features. He belonged in the room, as much as the Florentine drapes and classic architectural proportions. He moved at ease in this, his home environment.

Beside him, Barth loomed, half a head taller at least. Despite the fit and excellent quality of his tailoring, the hands that protruded from the edge of white cuff were still the huge, callused hands of a working seaman. The skin of his face and neck, not so much tanned as seasoned, glowed with a vigor completely lacking in the more civilized complexions that resulted from occasional tennis or golf. No one could doubt that here was a man who spent his time engaged in serious physical activity outdoors. No drawing-room creature, this: his vital masculinity succeeded, as it had in Miel's apartment, in making even James's spacious house appear a little too small. Women gazed and buzzed. Men, especially those who knew about the ads and had prepared a condescending smirk, shook his hand with a new and hasty respect.

Miel set down her drink on a narrow sideboard, hating suddenly to see James upstaged in his own living room. Barth, so obviously not one of the soft, pampered men standing around drinking cocktails, was as out of his element here as James had been aboard the *Yancy*. Yet in this case the contrast seemed to work to Barth's advantage. His sheer size and potency dominated every other male in the room and provided a pungent dash of spice to these otherwise bland gatherings. Now everyone was ignoring James, who was carrying on so gallantly despite his sudden loss of favor. The old protectiveness stirred. With a dazzling smile, Miel sailed in and carried her employer off to the haven of a little square-backed settee, where she put a plate in his hands and began resolutely filling it with tiny glazed sandwiches and marinated mushrooms.

"What's this?" James laughed, peering at the assembled dainties.

"It's your party too. Let them all look after themselves for a while. Time out for a little R and R."

"Really...."

"James, you're showing every sign of turning into a fusspot," she teased affectionately, wondering at her new daring. Her tiny gold earrings picked up light and glinted with every graceful movement of her head.

"Am I? Maybe I am."

His eyes met hers and crinkled in tacit recognition that on this occasion there was nothing to sell and no one's favor they had to curry. Popping a mushroom into his mouth, he seemed to relax and enjoy the comfort of his own settee.

"Honestly," Miel murmured, leaning closer, "it's good to see you back to your old self."

Maintaining that physical contact he had seemed to need from her since she had arrived, he reached over and squeezed her hand.

"Maybe better than my old self. Things have been happening. Changes for Crome's."

"What things?"

"Later. You'll find out everything."

His voice was faintly breathless, his eyes glowed with that fevered energy that had made her so uneasy before. She wondered if he was capable of doing something desperate in defense of the store but had to hold her questions in the press of people. James ate a few of the tidbits on the plate before pushing it aside, restless again, drawing Miel to her feet.

"Come on. We better go see if the Ferrers are here."

But Miel noticed that he sometimes frowned toward the softly lit hall or the imposing vestibule as if expecting to see some other, unmentioned person, who would not appear. Hildy, Miel thought. Only Hildy's dancing, nonconformist brilliance could have challenged Cora's hold here tonight. But Hildy, alas, was sadly holed up somewhere, with hardly a shred of brilliance left.

The evening wore on, with Miel and James moving in eddies of people from one group to the next. Miel did not get away until James was claimed by an indisposed guest apologizing long-windedly on the telephone. Glancing behind her, she gratefully escaped the hubbub through the French doors and onto the terrace where the scent of freshly cut grass and falling dew rose around her.

The silence outside was always a shock, as was the looming wildness of the Rosedale Ravine, rustling just at the foot of the garden wall and giving, even in the heart of the city, uneasy intimations of uncivilized wilderness. Miel sighed and stretched and walked to the shelter of a small grape arbor, where she leaned back to look at the sliding silver moon. She did not hear other approaching footsteps until a voice, husky and familiar, spoke at her shoulder.

"There you are. I wondered when you were going to get away."

Even as she started, she found masculine arms circle her waist and pull her back against a white-clad chest. Lips fluttered lightly along the glimmering curve of nape exposed by the dress.

"Barth, you shouldn't!" Miel gasped as an arrow of desire struck, thin and unerring, into her vitals.

"Oh, shouldn't I? Well, then, how about this... and this!"

Teasingly, caressingly, he nibbled her earlobe and ran his tongue down the velvet quiver of nerves that was the side of her neck. Weakness shot through Miel. In spite of herself, she pressed her head back against the side of his jaw and groaned, forgetting all else but the wonderful sensations.

In the shadows, Barth turned her to him, arms tightening, playfulness quickly submerged in the increasing intensity of his explorations along her cheeks and throat. He was reaching her lips, her breasts pressed tight against him, when there was a loud burst of voices, indicating that others were drifting into the garden. The moon, momentarily obscured behind a cloud, slipped out, shedding pale light on the scene. Miel caught her breath and managed to draw slightly away.

"Barth, there are people. How awful if we were seen doing this. James. . . ."

Barth's face darkened even in the obscurity of the trellis.

"You mean you haven't spoken to him yet?"

She turned her face away, looking uncertainly toward the brightness of that other world spilling out on the flagstones and exerting its pull.

"No, I haven't. With all the troubles at the office right now I just can't dump anything more on his head. Besides...."

"Besides what?"

Nothing could have been more damning than that weak trailing away of words and now Barth was stiffly urgent, his hands riding up to close upon her shoulders. Miel knew that he had sensed her hesitation, yet she refused to be coerced. Casting about for some answer, she heard the tick of heels upon the walk and then an ample figure swept out.

"Miel, there you are, dear. James is looking all over for you. Such a lovely couple, you and James. Go on now and don't keep him waiting."

Madge Ferrer, matchmaker-in-chief of Lillian's set, was a woman whose energetic creativity embroiled nieces, nephews, cousins, grandchildren and any suitable strangers who wandered within range. James had been a challenge for some years and now, although she had had no hand in the doing, her experienced eye told her at once that James and Miel were a pair. One anxious look from James had probably been enough to send her in search of the lost sheep.

"Yes, of course. I was just on my way."

She had already stepped away from Barth and left without looking at him or responding to the puzzled, speculative frown Madge gave her when she noticed the tall figure still under the arbor.

It wasn't long before the guests began to leave, in ones and twos at first, then all in a rush, as tended to happen when people discovered they might be in danger of being the last left behind among the empty sofas and abandoned drinks. Miel stood by James, saying goodbye to each until only a couple of stragglers were left, one of whom was Barth. He must have remained in the garden until the last minute, for there was the smell and coolness of outdoors about him as he now came forward, silent upon the carpeting. James was waving to Ruth Conning at the door as Barth stopped beside Miel, his fingers brushing her elbow.

"Well, free at last." He grinned but with something that was not quite amusement in his eyes. "Get whatever it is you came wrapped up in. I'll take you home and maybe we can have a few minutes to ourselves."

He spoke as if it did not occur to him that there was any other way the evening might end. Miel hovered then, knowing there was no escape, nodded and looked around for her clutch. James came back from the door in time to sense her intention and was by her in a minute.

"Don't go yet, Miel. There's something I have to talk to you about."

Barth frowned. "It's late, James. Surely her business day is finished."

"Not yet," returned James in an enigmatic murmur. "Be back in a minute. I just have to see to old Mrs. Cranston."

He stepped away again, leaving Barth impatient.

"Come on, Miel. Tell him you'll see him in the morning. We have things to talk about right now."

Miel backed away slightly as if to remove herself from the aura about him that affected her so.

"I can't. I have to stay."

"Have to? Like a good schoolgirl? Does he still have that sort of power?"

"You don't understand. I can't leave with you now. James wants me."

"So do I."

"Please, Barth." This was growing too much like a contest between two bulldogs—and she was the bone.

"Miel, come here a minute. Edna would like to say goodbye."

Casting a look of appeal over her shoulder to Barth, Miel hurried away to take the aged dear by her thin, beringed hands. When she had said her farewells she saw that Barth, now looking like a gathering thunderstorm, was himself heading for the door. At that moment, Cora, who had been powdering her nose in the mauve papered bathroom, swirled out and spotted him.

"Need a lift to the harbor, sailor?" she called out merrily. "I just happen to have a Porsche for two outside the door."

The invitation checked Barth in his stride. He looked at Miel, who did not move. A second later, he let Cora fix herself to his arm and whisk him off into the night.

There was nothing for Miel to do, of course, except blink and try not to identify that unmercifully tearing pain at the bottom of her heart. Several moments passed before she understood that the house was finally empty except for herself and James. He joined her in the archway, touching the gentle curve of her waist.

"It's so warm in here, Miel. I've poured us both a brandy. Let's step out into the garden and get some fresh air."

The ordinary words were belied by such nervously controlled excitement that Miel was awakened out of her trance to have a good look at him. He had unbuttoned his jacket, and his tie was slightly askew as if he had been in the middle of pulling at it and had forgotten what he was doing. In fact, he was in a very strange state, gazing at her with luminous eyes, unaccountably tense, yet charged with some obvious surplus of energy.

Accepting the snifter, she followed him across the living room and through the tall, white-painted French doors onto the terrace. Immediately the cool night breeze lifted the hair from her forehead. A chorus of crickets sang around them. James guided her down the walk to the lower terrace, which fanned out against the low stone wall, separating the grounds from the ravine. Through the fabric of her dress, Miel could feel his fingers tremble slightly.

Away from the light of the house, there was

only moonlight to silver James's profile as he stood silhouetted against the glow of the night sky. He appeared to be gathering himself. When he turned to the woman at his side, a great deal of the gentle courtier had returned.

"Miel," he said, an odd strain in his voice, "I've kept you back tonight for a very special reason. I want, finally, to ask you to marry me."

Miel practically stopped breathing. She had been so wrapped up in her quandary over Barth that she had missed the clues entirely. Anyway, she had not expected it like this—so baldly, so swiftly, so soon.

"James!"

"I know it's rather fast, my dear. I had intended to be more proper about it, with wine and a ring truly worthy of you, but something has come up. I've known about the possibility for some time, but the final word didn't come until today. Needless to say, I've been in something of a state."

"Possibility?" asked Miel trying to sort out this tumble of speech.

"Yes. You see, it doesn't really matter about the Gagnons now. Our salvation lies in the store itself. For three generations the city has been growing up all around, and the property now happens to have become a very valuable spot. There's this consortium getting together land for another office tower. The store occupies the front corner of the proposed site, and we're the last holdout."

Vaguely, Miel remembered all the closed doors and mysterious phone calls James had been receiving.

"I don't quite see...."

"Oh, yes you do," he burst out excitedly, gripping her by the hand. "I can sell out for a fortune! Enough to set up two other stores. Maybe even three. The start of that chain I've always longed for. And...you can't guess the crowning irony!"

"What?"

"The outfit I'm dealing with owns the building where Avery Selks is set up. They're willing to trade me the lease as soon as it's up for renewal!"

This last was delivered with a rather inordinate glee, though Miel ignored it as she tried, a little desperately, to take all this in and wondered why she herself had never thought of the enormous value of the property itself. Yet somehow the proud old Italianate building and James seemed fused together in her mind. Tradition was his lifeblood. She somehow couldn't imagine one without the other.

"That's...wonderful, but I thought you loved the store just as it is. And...what has all this to do with your proposal of marriage?"

He sobered completely and set down his drink on the wall.

"Why, everything. This is the biggest opportunity I'll ever see in my life. Yet I won't do it—I wouldn't be able to do it—without you."

"Me?"

He had turned his back to the moon so that

his face was shadowed, but even so, Miel could see the lines and planes becoming taut.

"Miel, even with all the money from the sale, both you and I know the risks involved. And the work. It's staggering. Until a year and a half ago I always worked with mother. I have to have someone beside me, Miel. I couldn't... there's just no way I could do it alone. I want that person to be you."

Miel stood speechless, forgetting about the drink in her hand, so James took it from her and set it on the wall beside his own. When nothing but the whisper of leaves answered him, he plunged on headlong.

"Naturally, I'd make you a full partner, Miel. Legally. Half of everything—the new stores, the stock, all the property—would be yours, even to your name beside my own on the door. As my wife, you could have no less—I'd see to that. As my partner, you'd certainly earn it. What do you say?"

It was a staggeringly generous offer that alone, if the new chain took hold, would make her a wealthy woman in her own right. And in the field of business, it posed a tremendously challenging opportunity.

The air lay heavy with the scent of dense greenery, and for a moment Miel was besieged by the memory of Barth's nearness, Barth's kiss. Yet it wasn't Barth beside her, it was James, expecting her to say yes immediately.

"Frankly," she managed, "I'm...flabber-gasted."

And thankful for the night, which veiled her own confusion—and the dismay that would surely show on James's face if she didn't accept at once. James did not move, and something caught in Miel's throat.

Why don't you say you want me because you love me and you can't live without me! Why don't you simply sweep me up into your arms and. . . .

Instant remorse curbed the rest. James was looking at her so earnestly in the moonlight, his head inclined in that inimitable manner of his, his blind need reaching out to her. Her heart made her realize that James had never before exposed the core of himself to her or to anyone the way he was doing now.

She swallowed hard as another realization came to her with the impact of a grenade. James was afraid! Secretly but dreadfully terrified by the magnitude of the opportunity that had suddenly leaped into his lap. An opportunity that would end up the supreme test of his courage and skill as a businessman. If he should take it and fail—for in the clothing business, failure was always but a breath away from glittering success—James as a person, as a man, would be completely shattered.

James, for all his competence and quiet command, was simply unused to being on his own. All his adult life he worked with Lillian at his shoulder. Upon her death, Miel had been promoted to a position of responsibility and power almost equal to his own. His proposal was the final step, taking her into full partnership with him. With her at his side, sharing decisions and worries and work, he would forge ahead with all the self-confidence in the world.

But without her....

One look at the tightness of his body told her that if she refused, he would not take the opportunity. He would send the developers elsewhere, hang on to the present store in its increasingly unfashionable location and slowly, gallantly, go straight down the tube.

An immense tide of loyalty nearly overwhelmed her. Everything she was she owed to James. Surely her life was here, her place at his side. Anything he asked of her she would gladly do. Firmly she slid her own warm fingers over his and closed her eyes. She could not, would not, ever let him down.

"James, I...I don't...."

The words, the acceptance that teetered on the tip of her tongue refused to take any other form than a tiny, painful gasp. Instantly, she felt James stiffen and she fought wildly, grimly, to gain control of herself, for she felt she would protect with her heart's blood the naked vulnerability James had revealed at such cost.

"I...it's just that it's such a surprise. I'm really too stunned to say anything yet."

Oh God, was this the best she could do? How could she ever forget the tremor, so swiftly repressed, of pain and surprise that passed through his body into hers. Hesitating was probably the last thing he thought her capable of, though he bravely masked the hurt on his face.

"Of course, of course, Miel. It's a very big decision, and selfish of me to want an answer on the spot. Get some rest and do your thinking. I'll be counting the hours."

He was about to let her go, but on impulse Miel pulled him close and kissed him, her mouth quivering with all the tender things she could not say. His lips were wooden, and in a moment, she drew herself away, a cold sense of failure in the pit of her stomach. As her hands fell away, James caught her.

"Miel?"

"Yes?"

"I...have to know as soon as possible. I mean—" he ducked his head so plaintively Miel could have cried "—the lawyers have put a limit on the offer. If I don't make up my mind by the end of the month, they'll cancel out and start putting together a new package across the street."

"Oh, that it should come to this," Miel breathed, and fled up the lawn and through the echoing loneliness of the house to the refuge of her car.

CHAPTER FIFTEEN

"Good morning, Miel."

James's greeting the next day sounded perfectly ordinary. Only the eager tilt of his head and the utter stillness of his body gave away the intensity of his expectation. Actually, it had taken all the fortitude Miel could muster to step into that corridor after a night of tossing and turning. Her mind had been alternately reeling from James's offer and tormented by the image of Barth sweeping off with Cora—though she tried to tell herself *that* particular jealousy was quite unworthy.

"Morning," she tossed back with awkward lightness, pausing at his office door. She was not prepared in the least for the way James looked—gaunt and weary, as if every single worry since that dreadful scene with Avery Selks had decided to take up residence in his eyes.

This project is terribly important to him, Miel thought with a thump in her chest. It's his whole life.

She met his glance bravely and bore the painful disappointment spreading across his face at her silence. Deep in her heart she knew what she must sooner or later do, even though the long dark hours had not managed to give her the right words to frame her acquiescence.

"Miel?"

She was just walking to her own office. Now she stopped, the back of her neck going tight.

"Yes, James?"

"You. . .haven't heard anything from Hildy, have you?"

"No. Not yet." She expelled a long sigh. This was the first time James had spoken of the young woman. Miel thought it was a good sign, though his voice labored awkwardly with the effort. Then she glanced over her shoulder and was shocked by the emptiness in his look. "Oh, don't worry. We'll find out about her when she's darned good and ready."

He nodded, staring past Miel, then down at the papers on his desk, as if somehow suddenly disoriented. Back behind her own desk, Miel sat motionless, looking down at her fingers in her lap. File folders were stacked on either side of her, yet thoughts of work seemed impossible. Outside, the maple chattered and rustled.

She was saved from a dismal morning by the appearance of Allison, bearing a large sheaf of papers.

"These papers ending the yacht lease contract are to go down to Mr. Tramande at the harbor. James said he wanted it all cleared away as soon as possible. Maybe I should put them in a taxi."

She looked uncertainly at Miel, for until then there had always been somebody or other, who could take messages, going to and from the

Yancy. Miel suffered a little twinge of fear at the mention of the yacht. Barth would be down there, and sooner or later he must be confronted. Calmly, perhaps as atonement for her cowardice with James, she put out her hand for the envelopes.

"I'll take them, Allison. I have a few errands around town today anyway."

The harbor was bright and restless, so bright it hurt the eyes. A smart, hot wind snapped all the leaves of the young willows in one direction and tossed little flecks of spume even from the waves close to Harbourfront. All of the boats tied up in the slip heaved and rocked like a flock of trapped water creatures eager to be away to sea.

Barth was perched cross-legged on the forepeak, cleaning the flukes of the kedge anchor. So heart-stoppingly handsome he looked in his old ragged cutoffs and oil-spotted T-shirt that Miel felt her breath knotting thickly in her chest. Somehow she found the courage to pad along the catwalk and approach him.

Some amazing telepathy warned him. He dropped what he was doing to look up before she was even halfway there. As he caught sight of her, sudden pleasure blazed across his face and he leaped up.

"Miel! It's about time!"

He sprang forward, extending one brown arm to help her on board. Instinctively Miel avoided it, for she knew the havoc his mere touch could wreak. She also avoided his eyes as she handed him the packet of papers she had brought from the store.

"Here. Now that the Gagnon thing has fallen through, James would like these signed and out of the way as soon as possible."

The papers remained in midair. Miel was forced to look up and see again that cloud of dark puzzlement descend upon Barth's face as it had at the party. Now it was mixed with the beginnings of a baffled anger.

"You came down here just to get me to sign some papers?"

"Yes. . . no. I don't know!"

Her voice weakened, her arm dropped, for suddenly she didn't know why she was here—unless some puritanical streak was turning her longing to see him into an excuse for self-flagellation. Almost instantly her mind rejected this as too perverse. No, it had something to do with her own basic honestly, forcing her to show herself, to try, even in the midst of her own confusion, to show him what was happening to her.

"Then I take it you have nothing important to say to me?"

She only lowered her head, stumbling slightly as the rolling motion of the *Yancy* tipped her dangerously toward the sunken cockpit. He still hadn't taken the papers, and now they seemed to burn her hand.

"Please, Barth, I. . . have to get these back to the office."

"I see. To James!" he said with swift cold meaning. Snatching the forms and the accompanying pen, he scrawled his signature in violently slashing strokes, thus severing all connection between Crome's and the *Yancy* forever. He thrust them back and they crumpled slightly.

"Don't be hateful, Barth."

"Damn it!" The jerk of his body actually caused the *Yancy* to shudder. "How can I be otherwise when after all we've had together I see you preferring that man's company to mine!"

His good nature, his control had evaporated in this temper flash. Miel let out a tiny gasp. A white, strained look crept over her.

"A lot of things have been happening between James and me."

"Like that long private evening last night after the guests had left?"

"That's a low blow!" Briefly, she lashed back, then her voice lowered and took on a rather pained tone of confession. "Last night was very special. You see, James made a proposal of marriage."

Barth's eyes widened, then narrowed, scanning her fiercely. His fist closed round a stay as the *Yancy* dipped toward the harbor. It took only a moment for him to register perfect, incredulous comprehension.

"You're actually considering it, aren't you?"

Again, she could not look at him. One part of her longed to cry out to him, fling herself into the strong circle of his arms. Another part drew back, bound by well-nigh unbreakable bonds of loyalty and gratitude and affection for James.

"He has a chance to sell the Bloor Street property for a huge amount of money. He—we—could open up a chain. It's been a dream of his all his life. He's offered me full partnership.''

Two children sitting on the concrete were making a game of holding up tidbits for the gulls to snatch. The birds were thick as confetti and dreadfully raucous, but not even this din could impinge on the labored silence that fell between the pair on the *Yancy*. Slowly Miel made herself look—and found Barth staring at her, a kind of horror in his eyes, as if he supposed that she was doing it for the wealth that James was offering her.

"He needs me, Barth,'' she cried out. "He needs me so much. He really. . . won't be able to make it on his own.''

Before her very eyes, the lines deepened ominously at the corners of his mouth. The horror in his glance fell away and was replaced by something masklike. *Say you need me,* Miel pleaded silently and from the heart. *Say you need me, too!*

But whatever had been on the tip of his tongue evaporated with the speed of storm clouds. He straightened in an oddly painful manner, as if all his joints had turned stiff and old. Grimly somber, his gaze bored into her.

"Then I was sadly mistaken that time about your enthusiasm for the *Yancy* and the sea.'' His tone implied that she was but a creature of the moment, swayed by whatever influence happened to be the strongest at the time.

"Barth, no! I do care. Very much. But. . . my

whole life is here. You've got to understand. Before James, I was nothing!''

"Before James, you were a bright, spunky, beautiful thing. And you'll stay that way now with or without your employer."

"But, James. . . ."

"James, nothing! Is being propped up by him all you can think about? One of these days you're going to have to grow up and learn to stand on your own two feet!"

The very cords of his neck stood out now and Miel, in dismay, backed toward the handropes. She was seeing yet another side of Barth—a hard man who made hard decisions and despised anyone who didn't. Now he was impatient and angry with her.

"Barth, I really don't think all this is fair!"

She was hugging the papers to her chest as if to protect herself. Her hazel eyes had gone so wide and dark Barth had to look away to avoid losing all control. He seemed to be drawing strength from the sunlight beating down upon him, cooling himself in the breeze that plucked open the collar of Miel's soft blue cotton blouse. When he looked at her again, his features were creased with a sadness and a sort of deep disappointment in her.

"All I'm saying, Miel, is that this is real life, and very often real life isn't fair. Sooner or later you have to make up your mind about who you are and what sort of future you want to choose. And make sure you mean it, because once you've passed the fork in the road, that's it.

Take control of your own life or play it safe—
it's entirely up to you, Miel. Only—'' the old
ominous note returned ''—I'd suggest you
decide soon. I've done the best I can. And a
sailor can only struggle so much against an op-
posing tide.''

Anguish tore cruelly, bitterly through her.

''Barth. . . I just don't know. . . .''

''Do you think any of us know? Do you think
it's something easy, with guarantees written in
gold? Nothing's like that, Miel. You choose
your partners and take the consequences. And
even when mistakes are made, there may be no
going back!''

Unaware, she had stepped toward him the
merest fraction and his hands shot out to grip
her shoulders. The next second he was kissing
her—but it was not a tender kiss. It was chill,
frightening and savage. There was anger in him,
a muffled fury that was already tearing them
apart. She had only an instant to glimpse the
black violence of his gaze before he thrust her
abruptly from him, turned on his heel and
vanished deep inside the cabin of the *Yancy*,
leaving Miel utterly alone on deck.

Fear welled up in her—a sudden, awesome
understanding of just what she would lose if she
stayed behind with James. Longing possessed
her body. Every instinct pounded at her to rush
into the salon after Barth and throw herself into
his arms. She suffered a humiliating desire to
plead and explain, which she fought grimly. He
had told her she must make up her own mind,

weigh the risk of what he felt for her against what she felt for him. He did need her. Oh yes, in his own way, even the strength of his anger was proof of that. But could he possibly need her in the same deep, totally essential way James did? Could he?

James. Clinging to the thought of him, she stepped from the deck of the *Yancy* and made her way to the concrete wall which, underwater, was fringed with bright green weed. The moment she stood on solid earth the yacht became a separate entity to her, endowed, somehow, with a life of its own. In the windy harbor, it plunged and tugged impatiently at its mooring, saying, perhaps in the only way a boat could, that it was tired of this tame idleness and longed for the tumbling challenge of the ocean once more.

And to Miel, the invitation of the slim white bow, the pull of the wanderlust was also excruciating. She shut her eyes against it, the siren song singing wildly to her, threatening to obliterate all else—especially the obstacles!

But equal to the longing came the fear. Barth had shown her treasures, but they lay at the bottom of an enormous cliff where the sea boiled furiously. To reach them she must dive fearlessly off, straight into the empty air and the cold, foam-lashed water, leaping purely for the thrill of hearing the wind whistling in her ears all the way down.

Desperately as she wanted Barth, Miel reeled from a dizzying thud of fright, exactly as if she had found herself exposed at the top of a great height with not so much as a thread between herself and the terrifying drop.

It would take courage, so much courage! Before Crome's, she had been peeling vegetables. Her whole identity, her painfully won professional pride, were all bound up in the store. Without those, what would she be? A passenger on somebody else's boat? A truant on a giddy holiday? And if that holiday should end, she didn't even have a high-school diploma.

Trembling, Miel backed away, for the *Yancy*, lovely as it was, seemed suddenly a very tiny and fragile shell in which to entrust her future. No. She turned very slowly and headed back to James.

CHAPTER SIXTEEN

NUMBERS. STOCK NUMBERS, INVOICE NUMBERS, wholesale, markup, markdown, preseason discount, sales tax, inventory numbers—all as familiar to Miel as the lines in her palm. Yet these numbers swam before her eyes, either refusing to make sense or presenting themselves in rows of such unutterable tedium that she wanted to fling her desk calculator clear across the room. She had worked through her lunch, very relieved that James hadn't come in to see her or to invite her out. He was restless, she knew, for she recognized his step a number of times in the corridor, either on his way to the coffee machine or simply pacing. Sometimes, the footsteps had paused outside her door, and Miel held her breath. Invariably, they faded away. After her morning scene with Barth, Miel couldn't have hidden her turbulent emotions.

The changed atmosphere didn't help either. Owing to a new nervousness Allison dropped pencils, and the office staff was depressingly silent. On the sales floors, Miel had already scented doom. Twice she had seen the salespeople, highly professional though they were, pursue shoppers just a little too eagerly. The would-be customers, sensing that unflattering hint of desperation, had put down the dresses they were looking at and politely fled.

And of course Miel knew the other reason for the general glumness—Hildy was not there. Miel had not realized until that very day how much the store had taken the unpredictable pixie to its heart. A number of times she caught herself listening for that delicious chime of laughter that had brought so much brightness to the place, that dancing step, that deceptively meandering chatter, which was always aimed at some clever, unexpected end. All of them missed the scandalous flashes of color against the civilized grays and tans of the decor. All of them wondered unhappily how Hildy was surviving her disastrous dismissal.

Miel worried, too, until late in the afternoon when the sight of yet another piece of paper threatened to give her a headache. She dialed Hildy's number for the umpteenth time and, for the umpteenth time, listened to the hollow, unanswered rings. Where *was* Hildy anyway? Miel crumpled an order form without even know it. Her heart went out to Hildy, but there wasn't a thing she could do to help until Hildy chose to make her whereabouts known.

Twice again the footsteps outside echoed, but they were definitely headed in the direction of Hildy's back-hall office. Miel was suddenly reminded of the way James had gotten into the habit of wandering down to Hildy's office for a break. More often than not, he would beam at her in proud bemusement as she happily selected one after another from her hodge podge of sketches to show him. Yes, James, too, had grown much more attached to Hildy than he had recognized, and now he bore very very heavily the responsibility for her dismissal. If only he weren't so rigidly old-fashioned in his ideas of honor and honesty. But even as she shook her head at the futility of his notions in today's dog-eat-dog business world, she knew she could not care for him half so much were he any other way.

The columns of numbers wavered before her eyes again and she lost track. She was supposed to be making a decision about percentages of color ranges to order in the lingerie lines. The project, something she could usually complete in an hour, now seemed as remote and incomprehensible to her as craters on the moon. She was staring moodily into the heart of the maple when a low rap at the door ushered in Jenny with yet another handful of invoices and a pair of trousers trailing from her arm.

"These are from the Breton shipment, Miel. They've all got wide cuffs instead of the narrow cuffs you ordered. I just thought I better let you see them before I send them back. They're kind of cute just as they are. I wondered if maybe we should keep them."

Jolted out of her thoughts and already strung out on nervous tension for the day, Miel lifted the pants and looked at them. The little factory had done a beautiful job, but the cuffs were not in the style ordered. For a moment, and for the first time since she had begun to work at Crome's, she could not visualize what the original style was supposed to have been.

"Oh, I don't know," she snapped. "Does it really matter? Do what you think best."

Only when she noticed Jenny looking at her with a sharply furrowed brow did Miel realize how irritable and dismissing she had sounded, as if what was on the racks at Crome's mattered not at all. Immediately she apologized, telling Jenny she might as well keep this shipment because the style in hand was quite as chic as the alternative.

As Jenny left, Miel's eyes slid to her watch. Four o'clock. Restlessness, accumulated nerves and chagrin at her latest faux pas made her scoop all her papers into the bottom drawer of her desk and grab her briefcase. She was deliberately avoiding James and accomplishing nothing here. She might as well go home.

In the parking lot, she revved her car, then stopped, deterred by the prospect of her own bleakly empty apartment. On impulse, she turned instead toward the Annex, a midcity section of stately old houses now converted mostly to airy apartments, where Hildy lived. Once before she had driven past Hildy's home, but the windows had been dark. Edging along Bloor Street to a place where the high-fashion shops gave way to a section of crowded Hungarian restaurants and Italian fruit stores, she plunged into a side street lined with immense maples and pillared porches from an earlier, more tranquil era. Remembering her fruitless phone calls, Miel was prepared to glide disappointedly past Hildy's apartment. One shrewd glance made her slam on the brakes and pull to the curb. The drawn blinds obscured any activity, but one of the windows was raised to let in the warm summer air. Hildy just had to be there.

She knocked twice and received no answer. Drawing her brows together, Miel hammered even louder.

"Hildy, it's me."

The silence inside continued.

"Hildy, I'm not going to leave, so you might as well just open up now."

More silence, then hesitant steps, so faint they might have been dry leaves skittering across the floor. The door opened a crack, and a small pointed face appeared in the space allowed by the chain. Miel swallowed a gasp at how bleak a face it was.

"I thought I'd come by and see how you were. There's been no answer on your phone."

Wordlessly, almost listlessly, Hildy released the chain so that the door swung open of its own accord. Without waiting to be invited, Miel stepped in and looked around. The apartment, which Miel had never visited before, was exactly what one would expect of Hildy. Perched on the top floor under a collection of tilting ceilings and pointed gables, the space was an exuberant grotto stuffed with Chinese paper kites, old glass bottles, gigantic cushions piled beneath hanging ferns and strings of camel bells on loops of red and yellow wool. Ivy, green and vital, covered nearly the whole of one window. Nearby stood an amazing fabric sculpture, which turned out to be simply Hildy's way of storing scarves.

Yet for all the cleverness there was a definite and depressingly immediate sense that the spirit had flown out of the place. The plants drooped for lack of watering, clothes lay where they had dropped, cups and glasses—it looked as if no plate for food had been used—sat stained and neglected on the kitchen counter.

The most shocking change, however, was in Hildy herself. Wan and thin, dressed in only a faded pink shift, Hildy resembled nothing so much as a once-beautiful tropical bird shorn of its plumage. The shift emphasized the delicacy of her bones, her cheeks were drained of color, even her very curls hung flat and limp.

"Hildy, you look awful!" Miel sputtered in a burst of tactlessness she right away regretted. Hildy slumped down in a fuschia bean-bag chair and said nothing. Miel sped over and bent beside her. Instead of merely suffering from unemployment, Hildy looked as if her best friend had died. "Come on, Hildy, if it's something worse than just being fired, you can tell me."

This seemed to prick the bubble of vacant depression. The young woman looked up quickly.

"I've lost my professional reputation, Miel," she said with haste. "I'm ruined just starting out. Who'll take me on when word gets around about Crome's?''

Ah, now Miel thought she was recognizing the dark side of Hildy's passionate and impulsive nature. The tenacity that made her brilliant could also dwell on a passing disaster with such doggedness as to wear her spirit thin. Miel began to feel older and vastly more experienced.

"Oh, don't be silly, Hildy. What happened was just...unfortunate. Everyone knows how talented you are. Why, you'd get another job in a minute if you made up your mind to look for one.''

"But I don't want to look for one,'' Hildy declared with enormous glumness. "I don't want to work anywhere else but at Crome's.''

To that, Miel had no answer. They both knew the impossibility of James's ever again letting her go back to her drawing board. Hildy hugged a small cushion, then tossed it down again in exasperation.

"Oh, drat it all, Miel, the thing that really hurts is being made to look so...so rotten in James's eyes. He has that way about him, you know. All of a sudden it starts to seem the most awful thing in the world to have disappointed him.''

Miel knew only too well. It was the secret of James's power. He naturally expected the very best from everyone and, as a consequence, one felt just dreadful whenever one fell short of his sterling standards.

"And then giving up the Gagnon line," Hildy burst out, growing increasingly warm to the topic. "That was such a futile, futile thing to do. He'll lose all those new customers we've just won over, and it'll be ten times as hard to get them back. The store just can't afford those kinds of losses. It's commercial suicide."

So that was part of it—her fear for what would happen to the business, even though this was the one problem, at least, that Hildy did *not* have to worry about. Miel hesitated, weighing Hildy's comfort against James's confidence, then decided to tell Hildy about the consortium's offer for the property. Hildy couldn't have been more astonished if she had just stumbled into a high-voltage wire.

"But . . . he's so attached to the store just as it is. Is he going to take it?"

Miel examined her knuckles carefully, trying to think how to frame an answer.

"Miel, *is he*?" Hildy demanded, looking feverish to know.

"It . . . depends."

"On what, for goodness' sake?"

This was a matter somewhat deeper than Miel was willing to go into. She shifted uncomfortably in the creaky little rocking chair she had taken and shrugged slightly, as if the outcome was quite beyond her. Tipping the chair back slightly, she became increasingly and uneasily aware that Hildy had focused every scrap of her attention on her and that those emerald, thickly

fringed eyes were burning into her. To her mor-
tification, Miel felt a deep hot flush creeping up
her nape.

"It depends on you, doesn't it?" Hildy cried.
"James would never take on something so
gigantic without splitting the weight with someone he could really rely on."

How had she ever expected to avoid the keen-
ness of Hildy's perceptions? Almost in fascination, she watched Hildy's eyes widen into huge
pools and her cheeks become dotted with color
as the woman reached the ultimate, inevitable
conclusion.

"James has asked you to marry him!"

"Yes," Miel replied simply, surprised she
could be relieved that someone, even someone
as distraught as Hildy, could at last share the
knowledge.

"And you're going to, of course."

"I . . . haven't said anything to him yet."

Miel had to lower her eyes with this admission
and this was just as well, for she missed the
waxen pallor that crept over the small face and
the tiny hands that folded into fists at her
sides—all signs of some terrible inner struggle.
When Miel did look up again, she found Hildy
in control of herself, so much in control that
some of her former vivacity seemed to have
returned, although this time it was with a fierce
rather than a flickering flame.

"You must marry him, Miel," she said with
slow, heavy force. "You must say yes at once.

Offers from consortiums don't stand around forever. And if he lets this slip through his fingers...well, that'll be the end.''

The unspoken truth between them was that through the offer Crome's might win untold prosperity. If the offer lapsed, the store might very well go under—leaving James in bewildered ruin.

"I have to think, Hildy. I know I'll say yes finally, but...I have to think.''

Confusion was obvious in the furrows of Miel's forehead and the hunch of her strong, supple, normally graceful body. Besides, Hildy's eyes silently told her what she thought of any woman who had to think over a proposal from such a generous, gentle man. In a moment, Hildy lit into her vehemently.

"It's that sailor, isn't it? Barth Tramande.'' And at Miel's wince, she threw back her dark mass of hair with a groan. "It's all my fault. I dreamed up that yacht campaign and threw the two of you together. I never dreamed I might be... messing up everything for James.''

THREE DAYS passed, each more agonizing for Miel than the one before. She had to endure not only James's beseeching, increasingly hurt looks, but Hildy's promptings too, for Hildy called her now, though not on the office phone, making it abundantly clear that she would think Miel utterly mad if she rejected James.

"This delay is foolish, Miel,'' she would say in that tight, halting, but chillingly determined tone her voice seemed to have acquired these days. "I can't understand why you're so reluctant."

Miel couldn't understand either. Finally, during the last call, Hildy had said ominously that, "Something has to be done!"

Yet for some reason Miel refused to voice what she had in fact made up her mind and heart to do. The final words rose a dozen times a day and always stuck at the back of her throat as if encountering some invisible barrier. She existed in a state of nerves, forgetting to finish her makeup properly, or dropping correspondence on the floor, or simply staring out at the patch of blue sky she could see above the maple until the phone or the door roused her from her reverie. She cared for James with all her heart. She *loved* him. They would have a good life together. She kept these declarations at the forefront of her mind and never once, in the darkest part of the smallest hour of the morning, did she allow herself to think of the beautiful white yacht in the harbor, bobbing and waiting.

What she also wished she could forget were the everyday details of running the store. Rather than finding escape in work, she found it a steadily increased strain that sometimes drove her to pace with terrifying energy or sit blankly making paper clips into a chain. Today, inevitably, just as she was forcing herself to concentrate, there came a rap at the door. A rather uncertain one, which caused Miel to look up and see Muriel from accounting standing there, an official-looking envelope in her hand.

"I have some checks here, Miel. I was instructed to make them out to you."

"Me? What are they?"

Wordlessly, Muriel handed over the envelope and stood waiting while Miel riffled through the contents. Miel saw at once that this was the money Crome's was paying to Barth both for his personal modeling fees and for the lease of the yacht. But the checks were not made out to Barth. They were made out to Operation Seawatch, care of herself. She swallowed hard, knowing that Barth was sending her a message that could not be mistaken. Soon, very soon, she must declare her mind.

"Thanks, Muriel," she managed. "I'll take care of this."

Muriel, who was very thin in her cotton batiste and who had worked very earnestly even before the Seascape disaster, now hung back.

"They're wondering in my department whether there's any new foreign line to replace the...uh, Gagnons."

The remark was just a little too awkwardly casual and Miel read in the woman's eyes the entire nervousness of the staff. In this rock-solid three-generation establishment, they all knew very well they were in danger of being on the unemployment line. Miel laid the envelope on her desk and let out a long long breath. Though Muriel couldn't have known her timid inquiry broke, at last, through the impotence that had gripped Miel since James's proposal. She must make a choice. Too many other people stood to suffer because of her indecision.

"We'll let you know, Muriel, as soon as we can."

As the door closed behind her visitor, Miel stood up, pacing restlessly. Her stomach grew tight as a clenched fist and she began to shake. She knew what had been keeping her frozen these last days—it was fear, a terrible fear of having to look into herself, of having to find the truth, of having to experience the codes she lived by shift and dissolve.

I must face it. Whatever it is, I must face it now!

She looked around the spacious office. An even larger one would be hers. Whole stores for her to command. Decisions involving dizzying sums of money handled in equal partnership. That large, gracious gray stone mansion. Even a car with a chauffeur, should she so desire. The way was open to every material thing a woman could want, wrapped in all the kindness, respect and gratitude that James could give. The pinnacle achieved of her long struggle out of Bay Point. Why then had she not run straight to James that evening in the garden?

Because you can't, said the little voice she had been smothering with all her might since the cocktail party. *It isn't James you want. It's Barth Tramande!*

The shock rocked her and almost rumbled with the frightening clamor of her carefully constructed world's cracking about her ears. Frantically, she backtracked, trying to hold up the crumbling walls.

"James needs me," she whispered. "James

wants me. He can't possibly survive without me. All his wonderful dreams, all those people depending on him for their jobs...."

It was no use. She could only think of the snap of the mainsail and the long foam-streaked rush of the waves. All she wanted was to stand barefoot on the deck with Barth beside her. The call in her blood was so strong that she sank down in her chair and put her hands over her face. This was love—not the compassionate fondness she felt for James, but this awesome longing, this ache, this joy that would never be fully realized until she was folded forever into the haven of Barth's arms. How had she been such a fool as to think she could deny it?

Motionless in the sunlit room, she knew she was by her very thoughts consigning James and the business to probable ruin, yet there was nothing she could do about it. Her best effort, her noblest sacrifice would not now deceive James and she would not dishonor them both by even trying. She must go away to her own true love—but oh how dearly bought was the knowledge of her heart's desire.

She was stirring, moving to get up, when a tap at the door was followed by James, delivering one of their quarterly policy statements. One look at her face made the green folder slide unheeded from his fingers.

"You've decided, haven't you?"

Her skin felt very tight over her cheekbones as she nodded. Even before she spoke, her eyes conveyed the message.

"I . . . can't marry you, James. I'm so sorry."

Her blood seemed to change to ice water and she felt all weak and cold. James simply stared. When she wobbled visibly, he leaped forward.

"Miel!"

His cry was half plea, half shock and Miel stepped hastily back out of reach of his extended hands. She faced him with wide and stricken eyes. If he tried to change her mind, she would simply die!

"I love somebody else. I didn't realize how much until just now. I can't help it."

His hands dropped to his sides in a clumsy, blundering motion. Like an automaton, James spun and walked over to the window that looked out over the roof garden of the Scandinavian restaurant next door. He stood staring blankly, from time to time reaching to push back a non-existent wisp of hair. Watching him, Miel was overcome by compassion. Softly, she went to him and laid her fingers upon his shoulder.

"I won't blame you if you hate me. I tried so hard to be what you wanted but I'm just a different kind of person. I just—" she shook her head "—it wouldn't work for us. It couldn't. Not . . . now."

He remained motionless as stone under her touch, making Miel wonder just how deep the wound had gone. Sweet James who had waited all these years with such decorum and ritual, to whom giving himself was such a serious matter. Aching for him, Miel wished everything could have happened in some totally different way.

The silence lengthened, growing heavier and heavier, yet when James finally did shift around to face Miel, he appeared stunned rather than crushed—and he had recovered his customary gallantry.

"It's Barth Tramande, isn't it?" he asked in a low, questioning voice.

Mutely, Miel nodded. James lifted her hand and held it in his own. Never had his touch been so gentle and so tender.

"If you love him, my dear, then of course you must go to him. Don't mind about me or the store. We shall make our own way regardless."

And she saw from the look in his eyes that the offer from the consortium was in grave danger already. She drew in a breath, about to plead with him to take his future anyway, but he touched a finger softly to her lips. Truly, there was nothing more for them to say. They had reached the fork in the road. They must each take a different path, no matter what the consequences.

His fingers moved from her mouth to the side of her cheek in a gesture of quiet, unchangeable farewell.

"Go on. He's in the harbor waiting. Hurry before I say something maudlin and spoil this very special moment."

Completely unable to speak because of the lump in her throat, Miel kissed him and hugged him one last time and sped from the building, barely even stopping to pick up her handbag.

CHAPTER SEVENTEEN

How GAY AND VITAL she suddenly felt. What a mad, headlong drive down to the harbor. She slipped the car into one of the precious Harbourfront parking spaces and dashed, full of joyous anticipation, toward the slip where the white form of the *Yancy* would be waiting to bear her away. So naturally she let out a low, chagrined cry when she found the familiar mooring occupied by a heavy-looking cabin cruiser with an American couple aboard. In answer to Miel's queries, they shrugged kindly but blankly.

"Haven't seen any such boat. This spot was empty so we had it assigned to us when we came in. Better go ask at the office."

Miel's pulse began to thud erratically. Of course she couldn't expect the *Yancy* to be sitting there every single minute. There were a hundred places Barth could have taken it out for a spin.

But if he had, why would he have given up his precious mooring place in the slip?

Climbing the concrete wall, she peered anxiously out across the water, for the first time noticing how hot and hazy the day was, how much it would tempt one to escape by sail—as the flock of boats in the harbor readily attested. Not one of the nautical shapes was the pale silhouette of the *Yancy*. Where was he?

For a while, Miel just stood there staring, her heart stuttering into a slow, muffled drumbeat as she tried to ignore what the presence of the cabin cruiser was saying. Then, struggling with a dark premonition, she approached the small office that looked after moorings.

"The *Yancy*," she asked. "Where is it?"

A squat man with mottles on the back of his hands thumbed through some pages and then thumbed his lip.

"Checked out for the Seaway this morning. Fellow laid in a lot of stores and seemed in a hurry. Him—" a fat-lipped smile curled across the man's face "—and that redheaded woman who got on right behind him."

Redheaded woman? Miel blinked and looked uncomprehending. Then something happened to the backs of her knees.

Cora!

The name, the realization was a mean, cold blow to the stomach, numbing Miel, staggering her, jarring her powers of reason and leaving her barely the strength to make it to the back of the marine store, where she limply sat on a crude lump of concrete.

A blowing napkin on the ground faded in and out of focus as it fluttered to disintegration in the harbor water. A gull's cry, making a thin, agonized needle of sound, barely penetrated the roar mounting dully in Miel's ears. All her years of work and struggle, all her fierce self-discipline had come to nothing. The wound deep in her heart that she had imagined stitched so firmly over by time and maturity ripped wide open, spilling again the ancient pain—the pain of being totally abandoned.

Barth was gone. Barth and Cora Fowler. He was nothing more than a raffish womanizer after all.

Had it been any other man on earth, Miel could have coped. But this was Barth, the passion of her youth, the man to whom she had just irrevocably committed her heart. She closed her eyes. Instantly, without will, she was transported back, back to Bay Point, back to the blackness of that long night after she had been thrown off the *Yancy*. All of the misery surged over her, forcing her to relive the despair as if it had never left. With slow, horrifying vividness, she could recall the cheap, grainy weave of her pillowcase as it ground into her cheek, the heartless, hollow tick of her big old alarm clock accompanying her sobs.

"He promised to be here for me," she whispered haltingly, making a passing child stare, then scuttle to his mother. "He promised! And now he didn't even wait to find out if I wanted to come for sure!"

Her mind had plunged into a deep shock, able only to turn over and over again, impossible as it seemed, that for a second time Barth had run out and left her on the shore.

At first she sat motionless, uncaring that her plum-colored cotton pantsuit had begun to stick to her in the heat, unaware that her slack mouth and slumped shoulders were making her an object of comment among the patrons on the outdoor deck of a restaurant a few yards away. Finally, when she began slightly to rock back and forth in the age-old attitude of a woman keening, a waiter stepped quietly down the weathered steps.

"Are you all right, ma'am? It's terribly hot out here in the sun. Perhaps a glass of water?"

Her head jerked around, her eyes flew wide. A strange man was bent forward saying something to her, something she was unable to understand because mere words just broke into fragments in her mind.

"Ma'am?"

"No. Go away. I don't want anything. I don't want...anything ever again from any man!"

Getting up, she stumbled away, this time to the shady side of the building where she found relief for a moment from the beating of the sun upon her head—but not from the beating of the pain inside her. Soon it would be unbearable unless she could find something to distract herself.

For several minutes, she stood there confused and disoriented. Nearby, foraging ducks tipped themselves up, to expose feathery white bottoms. Then instinct took over. Blindly, she began to walk quickly toward the two sailing dinghies still kept ready for the use of the advertising staff. Sailing had been the one solace of

her young days. Now she turned to it with
natural need. Oblivious to her immaculate business outfit, she untied the painter and pushed
herself out onto the oil-smooth water of the harbor.

The air was muggy and almost dead calm,
hardly a breath to flutter the sail. Miel didn't
care. She worked the tiller a bit, and that got her
out far enough so that the boat drifted slug-
gishly away from the pitted concrete edging the
slip.

As she maneuvered farther into open water,
the close heat of the afternoon, which could
make Toronto like a steam bath in summer,
curled around her like a heavy hand. The haze
was slowly turning the sun to a white burning
smudge, and the water, a murky, glassy olive,
seemed to lack the energy even to dimple. The
ducks gathered into small flotillas under over-
hanging willows, and the pleasure parties on the
larger yachts began to abandon the blistering
decks in favor of cooler pleasures below.

Hauling up the jib and then the mainsail, Miel
ignored the other becalmed sailboats dotting the
water. After a few moments, she managed to get
away far enough to be in the path of any breeze
should it choose to come. The sails hung creased
and discouraged, and the city skyscrapers
bunched behind her like a solemn, monstrous
tribe, all wanting to put their feet into the water.

Soon her efforts were rewarded. The sail bellied out just enough to set the dinghy into a hint
of a glide. At such slow speed, there could be lit-

tle maneuverability, though Miel was luckily clear of the ferry paths and the spot where the little seaplanes put down like noisy gnats upon the water. In the somnolent afternoon, Miel sat perfectly still at the tiller, shoulders drawn up against the seeping misery as she tried to make her mind into a smooth white blank. If only she could sit there forever and never have to go back and face a life made empty and meaningless once again, for Barth was gone, and she could never again return to the store after so dramatically refusing James. She would not be able to stand Hildy's reproaches as the store slid downhill. She would not be able to tolerate the responsibility for her part in the mess. But most of all, she wouldn't be able to bear the pity that would glow so sincerely in James's dear brown eyes.

Under the incandescent sun, she gave herself up to the almost imperceptible dip of the dinghy, while her downcast eyes watched pieces of waterweed float by and, now and then, an iridescent feather shed by a water bird. Opposite her, the CN Tower, dominating the city here as it did from every other angle, rose up like a gigantic, burnished needle, its rings of metal-work glinting hotly, drenched in light. No romantic mist obscured it now. That had all been burned away as effectively as her own ridiculous illusions.

Miel lost track of how long she sat lulled by the intermittent flapping of the sails. She drifted nearer to the island, where a pair of energetic canoeists could be seen hugging the shore in a yellow canoe. Away to her left the triangular Royal Bank Plaza shone like molten gold, just as designed, for several hundred ounces of the precious metal itself were said to have been applied to those sheer cliffs of glass. Then suddenly a small puff of wind sent the dinghy into an almost startled lurch as the water all around became a living skin of ripples. Automatically, Miel gripped the tiller in order to take advantage. The sail quickly sagged, but within a few minutes filled out again with a second gust, which propelled the boat quite vigorously forward.

Now she was out of the doldrums. A third gust ensured the progress of the craft as Miel guided it past the narrow channels separating the smaller islands making up the island park. Soon she reached the business end of the harbor, where the commercial docks serviced the many freighters lying with their black blunt bows and white superstructure at each end as spidery cranes leaned over to fill the holds. Rainbow hints of oil upon the water and the dark ships reminded Miel too vividly of her grandfather, so she tacked around in a wide half circle to begin her trip back along the inner edge of the island's green scimitar of trees. This time, because she was beating against the steadily reviving breeze, she had to proceed close-hauled. The effort roused her a little, taking her inevitably toward the Western Gap. The noise and jolt of being buzzed by a descending Cessna determined that she would continue straight ahead in her quest for solitude.

The breeze was quite brisk now. It played through Miel's hair and filled the sail so much the dinghy heeled nicely, even leaving a narrow trail of foam in its wake. Very slightly, Miel's blood stirred and she grasped for the old comfort of sailing. Skimming past the low square airport building, crossing the country's shortest ferry route, which gave access to the island airport, she decided to slip, just for a little while, out into the wide freedom of the lake.

It was a bit of a tricky maneuver to negotiate the longish channel, especially with the prevailing wind—the breeze could now be fairly termed a wind—working against her. Miel succeeded with one object in mind—a long, unimpeded run with the wind at her back around the outside of the island before turning in at the eastern ship channel and taking to safety again.

Inexperienced sailors were always sternly warned not to take something as fragile as a sailing dinghy out of the shelter of the harbor into the rougher, more unpredictable waters of the lake. Races held outside the island's shelter were always under strict supervision. Small boats scurried at the first sign of chop. Such warnings, however, held no strength with Miel, familiar as she was since childhood with the temper of the lake and able to make a boat almost a part of her. Indeed, the dinghy, like a caged thing spotting freedom, burst merrily out past the ranked yachts of the Ontario Place marina and, once more ahead of the wind, began the wide, curving run to the east.

There were water-skiers just off the beach, and the laughing cries of bathers grated on Miel's nerves, their very happiness an affront. She swung the boat very far from them, out so that their figures became distant and sticklike and their sounds reached her not at all. The breeze, which had been strong behind Miel, dropped, then sprang up from a slightly different direction, easing Miel farther from shore until she finally noticed and adjusted to aim at the ship channel. This erratic changeability was not a good sign, but Miel was too absorbed in her own misery to worry. Freed of the necessity to watch for ferries, tour boats and seaplanes, she pushed the dinghy to its limit, unconsciously and ironically proving every advertising claim.

She ended up almost where she expected to end up, yet just as she was working around for the harbor entrance, the wind direction swung sharply, jibbing the sail with such a vicious snap Miel barely avoided being swept overboard by the whipping boom. At once, the dinghy fought the tiller like a balky little mule, refusing to make headway. Beside them, small whitecaps began to edge waves that swelled up in a curious rolling motion that made the lake look as if it were slowly beginning to breathe.

"Okay, okay," Miel said aloud. "Forget the ship channel. We'll go back in the way we came out."

As she tightened the main sheet, the dinghy

was caught by a gust that heeled it over so suddenly Miel was thrown against the gunwale, almost losing her grasp on the tiller. Recovering instantly, she thrust herself onto the opposite side to correct the tipsy angle of the boat and get the sail under control. Then she looked up and gulped at what she saw.

The sky, which had gradually turned to a pale off-white because of the heat haze, was now a livid gunmetal illuminated weirdly from behind by a totally invisible sun. From hiding, their approach obscured by the wall of city office towers, came a march of purple thunderheads boiling ominously upward from a smudgy, darkening horizon. Recognizing the edge of one of those galloping summer storms that are the terror of small-boat sailors, Miel knew she had better run for cover as fast as she could.

In the few minutes it took to note all this, the wind, like the hot, damp breath of an unfriendly giant, rose strongly enough to almost swamp the dinghy in such exposed waters. In the distance, Miel could see the tiny figures of bathers snatching their possessions into bundles and making a run for it across the island to the ferry docks.

She set out at once for the Western Gap, even though each swell was strong enough to lift the little boat up and bring it down on the next with a resounding slap against the hollow hull. A wave struck from astern, sending an arc of spray across Miel's back, but she could not spare even a second to shake herself as she applied all her skill to fighting her way back to safety.

All her skill soon proved quite useless. The wind, though it shifted treacherously and struck in dangerous gusts, came directly off the shore. Try as she might, Miel could not sail into the teeth of it to get back to the harbor entrances. And when she tried running parallel, hoping to slant obliquely aground on one of the beaches, the nose of the dinghy was slowly, inexorably thrust out toward open water so that she ended up running far behind the harbor altogether. Running parallel also put the boat broadside into the path of rapidly increasing waves. It wallowed heavily and took water in the bottom from the crests of swells breaking over the side.

Miel, fully alert now, cursed herself both silently and aloud for being such an idiot as to take the dinghy out of the harbor. If only she'd bothered to look up, she could have guessed what the weather presaged. Now she had the mainsail reefed down to almost nothing, and still the dinghy tipped crazily into the foam every time the wind gave it a cuff. Soon the sails would be too dangerous to use at all.

She kept her parallel course until it became impossible. As it was, she was forced to start bailing, soaked to the thighs and her Italian leather pumps awash in a corner where she had kicked them off to thrust her feet all the better under the hiking straps. Alarm shrilled through her. There was no more time for fooling around on her own. She had better see what she could do about attracting help.

Keeping a tight hold on the tiller, she half

stood, precariously peering about, ready to hail any nearby vessel. There were, however, no vessels within hailing distance. They had all scuttled, under motor power, back to their moorings at the first hint of trouble. Nevertheless, Miel waved her arm and yelled at the top of her lungs, her cries carried away to nothingness by the wind. The thunderheads were piling into awesome battlements overhead, and a twilight kind of gloom was prematurely darkening the day. Yet what frightened Miel the most was the vast, eerie purple-gray arch stretching from horizon to horizon and preceding the clouds. Never in her life had she seen anything like it, though such an arch figured vividly in her grandfather's tale of a three-day killer storm that had very nearly taken his life. Chillingly, Miel realized that if she didn't get to shore soon, she wouldn't stand a chance.

A white-topped wave crashed against the side of the dinghy, sending an alarming amount of water sloshing around Miel's feet and making her leap back to her post and begin to bail. At the same time a gust of wind almost laid the dinghy over on its side. Hastily, Miel dropped the bailing can and furled the mainsail completely, knowing that if too much surface was left exposed the boat would be "knocked down," or made to capsize, for sure.

Also, Miel knew that with so much water coming in, she could no longer leave the dinghy abeam to the waves. That left two choices. The first was to turn around and run before the storm directly into the vast heart of the lake—and probably oblivion. The second was to put the bow toward the city and, with a bare mast, try to hold her position until someone came to her rescue.

At this point the jib head tore loose, making the first choice impossible, for she would have needed the jib to keep the head steady if the wind was at her back. Managing to release the other lines so that the jib was whipped overboard and floated away in a pale, churning, waterlogged mass, she wrestled with the tiller until the bow was pointing straight into the teeth of the wind. Between spates of bailing, she concentrated grimly on keeping more lake water from washing in. The only other boat she had seen was a blurred stern vanishing through the channel of the Western Gap.

As the waves grew higher and higher, the dinghy alternately balanced on the crests, then slid precipitously down into the troughs. Since the tiny anchor was useless against such forces, the dinghy, no matter how hard it strove to hold its position, was driven slowly back and back by the head-on wind. Already, the island was beginning to recede into a low mass of whipping trees edged with a froth of white along the shore. She could only pray that someone would notice her before she was out of sight altogether, and refused to remember how she had taken the dinghy out without a word to a single soul.

This, of course, was how accidents happened

on the water. Nor was it surprising that a small
boat should have to battle for its existence within sight of the entire city of Toronto. Miel,
clinging to the tiller and the hiking straps in the
shallow fiberglass hollow of the hull, was too
preoccupied to think much about her situation.
If the wind and cloud proved to be a short
squall, she knew she was good enough to ride it
out and, when conditions calmed, make it back
to shore. But if the disturbance was the prelude
to a once-in-a-decade Great Lakes blow, then
she was in the most terrible trouble of her entire
life.

CHAPTER EIGHTEEN

As THE GIGANTIC STORM ARCH dipped toward the distant lake behind Miel, the daylight was being rapidly blotted out, and that was what worried her as much as anything. Already she was nearing the shipping lanes. If she was out without so much as a light in the pitchy darkness, not only would she not be able to see where the next breaker was coming from, but also she could quite easily be run down by some freighter wallowing through the night.

The wind continued to increase until it stung her ears with its noise. The clouds, charcoal and basalt, roiled and tumbled until the entire sky was covered. The waters of the lake turned greenish black, throwing into intense relief the almost phosphorescent crests of foam that boiled and crashed around the blow of the dinghy. All that could be seen now of the little craft was the occasional wet gleam of the metal mast and the forlorn dull orange of Miel's life jacket.

Sometimes a large wave would send gallons spewing into the interior of the sailboat. Miel then would have to clutch the tiller with one hand and bail frantically with the other, all the while trying wildly to keep her balance as the dinghy was tossed and tipped, making Miel sometimes feel she was up to her armpits in a heaving wilderness without even a boat beneath her. A sharp rain began to fall, stinging like watery shrapnel and promising a deluge later on. The lights of the city were now but a smear on the sullen gray curtain of murk gathering around her. Finally, she had to face it.

No one in the whole world knew she was out there!

Miel gripped the tiller so tightly her knuckles ached, and gallantly thrust her head forward in the wind, refusing to admit that, for her, this looked very much like the end.

In a short time the air had thickened with such gloom that Miel was battling almost blind against large combers that again and again rose up out of nowhere and struck the bow with vicious, impersonal rage. The boat was a cockleshell, a sunny-day toy meant for a playful breeze and a cottage lake no bigger than the harbor. It was now out in weather far beyond its capacity, and only Miel's marvelous reflexes kept it from being swamped outright and sinking underneath her. She knew, however, that it was only a matter of time. The wind and waves were building into a massive tempest that would soon swallow her and the dinghy in its giant maw, as if they were no more than bits of twig adrift.

The worst part was the time passing by— hours or minutes, Miel couldn't tell except for the thickening darkness, the ache in her arms, the fear as the scrap of fiberglass faced each attacking wave. The bow climbed up and up and up with agonizing slowness, hesitated, then plunged down through an avalanche of foam onto the glassy slope while Miel madly tried to keep the dinghy from slewing sideways and tumbling out of control.

The struggle went on and on as Miel fought a slowly losing battle with the bailing can. The whole bottom of the dinghy was full of water, making it lumber ponderously, more and more sluggish in response to the tiller. She had taken to shutting her eyes briefly against the now-heavy rain. She opened them on increasingly tormented gloom until one time a sweeping light so dazzled her that she almost dropped the tiller in surprise.

A ship's searchlight! Her heart practically leaped through her chest. Had the harbor police or the Coast Guard finally stumbled across her in the dark?

The searchlight glanced away. Through the wind, Miel picked up the growl of diesels. Running lights appeared, and then a sleek white shape driving up through the rain with a man at the wheel.

Barth! Barth and the *Yancy*!

Miel's fingers convulsed on the tiller as she felt a surge of hysteria mixed with joy. Frantically she worked the dinghy into the lee of the large yacht, balancing like an acrobat. Crouching, she waited until a wave had lifted the dinghy up, then sprang with all her might toward the rope ladder Barth had swung over the side. The instant she grasped it, a strong hand clamped on her wrist and hauled her up until she was flipped like a fish on the sopping deck. The dinghy, bereft of guidance, spun sideways, took water and capsized. Barth, still gripping Miel fiercely, stumbled with her into the cockpit, where he clasped her to his chest.

"Miel! You're all right! You're really all right!"

He was shouting above the tumult of the waters, and all Miel knew was that by some miracle she was in Barth's arms, safe and saved. She shivered with the dizziness of relieved strain and clung to him, feeling his wonderful, wonderful solidity next to her own.

"Yes, oh yes! Oh Barth...I thought.... How did you find me? How did you get back to...."

A hair-raising squeal of metal rose from the stern of the *Yancy*. In an instant, Barth had jammed the wheel into Miel's hands while he raced to the engine switch, swearing wickedly. They both knew what the sound was—the capsized dinghy had fouled the propeller. Now the motor was out of action entirely.

Within seconds, Barth was back and had Miel strapped into a safety harness, which had a longline snapped to the front. Good thing too. The moment the engine stopped holding the yacht on course, the wind took it and began to swing it hard abeam so that, without any kind of control, it was plunging helplessly. In a moment they would be in the most dangerous of situations—lying broadside to the waves so that the full, towering weight of the water crashed against it. Larger boats than the *Yancy* had been smashed to matchsticks by the lake or turned upside down in the blink of an eye. Immediately, without speaking, Barth and Miel knew what had to be done. Miel grabbed the wheel and fought with all her strength to swing the bow back into the waves while Barth, clutching stays and handropes, made his way inch by inch up the slick dark deck.

As the yacht plunged like a frightened colt, Miel felt as if her arms were being loosened in their sockets. She clenched her teeth and gradually the *Yancy* came around, heaving up and knifing down through the black, foam-capped swell. Twice her heart shrank painfully as she saw the figure of Barth, lit by approaching flickers of lightning, silhouetted against the heavens as the prow rose up and up until he seemed suspended on the very last precarious inch of tilting deck.

The first thing he had to do was make his way to the forestay—the piece of rigging that ran from the tip of the foremast to the end of the bowsprit. There, he would attempt to set the storm jib, a small, tough, triangular sail attached to the forestay, which acted much like the tail of a weathervane to keep the yacht parallel to the direction of the wind.

As the strength of the storm steadily in-

creased, sharp gusts of wind cuffed the vulnerable craft this way and that. Miel clutched the
wheel tightly with both hands, bracing herself
against the kick of the rudder and the forces of
the storm seeking to draw the vessel into their
watery grip. She reacted with a sailor's instinct,
doing her best to control the wild lurching,
straining from the partial shelter of the cockpit
to see where the next wave was coming from
and, at the same time, keep watch on Barth
struggling with the jib, which whipped and
jerked in his hands as if it were violently alive
and determined to be free of him.

The other source of illumination was the yellow light seeping from the portholes, which gave
strangely dissociated glimpses of the man battling for purchase on the rain-lashed decks. Miel
gasped as he seemed to stagger back, his weight
more than once taken by his safety line. Then,
with a crack like a gunshot, the white triangle
snapped taut. The *Yancy* immediately straightened with a style that brought a thrill even in the
midst of the immense relief of getting the yacht
in hand again.

Barth worked backward toward the mainmast, becoming more visible in the glimmering
light. The wind buffeted him, and spray driven
across the open deck soaked him so that his
clothes were glued to him, showing clearly the
interplay of straining muscles underneath. Apparently heedless of the turmoil around him, he
dropped into the cockpit with a sound completely lost in the scream of the wind. His arms

seemed to encompass Miel and the wheel at the same time.

"We don't have a prayer of making it into the harbor without power," he shouted almost into her ear to make himself heard. "We'll have to make a run for it straight before the wind and hope this blows itself out before we end up aground on the opposite shore. This is just about as bad as anything I've ever seen at sea."

Miel nodded, hanging on tightly as the stern of the yacht was tossed up by a passing wave. She knew very well that no sailboat could maneuver the narrow harbor entrances in such a high wind without being smashed against one or the other of the retaining walls. Miel's grandfather used to maintain that more boats were wrecked foolishly trying to race for shelter when it was too late than had ever been taking their lumps bravely in the open.

Barth took the wheel from Miel, but still held her within the magic circle of his embrace as if she and the yacht were one. Miel leaned against him, feeling his body warmth flow into her, his strength steadying her as the faintly lit bow rose up and up, teetered, then, in the darkness, appeared to crash down into a terrible void boiling with geysers and eruptions of white foam. The wind was dead at their backs now, turning the *Yancy* into a driven thing plunging perilously from crest to crest.

"Go below," Barth ordered above the scream of the rigging. "Get out of this. I'll handle it."

Miel only clung more tightly to the wheel. Never, never again would she leave him.

"No. I'm staying right here to help. We're going too fast. You'll have to put out warps."

He made one more effort to pry her away, but she refused to budge. Using her considerable strength to resist him, she turned so that he saw the dogged determination on her face and was convinced. Their eyes locked for a second and then she was sure she saw the incredulous flicker of teeth. He gave her the wheel completely again, an act of trust no less significant because in that seething weather there was very little choice. Without exchanging a word, both knew that without the help of the motor they had been flung straight back into the days when a boat had to face the elements with nothing but a small triangle of canvas and the courage of its crew. And in all her life at Bay Point, Miel had never seen anything like the fury that now lashed the lake.

"Keep dead on that heading. I'll be back with you as soon as I can."

When he relinquished his hold, the wheel twisted savagely, but Miel held firm; danger and Barth's presence had given her the strength of ten.

Barth vanished briefly through the companionway hatch and reappeared with a coil of rope the thickness of his arm. Tying down the ends, he tossed the excess over the taffrail so that the huge loop would drag behind them in the water, acting as a sort of impromptu brake on the headlong, perilous rush of the yacht, a process known as trailing warps.

At once, Miel felt the slowing effect and knew that the immediate jeopardy was over. Now everything would hinge on keeping the bow of the *Yancy* pointed straight into those waves. Should they slide sideways and take the full weight of one of those massive breakers, they just might splinter like a child's cheap toy.

Barth dropped back beside her, water streaming from his limbs. He took the brunt of the wheel from her but they both stood, locked together, their grip tight, sharing the hold on the mahogany spokes. Miel had already spent hours struggling against the lake, her fingers numb with weariness. Now she was holding together on the pure adrenaline pumping through her body.

"How did you...find me?" she shouted against the din.

"What?"

"How did you find me?"

"Coast Guard. Message." The yacht bucked, jarring Barth sharply against Miel. "Heaven knows how...."

They were pitched back the other way and the wind sucked up the rest of Barth's words. It was next to impossible to talk. Miel grappled only briefly with news of a mysterious and life-saving message before a maverick wave sent an arch of spray high over the gunwales, soaking them both to the skin for the umpteenth time. Miel's beautiful pantsuit was plastered to her body, revealing every curve in the yellow sheen of light from the interior. Barth tried once again to get her to go below, but she refused.

"Not stirring an inch!" she flung back, getting the idea across more by the vehement shaking of her head than by her words. It would take the two of them to nurse the *Yancy* through this uproar, and they would be lucky if only two could manage it. Miel could not but be aware of all the disasters that could strike a lone sailboat, even one as magnificently equipped to be sailed single-handedly as this one was. She clung to Barth and the wheel, stubbornly ignoring the fear that clutched at her heart, reasoning that it was directly in the interest of saving her own neck to stay topside and keep the *Yancy* going.

Knowing the short temper and imperiousness of seagoing types under stress, Miel braced for a blast. When the heaving of the boat flung her around again, the last thing she expected to see on Barth's face was a grin—but grin he did, gripping the wheel with one hand, reaching out with the other to steady her on the slippery cockpit sole from which the residue of the last wave was just draining away.

Suddenly, wet and jolted and aching as she was, Miel could feel neither cold nor tired. The strong, hard bulk of Barth put courage into her bones and hot, revitalizing energy into her veins. The *Yancy* shuddered, then planed recklessly down one of the black, tormented slopes of water.

"Shouldn't we call for help?" Miel cried into his ear as they thudded into the trough.

Barth shook his head against the lashing of the wind, the muscles of his wrists bulging against the forces seeking to tear the wheel from his grasp.

"No use! Coast Guard's too busy."

"They're what?"

"*Too busy!* People...boats in trouble...fend for ourselves...."

Miel picked the few words she could catch out of the gale and put them together. Of course. The rescue units, suddenly overstrained by the havoc of this storm, would be concerned only with boats that were actually going under. Any vessel equipped to ride it out, such as the *Yancy*, would be left to look out for itself. Anyway, Barth would never, except as the very last resort, abandon the *Yancy*.

The two hung on while the wind screeched and wailed through masts and rigging bare of all sails except the tiny jib keeping them on course. Miel began to shake slightly as it occurred to her just how astronomical the chances had been against Barth's finding her in the midst of that night-shrouded, heaving waste. Only the shrewdest calculation of time, current, wind direction and sheer, mind-boggling luck could have led him to her, all the experience of a lifetime at sea thrown into this attempt to bring her to safety.

But who had had the call put through? Who?

Another wave, like the glistening back of a monster, lifted them up while Barth, feet planted firmly, guided the bow unerringly through the darkness. He was going by sound, Miel thought, for if the head swung but a few degrees either way off the direction of their run, the din among the stays and halyards drowned out everything else.

"Hot soup in the galley." Barth's face was but an inch from Miel's ear as the *Yancy* heeled heavily to port. "Thermos! Get it for us both!"

This time, certain she wasn't being banished, Miel let go of Barth and edged forward to the companionway door, which flew open then slammed ferociously shut behind her just in time to prevent the dregs of a wave from accompanying her. Light and dryness immediately greeted her and the roar of the storm was muffled. The motion, however, was unaltered, and she had to clutch the conveniently placed handholds in order, as the sole reeled and jumped beneath her, to make it to the galley.

Here, when her eyes had adjusted to the brightness and scanned the salon, she saw that everything had changed. All the evidence of clutter from the ad campaigns and Barth's casual living had disappeared. The galley had been stripped down for rough weather, all utensils and loose articles stowed out of sight, all hatches and doors—many of them fading invisibly into the paneling—now tightly closed. The *Yancy* had turned into a gleaming example of spare, precise efficiency—just as she suspected Barth's life would be when he turned his mind to serious business.

She groped around until she discovered the thermos, firmly secured as was everything else aboard the pitching boat, and gulped some of the hot, nourishing broth. She did not even consider a change of clothes, for anything fresh would soon be as sopping as the expensive cotton that left a dripping trail behind her. Allowing herself only a moment to lean against the counter while the soup restored her energy, she struggled out into the squall where Barth still manned the helm.

Hanging onto the binnacle tightly with one hand, Miel handed over the thermos with the other. While he drank, he balanced with that marvelous agility of his, retaining, as always, command of the vessel. It had been smart foresight on his part to have prepared the thermos, for any cooking would, of course, have been totally impossible. In two hungry gulps, he downed the contents, and a good thing too. As he lifted the thermos away from his mouth, an arc of spume flashed like a fist and knocked it forever into the jaws of the lake.

Her confidence slipping again, Miel let out a low, sharp cry. Barth's head came around. By the time he looked at her, her mouth was firmly shut and her hand raised in an "I'm okay" gesture. She felt she would rather drown than let Barth guess the terror that was again slowly welling up in her. She fairly trembled at the sight of those lunging swells that each time picked up the *Yancy* as if it were flotsam and tossed it forward, doing their best at the same time to suck the yacht under in an avalanche of foam.

The wind grew yet more violent, ripping a halyard loose and whipping it against the mainmast so there would very soon be a terrible tangle of lines and rigging if it was not soon lashed tight again. Speaking was now impossible, but Barth pulled Miel behind the wheel and went forward to catch the frenzied line, oblivious to the tumult around him and moving with that lithe, sure ease.

When he returned, dripping, even the weak cabin light revealed that there was color under his tan, as if from exhilaration. He did not take the wheel immediately but hung back on the handropes, watching Miel battle to retain control and yet, at the same time, inevitably taste the enormous sense of power to be gained only at the wheel of a large sailing vessel in a storm.

The weather, however, was now past squall proportions, and increasing steadily in strength and fury. Storms on the Great Lakes were often more treacherous than on the ocean itself, both because of rocks and shoals and because the shallower bottom drove the waves up into wild, towering shapes. As she grappled with the wheel, Miel knew that her terrors were well justified and had a healthy respect for Lake Ontario's temper. The bottom was strewn with hundreds of wrecks, from old wooden brigantines to modern freighters picked bodily up and twisted into broken metal before plummeting into the deep.

Now the illumination from the portholes and running lights only served to make the sooty blackness more impenetrable. Nothing beyond the bow could be seen at all save, now and then, the mottled churning side of a wave rising up from nowhere for a battering assault on the hull. Besides the nerve-tearing wail of the rigging, all around echoed the natural but frightening creaks and groans of a wooden vessel absorbing stress. Behind them, erratic, eerie flickers had been revealing more and more of the low, turgid clouds.

Suddenly, Barth lunged for the wheel.

"Hang on!" he bellowed, "I think. . . ."

Without warning, the heavens opened and a mighty, yellow-white tongue of fire seared down to the tip of a wave not a hundred yards away. The horrible crackles melded with a roar of thunder that sounded as if the fabric of the sky were being ripped apart directly above their heads.

Miel gasped in elemental awe, face, hair and body momentarily white in the blinding glare. Barth recoiled at the helm, then went as still as Miel as the last growl was whirled away in the wind. For one moment in which the whole world seemed suspended the two stared at each other. Considering the danger of being caught out on the lake in a thunderstorm, they ought to have worn expressions of mortal dread. Instead, reckless glance met reckless glance. Incredibly, they both began to laugh.

"In for it now," shouted Barth. "Might as well . . . enjoy the ride."

"What?"

"Enjoy the ride!"

Yes, Miel nodded, lurching into the binnacle. Yes, yes, yes!

And she felt Barth's arm leap to her waist in a rapid squeeze before he had to grab the wheel again.

It was at the same time a kind of madness and a bond so strong it felt like a tangible physical link. No amount of skill or effort could make a difference to a lightning bolt, so fear became useless baggage. Miel and Barth threw fear away and gave themselves up to the wild exaltation as lightning not only hissed into the water but also hurdled from cloud to cloud, converging flash on flash on flash until it seemed the entire firmament was ribbed and veined with aerial rivers of incandescent fire. The very electricity charging the air poured its energy into the two figures braced in the cockpit of the bounding yacht. Miel laughed again and gripped Barth's elbow as the pyrotechnics lit up boiling thunderheads and a seething, tormented disorder of waves from horizon to horizon.

The *Yancy* seemed born for this. With every wave it proved the style and seaworthiness that made Barth love it so. The long keel kept it balanced as delicately as a ballerina, yet the abominable pounding could not get the better of the stoutly fitted planks. Through cannonades of spume and the weight of combers hurtling across the decks, the bow sliced imperturbably on, true to the helm where Barth stood, blond hair flying back, exactly like the Viking king a younger Miel once imagined him to be.

Miel lost all track of time as she kept to the cockpit, often held in only by her safety line and the solidity of the man at her side. Now she understood the uses of Barth's enormous physical strength as he kept continuous and unrelenting control while the yacht climbed, in agonizing slow motion, the sheer face of every wave, teetered on the crest and then, after a horrifying pause, tumbled and slithered downward in the breaking surf until it dropped into the black, yawning trough. From here it would skid toward the next towering wall, where the whole process would begin all over again.

Nothing could be heard over the tumult. The rain came in earnest, indistinguishable from the masses of water already pouring over them, and driven horizontally like buckshot in a wind so fierce it was tearing the tops of the waves to smoke. Suddenly there was a crack like gunfire, and the *Yancy* began to shiver and veer.

"The jib! Migod!"

Once again Miel was thrust bodily behind the helm while Barth climbed out of the cockpit and into a determined crawl forward on the slippery, bucking deck. The jib sheet, the line that held the inner corner at the correct angle to the wind, had broken loose and the small sail was jerking like a soul in torment. Miel stiffened. If Barth didn't get it under control in a very few minutes, it would be blown to ribbons, and the *Yancy*, without the jib to guide it, would be in real danger of being knocked sideways under one of the approaching waves.

With intense concentration, Miel steered while Barth inched forward, utterly exposed to the brute pounding of nature. As he reached the bow, Miel shifted the yacht slightly so as to send the flying line within his reach. Neither had time to remark on this wonderful display of mutual skill, for when Barth grasped the sheet and was just trying to secure it again against the fearful force hardening the sail, Miel looked up and saw it coming. A graybeard!

Graybeards were the stuff of legend and the greatest dread of those who sail small boats. A graybeard is a wave—a wave like no other. It is a freak, a fearful fluke of nature, a rare coincidence of unleashed powers that produce a rushing leviathan of water, making nearby waves appear as dimples on a pond.

This one, lit by retreating forks of lightning, bore down—a massive, glittering precipice that advanced with the snarl of a locomotive and spewed a savage frill of foam from its terrifying crest. So fast it came that Miel had time to do no more than clamp herself to the wheel convulsively and scream warning at the top of her lungs.

The monster broke over the *Yancy*. One moment Miel breathed clean, sweet air, the next she found herself engulfed as ton upon ton of lake water toppled onto her. The *Yancy* was stopped in its tracks by the blow, shuddering from bow to stern as if every seam was bursting. As the vessel tilted crazily, Miel felt as if her arms were going to break. The only impression she had was that she and Barth were going down through a whirling caldron to their doom.

She did not, however, let go of the wheel, for the helm was her only connection to life on this earth. She hung on with mindless intensity though the great spokes ground into her ribs and bruised her fearfully just along the hairline. She clung as the *Yancy* righted itself, hung suspended, thrust its bow upward and, rather like a large, surprised dog, shook its entire, glistening bulk free of the flood. As the yacht rose, the water from the graybeard parted in the middle and rolled in thundering cascades off the deck and into the lake.

As soon as the cockpit cleared, Miel sucked in huge, sputtering lungsful of air and opened her eyes. The companionway door had held and so had all the other hatches. The masts had survived and the rigging and even the jib. But Barth?

Oh God, where was Barth?

Miel gazed wildly about, seeing only empty deck. Barth had had a safety line, of course, but what was a mere rope when one of those Goliaths could rip the superstructure from a tanker! Her hands still gripped the wheel so tightly her knuckles stood out in bloodless lumps. And even as she scanned the scene before her in total panic, she unconsciously worked the helm to steady the stunned boat back to a safer course.

Panic changed to absolute terror when a spurt of lightning lit every sliver of the yacht, and still there was no Barth to be seen. Dear heaven, had that monster swallowed him as if he were but a broken bit of waterweed?

Lightning, weaker this time, flickered again, and Miel caught sight of an arm wrapped tightly around one of the rope stanchions opposite the mainmast. Nothing else could be seen, only a disembodied arm.

With a speed she didn't know she possessed, Miel slipped the becket, a small loop of rope designed for lashing the helm, over one of the spokes and dashed forward. Barth hung, trailing from the side of the boat, all his attempts to haul himself back aboard useless because his safety line was fouled.

Heedless of danger to herself, Miel knelt, grasped the safety harness, and by sheer will lifted him high enough so that she could flick the line free. The minute the constraint was gone, Barth sprang like a panther back on deck and gathered Miel into a rib-cracking hug against the streaming expanse of his chest. Miel grasped him instantly and in that single moment all the frantic, almost superhuman strength she had found to save him was transmuted into one enormous jolt of emotion. The two were welded together into one, forged from the joy each felt that the other was alive. Nothing else mattered to Miel in the whole watery world, but Barth tore suddenly away.

"Get back to the wheel. The boom's come loose!"

Miel scrambled back to her post, flipping off the becket and taking over the helm. Her job was to try to turn the yacht partway off the wind, so that the heavy boom would not swing so wildly that it threatened to tear itself, the furled mainsail and the most important of the rigging to bits.

Leaping for the line that controlled the boom, Barth grasped and by sheer brute strength held it against the rage of the wind until Miel had jockeyed the *Yancy* into position. Until the last moment he crouched. Then the yacht heeled toward him, sheltered in the trough of a wave. The boom snapped toward him enough for him to flip the erring mainsheet down over the cleat and turn it fast. After that, he had to finish with the shivering jib and fight his way over the perilous open spaces back to the safety of the cockpit.

The cockpit, self-draining, had already shed the volume of water left by the graybeard, but the two occupants were utterly drenched. Miel shook from exertion and from fright, though no one would have known it from the way she handled the boat. She also trembled from the surge of feeling that had possessed her when Barth had taken her into that brief, agonized embrace. Barth seemed energized by the very elements that had almost gulped him up. He took Miel by the arms his gray eyes alight.

"Well done, Coconut Princess!"

That was all he needed to say. Miel knew she had won his final respect—as companion and as sailor, her courage proved, her skill admirable. Her blood sang with rejoicing as she again relinquished the helm.

The graybeard had been the dying convulsion of the tempest. As suddenly as it had arisen, the wind began to die. Within half an hour, the savagery was gone and the direction shifted enough so that Miel and Barth were able to get the *Yancy* turned around and pointed back toward Toronto harbor.

"Got to change the jib."

"Want any help?"

"No."

"I could slip on the becket."

"No. You're doing fine. Won't take me a minute."

Speech was now possible over the churn and slap of foam, yet Barth had turned oddly silent. Instead of the exuberant grins Miel had expected from him when they finally bucked over the swell in a half circle and were safely headed for home, he quite brusquely hurried forward to replace the tiny storm jib with a larger one and then to examine inch by inch the vital mainsail rigging to see if the runaway boom had damaged anything. Miel's happiness receded just the barest fraction as she watched him moving around, only parts of him visible in the weak yellow light from the portholes.

By now all that remained of the gale was a

stiff, rain-scented breeze, and the *Yancy* angled across it over a still rough but manageable swell. The downpour had stopped with the graybeard, though distant flickers of lightning could still be seen like thin mad dancers retreating over the horizon. Barth lifted his head, testing the air and judging it ready for him to run up the mainsail. He grasped the halyard, and in a moment the great ghostly wing rose up above their heads. Immediately the *Yancy* steadied and heeled and ploughed with purpose through the ragged chop. A moment later the clouds parted like marbled smoke to reveal a shining moon.

"Oh, Barth," Miel cried, entranced. "Oh, it's unbelievable. When we get back...."

"Sssh! Don't!"

He was behind her now, his arms around her waist, pressing her back to him even as she remained at the wheel. She could feel the outline of his cheekbone against her hair, which was beginning to dry into a mass of shockingly undisciplined curls.

"But...."

"Miel, magic moments are all too brief in life. Let's not spoil this one with talk."

Something almost painfully urgent in his voice made Miel stiffen, but further words died away as his embrace tightened and he held her against his body, his cheek resting on the top of her head. The nearness of him sang like glory through her being, making her delight even in the soft clink of his safety harness and the feel of the smooth solid planking beneath her bare feet. The invisible flame of her love recovered from the faint alarm of his tone and burned sure and bright. They were together on the *Yancy*. What else mattered in the world?

The night became truly magical as the waves shimmered alive with moonlight, and the *Yancy*'s silver wake spilled away over the dark water behind them. The yacht dipped over the rollers at an intoxicating clip as the great sail rustled and murmured high on the mast. Miel felt the wheel sweet in her hands and the intimate, sheltering warmth of Barth coming to her, skin to skin through their clinging, spray-soaked garments. She nestled herself against him, so close she could feel the strong, oddly uneven rhythm of his breathing.

Forever, she thought. *Let us just sail on and on just like this, and never come to shore.*

CHAPTER NINETEEN

THE LIGHTS OF THE CITY, at first a careless scatter along the edge of the sky, brightened in the clearing air. Closer, they formed themselves into luminous honeycombs of white and gold, rearing up higher and higher into soaring columns until they peaked like a wave against the flashing beacon of the CN Tower.

The *Yancy* slipped through the gap just as the pink of dawn washed in from the east and caught in the droplets still beading every inch of the yacht's deck and rigging. Without benefit of the engine the entry was tricky, and it took considerable effort to work the *Yancy* to its mooring. Behind them, the lake was slowly quieting into its former tranquillity. The harbor seemed smooth as a duckpond after what they had just been through.

Miel leaned against the mainmast, a little tottery with fatigue but smiling with a smile that lit her from deep inside. Barth tested the last line, then stepped up beside her. His shirt had dried on his back and was heavily marked where his life jacket and safety harness had bit into it. His hair lay in a springy, disorderly tangle just the way the wind had left it, and he was ruddy as with the afterglow of battle. Yet as he turned to Miel, there was a darkness in his gray eyes and a terrible tightness to his jaw, which she didn't see because she was staring past him.

"Lord, look!"

Whole limbs had been torn from the island willows and lay half submerged at the waterline below uneven gouges in the shoreline. In the city, small figures scurried around, dragging sheets of plywood to the myriad blown-out windows. Far down, on the shoulder of the Quay, a van lay on its side, and in the slip several boats floated crazily and slammed into one another. One cruiser was so filled with water that only the bow and the cabin roof were still above the surface.

The magnitude of the disaster began to penetrate. Miel snapped around to face Barth.

"Hildy and James. They must be...."

She caught the grimness in his expression then, and stopped.

"Not yet. There's someone else we have to see to first."

Someone else? Miel blinked and realized she had completely forgotten Cora. And very quietly all her ecstasy crumbled into ash.

Without speaking, they descended the companionway and passed the main salon in which Miel, earlier, had not spotted the least trace of another woman. Just outside the door of the stern stateroom, Miel caught a low, barely human moan. Barth pushed the door open so that light spilled in. Nothing different could be seen here either save a large, elongated lump on the nether berth. Miel let out a cry and bolted over, horror overcoming even her heartbreak as she realized that what she was looking at was all that was left of Cora Fowler.

The groan rose again—a thin expression of utter misery. Miel snatched up a hand that lay like an exhausted mackerel and felt exactly as clammy.

"What on earth...?"

"I'm afraid she doesn't take well to the water."

Indeed, the normally so animated face was a dim shade of green, set against the wild incongruity of vivid hair. The light, Indian cotton coverlet had been writhed into knots, and bands of strapping, meant to prevent a sleeper from being tossed unexpectedly across the cabin in nasty weather, were fastened across the inert twisted body. Miel wondered if it were possible to actually die from seasickness.

"Shouldn't we call an ambulance?"

"Noooo. Don't you...dare." This was the first sign of conscious life from Cora, and the thick lashes opened a centimeter. "I couldn't bear to be moved one *inch*...oh...."

The following groan conveyed volumes about Cora's queasy dread of being shifted from the mattress. Barth loomed up behind Miel, and even his face softened a little in compassion.

"Nothing to do but let her sleep it off."

"How long has she been strapped in?" Miel

asked, cringing at the torment Cora must have endured down here in the insanely pitching interior.

"Almost since the first moment I found her. And no matter how she begged, I wasn't putting back into Toronto harbor. Not for any damned reason!" he added with such unexpected vehemence that Miel started.

"Found her?" she said, allowing a wretched little wraith of hope to rise. "You didn't know she was aboard?"

"Bloody right I didn't. I have no idea how she knew I was leaving."

"Bribed the dockmaster, dear," came a voice from out of the heap that was Cora. "Stowed away for the...aaaah...the hell of it. Oh... ugh...I'll never touch another sailor as long as I live. Never...."

The heap made a feeble effort to lift its head before going limp again. Miel felt Cora's forehead, and it seemed to be the very opposite of a fever—beaded and damp with cold. Yet already the spark of Cora's personality was flickering, making Miel want to take care of her.

"Can I get you anything, Cora? A drink, maybe? A glass of water?"

She rolled away to hide her face in the much-tortured pillow.

"No, oh no. Just go away, pleeeease."

Miel straightened. The short, violent beating inside her at hearing that this was merely another of Cora's escapades died down. Whether or not

Barth had known Cora was there, he had still been leaving. And as for his wild search on the lake—well, wasn't it the duty of any mariner to help another in trouble? That apparent charm and sincerity had fooled her once again. When he got tired of the game, he simply packed up and sailed away.

When they got up on deck again and Miel looked over the chaos of the slip, she fought a dizziness rising within her and grasped at a hand-rope. How often, how often could a person's world fall out from underneath her before she went mad! She appeared so haunted Barth reached for her elbow.

"Look, Miel, that woman is merely a stow-away...."

"Stop it!" Miel hissed, feeling herself to be a mass of nervous confusion. "It it wasn't Cora it would be somebody else. You make a habit of skipping off to sea whenever and with whomever you please. Why should I expect anything to be different now?"

"You know damn well it's different. This time...."

"Oh, spare me, Barth!" Miel whirled on him. "Go and have your fun, but at least have the dignity to stick by your own actions. You don't have to explain a thing to me. After all, it's not as if... we'll be seeing each other again!"

Her own words seemed to explode in front of Miel, impressing upon her the terrible fact of her altered future. Barth stopped as if struck, his whole body seeming to shudder. The look of hope he had worn since the graybeard completely disappeared.

"So it's true, then. You really are going to stay in the city?"

"Of course I'm going to stay. In view of the circumstances, it's the one choice left to me, isn't it?"

To someone more detached, her proud, bitter, tormented cry might have been taken as an agonized appeal. Barth only stiffened, inside of a moment turning into the closed, hard-bitten man who bossed the salvage crews. All trace of vulnerability evaporated.

"I thought you had changed, Miel. Really, I did."

"Ditto here, sport. The joke's on both of us!" Miel stepped doggedly off the *Yancy*, knowing that if she didn't keep moving she would be beside herself with grief. "Come on. James must be half out of his mind if he has any idea we've been out in this."

Pain skittered across Barth's features. He would have vanished back down the companionway had he not seen Miel's hand shaking badly as she fumbled for her car keys.

"Give me those," he said grimly. "Now that you're this close, James wouldn't want you run over in the traffic."

Miel's car, by some miracle, still sat undamaged among the torn greenery of Harbourfront where she had parked in that joyful race for the harbor that now seemed so very long

ago. They roared up Bay Street past the deserted
expanse of Nathan Phillips Square and the massive dark red sandstone of the Old City Hall. A
red-and-white streetcar on Dundas barely
missed them, but Miel paid no attention. She
was speeding like a rabbit to the one place that
had always been refuge to her—the store.

Though it was almost an hour before the
working day began, she knew James would be
there. In a few minutes she and Barth pulled
into the parking lot and were striding through a
magically silent realm that smelled of eternal
newness and which, as yet, no customers had
disturbed. Up the unmoving escalators they
climbed and then the little set of stairs leading to
the executive floor. The door of James's office
was tightly closed, but a long sliver of light
seeped out from underneath it. Without stopping to knock, Miel, from old habit, flung the
door open and strode in, Barth at her heels.

"James...oh!"

She stopped so sharply that Barth all but
knocked her over from behind. If, at the back of
her consciousness, Miel had harbored some idea
that James might comfort her, it vanished at
what she saw. Nothing could have prepared her
for the scene.

James was not at his desk, but in the over-
stuffed Edwardian wing chair in which Lillian
had liked to rest her aged bones when business
got too hectic. His suit coat was off, his shirt
was open almost to the waist and his tie—the
only time Miel had ever seen it disarranged—

was draped over the filing cabinet. His face, palely drawn and speckled with a day's growth of beard, looked as if he had, quite frankly, been through hell. And yet in the split second before he became aware of Miel's presence, she realized she had never seen him quite so happy.

He had been asleep, obviously the fitful, exhausted sleep of a long vigil. But through the weariness a faint smile played on his lips—for curled in his lap, nestled against his heart and cradled in his arms like the most precious of objects, lay Hildy, still clad in a much-creased pink eyelet dress from the day before.

Their eyes flew open at the same instant and they both sprang to their feet like scalded cats. Guilty scalded cats, Miel could not help thinking. Dazed, they stared at the pair invading the office until comprehension burst upon their brains.

"Miel! Barth! Hey, you're here! You're all right!"

For a few minutes everyone was lost in a startlingly uninhibited barrage of hugs and back slaps and handshakes and giggles choking on the edge of tears. The wastepaper basket got tipped over in the shuffle and Lillian's sacred pen-and-pencil set was knocked askew. Miel was so overcome by this emotional greeting from her friends that she forgot her own troubles for the moment to struggle with the lump in her throat that was growing unbearably large. She sniffed into James's linen handkerchief, then held him at arm's length in mock ferocity.

"Now that you see we're in one piece, what about the charming spectacle that Barth and I blundered in on?"

The last thing she ever expected to see on James's face was an outright blush, yet there it was, a lovely mottled scarlet climbing past his eyes clear up to his hairline. His fingers flew to the shocking gape in the front of his shirt and began buttoning rapidly.

"Oh, go on, Jimmy. Tell them. They ought to be the first to know."

Jimmy! Miel gasped aloud and stared. Hildy, who looked both smug and grateful and ecstatic all at the same time, gave James about ten more seconds, then took charge herself.

"We're in love," she announced, seeming to tremble blissfully on tiptoe, as if she were no longer connected to the ground. "We decided about five o'clock this morning when we heard the wind go down."

"And I can't believe it. I still...." James lost his grip on the sentence and stood there swaying slightly on his heels, his aristocratic features still pink with incredulity.

"He'll believe it all right, just as soon as I get him home."

Hildy took James's shirt-sleeved arm with such natural pride of possession that Miel was treated to a scandalized vision of the little artist leading James up the stairs of his gray stone mansion straight past the horrified gaze of Mrs. Howland, the housekeeper. Romance would have to be interrupted to deal with Mrs. Howland's heart attack.

Hildy's laugh bubbled up like fresh champagne, oh so very good to hear again. Then, when Miel still could not speak, she grew concerned.

"You really don't mind, do you, Miel? I mean, you did give him up, and I've never been so happy in my entire life."

"But when. . . ."

"Oh, I don't know. The first day, I think. My original reason for wanting to work here was to get back at my stepfather, but when I met James, well, something just sort of clicked for me. Of course, he didn't give me a sideways glance at the time."

"So that was why you were less than enthusiastic over those roses," said Miel, as at least a couple of the crazily jumbled pieces of the puzzle fell into place.

"Less than enthusiastic! I thought I'd die. I knew how pigheaded James was. Once he had made up his mind he wanted you, I was afraid there wouldn't be any way I could change it."

"You didn't try," put in James, sliding his tie surreptitiously from the edge of the Accounts Received drawer. "How was I to know?"

"Didn't try!" Hildy tossed him a glance loaded with pity for the obtuseness of the entire male sex. "I thought up that advertising campaign, didn't I? I know a lurching juggernaut of masculinity when I see one. I practically threw Miel bodily into Barth's arms.''

Here Miel remembered everything and winced visibly. Lifting her hand to her temple, she ran her fingers along her wind-burned skin.

''I...I'm having a hard time getting used to this, Hildy. If you were so in love, why, only last week, were you begging me to forget Barth and marry James myself?''

James stopped in the middle of looping his tie knot and stared at her in astonishment.

''Hildy! You what?''

Hildy leaped up in a lacy swirl of skirt, immediately sober and defiant.

''It's true. After the way you fired me, I thought you'd never even look at me again. And I knew you'd never take that wonderful chance the consortium was offering unless you had... *somebody* to be a partner.''

''You found out about that? You *schemed* to have me marry someone else just because of the store. What did you think—''

He broke off, stepping angrily. Then, realizing what a desperate, hopelessly gallant act Hildy's plea had been, his face contorted with the kind of naked, passionate longing Miel had never even remotely considered possible for him.

''Hildy, I never imagined. Stupid me, how could I ever have guessed you care so much....''

He gathered the small form to him, oblivious now to all others in the room. Hildy snuggled her head against his shoulder in a gesture of total confidence that, for a moment, filled Miel's breast with a terrible, aching emotion. She clenched her teeth against it until James broke away, evidently realizing what he had just implied about Miel.

"I'm sorry," he said to her, swallowing. "I was really pushing you into a corner. I had no idea what love—the real thing—would be like."

"It's all right, James. I understand. I honestly do," said Miel, trying not to think how deeply, how painfully this was true.

Those brown eyes spoke to her fondly, as if he remembered how long and how earnestly he had paid court. The ties were broken, but habit clung enough to make him run his hand over his hair without caring who saw the vulnerable bald spot.

"Don't ask me to explain it," he said helplessly, no doubt thinking of all those roses and dinners and oddly stiff caresses stolen behind this very office door. "It must have been going on inside me since the day I hired Hildy. Nature slugged me between the eyes and told me it was time, and I instinctively turned to you. I've always admired you so very much. Besides, I just couldn't bring myself to believe...."

He was too much of a gentleman to finish aloud, and his bedazzled gaze returned to Hildy, who could look so bewitching in strings of cowrie shells and yellow vests made from old tapestry. She would have given Lillian apoplexy, and James could have had no more idea how to cope than if a bird of paradise had some-how gotten loose in his hall. Now here he was, moonstruck and motionless.

"She'll be very good for you," Miel said sud-denly and from the heart. "You're very lucky. She's the real brain when it comes to merchand-izing."

More so than I, she added silently, knowing her own career was quite ruined by this madness for the sea.

"I think I know that now. The truth dawned on me when she came back to get her things and went frantic thinking both of you might be out there in that storm. After we're married, I doubt things will ever again be dull."

Hildy popped out from under his arm, smil-ing and subdued, though her eyes were suspici-ously bright.

"Well, it took you long enough to decide, James," she murmured half teasingly. "And don't think I'll let you forget it. Lucky for me, Miel picked Barth in the end anyway."

Miel shrank as these last words struck the air and hung in sudden, dreadful silence. Oh, to have her humiliation revealed at the very last moment. Her eyes dropped. She couldn't bear to look at anyone. Behind her, she seemed to feel Barth's presence loom, huge and brooding, making her acutely, agonizingly conscious of what she must give up.

"She what?" he asked in a voice filled with shivering little wires.

"She decided to marry you after all," put in

James affably. "After all my efforts, she turned white as paper yesterday and announced it was you she had to have. I don't think I knew it at the time, but I was secretly relieved. I gave her my blessing and sent her on her way."

"But I thought...I was given to understand...." The bewilderment in his voice was swiftly replaced by a deadly, steel-cold quietness. "Hildy, after what you told me down at the slip, I think you had better explain!"

After one stunned second, Hildy let out a yelp and jumped away from the crook of James's arm.

"I did explain. Everything! To that man handling the Coast Guard radio. He just had to tell you how sorry I was about sending you off like that when Miel hadn't even given James her final word."

"You what?" Miel felt a wild beating start up inside her, and she stared at the little art director. "I think somebody better start this story from the beginning!"

Hildy gazed from one to the other, still breathless from James's embrace. The wide-eyed half smile faded, replaced by a creeping horror as she slowly read their faces. Her hand flew to her mouth, and she backed up against the edge of James's immense rosewood desk.

"Oh, my God! They didn't tell you! They didn't explain a thing!"

"The Coast Guard is hardly in the business of passing on personal messages, especially not in heavy storm static. All I heard was that a Ms

McCrae was out alone in a sailing dinghy and, given the circumstances, they'd appreciate all the help they could get.''

The dryness of Barth's words contrasted with the violent grip he had taken on the back of one of the guest chairs, as if he meant to rip the tasteful upholstery to pieces. James regarded him earnestly.

"After she refused me, Miel went down to the harbor straightaway, where she supposed you were waiting for her. Then Hildy came to get her belongings and when she heard that Miel was off to find you, she nearly fainted. All I could get out of her was that you had already gone. Naturally, we both raced down to the harbor to try to cushion the shock. When we saw that one of the dinghies was gone, we knew right away that she was out there alone in that storm.''

"And that's when we really went into a tizzy,'' continued Hildy. "There were boats capsizing all over the place. We knew that somebody had to rescue Miel and you were the best candidate. You would have been so proud of us, jumping up and down and demanding all kinds of attention from those poor harassed harbor police.''

Miel's mind reeled through all this, only understanding that in spite of all the words flying around, the basic facts had not changed. She had thrown over everything only to find that, once again, Barth had left her on the shore. Her features remained tight with hurt until Hildy noticed.

"Barth, for heaven's sake! Tell her why you left before the poor girl expires from misery!"

This was too much. Miel gathered her dignity and flung up her head. Her pride returned to her along with the strength that was the legacy of those dynamic years at Crome's. Let him say it to her. Let him explain to her face exactly why he had decided she was no longer worth taking along.

Slowly, she turned to look at Barth, determined to match him, her energy against his own. Her eyes were enormous, her mouth stark, her cheeks taut, as if cut from wood. Yet her mass of wind-dried hair and the new, storm-won freedom of her body added a beautiful wildness, the wildness of her Bay Point youth, which none at the store had ever seen before.

"Yes, Barth," she whispered softly, accusingly, "tell me. Why did you sail away from me this time?"

His nearness enveloped her like some shimmering, invisible cloak. The gray eyes, unwavering, burned into her own.

"I left because I thought there was no more hope. Hildy came down to the boat that morning and told me you had decided to marry James."

Miel choked and almost lost her footing. She hadn't heard that right. Surely not! But then—there was Hildy at her elbow, small hands clutching her like a plea.

"Oh, Hildy...."

"I know. I deserve everything you're thinking

about me, but honestly, I was sure it was only a formality to get you to agree to James. Barth was a distraction I'd set up, so it was up to me to get him out of the way.''

A distraction she'd set up! Gasping, Miel suppressed a manic sputter of laughter. For once poor Hildy had wildly overestimated her ability to arrange other people's fates. Neither she nor James had the slightest idea of the past Miel shared with Barth or the power of the currents that had picked them up and swept them together at the first opportunity.

As the enormity of her interference began to sink in, Hildy began to apologize all over again in increasing distress. Miel no longer noticed. Floods of trembling emotion welled up in her as the glorious possibility, the possibility of Barth's love, began to sink in. It seemed to take an age to meet his gaze. When she did, it was like being wrapped in fire, so bright it was, so full of passionate hunger.

''Barth. . . .'' she breathed, then found the rest of her words smothered by the constricting bands around her chest. The very air felt so laden with urgency she could hardly breathe. She felt dazed, propelled into some new reality her senses had been unable to perceive before.

''So you did come,'' Barth cried. ''Why didn't you tell me? Why, just now in the harbor, did you say you were going to stay in the city?''

''What else could I say? I thought you'd left me. It was just like in Bay Point—only a thousand times worse. All I could think to do when I found out was to get into the little boat and sail. And then, when everything looked perfect, there was Cora...."

Her expression was a combination of remembered anguish and uncertain hope. Barth stood up.

"Poor Miel! Sailing always was the one place you would go for consolation."

"Barth, if you ever leave me, ever again...."

Her hands dropped weakly at her sides, by that single gesture indicating all the devastation that would engulf her if she were abandoned. Barth was by her side in a single step, his hand fiercely on her shoulders.

"I won't. I swear it!"

For several moments neither of them seemed able to speak. A pulse beat visibly at Miel's temple as she tried to make herself believe her good fortune. Barth, too, struggled with a new reality and he bent his head. His voice came out in a thin whisper, as if he still expected his happiness to be snatched away.

"Miel, are you really sure about this? I know how much the store has come to mean to you. I pressured you an awful lot, I'm afraid, and I shouldn't ask you to leave it...."

"Ask! *Ask!* Don't you know that's all you have to do, you big gorgeous sea dog? Ever since I was five years old I've wanted to run away in a boat. I'll go now even if I have to drag you aboard myself!"

Barth could not have been more surprised.

"Really?"

"Really!"

A grin spread across his face as the actuality of her love sank in. Then Miel was swept into the paradise of Barth's arms. She was drowning, floating, laughing weakly, giddily with joy, thinking how absurdly fine his T-shirt felt against her cheek. He was kissing her so feverishly his mouth kept missing hers, catching her cheekbones, the side of her nose, her upturned chin. When his grip loosened a little, Miel was hardly surprised to discover tears watering the corners of her lashes.

"Hey, you two better get out of here—" James grinned "—*before* this gets embarrassing!"

The footsteps and muffled voices of the arriving staff emphasized his point. Sooner or later, someone was going to open the office door and probably shriek. Too bad to miss the fun of watching the usually impeccable, now thoroughly disheveled, James make his explanations.

"Come on, sweet. We have a lot of catching up to do," Barth whispered, managing to loosen his arms just enough so that she could move.

On the way out, Allison did shriek, though softly, almost soundlessly, as befitted a front-line employee at Crome's. Miel and Barth descended the elevator and then the now-operational series of escalators, too caught up in each other to notice the astonishment of the salespeople and the early-morning shoppers.

Only on the ground floor did a mirror reveal to Miel that her pantsuit was a plum-colored disaster of rips and stains and wrinkles quite in keeping with Barth's shapeless T-shirt and raveled cutoffs. Nevertheless, she gave a wink to the stone-faced nymphs at the door. Never had she felt more totally, desirably chic.

CHAPTER TWENTY

HOURS LATER, the *Yancy* still lay where it had been moored. The sail cover had not been slipped over the furled and valuable mainsail and, to tell the truth, the jib looked a little untidy too. Since the arrival of the young couple about ten o'clock, no life had been seen aboard the yacht, except for an impressive, redheaded woman who had tottered out and been helped into a taxi. Nevertheless, she had managed to call out a good-luck wish so cheerfully that coffee mugs and screwdrivers had dropped onto decks over a good half of the slip. Now a pair of gulls had possession of the wheel, and a convoy of ducks poked around under the bow for delicacies stirred up by the storm.

Inside, in the master stateroom, Miel lay in bliss, draped across Barth's chest, tormenting him gently by running her fingertips in circles just beneath his hipbone.

"I had no idea you had three moles pointing the way to your belly button." *Or that you could release the very stars of heaven,* she added silently, still dazed by the revelation.

"You didn't tell me that you have skin that tastes like almonds and cloves or that you mis-

pronounce my name at the height of passion.''
And when she blushed, he laughed and caught
her to him. ''I knew it anyway. I sailed halfway
round the world just to get to hear it.''

They had thrown aside the coverlet, which had
Indonesian dancers on it. Barth's limbs, naked,
were uniformly dark and of heroic proportion.
Miel's arms and legs were a rich tawny color, but
her torso remained the creamy ivory of habitually covered skin. She looked as strong and as
beautiful as a young Amazon as she gazed upward, thinking how she would have to get used to
being watched by those carved mermaids floating on the ceiling. They seemed very dreamy, as
if they already shared with her the knowledge of
just how high one could be tossed on the crests of
this marvel known as lovemaking.

Barth ran his hand from the tip of her breast
down the long taper of her waist to the top of her
thigh.

''We'll have to do something about the color
of you. You should be as brown as one of those
tall island women and run barefoot in the sand. I
know this little cove on the south of Fiji. The
sand sparkles in the moonlight, and in the forest
you can find orchids as big as your fist.''

''You'll bring me coconuts?''

''And breadfruit and mangoes, and pineap-
ples and adoration.''

''We can just loll in the sun and bake a fish for
breakfast?''

''With banana pancakes over a fire of coconut
husks.''

His hand found her hair and brushed it back with a tenderness that made her throat ache.

"You promised me a year."

"I promised you forever, lady. I'll prove it to you as soon as I get you alone in that pretty green lagoon."

"And you won't abandon me on any more docks?"

She raised her head and looked at him. His eyes were gray and soft now, but she had very recently seen them charcoal with desire. She was only teasing him, for she felt so warm now, so secure, so much a part of him that she had trouble remembering what her former panic had been all about. Instantly, she was sorry for the brief spasm that tightened his lips.

"Never, my love. Never again!" His voice was so filled with emotion, Miel knew it was coming from that deep part of him that she alone had the power to touch. He lifted himself and hovered above her as if offering the protection of his massive shoulders—and his heart. Oh, that it should always be.

Barth kissed the exposed softness of her arm, and his touch ran through her like a steeple bell. She twisted in his embrace, thrown against him by the soft sway of the *Yancy*.

"Let's go to that lagoon," she said earnestly. "Now?"

Laughter returned to his voice and he rolled over onto his back again, his head making a deep dent in the oversize pillow.

"Right now. This minute."

He saw that she meant it, and the corners of his mouth turned slightly down.

"What about your job?"

"What job? That ended the minute I said no to James and walked out."

"And your apartment? All your plants and wicker chairs and those funny-looking elephant end tables?"

"I'm leaving it all to Hildy. She can scatter the stuff all around James's mansion and listen to him scream."

"Poor fellow. Do you really think those two can make a go of it together?"

"Strangely enough, I do," Miel said, sliding her fingers with pensive fascination through the crisp, sun-bleached hair on Barth's chest. "She really is a genius, you know. If he follows her lead, they might make millions. He needs to be kept shaken up and full of fresh ideas. If I'd married him, we would have simply ossified together."

"If you'd married him, you wouldn't be here suggesting we run off to the South Pacific. Next time I came back, I would have had to carry you off, like a pirate."

The thought of not being there with Barth that moment was too enormous to consider, so Miel began to nuzzle his ear and the tip of his collarbone.

"Hey, hey," Barth chuckled, twisting his head around to look at her. "What about your car, parked out by the side of the road?"

"I'll leave the keys inside it and a note: First come, first served."

"Lord, I believe you. I bet you'd even go without your clothes. And after all that fashion!"

Deep in her throat, Miel laughed—a husky, sensuous sound that made Barth's eyes darken involuntarily. Her mouth found the soft part of his underjaw and nibbled there.

"Fashion? I plan to wear a grass skirt or maybe a sarong. Most of the time, however—" her lithe body slid until she lay along the length of him "—I plan to wear absolutely nothing at all."

Barth eased her weight on top of him so that he could look deep into her hazel eyes, making her weak inside for gladness.

"That's quite a bribe, my sweet. We'll get up and cast off immediately."

She laughed again and kissed him, and the quiet creaks of the *Yancy* spoke to them as if it knew what a precious cargo of love it bore in its hold. Slowly, hungrily, Barth drank in the glory of Miel's smile, the warmth of her supple body. His hand slid down her back, the whisper of his palms on her skin making her gasp and suddenly drop her mouth to his. With matching ardor, he groaned and crushed her to him.

And despite their best resolutions, it wasn't until the pale lemon tinge of the following dawn that the *Yancy* stole finally from the harbor.

ABOUT THE AUTHOR

Margaret Gayle is not unlike her heroine, Miel McCrae. Like Miel, Margaret grew up in a small rural community in Southern Ontario, which she then left for the big-city bustle of Toronto. Armed with an Honors B.A. in English, she tried teaching first, then copywriting, until the same wanderlust that haunted Miel worked its magic on Margaret and off she went for an extended adventure to Africa and Europe. Sometime later, Margaret spent three months in the Sahara, resulting in her first Superromance, *Precious Interlude*.

Although she loves to travel, Margaret's real passion is writing romances, and in 1982 she won the Air Canada Young Writer's Award.

Determined to have the best of both worlds, Margaret divides her time between a home in Toronto and her parents' farm near Demorestville, where she loads hay and tends a vegetable garden when she's not busy writing.

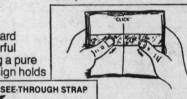

Yours **FREE**, with a home subscription to

HARLEQUIN
SUPERROMANCE ™